GILDED BLOOD: BOOK 1

Inked

RACHEL RENER

Inked • 2

© 2023 Lightning Conjurer Books, LLC

All rights reserved. No portion of this book may be reproduced in any form without permission from the author, except for the use of brief quotations in a book review.

This is a work of fiction. Names, characters, businesses, places, events, locales, and incidents are either the products of the author's imagination or used in a fictitious manner. Any resemblance to actual persons, living or dead, or actual events is purely coincidental.

Edited by Sara Lawson
www.sarasbooks.com

Cover Design by Miblart
www.miblart.com

Inked typography by Allegra Pescatore
www.facebook.com/groups/allegrasartalcove

Interior illustrations by Rachel Rener
www.RachelRener.com

"Tattoo" words & music by Van Halen, *A Different Kind of Truth*
© 2012 Warner Bros. Interscope

ISBN: 9798405621791
ASIN: B09P7BNJPP

TW: Themes of bodily autonomy, and lack thereof, are explored throughout this book.

Other Works by Rachel Rener:

The Gilded Blood Series
I. Inked
II. Jinxed
III. Linked
IV. Synced
The Gilded Blood Limited Edition Omnibus

The Lightning Conjurer Series
I. The Awakening
II. The Enlightening
III. The Christening
IV. The Reckoning
The Complete Series Collection

The Bone Whisperer Chronicles
I. The Girl Who Talks to Ashes
II. The Boy Who Lurks in Shadows

The Little Morsel

The Precipice of Sin
(As part of the *From the Shadows* Anthology)

Autographed Books Available at
~ www.RachelRener.com ~

Table of Contents

- Butt Cobras 8
- The Jewish Mother Zone 19
- A Snake in the Glass 32
- Bringing Art to Life 44
- Hidden Messages 55
- Interdimensional Filing Cabinets 64
- Gold Blood 73
- Uninvited Guests 87
- The Plight of the Incubus 96
- A Jilted Glaistig 110
- Dawn of the Cerulean Sun 130
- What the Fachan? 143
- The Waypoint 156
- Cliffs at the Edge of the World 165
- A Seder With the Satyr 179
- Sol's Dominion 194
- Alabaster Delphiniums 208
- A Hot Pursuit 226
- The Stowaway 241
- Home Again, Home Again 246
- The Early Bird Gets the Ink 259
- Unchained 270
- Purple Banshee's Majesty 287
- Rubies and Emeralds 298
- New Beginnings 312
- Common Blood Types and Their Magical Classes 330

Glossary For the Goyim	332
A Dirge of Salt and Sin	336
The Gilded Blood Series	338
The Lightning Conjurer Series	339
The Bone Whisperer Chronicles	340
The Little Morsel	341
Acknowledgements	342
About the Author	345

Inked • 6

"To love a person is to see all of their magic and to remind them of it when they have forgotten."

– Unknown

I.
BUTT COBRAS

The rotund, dimpled butt cheek jerked and wriggled beneath my fingers, eliciting an exasperated sigh from me, the stalwart curator of said derrière. It belonged to a squirming fifty-something-year-old gentleman whose leather motorcycle chaps had been bunched up just beneath the crease of his glutes so that I, his illustrious tattoo artist, could add a rattle to the tip of the cobra's tail, which started at the top of his shoulders and ended right there on his exposed bottom. Yes, I realize cobras don't have rattles. And no, it wasn't my idea. Apparently, my original snake design – which boasted kickass, glowing red eyes and three-inch-long, venom-dripping fangs – wasn't intimidating enough. Hence the ill-advised conception of the rattlesnake-cobra abomination.

Hey, the customer's always right. Or so I'm told.

As the burly man quivering beneath my electric needle let out another pitiful whimper, I was forced to look up from the impeccable line I was pulling. "You doing okay over there, Roy?"

"Uh-huh." His arms were wrapped around the chair he was straddling as though he were clinging to a life raft. "Doing great."

"Okay, so, the good news," I regarded the empty plastic container on the stand beside me, "is that we're like ninety-eight percent finished. The bad news is, I just ran out of brown ink. Why don't you take a breather while I head to the back and grab some more?"

His eyes rolled backward as he sank face-first into the vinyl pad he was smothering. "Thank you, sweet baby Jesus."

"Talia is fine," I quipped.

He snorted into his seat. "You know, I meant to tell you yesterday that I got a nephew about your age, just turned twenty-five. He's funny, like you, and a good looker too – kid's got tattoo sleeves from his jaw to his wrists, just like his uncle."

I coughed to try to conceal my laughter. "My mother would have a conniption fit if I brought home another gentile with a neck tattoo. So, unless your nephew's last name is Lipschitz—"

"Gentile? That some kind of lizard?"

"Depends on the gentile," I grinned.

I set down my tattoo gun and peeled off my gloves, stretching my fingers as I did. Apart from Roy, the shop was totally empty this afternoon. He'd sent his biker buddies over to the dive bar next door once it came time for me to shave his right butt cheek – one of the many "perks" of my day job – and Zayn, my boss, hadn't shown up to work this morning.

Chewing on the inside of my cheek as I trudged to the back room, I glanced down at my phone's empty screen for the hundredth time that day. It wasn't like Zayn to go AWOL. In fact, he'd only ever missed a single day of work since hiring me two years ago, and even then, he'd been bombarding me with nonstop texts the entire morning: *Is the register locked? Do you have enough singles in the drawer? You're not doing tequila shots with customers again, right??*

I pulled up his contact information in my phone, feeling my stomach do a little flip as it always did when his stupidly gorgeous photo appeared on the screen. The man drove me crazy with all of his neuroticisms – sort of reminded me of my mother in that respect, now that I thought about it – but hot damn did he have a beautiful face. Wavy black hair, high cheekbones, a year-round dewy glow that made me suspect he visited tanning beds on his extended lunch breaks. And those eyes! They were like polished emeralds – sometimes dark, sometimes gleaming, depending on the light and his ever-changing moods. They made my own green eyes look like a mucky swamp. My thumb hit the CALL button as my free hand rummaged through the cabinet, looking for #17 *Dulce de Leche* brown.

Maybe he just slept in, I told myself as the first ring trilled in my ear. *I mean, even workaholics gotta have benders from time to time.* Except Zayn didn't drink. Or party. Or indulge in so much as a single Reese's Piece, lest his perfect six-pack be chipped away by a morsel of smooth, peanut-buttery goodness.

The line rang and rang. Meanwhile, that stupid shade of brown was nowhere to be found.

"You've reached Zayn," a deep, husky voice finally answered. *"Don't leave a message—"*

"—because you never check your voicemails," I finished, having heard that same greeting twelve times that morning. "Yeah, yeah." I slammed the phone on the counter, only semi-concerned about the replacement screen I'd just gotten for, you know, repeatedly slamming my phone on hard surfaces. Telephonic devices don't last particularly long in my custody.

"Hey Tal, what's the hold up? I gotta pee!" Roy hollered from the other room.

"Don't you dare pull your pants up!" I yelled. "They're not sterile!"

"Fine, but I got maybe ten minutes before my bladder explodes!"

"Okay, okay, I'm coming! We're almost done – just hang tight!"

He gave an annoyed grunt in response.

Craaaaap. My hands raked through the scattered ink bottles on the counter. I'd dumped out the entire cabinet but there was nothing – not even a darker brown I could blend with white. I rubbed the bridge of my nose in aggravation. Running out of ink nine-tenths of the way through a five-hour session was such a rookie move. My cheek chewing intensified further as I eyed Zayn's locked office door. I knew he had an entire stash of expensive, exotic ink in there that I was strictly forbidden to touch. Zayn himself only used it for special VIP clients who paid him something outrageous to engrave these weird-looking symbols all over their body. I'd asked him about them once – both the clients and the elaborate squiggles – and his answer had been clear: none of my damn business.

"There's an empty water bottle out here – can I use that?" Roy hollered.

"For drinking?"

"…No."

"No, you cannot 'use' that!" I shrieked, thinking of the beautiful bedazzled thermos my mother had gotten me last Hanukkah. "Just *hang on*, I'm coming!"

Without another thought, I snatched an expired credit card from my wallet and jammed it between Zayn's locked office door and the frame, expertly jimmying the handle as I made a sawing motion with the card. When the lock finally caught, I swung the door open triumphantly. Zayn's office was cast in darkness, but I didn't bother turning on a light as I made my way to the metal filing cabinet behind his desk, where one of the cool symbols he was always doodling had been etched into the metal. By some miraculous turn of events, the top drawer was unlocked and slightly ajar, displaying a beautiful cache of tiny glass bottles clustered at the bottom, just waiting to be injected into someone's butt. I flicked on my cell phone flashlight as I rummaged through Zayn's clinking treasures like the amateur burglar I was, my fingertips brushing over the fancy labels until I found the one I needed: a light brown pigment aptly called *Fawn.* The name was hand-painted in fancy calligraphy, with grand flourishes on the F and n.

"Are these seriously stoppered with corks?" I marveled, rolling the bottle in between my thumb and forefinger. "How weird."

I could practically hear Zayn chastising me: *Tal, you'd better put that the hell back and walk away. A year's worth of paychecks wouldn't cover the cost of that one bottle!*

I'll just use a tiny bit, I silently promised my conspicuously-absent boss, clutching the itty-bitty vial in my hand. With a fleeting twinge of guilt, I shut the door and made my way back to the hairy full moon my customer was casually baring in the lobby.

"Sorry, sorry!" I breezed as I slipped on fresh gloves and carefully refilled the ink chamber, making sure to be as stingy as humanly possible. "I'll have you inked and Saran-wrapped before you know it. Just don't jerk around this time!"

Roy let out an unintelligible grunt as I used a mag needle to whip shade across the rattle on his rump, switching off between blotting and filling in the shading as quickly as possible. The ink was smooth and creamy, its pigment vibrant and vivid despite being a yucky brown shade. Ignoring his persistent griping and fidgeting, I smeared some ointment on the new lines, then quickly swapped in the 5R liner to re-sculpt the old #17 *Dulce de Leche* lines running across the snake's belly, marveling at the quality. Zayn had been right to hoard this stuff!

I jumped up from my chair as a brilliant idea struck me. "Be right back!"

A moment later I returned with two more bottles from Zayn's stash: *Onyx* and *Ruby*. After cleaning out the ink cartridge with distilled water, I quickly touched up the rest of my creation, awed by the ease in which the black ink spread across Roy's skin with perfect coverage, making the scales of the snake pop and whisper as though brushing past one another as it slithered. Meanwhile, the red ink had the perfect viscosity for meticulous precision, allowing me to pack color into those wicked crimson eyes with unbelievable depth and emotion.

"Yessss," I hissed, hunched over my brilliant work like a mad scientist.

"How's it look?" Roy asked, squinting at me over his shoulder to examine the progress of his Franken-snake.

"Terrifying," I grinned. "He looks like he might leap right off your back and bite me!"

As I wiped away the excess ink and cleaned the tattoo site, I had to take a minute to admire my artistic prowess. I mean, sure, it was a stupid cobra with a rattle, but in terms of quality, it was one of my better creations. The scales were slick and black, gleaming like oil beneath the fluorescent lights. The eyes were narrowed and lively, crimson danger seething behind slanted irises. And the rattle was so realistic, it was practically quivering. In fact, the lights on the ceiling must have flickered, because for a second there, it really did look like it was moving.

Or maybe that was just Roy twitching from a raw butt and a full bladder.

After snapping a quick photo for my portfolio – minus his butt crack, for the sake of the children – I quickly cleaned and reapplied a layer of tattoo ointment to all five feet of snake, then held up a mirror for Roy to admire the work of art on his backside.

"It's perfect!" he grinned, taking it in from fang to rattle. "My wife's gonna love it!"

"Yep, Dottie's a lucky lady," I chuckled, deftly pressing a sheet of adhesive tattoo film to his posterior before helping him pull up his pants. Without bothering to re-fasten his belt, he half-ran, half-waddled to the bathroom, letting out a prolonged moan of relief that I could hear through the door the moment it clicked shut.

After taking one more glance at my phone – no missed calls, except the usual three or four from my mother – I got to work cleaning up my station: gloves, leftover ink, and ink cups went in the trash, used needles were placed in the biohazard bin, metal stand was cleaned and disinfected with MadaCide, and hands were thoroughly washed with surgical-grade soap. I'd just started cleaning off my tattoo machine when another moan sounded from the bathroom, this one heartier than the last.

"Jesus, Roy," I muttered, shaking my head in disgust. "Turn on the damn fan."

The shrill, blood-curdling scream that followed made me jump half a foot in the air.

"Roy?" I shouted. My half-cleaned tattoo gun clattered on the stand as I tore across the shop. "Roy! What's wrong?!"

"Help! Get it *off!*"

"Roy!" I jiggled the handle, then banged on the door with my fist. "Unlock the door! *Roy!*"

"Help me!" he yelped. "Please—*augh!*" His voice cut off with a loud choking sound. Something heavy thudded against the floor, followed by skin-prickling silence.

"Roy?" I shouted, kicking the door. "Roy!"

No response.

I yanked out my cell and dialed 9-1-1, cradling the phone between my ear and shoulder as the line rang. Then I snatched up the same credit card I'd used to break into Zayn's office and forced it into the door jam, jiggering the handle violently.

"Nine-one-one, what's your emergency?" a female voice answered.

"Um, hi, how are you?"

In the beat of silence that ensued, an unwelcome memory of the first time I'd called 9-1-1 flashed through my mind. I was eighteen years old and had just gotten home after my last day of high school. Excited for that one and only parent-sanctioned shot of tequila my dad had promised me if I got through my final exams, I burst into the kitchen to find him passed out on the kitchen floor. It was the first of several times I'd find him like that, though the cancer diagnosis wouldn't come for a few more years.

"Ma'am, what is your emergency?"

Grimacing, I roughly shook the memory away. "I think my customer is having a heart attack!" I grunted, using my shoulder to push against the door as I jimmied the lock. The credit card caught, then slipped past. "Dammit!" I yelled. "C'mon!"

I could hear the woman clattering information into her keyboard. *"Ma'am, I need you to calm down. What's your name and location?"*

"T-Talia. Talia Kestenbaum. I work at Flourish and Dots Tattoo Parlor in Wynwood – er, Miami," I added for good measure, yanking down the handle just as the card caught the edge of the latch. *Yes!* I shoved against the door, but it only budged a few inches. Roy's body was blocking it from opening any further.

"Dammit, Roy!" I wheezed, pushing on the door with both hands. No luck.

"Please tell me exactly what's happening, Talia," the dispatcher was prompting me.

I pressed my back against the door and heaved with my legs, which slid uselessly across the linoleum tile. "My client had to pee so he went to use the toilet," I groaned. "Single stall." The door still wouldn't budge so I started doing backward thrusts with my hips, pounding my ass into the door battering-ram-style. "Few—" *thump* "—minutes—" *thump* "—later—" *thump, thump* "—he started screaming—" *thump, thump, THUMP* "—ugh, dammit!" Butt throbbing, I sank to the ground.

"And then what happened?"

"Then he, I don't know, fell, I guess…?" My articulate and incredibly helpful explanation petered out as I peered into the five-inch crack between the door and the jamb. Roy's bare legs were splayed out on the ground, leather chaps bunched around his ankles. Behind him, near the toilet, something small and dark darted across the floor.

"What the…" I whispered.

"Ma'am?"

A strange, discomforting sound was emanating from the general toilet area – a soft hiss, almost like the whisper of wind. *A gas leak?* I wondered idly. But I couldn't smell anything. I turned my ear toward the crack, holding my breath to listen. There was another weird sound on top of that, an intermittent shaking sound that reminded me of a maraca – one that was being rattled at a million times per second by an angry, tight-fisted mariachi player. Which of course didn't make any—

"Ma'am, please, do you know if your client is breathing?"

"I'm trying to find out," I snapped, craning my neck to try to get a better look inside. A movement just behind Roy's legs made me jump and smack my head on the door jamb. *"Ow!* What the—" I started, then abruptly choked on my own question as a flat head rose up from the tiled floor. At the end of its long, black, serpentine body, a fawn-colored rattle quivered a spine-chilling warning that made every hair on my body stand on end and my throat seal shut, much like the last time I'd eaten a strawberry – only to realize that I'm deathly allergic to them.

Somehow, I didn't think an EpiPen was going to save me this time.

"That's not possible," I tried to say. Instead, an unintelligible, strangled noise croaked out of my fluttering mouth. The cobra's head bobbed from side to side, its red eyes boring into the depths of my soul.

"Talia, officers are currently on the way, but I need you to provide me with additional information in the meantime. What is the victim's name and age? Is he conscious?"

"Sn…sn…" I stammered.

With a hiss that sliced through the air like a whip, the creature's jaw unhinged to reveal the largest, sharpest fangs I'd ever seen and a forked tongue darting in and out between them. It pulled its head back as though rearing to strike.

"Snake!!" I screamed.

"Wait, did you just say—"

"There's a giant-ass snake in the bathroom!" I shrieked into the receiver. "It's – *oh, shit!!*"

My cellphone clattered to the floor as the black serpent rose up from the ground, its three-inch-long fangs dripping with venom and malice, and its brown rattle shaking menacingly.

Before I could choke out another four-letter word, the snake lunged.

A high-pitched, little-girl scream tore from my throat. In a fit of panic, I toppled backward, smacking my head on the tile with a terrible *thwack* that immediately blotted the fluorescent ceiling lights into inky black darkness.

II.
THE JEWISH MOTHER ZONE

"...BP is one-nineteen over seventy-five," a man's voice was saying from somewhere above. "No signs of external injuries." A blinding white light shone into my left eye, and then the right. "Pupils look good."

"Zayn?" I mumbled.

"Nope, my name is Nick," the voice replied. "You fell and hit your head. Can you squeeze my fingers for me?"

"Did I lose a lot of blood?" I murmured.

"None at all, as far as I can tell."

"Oh, thank God." I squinted one eye open and then the next. A decently attractive red-headed guy was kneeling over me, holding my hand in both of his. "Did you just propose?" I asked, wincing as I tried to hoist myself up on an elbow. "Because I generally prefer dinner and a movie first."

Like most good-looking men, Nick rolled his eyes and ignored my comment. "Squeeze my fingers, please… Good. Can you wiggle your toes?"

I nodded.

He patted my freshly de-sneakered foot, then arched an eyebrow. "Out of curiosity, why were you asking about blood loss?"

"Crazy rare blood type, all transfusions are a major no-no," I muttered as I looked around the room, trying to remember where I was. When my eyes landed on the wide purple wall sporting hundreds of polaroid photos of fresh tattoos, it dawned on me that I was at work. But unlike most Tuesday afternoons, various men and women in police uniforms were shuffling around the tattoo parlor, including a pair of burly dudes from Animal Control.

"Roy!" I gasped, sitting bolt upright. "Where is he? Is he okay?" My eyes widened as the events from earlier that afternoon came careening back. "There was a snake!" I cried, gripping Nick's arm. He gently leaned me back against the wall.

A female officer who had been standing a few feet away turned her attention on me. "Wait – so you also confirm there was a snake?"

I nodded meekly.

"Hmm." She pulled a notepad from her breast pocket to jot something inside. "We didn't see any evidence of one, but the guy on the stretcher kept insisting there was one in the bathroom."

My head whipped to the front of the store, where all of the blinds had been opened to provide a clear view of Roy being carried into an ambulance outside. Head bandaged, he was sitting bolt upright on the stretcher, gesticulating wildly as he shouted at the three EMTs who were straining to lift him into their vehicle.

"He did have two long scratches on his backside," Nick remarked. "That might be where a hypothetical snake could've grazed him." He pulled a radio from his pocket and spoke into it. "Hey, Jen, put a pressure immobilization bandage on that scratch on his left glute. He may need a round of antivenom at the hospital."

"Wait – is he okay?" I tried to scramble to my feet, but Nick's surprisingly firm hand held my flailing shoulder down. "What the hell happened?!"

The police officer knelt beside me, a touch of sympathy softening her otherwise stern expression. "It's Talia, right? My name is Officer Wilcox from Miami PD. From what we can gather from your customer's intoxicated explanation, there was a snake in the toilet. When he saw it, he passed out, hitting his head on the sink."

Intoxicated? I frowned. *Roy knows better than to drink before getting a tattoo.*

"He's fine," Nick quickly added. "Just a mild concussion and those shallow lacerations on his backside. We've already notified his wife that we're taking him to the hospital. By the way, how many fingers am I holding up?"

"Four." I watched Roy's ambulance depart in a blue and red flurry of sirens, feeling my stomach sink. "What do you mean, there was a snake in the toilet? Did you catch it?" My eyes trailed to the two gentlemen standing beside a rather large kennel.

Officer Wilcox shook her head. "As I was saying, there was no sign of a snake when we arrived—"

"And when was that?" I blustered, feeling increasingly belligerent.

"About six minutes ago."

My mouth dangled open. *How long had I been out?*

Wilcox shrugged a padded shoulder. "Most likely, Roy flushed the snake back down the toilet just before passing out. I'd like to tell you this is an anomaly, but here in Miami, you'd be surprised. That said, we'd be happy to have Animal Control search the rest of your shop to be safe. Are you the owner?"

"No," I replied, massaging the growing bump on the back of my head. "Um, he didn't show up today." My eyebrows stitched together as my full wits slowly started to return. That snake wasn't in the toilet, it had been on the ground. And since when did cobras live in Miami? Because that's definitely what that snake was, right? Flat head, flared hood on the sides. I mean, I would know, since I'd literally just drawn one that was pretty much identical to the cobra that tried to kill Roy in the bathroom…

A lump the size of a tennis ball reappeared in my throat.

"Could you please provide me with the owner's name and contact information?" Wilcox asked, pen poised above her notebook.

I struggled to my feet, my head spinning as I did. Nick took my elbow and gently helped me up. "I mean, I'd be glad to, but he hasn't picked up his phone all day. I'm…I'm actually worried something might have happened to him."

Wilcox's own eyebrows furrowed as she scribbled another note in her pad. "How long has he been missing?"

"Since last night."

She let out a hearty laugh. "Okay, well, give us a call if he doesn't show up in another forty-eight hours. In the meantime, with your permission, we'll do a quick sweep of the place and then be on our way."

"Um," I started.

"Yes?"

I chewed on my lip, acutely aware of how ridiculous I was about to sound. "I'm not a Florida native, so forgive me if this is a stupid question, but…are there cobras in Miami?"

Officer Wilcox raised an eyebrow. "Not legally, no. But just ask Hank and Russ," she gestured to the gentlemen from Animal Control who were currently shining flashlights into every nook and cranny of the shop. "People smuggle in all types of animals from overseas."

She turned to leave, but another one of my inquisitive squeaks stopped her. "Um, sorry. But these cobras that people smuggle in, are any of them jet black, with, uh…with like, rattles on their tails?"

"Rattles?"

"You know, like, um. Like a rattlesnake. But…on a cobra. With glowing red eyes."

Officer Wilcox and Nick exchanged raised eyebrows. "Not that I've ever seen," she replied carefully. "Nick?"

His mouth pinched into a thin line as though he were suppressing a laugh. Or a snarky remark. But because he was a nice person, he just replied, "No, ma'am. I have never seen a Floridian cobra with a rattle and glowing red eyes. But who knows? Maybe they have 'em in South Beach."

Yep, they both thought I was a complete whack-a-doodle.

"Do you want us to escort you to the hospital?" Nick casually asked as he packed up his medical equipment. "Your vitals look good, but I'd be happy to take you in as a precaution."

"I'm fine."

He didn't look remotely convinced. In fact, once Officer Wilcox had excused herself to join the rest of the snake hunt, he pitched his voice lower. "Not trying to offend you or anything, but were you or your customer partaking in any, uh, recreational activities, before we arrived?"

I frowned, seriously considering his question. "Um. No. Not that I know of."

"Just checking," he smiled, gathering the last of his things. "You never know in Miami."

As he turned to leave, I suddenly remembered something. "Hey – please make sure Roy keeps that tattoo covered and clean at the hospital. That bathroom floor isn't exactly sterile."

"What tattoo?"

"Uh, you know, the massive snake tattoo that covers his entire backside?"

Nick was staring at me as though a polka-dotted unicorn horn had sprouted between my eyebrows. "There was no tattoo on that man's back," he finally answered, frowning deeply. His eyes crept back to where Officer Wilcox was standing, as though he really did think I was on drugs. "Hey, Wilcox, maybe you'd better come—"

"I'm joking!" I blurted out, a borderline-maniacal laugh slipping through my lips. "You know, just your typical tattooist humor. I'll just, um…I'll get out of everyone's way," I forced a plastic smile on my face to accentuate my perfectly sane demeanor. "You know, what with the missing reptile hunt and all of that. Thanks for, you know…yeah."

With that, I spun on my heels and fled to the unoccupied back room, cheeks flushing hotter than a shot of cinnamon whisky while Nick's dubious expression burned a hole into the back of my head.

The officers stayed for another twenty minutes or so, searching the place for "snakes" – though by that point, I was fairly certain they were looking for the hallucinogenic drugs

Roy and I must have been partaking in. Luckily, they found neither. And so, they bid me good day after I refused them entrance into Zayn's office and they refused me information about which hospital Roy was carted to even after I'd lied about being his niece. I guess they didn't see the resemblance.

Once all of the police cars had scattered, I made one more anxious lap to check for stray cobras, then flipped the sign on the front door to CLOSED. With a huff of determination, I burst into my boss's office, squaring my shoulders in an attempt to feign bravery. The filing cabinet of exotic ink was still unlocked, its open drawer beckoning to me.

"Okay, Talia, let's work through this logically," I said aloud to myself as any sane, not-crazy person would do. "You just spent, what – five hours? – tattooing a custom-designed, *imaginary* cobra-slash-rattlesnake onto a man's back. Just as you've done six days a week for the last two years and four months." I flicked on the fluorescent ceiling light, scanning the floor for stray, not-so-imaginary serpents as I made my way to the cabinet. "As far as you know, you have not done drugs, unless that ink had some sort of weird inhalant, which would be a really bizarre thing for Zayn to have in his possession…"

I peered into the drawer, which must have had a hundred bottles of ink, all perfectly arranged by color and hue, from white to black and every color in between. After triple-checking the area for snakes, I pulled the ink bottles out of the drawer one by one, assembling them on Zayn's immaculately clean desk so I could sit in his leather chair and examine them. Picking the nearest one up, a bright pinkish-orange color, I brought it to my nose to carefully inspect its label. Except there was nothing to inspect.

"What the hell?" I muttered, turning the bottle over in my hand. Apart from the elegant script that read *Daylily*, its label was otherwise blank. Where was the ingredient list? The expiration date, the company information, the safety warning? I picked up the next bottle, *Hyacinth*, and the next one, *Peacock*. Nothing! No info, no instructions, no—

Wait a minute.

I held *Peacock* up to the light, squinting at its contents. As I twirled the bottle from side to side, the ink inside shimmered like the iridescent surface of a bubble: royal blue, emerald green, and deep purple all swirled inside the glass like an actual peacock feather glinting in the sunlight. Eyes bulging, I yanked the stopper off and peered inside.

"How is that even possible?" I asked no one in particular. "Tattoo ink isn't iridescent. It's not like you can just stuff multiple colors in a single bottle!"

I snatched another vial from the desk – *Opal* – and nearly choked when I yanked out the cork. Its contents were pearly white and opalescent, with flecks of every color of the rainbow twinkling beneath the harsh fluorescent light of Zayn's office.

"What the hell *is* this stuff?" I leaned back in my stolen chair, taking in the assortment of pigments displayed on the desk. Some were metallic, others looked like literal gemstones. One, aptly named *Galaxy*, glittered like thousands of twinkling stars, and another one of them – *Spectral* – had every color I'd ever seen in my life packed into one bottle, including a purplish-but-not-quite-purple color I was fairly certain was not an actual color.

Part of me started to wonder if I'd made some sort of terrible mistake, thinking these strange dyes were for human skin.

But they are! I shook my head vigorously, then winced at the throbbing ache it brought on. I'd seen Zayn use them with my own eyes. Just last month, in fact, when I'd been forced to stay late rebalancing the cash sheet after the register was off by eighty dollars – I may or may not have given someone change for a hundred instead of a twenty – one of his strange-looking, late-night clients came in. A tall, athletic-looking chick with overly-bronzed skin the color of glittering honey and hair so green it looked like sour apple candy. She stuck up her nose when I greeted her and went straight to Zayn's chair, where he wordlessly etched those strange symbols across her shoulder blades using the ink from these very bottles…

"Ack!" I nearly toppled off my chair as the phone in my pocket buzzed. Snatching it from my jeans like a hot potato, I couldn't help but be disappointed when I saw it wasn't Zayn.

After fumbling to hit the green button on my cracked screen – *Again?!* When did *that* happen? – my mother's shrill, New-York-tinged voice filled the empty office before I even had time to say hello.

"I have been trying to reach you all day!"

"Why are you yelling?" I shouted back, yanking the phone away from my ear to adjust the volume to the bare minimum, just like I always had to do when she called.

"I'm not yelling, that's just how I talk!"

"Okay, fine! But why are you calling me right now? You know I'm at work!"

"Still? Why does that horrible man work you like a pack mule?"

I set the phone on the desk, not bothering to put it on speaker since I could hear her just fine even with the volume turned all the way down. "First of all, Zayn isn't horrible – he's not even here! And second of all, it's three-thirty in the afternoon!"

"Well, if he's not there, why should you be?"

I rolled my eyes. "Why have you been blowing up my phone all day? Did someone die?"

"Oy gotenyu, bite your tongue! Of course no one died – there's no one left to die but me, and if I were dead I wouldn't be calling you, would I?"

I rubbed the growing ache in my forehead with my palm. "Ma—"

"Are you coming over for dinner tonight or not? I'm making chicken parmesan, your favorite!"

"Ma, I already told you, I can't come to dinner tonight," I replied, absentmindedly twirling 'Galaxy' in my fingers while simultaneously trying to figure out how the heck someone could make the indigo-slash-black ink sparkle like that. It's not like you can just inject glittery microplastic under someone's skin. *Well, not safely or legally, at least,* I sighed in frustration. "And I can't eat chicken parmesan anyway! I'm lactose intolerant!"

"What are you talking about! Chicken parmesan doesn't have lactose in it!"

Releasing my grip on the ink, I pressed my forehead to the cool, smooth wood of Zayn's mahogany desk and stifled a groan. "Mother. Go to your computer. Pull up Google. Type in 'parmesan cheese' and 'lactose' and see what comes up."

"You know I don't know how to use that farkakteh Google!"

"Okay, Mom, look. Forget the parmesan." I took a deep breath, trying to make sense of a day that frankly reminded me of the time I ate two of my ex-boyfriend's "special" brownies without asking him first. It was the only other time in my life I'd been seeing things that may or may not have been real. Which, for whatever reason, gave me an absolutely insane idea. "Listen, I have a serious question to ask you."

"What's wrong?"

"Nothing's wr—"

"Are you finally dating someone? Has he proposed?"

"What? No!"

"Oy! How could you not tell me you were dating someone! What's his name?!"

"Ma!" I shouted. "I'm not dating anyone!"

"Are you at least pregnant? If the father's Jewish, I won't be mad!"

"Ma," I sighed, peeling my forehead off of Zayn's desk to lean back in his chair. "Look, I just wanted to ask you, even though I'm a grown-ass woman, how angry you would be, on a scale of one to homicide, if I, um…" I trailed off, tugging on the gold locket I always wore around my neck – an anxious habit I'd developed years ago, when my dad was first diagnosed with cancer.

"How angry would I be if you what?!"

"Ugh! If I got a tattoo, okay? Not a big one or anything," I quickly added, warily regarding the long line of vials stretching before me, "just, like, a little tiny one that's super inconspicuous. Hardly noticeable. Itty bitty."

I was shocked she actually let me get the whole sentence out without interrupting. In fact, the line had gone silent for so long, I checked to see if the call had dropped.

"Mom?" I asked, bringing the phone back to my ear. "You there?"

"Oh my God," she wailed, nearly causing me to drop it again. I gingerly nudged the cellphone far away, to the far corner of the desk, while her shrill lamentations broadcasted throughout the entire room. *"I knew it. I knew working at that place would turn you into a Hell's Angel. God made your body a temple, and now you want to go and desecrate it? You're supposed to leave this world as you entered it, in one piece and unblemished – like a rental car! Not covered in cheap bumper stickers like some used Volkswagen!"*

As she carried on, I traced small circles on the desk with my finger, not even bothering to interject. She was deep in what I liked to call "The Jewish Mother Zone" – or JMZ, for short – a hysterical state where she became untethered from the natural world, unmindful of all other stimuli and lifeforms, and as undeterred as a wild snowball careening down Mount Everest…

"Who goes around graffitiing rental cars before returning them? Did your new boyfriend put you up to this mishegas?"

"*Ma!* For the thousandth time, I don't have a boyfriend!"

"Oy, you really are meshuggeneh! First you move twenty miles away from home, then you dye your beautiful hair to look like a fire hydrant—"

"Fire hydrants aren't burgundy," I muttered, fingering my ponytail.

"—at some schlocky tattoo parlor in the worst part of town—"

"The art district is the worst part of town?"

"—and now you want to get gang sleeves like the Bloods and Crips. What happened to your supposed needle phobia that I used to hear so much about?"

"I—"

"Oh, God," she moaned. *"I don't know how much more of this my heart can take. Dr. Feil already told me that a drop – a drop, Talia! – of added stress could make my heart explode like a microwaved egg!"*

Knuckling my forehead, I stifled a groan. If I didn't nip this diatribe in the bud, it would last through midnight. It was time for evasive maneuvers.

"What?" I suddenly yelled into the empty shop. "Oh, sure, yeah, I'll be right there! …Well, if you're bleeding *that* badly, you gotta apply pressure to the wound!" I added for good measure as I brought the phone back to my ear. "Aw shoot, Mom, a customer just walked in and he's severely hemorrhaging."

"What?!"

"Anyway, love-you-more-than-life-itself-gotta-go-bye!" I said that last part in a single, rambling crescendo, then hurriedly switched off the phone before she could launch into a bonus feature, director's-cut conniption fit.

After another long sigh, aimed more at my current situation than at my fruit-loops mother, I reached for an ink bottle labeled *Platinum,* whose silvery contents were shimmering like liquid metal.

"There's only one way to test all of this," I murmured, eyeing the ring finger of my right hand. My clients had always teased me for being the only tattoo artist in the world with zero tattoos. Well, this would shut them up *and* prove I wasn't crazy. Probably. And, sure, I'd have to wear a glove around my mother for the rest of my life. Or, at least, the rest of *her* life. But if Harley Quinn could do it, so could I.

With a determined huff, I snatched two more vials from the desk and made my way to the front of the shop. Either this was going to work, thereby proving my sanity, or I would call Nick back and ask him to personally escort me to the nearest mental institution – a comforting thought, really, since asylums usually have guards, and that meant my mother couldn't follow me inside and strangle me to death for what I was about to do.

III.
A SNAKE IN THE GLASS

I stared at the tattoo gun I was clenching in my left hand, its ominous 3RL needle gleaming in the light like the cursed spindle in Sleeping Beauty. My hand was shaking like crazy, partially due to the fact that I'm most definitely not left-handed. (No way was I going to tattoo a diamond ring on my wedding finger!) But, as my mother so astutely pointed out, the primary reason for my uncontrollable trembling was that I'm actually terrified of needles – the ones that are aimed at *my* body, at least. That's why Zayn had been amazing enough to outfit our shop with brand new, pocket-sized, wireless rotary tattoo machines that most clients mistook for hearty vape pens. The design honestly made me forget I was clutching a needle in my hand – until, of course, the scary, pointy bit was directed straight at me.

Bordering on hyperventilation, I sucked in one deep breath after another, trying to calm myself down. Despite the AC being set to its highest, sub-Arctic setting, beads of sweat kept appearing above my brow, and the salt was making my eyes sting no matter how furiously I tried to shake the droplets away. Top it all off with the forthcoming, dramatic reappearance of the bowl of Lucky Charms and almond milk I'd eaten that morning, and my "brilliant" plan suddenly didn't feel so brilliant anymore.

Setting the gun beside the three unopened vials of ink, I removed my nitrile glove to rub the bridge of my nose. A few minutes ago, my idea of etching a multi-carat-diamond-and-platinum ring onto my finger to test the magic ink that I was fairly certain had brought Roy's tattoo to life had seemed brilliant: If I was wrong, I'd just end up with a permanent ring on my right hand that would be easily concealable. If I was right, I would have a lavish piece of jewelry that I could auction off to gift myself a Maclaren 720S in mauvine blue while still having leftover cash to undergo emergency tattoo removal before the High Holidays.

However.

After putting a little more thought into it – specifically, the thought of my mother's heart exploding like a microwaved egg, as she so vividly put it, paired with an acute case of trypanophobia – I was beginning to have my doubts. I mean, assuming I wasn't inadvertently high on drugs or in a coma, I had just witnessed a man get attacked by his own butt cobra.

Probably better to play it safe than bitten.

Two minutes later, with a freshly sharpened #2 pencil in hand, I pulled a blank piece of paper from Zayn's printer and sketched out an image of a diamond ring with sharp lines and cute little flowers embedded in the band, much like the engagement ring I'd one day drop nonchalant hints about if I ever managed to nab myself a serious boyfriend. After outlining it in black ink and erasing the pencil marks, I retrieved a purple, green, and blue feathered quill from Zayn's top drawer, which I anxiously hovered over an uncorked vial of ink called *Diamond Dust*. Aptly named, the glass-clear pigment actually threw rainbows onto the walls when I twirled it in the light. With a deep breath and a mostly steady hand, I dipped the quill into the ink and began filling in the gemstone on my sketch, admiring how each facet glinted and sparkled as though three-dimensional. Once I was finished, I re-corked *Diamond Dust* and uncorked *Platinum*, coloring in the band and its delicate etchings while adding highlights and shadows with *Snow* and *Onyx* – the same black ink I'd used on Roy's tattoo.

After thirty minutes of filling, shading, and wiping drops of stress sweat from my brow, I held up my finished creation in front of me, marveling at the realism. The platinum band glinted like buffed, shining metal. The diamond glittered and flashed like a real million-dollar stone. And the floral decorations engraved along the band looked so real, I half expected there to be smooth bumps and edges as I ran my finger across them. It was so realistic-looking, I was honestly waiting for the ring to tumble off the page and into my outstretched, greedy palm.

Except nothing happened. The fancy grandfather clock that I'd helped Zayn schlep into his office last year ticked and tocked from the back corner, as though *tsk*ing my silliness with every passing second.

Determined nevertheless, I carefully set the paper back on the desk and smoothed out the edges, willing it, *envisioning* it, as my therapist often said, to be real. My jaw locked and my eyebrows creased with concentration as I stared at my magnificent ink creation. Ten minutes went by, and then twenty. By the time the clock struck four-thirty, and the noise of the gong nearly startled me out of my seat, I was starting to feel pretty foolish.

Tattoos don't just come to life, I chided myself, cheeks burning with embarrassment. *But snakes really do pop out of toilets. From time to time, at least.*

Plus, I never actually saw Roy's supposedly-empty backside after passing out. Nick merely asserted that my client didn't have a tattoo there, which could have been a mistake, or a dumb joke, or, hell, maybe *he* was the one on drugs. After all, this was Miami.

I nodded resolutely. Roy's tattoo was still on his back, just like the hundreds of other tattoos I'd designed for people over the years. A random snake crawled out of the toilet and freaked us both out because that's just what happens in Florida. And the only reason I'd mistaken it for some imaginary cobra-rattlesnake monstrosity is because I'd been staring at my own creation for five hours straight, thereby subconsciously influencing the panic-related delusions I'd obviously been suffering from.

"Yep," I said out loud as I recorked the ink pots I'd been using and carefully began transporting them back to Zayn's drawer one by one. "The simplest explanation is almost always the right one. Tomorrow, Zayn will be back and everything will be fine. Well, save for all the money he's gonna deduct from my paycheck for borrowing a few precious drops of his fancy-schmancy ink."

Ink that changes color and glimmers like galaxies and gemstones, a sullen voice muttered in the back of my mind.

"Nope, all in my mildly-concussed head," I replied dismissively as I did my best to arrange the colors the way I'd found them, from *Snow* to *Onyx*. I didn't bother taking a closer look at the fancy vials because my mind was firmly made up.

Once the bottles were just about as perfect as I could make them, I shut the drawer, grabbed my failed sketch, turned off the light, and locked Zayn's office door from the inside, letting it click shut behind me. Then I turned off all the lights in the shop, left the register drawer uncounted since Roy had never actually paid me, and walked out the front door an hour before my shift ended because no one was there to tell me not to.

I whistled as I made my way to the alley where I always parked my beat-up brown Mazda, enjoying the balmy air and sunshine, even if the smell of booze and urine somewhat tainted the atmosphere. Less than ten minutes away, my studio apartment was waiting for me, full of boxed wine, leftover brisket from Mom, and a soft, cushy bed where I could sit and binge Netflix until the wee hours of the morning. Tomorrow, Zayn would be back and we would laugh about everything that happened today, and he'd be so relieved that I hadn't been bitten by a snake that he would forget about the ink I took without permission and instead give me a raise for my troubles.

Yeah, I thought, smiling to myself as I stepped around the homeless person who was napping outside the brick alleyway. *Tomorrow's gonna be a great day.*

Tomorrow was not a great day.

After sleeping in, stumbling out of bed, throwing on a white tank top and a pair of low-rise jean shorts, and then giving myself a stupid papercut while admiring my very two-dimensional and *not*-real diamond ring sketch, I got in my car and sped to work, brushing my teeth one-handedly and spitting into an empty Slurpee cup like any functioning adult does while driving. After nearly squishing the aforementioned napping homeless person as I peeled into the back alley – turns out his name is Brett and I gave him my homemade iced coffee for the trouble – I arrived at the shop twenty-seven minutes late, only to find the door locked and lights off.

"You've got to be kidding me," I moaned. There, on the inside handle of the shop, was my stretchy hot pink bracelet, the shop key dangling from it. Pressing my face to the door, I banged on the glass with my palm. "Zayn!" I hollered. "Zayn, come on – open up!"

Weirdly enough, all was dark and still inside, just like it had been yesterday morning…until something long and black scurried across the tile directly in front of the door, making me leap three feet backward.

"What the—!"

My words cut off in a terrified yelp as a pair of glowing red eyes flickered open and peered at me from the darkness within. With shaking fingers, I pulled my phone from my pocket, fumbled with the cracked screen, and flipped on the flashlight. A strangled gasp lodged itself beside the knotted mass of obscenities that were jammed in my windpipe.

There, coiled on the floor, barely two feet in front of me and clear as day, was a jet-black cobra with glowing red eyes and a brown rattle, the sound of which I could faintly hear through the half-centimeter of glass – the only thing separating me from its long, curved fangs, which were jutting out and poised to strike. I took a single step back, and then another. I seriously considered calling the police, or maybe animal control, or at least taking a photo to use as evidence for when they inevitably tried to lock me away on insanity charges.

But when the snake reared its flattened head, all logic was left behind.

I bolted, racing down the sidewalk and across the alley, straight past Brett who was happily slurping away on my iced coffee, and into my car, which I'd conveniently forgotten to lock. I fumbled as I thrust the key in the ignition, revved the engine the moment it turned over, and hauled ass out of the graffiti-decorated alley – but not before politely returning Brett's wave because I'm not a savage. I raced away from the art district, past the Miami Selfie Museum and across the causeway, barely registering the assortment of people and palm trees that flew past as brief, inconvenient blurs. I was on autopilot, making my way to a cushy apartment complex located in South Beach that I'd only visited once, though that particular visit had been permanently engraved into my memory.

But I wasn't going to think about that.

When I finally arrived at Zayn's posh high-rise that overlooked Biscayne Bay, I pulled into the first spot I found, not bothering to check whether it was paid parking or not, and ran across the well-trimmed lawn, past the dolphin fountain, and into the marble lobby where the snazzily-uniformed doorman gave me a quizzical look.

"I'm here to see Zayn Bahrami!" I shouted over my shoulder as I made my way to the elevators.

"That's apartment 14-F. Uh, excuse me, Miss…?!" he called after me, clearly trying to decide whether or not he should try to intercept me.

But it was too late. The elevator doors opened and I skidded inside on the toes of my candy-apple-red converse sneakers, ramming the button for the fourteenth floor until my knuckle hurt. The moment the doors slid open, I flew out, arriving at 14-F as a gasping, sweating, hyperventilating mess who was kicking herself for leaving her inhaler in the car. Any other day, I might have stopped to powder my nose or properly catch my breath – but given the circumstances, I skipped the preamble and went straight to banging down my boss's door.

"Zayn!" I shouted. "It's Talia – open up!"

Out of the corner of my eye, I noticed a faded blue symbol that had been hand-painted on the inside of the door frame, much like the geometric scribbles he tattooed on his ultra-rich, late-night clients – when he wasn't obsessively doodling them on sticky notes that he left all over the place. The placement reminded me of a Jewish mezuzah, a religious decoration nailed inside the door frame to protect one's home. Not that a little blue squiggle was of any consequence to me at that particular moment.

"Zayn!" I hollered, not caring who heard me, so long as he did. "C'mon, Zayn! Answer the door!"

I knocked and knocked, and called and called, and even rang his cell five or six times, but there was no answer. As I slumped against the outside of his door, a little green gecko scurried across the opposite wall, much like the gecko that brought about our first meeting.

Just over two years ago, shortly after I'd dropped out of art school less than a month before graduating – turns out crippling grief does wonders to one's common sense – I followed my mom from Brooklyn to Miami. She and I were unsuccessfully sharing a one-bedroom apartment in Edgewater, with me sleeping on the couch, and both of us driving each other up the peeling wallpaper. One morning, after a particularly shrill shouting match stemming from the adorable, tiny gecko that had climbed into her oatmeal – she wanted me to get rid of it, and I obviously wanted to keep it as a pet and name it George – I found myself traipsing through the neighboring district with my portfolio in hand. It was the gorgeous array of spray-painted murals and colorful street art that had drawn me to Wynwood, desperately searching for literally *any* kind of artsy-fartsy job that would pay me enough to rent my own place. That was when I impulsively walked into Flourish and Dots after noticing the HELP WANTED sign taped to the door, despite having no prior tattoo experience whatsoever. When the dark-haired Adonis at the front desk identified himself as the shop owner, I went completely tongue-tied, botching the impromptu interview worse than a backyard Brazilian butt lift. Miraculously, Zayn hired me as his apprentice on the spot, explaining that my bulging portfolio of drawings and art school credits were a good enough starting point. Paired with the generous salary he offered – despite the fact that rookie tattoo apprentices are almost always expected to pay their mentors – I'd have been a putz to decline, needle phobia or no.

Now, after more than two years in the tattoo industry, I truly appreciated how lucky I was to have stumbled into such an incredible opportunity, bare butts and all. I owed Zayn everything – my sweet studio apartment that was smack-dab in the middle of a happening art district, my tattoo license, my financial independence. My whole lifestyle, really, was thanks to his totally misplaced faith and generosity. If it wasn't for that, I'd probably still be wandering around aimlessly, jumping from job to job, trying to figure out what I want to be when I grow up. That was why I had to figure out what the hell was going on – both inside and outside the shop.

A muffled voice coming from inside Zayn's apartment made my ears perk up. Pressing my ear to the painted steel, I held my breath to listen. At first, it was completely silent, as it had been before, and then—

"Help!" a voice shouted. It sounded like it was coming from somewhere deep inside.

"Zayn?" I gasped.

"Help me!" the voice shouted again, this time more frantically.

"I'm coming!" I cried, jumping to my feet. I jiggled the handle, expecting to have to play amateur cat burglar again, but to my surprise, the door swung wide open.

Tentatively, I stepped inside the swankiest, most impeccably clean bachelor pad I'd ever seen. With floor-to-ceiling windows overlooking the sparkling blue bay and distant sailboats, spotless marble floors boasting expensive-looking tapestries and exotic rugs, and ultra-modern, white furniture that my clumsy ass would have ruined before brunch, it looked like something straight out of one of those posh home design magazines.

"Zayn?" I called, my voice echoing against the towering white walls. "Where are you?"

"Help!"

I frowned. The voice *sort of* sounded like Zayn's, if Zayn had recently picked up a helium-balloon-sucking habit.

"Zayn?" I repeated uncertainly, taking a tentative step toward the dramatic archway that led into the kitchen. "Is that you? What's going—*aaaahh!!*" I screamed, flinging my arms over my head as a multi-colored, airborne blob hurtled out of the kitchen and dove straight at my face.

"Help me!" the thing shouted as it sailed past me like a gay-pride missile.

I spun around like a top, scrubbing strands of merlot hair from my eyes. "What the f—"

My voice trailed off as a large blue and green parrot landed on the back of the white leather couch directly in front of me, shaking out its massive iridescent wings before gracefully tucking them back into place. Long, rainbow-colored tail feathers trailed behind it, nearly sweeping the floor, as its wide eyes took me in.

"Help me," it whimpered, lifting a trembling claw.

I stood there in shock, unable to move or speak – not from the surprise air offensive launched by the most stunningly beautiful creature I'd ever laid eyes on, or even the fact that this parrot, not Zayn, had been the one crying for help. No, what was most shocking was that I was fairly certain I'd seen this parrot before. From its big, gold-speckled, black eyes to its lustrous turquoise body and intricate feather patterns, all the way down to its impossibly colorful tail that transitioned from royal purple to crimson red with every color of the rainbow in between. I took a cautious step forward, watching my own reflection in its large, unblinking eyes. Its head feathers ruffled and then unruffled as it took me in, no doubt sizing me up in the same way I was sizing it up.

Yes, I was absolutely sure I had seen this parrot before, because it was all but a photocopy image of the crowning element in the intricate tattoo sleeve that Zayn sported from his right shoulder to his wrist; one that featured a gorgeous exotic bird whose long rainbow tail curled around Zayn's muscular bicep and forearm, ending in an exquisite splash of symbols and runes – the meanings of which he never saw fit to explain. This parrot had to have been the inspiration for said tattoo, though my boss had never mentioned owning a pet bird before. And a creature like this certainly deserved to be mentioned, because it was like nothing I'd ever seen before – some sort of hybrid between a rainbow macaw, a bird-of-paradise, and one of those mythical phoenixes I'd seen in that movie about the boy wizard.

Already bored with my basic wine-colored head feathers, the parrot turned its own head 180 degrees to preen the teal fluff on its back. Entranced, I took another step closer, marveling at the radiance of its plumage, which shimmered like the iridescent surface of a bubble: royal blue, emerald green, and even a flash – I gulped, recognition suddenly dawning on me – of deep purple… just like the color-changing *Peacock* ink I'd held in my hand the night before.

As the parrot inclined its head at me, understanding clicked into place. This parrot wasn't the inspiration for Zayn's tattoo.

This parrot *was* Zayn's tattoo.

IV.
BRINGING ART TO LIFE

"You've gone insane." I rubbed my eyes, grateful that I'd forgotten to put on mascara that morning. "Tattoos don't just come to life."

Yeah, and cobra-rattlesnakes don't exist, Inner-Voice Talia replied haughtily.

"Hello!" the glittering rainbow chicken exclaimed, lifting its claw in an amiable gesture that looked remarkably like a wave.

"Um, hello," I waved awkwardly. "And who might you be?"

It ruffled its turquoise head feathers, then shook them out. "Biss-kiss!"

"Huh?"

"Biss-kiss!"

"Are you saying 'biscuit?'" I frowned. "Is that supposed to be your name?"

"Biscuit!" it chimed, tail feathers wagging.

"Um, hi, Biscuit," I replied, feeling fairly idiotic. "I'm Talia."

It let out an excited screech. "*Tal*-ya!"

"TAL-ee-yuh," I repeated.

"Tal-ya!" Biscuit beat his wings twice. "Want almond!"

"Are you asking if I want an almond?" I blinked stupidly. "Or, er, do *you* want an almond?"

Biscuit cocked his head at me – I'd arbitrarily decided just then that he was a boy – then spread his wings and launched right past me, his magenta-pink wingtips grazing my cheek. He sailed under the high archway, landing gracefully on Zayn's spotless white countertop in his spotless white kitchen. "Talya! Come here!" he squawked.

Not knowing what else to do, I went.

Biscuit tapped his beak on one of the white cabinets as I approached. "Want almond!"

Hand trembling – seriously, where the *hell* was Zayn? – I opened the cabinet door to find an entire Ziploc bag of raw, unshelled almonds. When I took it out, Biscuit let out a high-pitched screech and started pacing back and forth on the countertop, which I could only interpret as extreme impatience.

"So, um, where's Zayn?" I asked, taking an almond from the bag.

"Almond! Want almond!"

I sighed in frustration. "Zayn! Where's Zayn?"

"Help me!" Biscuit screeched. "Want almond!"

"Fine! Here," I said, thrusting the nut at his fairly intimidating beak; much like my mother's temper, I didn't ever want to be on the wrong end of it. "In fact, take a few more while we're at it," I added, gingerly placing an extra handful in front of him.

As he greedily attacked the mound of nuts, I rummaged through Zayn's cabinets until I found a small metal bowl, which I filled with fresh water and set in front of Biscuit. He was already annihilating his third almond by then, sending bits of broken shell ricocheting across the counter. But when he saw the bowl, he immediately hopped over and practically dunked his entire face in it, filling the lower part of his beak with water and tipping his head back several times to drink. A pang of sympathy made my breath catch. When was the last time the poor creature had eaten or drunk anything?

Then again, does a tattoo even need food? Or a cage? I frowned, now 99.999% sure that Zayn's colorful bird tattoo had indeed flown the coop – er, sleeve. Well, whatever it was – exotic animal or ink – I hadn't seen a cage or any other bird supplies in the apartment.

I shook my head at the absurdity of it all as I wandered out of the kitchen, feeling like a total creep. I hated this, skulking around my boss's empty apartment like the unwelcome intruder I most definitely was. If he walked in right now, what could I even say to defend myself? Oh, God, what if he had a silent alarm system that notified the police of a break-in?

What if they're already on their way? I fretted.

I tried to push that discomforting thought to the back of my mind as I made my way through Zayn's home, careful not to touch a thing while I kept an eye out for hints of where he may have gone. Not that there was much to touch, apart from the posh furniture and an almond-addicted bird. Despite his fashionable clothing, perfectly sculpted hair, and abundance of flashy tattoos, Zayn evidently lived as a minimalist, with just the random ornamental bowl or rug for decoration. Which made my sleuthing all the more unnerving. There were no dirty dishes, no sticky notes, no signs whatsoever that anyone had even lived here recently – save for one mug of coffee sitting on an end table, which was half empty and completely cold. The longer I searched, the more anxious I became. Why had his front door been unlocked? Had someone broken in? What if he'd been kidnapped?

Well, that *might be a stretch,* I reasoned. After all, I'd personally witnessed him cuff one of my troublesome clients straight in the jaw, knocking all six-plus feet of boob-groping perv straight to the ground.

I had to smile at the memory, though it quickly faded as my brain went into full-on neurosis mode. Was Zayn sick? Had he slipped and fallen in the shower? *Oh, God, what if he hit his head on the side of the tub and drowned??* I felt queasy at the thought.

When I finally mustered the courage to stick my head in his bathroom ten minutes later, I was shaking like a leaf, absolutely positive that I was going to find a gut-splattered crime scene. Luckily, all I found was a tin of cinnamon potpourri sitting on top of the toilet. Still, as I resumed my search, every possible combination of scenarios that could have gone horribly wrong played out in my head, each one worse and more gruesome than the last.

By the time I approached his bedroom door, the last room in his apartment, I was two ragged gasps away from a full-on panic attack. I nervously reached my hand for the knob, then hesitated, fingers hovering over the brushed nickel. My heart was pounding against my ribcage like a battering ram while my stomach felt like a tiny, violent chef was flipping lead pancakes in there.

I'd spent the past two years trying – unsuccessfully – to forget about that night. And yet, here I was, about to enter Zayn's bedroom.

Again.

The first time had happened a few months after he'd offered me my apprenticeship. We were locking up after an exceptionally shitty day – the same day he'd knocked an ex-client to the ground for groping me, as a matter of fact – when he spontaneously invited me to go get a drink. Startled, I'd briefly considered saying no. After all, he was my boss, and an incredibly professional, generous, and emotionally-aloof boss, at that. Furthermore, I didn't want to do anything to mess up our rock-solid dynamic, given my admittedly long and sloppy list of amorous casualties. But something in Zayn's expression made me reconsider – maybe it was the hint of sadness I saw reflected there, or some brief flicker of urgency that crossed his eyes. Hell, maybe it was my own over-zealous, sex-starved imagination. Whatever it was, it didn't help that said expression was situated on the most gorgeous face I'd ever laid eyes on.

Frozen at the threshold of Zayn's bedroom, my hand hovering over the knob as though it were a nuclear launch button, my breath hitched as all the forbidden memories from that evening came flooding back. Memories of us tearing each other's clothes off like animals before the front door had even closed behind us. Memories of how we had stumbled around in the dark until we arrived here, at his bedroom door, where he lifted me up like I was nothing, pressing my bare back against the cool wood. How he'd kissed me deeply, knotting his perfect, skillful fingers through my tousled hair as his tongue danced over mine. How his other hand slid up my skirt and beneath my thong, clutching my ass with a hunger and urgency rivaled only by my own. As I moaned with pleasure, my trembling hand reached down to fumble for the doorknob…the very same one I was now too shy to touch.

I pressed my forehead against the cool wood as a hot flush of longing and embarrassment spread across my face. The memory felt as fresh as the following Monday morning, less than thirty-six hours after our forbidden tryst. I'd shown up to work ten minutes early – a veritable weekday miracle – with a big, doofy grin on my face and two homemade iced coffees in my hands. But I quickly realized that I was the only one smiling. Apart from a curt "Thank you," Zayn was completely silent. And he would remain completely silent for the rest of the day, his soft, perfect lips pressed into a permanent scowl. I was too stunned, too humiliated, to ask what had gone wrong between Saturday night and Monday morning, instead giving my neurotic brain free rein to concoct a dozen different explanations, each one more mortifying than the last. Thankfully, after a few days of awkward silence, business at the shop continued as usual, and Zayn and I fell back into an amiable rapport – though we never discussed that night again.

In my mind, at least, sparks still lingered between us, smoldering in sideways glances, swallowed words, and brief brushes of contact that sent electrifying jolts through my body, but that was it. And that was all it would ever be. It didn't matter what I thought or how I felt. Because even though he never said it, I knew he deeply regretted that night. His silence on the matter had said it all.

But that was then, and this is now, a wistful sigh escaped my lips. *So, suck it up.*

With a deep, trembling breath, my fingers clasped the knob, then turned. The spicy, intoxicating scent of his cologne was the first thing I noticed, concentrated and magnified within those four walls. His king-sized bed was the second, as my eyes trailed to the black satin comforter that once lay tangled beneath our naked bodies, now neatly folded and tucked beneath the edges of the mattress. There were no clothes draped on the chair or dirty socks in the hamper. There were no empty bags of chips on the nightstand or scattered papers on the desk. The bed was empty. The room was empty. The attached bathroom was empty.

He wasn't here.

A sudden wave of emotion hit me, a big, messy tangle of worry and grief and longing and despair. Leaning against his door frame – while vaguely noticing that this too had a strange symbol painted on the upper corner – I slid to the floor, pressing my forehead to my knees. "Zayn," I whispered, "where are you?"

A colorful flurry of feathers landed at my feet. "Help," it cooed.

A sharp stab of fear hit me in the stomach. "Why do you keep saying that?" I demanded. "Where did you even learn it?"

Biscuit fluttered from the floor to the back of the wooden chair beside Zayn's desk in a single, graceful flap, then cocked his head at the lone item resting atop the polished surface: an old, leather-bound book that looked entirely out of place in the ultra-contemporary apartment. "Help," he repeated, his left eye trained directly on me.

"Was Zayn calling for help?" I asked, rising from the ground. "Is that why you keep saying that?"

The parrot jumped off the chair and landed neatly on my shoulder, where he began taking loose strands of hair from my messy bun and gently preening them with his beak. "I guess that means you like me, huh?" I sighed. "Still wish you could tell me what happened to Zayn, though."

Already growing bored with preening my hair, he fished around my collar and began tugging at the gold chain on my neck.

"It's a locket," I said, pulling the charm out to show him. "My dad gave it to me."

Biscuit didn't care. "Head scratch?" he cooed, using a claw to point to his head.

"Uh, sure," I replied, absentmindedly ruffling his feathers with one hand while reaching for Zayn's peculiar book with the other. "Huh," I frowned, running a finger across the cover.

It was old; that much was certain. The rich, faded leather was soft and worn with age, and the intricate, gold-embossed patterns that curled around the cover were faded and flaking. Embedded among the curls and flourishes, an ornate script spelled out an illegible title in a language that was like nothing I'd ever seen – geometric lines with partial triangles and hollow dots that may as well have been Martian. Zayn's distant ancestors were from Persia, that much I knew, but I was fairly certain this wasn't Farsi. Based on the way the dots were arranged beneath the triangles, it reminded me of Hebrew – vowels, maybe?

As my fingertips traced the text, the gold symbols glinted against the light coming in from the window. Or, at least, I'd thought that was the case; but when I glanced over my parrot-free shoulder, I realized that Zayn's curtains had been pulled shut. Leaning forward, I peered more closely at the letters. They were definitely glowing, but from what source?

Biscuit promptly hopped off my shoulder and landed beside the book, almost as though he was also inspecting it. I couldn't help but laugh. "Hey buddy, whatcha do—*oww!!*" Pain sliced through my index finger. For absolutely no apparent reason, the little shit had lurched forward and *bit* me, breaking right through the skin on my knuckle.

"What the hell!" I yelped, yanking my hand away. As I did, several drops of blood splattered across the cover of the book. I sucked in a ragged gasp as text and symbols that definitely *hadn't* been there before started lighting up the leather like the freaking scrolling marquee in Times Square.

"Gold blood," Biscuit shrieked, flapping his wings. "Talya! *Squawk!* Gold blood!"

I staggered backward and away from the malfunctioning psittacine until I nearly tripped over Zayn's bed. "What the hell does *that* mean?"

Biscuit started beating his wings furiously. *"Gold blood!"*

"Stop!" I yelled, shielding my face. When my back pocket started vibrating, I let out a literal scream.

With a parroted screech that surpassed even my own, Biscuit leapt from the desk and tore out of the room, screaming "Gold blood!" over and over as he careened down the hallway.

"This cannot be happening," I whimpered.

Despite the tender throb in my finger, I pinched my arm – hard – and winced at the pain. Nope, still not a dream. Which meant I should probably answer my phone. Keeping my petrified eyes glued to the illuminated text of Zayn's haunted textbook, I fumbled to answer the stupid cellphone, leaving a macabre streak of blood smeared across the splintered screen as I did.

"Hello?!" I blustered.

"What's wrong?" my mother demanded.

"Nothing!" I replied shrilly. "Why does something have to be wrong every time I answer the phone? Can't a person be allowed to answer their phone without you automatically assuming something bad has happened?!" My voice was getting higher and higher with every word, noticeably cracking on the last.

"*Oy, God help me with this meshugge child!*"

"Ugh!" was all I could muster in response. Still, I felt somewhat emboldened by having my mother on the line, immensely aggravating though she was. I took a wary step toward the faintly glowing book, which was becoming dimmer and dimmer by the second.

"*Have you given yourself tetanus yet? Or gangrene? I already warned Doctor Feil just in case, and then I called Rabbi Friedmann and said we might have to move the family plot—*"

"Ma, I have no idea what you're talking about!"

"*I'm talking about that farkakteh tattoo you gave yourself!*"

My hand flew to my back pocket, where I'd shoved the crumpled-up diamond ring design before leaving for work that morning. "First of all," I retorted, snatching up the wad of paper, "we keep an extremely hygienic shop, so no one is getting gangrene! Second of all," I continued, carefully unfolding it, "I never even got the stupid—"

Something small and metallic clattered to the floor.

"*Never got the stupid what?*"

"No way…" I inhaled sharply as I stared at the piece of paper I was clutching, which was now completely blank – save for a tiny splatter of blood from the papercut I'd given myself that morning.

"*Talia!*"

"Hang *on*, Mom!" Forgetting Zayn's book altogether, I knelt to the ground, fumbling to find whatever had just fallen. My fingers closed around something cool and circular. "No way," I repeated, staring at the gleaming object resting on my sweaty palm. "There's no freaking way."

"*Oy, Talia! You're giving me a heart attack! What's wrong? Should I call the police?! Cough twice if you're in trouble—!*"

"Nothing's wrong," I swallowed, slumping backward on my butt. "I just…I need a second." Leaning my head against Zayn's satin comforter, I breathed in his familiar, comforting scent as I gazed at the impossible treasure I clutched: a platinum ring with a massive diamond that was glittering and flawless – save for the tiny patch of dried blood encrusted on the gemstone. My blood.

Gold blood.

The pitter-patter of tiny claws made my head shoot up. Biscuit was sticking his head in the doorway, looking at me with the equivalent of big, black, puppy-dog eyes. "Head scratch?" he cooed plaintively, pointing a claw to the ruffled feathers on his neck. "Talya do head scratch?"

I glanced from him, to the book on Zayn's desk, to the five-carat diamond ring I was clutching in my hand.

"Ma, I'm gonna have to call you back."

V.
Hidden Messages

I'd like to tell you that I steadily rose from that cold marble floor, hands clenched with purpose and conviction as I prepared to unlock the secrets embedded in the magical pages beckoning to me from my boss's desk. I'd *like* to tell you that. Instead, I promptly scrambled to my feet and raced to the bathroom, since the last twenty-seven minutes of havoc and anxiety had gone straight to my delicate bladder.

But immediately after my bladder was satisfactorily emptied and my brand-new, diva-worthy bling was placed on my freshly-washed and bandaged ring finger, I marched straight back to that bedroom and snatched the heavy book off the desk, my heart thrumming with determination. I settled myself onto the foot of Zayn's bed, eyes glued to the flickering lines of symbols and runes that definitely hadn't been there before my "gold blood" lit up the front cover like a Hanukkah bush at the Zuckerberg mansion.

My bandaged finger's sharp-beaked offender landed on my shoulder and began preening my hair as if he hadn't just tried to amputate one of my digits mere moments ago.

"Jerk," I muttered sullenly as I opened the book and flipped through its many hundreds of pages while a tie-dyed seagull plucked at my scalp.

Unfortunately, there would be no secrets to unlock today, because just like my high school German textbook, the entire thing was written in some strange, indecipherable language that may as well have been Klingon. Foreign, hand-scrawled script surrounded each entry, filling every square inch of the weathered parchment. But I was enchanted nevertheless as I traced my fingers over the elaborate designs that filled the book from cover to cover. There must have been a thousand pages crammed into that spine, but at the center of every page lay a different symbol made up of overlapping triangles and circles and intersecting lines that vaguely reminded me of crop circles, except much more colorful and complex.

"Hey, I know this one," I murmured after thumbing a third of the way through the book. It was the exact same blue design that had been scrawled on Zayn's front door.

If only I could read the description, I sighed, then rubbed my eyes. My vision was blurring, making the letters bleed together like that time I developed an ocular migraine in the middle of aforementioned German class. Except the letters hadn't been dancing across the page as they appeared to be doing now. Or forming words that I was beginning to recognize, even though I'd never seen this language before in my life.

"Gold blood," Biscuit bawked, cocking his head to peer at the page I was squinting at.

"Holy shit," I whispered as the words once more blurred into focus. I had no idea how, but I could read them now, perfectly, as though the book had been written in plain English this entire time.

Protection Ward, Used to Defend Against Malignant and Malevolent Miscreants

My eyes widened as the rest of the page described, in painstaking detail, the order of strokes, exact measurements and angles, and specific ink shade ("Hydrangea") that needed to be used when creating said – *gulp* – "Protection Ward." More curious than convinced, I stepped off the bed, carefully cradling the book in my arms and balancing the bird on my shoulder as I strode through the apartment to the front door, where I cracked it open to inspect the symbol Zayn had etched and painted into the frame. Every line, every angle, every stroke was absolutely perfect, matching the illustration inside this book to the exact millimeter.

When I shut the door behind me and gazed around his apartment, I suddenly recognized what my eyes had overlooked when I first arrived – dozens of small, complex runes scrawled all over the place: the top corner of the picture window, the inside of the kitchen archway, the edge of the dining room table…even the abandoned mug of coffee.

"Huh." I crouched beside the end table to get a closer look at the otherwise plain, white mug. This symbol wasn't drawn cleanly or precisely like the others. It was scrawled on there with permanent marker, and hastily so. "I know this one, Biscuit," I declared, no longer caring a whit that I was openly conversing with a bird. "I've seen it, on the filing cabinet in Zayn's office."

Biscuit hopped off my shoulder and began foraging around the underside of the couch. A moment later, he flapped onto the armrest and dropped an uncapped black marker into my hand with a helpful squawk.

"Thanks, buddy," I murmured, examining it. The tip was still wet, which meant it hadn't been uncapped for long.

I knelt down and rooted around the couch until I found the cap. After replacing it, I handed the marker back to Biscuit to play with, then turned my attention back to the mug. My eyebrows knitted together as I swiveled it in my hand, careful not to slosh cold coffee on the rug while examining the design. The lines were uncharacteristically sloppy and rushed, as though Zayn had been in a hurry to leave. But if he was in such a rush, why on earth would he stop to scribble this particular symbol on the one thing in his apartment that he'd left out of place? Sure, Zayn was an idle doodler – most artists are – but I'd never seen him ruin a perfectly good coffee cup.

No, I shook my head. This definitely wasn't left here by accident. And whether it was left for me to find or for someone else, it didn't matter, because I was the only someone who was here.

"C'mon, Biscuit," I held out my hand, which he happily hopped on. "We've gotta go."

With Zayn's heavy book tucked safely beneath my other arm, I spun on my heel and made a beeline for the exit. But just as I reached the front door, Biscuit tugged on my ear.

"What?"

"Almond!"

I let out an aggrieved sigh as I headed back to the kitchen to grab the Ziploc baggie full of almonds, handed him another one, and patiently waited for him to finish so I could clean up the mess he made. Finally, after the bird had been fed and the trashcan had been located, Biscuit and I were on our way.

You'd think that a speeding, Britney Spears-blaring Mazda with a dancing parrot rocking out on the dash would attract a lot of attention on a Wednesday morning, but not in downtown Miami. And even though I'd been prepared to receive a lot of ogling and unwelcome attention once we emerged from the car, I was pleasantly surprised to see an even odder sight drawing the usual crowds toward the end of the block: an old man wearing Daisy Duke cut-off shorts and thigh-high fur boots playing the accordion while his partner, a topless middle-aged lady sporting a live iguana as a headpiece, did a little dancing jig.

Hey man, to each their own.

Anyway, thanks to that fascinating spectacle, my colorful companion and I were able to park and walk right up to Flourish and Dots without any fuss – until I got to the front door and suddenly remembered that the shop had been locked from the inside by some keyless halfwit, a.k.a. me.

"Shhiiiiiit," I sighed, staring at the keys that were dangling on the inside handle, glinting antagonistically in the midday sun.

"Shhiiiiiit," Biscuit parroted, adding a fancy whistle at the end just to be extra. "Head scratch?"

"No head scratch! I have to figure out how to break into my own store without getting arrested," I grunted, setting Zayn's book on the concrete while I considered how one might smash a window inconspicuously.

Biscuit hopped off my shoulder and landed beside the cover, which he nudged open with his beak. I couldn't help but snicker as he flipped through the pages like a little human, acting as though he could actually read—

"Raaawk!" he squawked, tapping one of the open pages with his beak.

Eyes wide as saucers, I knelt beside him and gaped at the page upon which he was excitedly hopping up and down:

Chaining Rune,
Used to Bind, Bolt, and Bond

And there, on the adjacent page, was a similar rune, but with the opposite – and extremely convenient – function:

Unchaining Rune,
Used to Unbind, Unclasp, and Unlock

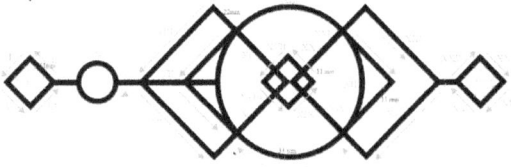

"B-But, how did you—?" I sputtered.

He scratched at the side of his ruffled head with a juddering claw, just like a dog would attack a floppy ear, then looked up at me with big, black-gold eyes. "Almond?"

I blinked, then shook my head in disbelief while I fished one from my purse. "Here you go – thanks for the, um…suggestion."

He happily broke apart his nut while I stared at the disconcertingly specific rune he'd uncovered. It was one of the less complex ones, with just a few overlapping diamonds joining inside a circle. I didn't have the ink it called for, *Stardust*, but I did have the permanent marker from Zayn's house in my back pocket. After pausing to admire the way my massive new diamond ring sparkled in the sun – priorities, I know – I unscrewed the marker, clenching the cap between my teeth, and knelt in front of the handle to vandalize my own storefront.

"Here goes nothing," I muttered, all the more relieved that the nearest crowd was at the end of the block, snapping photos of the scantily-clad iguana couple.

Balancing the open book precariously on one knee, I carefully drew the "Unchaining Rune" one line at a time, following the ridiculously complex instructions to a T. Every stroke had an order of operations. Every angle had a specific measurement. Every line had to be copied to the millimeter. I scrunched my face in concentration, trying my best to force my attention-deficit brain into submission, but let's face it, there's a reason I opted for art school instead of a titillating career in geometry.

After twenty-five painstaking minutes, Biscuit was tugging at the collar of my shirt impatiently. I wiped the sweat from my brow as I squinted at my less-than-perfect creation.

"So, now what?" I asked dubiously.

Instead of being helpful and offering another suggestion, Biscuit began meticulously preening the magenta-and-purple feathers at the top of his wings. Not knowing what else to do, I awkwardly knelt by the door, trying to envision it unlocking from within. I even offered a few words of encouragement to the rune because, hey, a little positivity never hurt anything – or so I told my withering houseplants. But after several minutes of staring at the handle like a complete boob while the noonday sun toasted the back of my neck, I began to feel more than a little foolish.

I glanced at Biscuit, who had abandoned his feathery ablutions to cock his head at me, the incompetent human. "What am I doing wrong?"

"Gold blood!"

I rolled my eyes in exasperation. "Look, tiny dinosaur, if you say that one more time—"

"Hey, what kind of bird is that?"

I whipped around so fast, Biscuit let out an indignant squawk, rudely clamping down on my earlobe for balance. A heavily spray-tanned guy in bright pink shorts was standing behind us, lowering his aviators to gawk at the neighborhood vandalizer and her weird looking parrot.

"Oh, he's a, um, Tasmanian rainbow, uh, guinea…fowl."

"Dude, that's so sweet! Hey guys – come look at this crazy-looking parrot!" he shouted at his throng of neon-clad buddies across the street.

"Biscuit!" I hissed, tucking a sweaty piece of hair behind my ear. "What do I do?" Without warning, the little shit *bit me again*, drawing a gnarly gash across my pinky. "What the hell!" I shrieked as I yanked my hand away.

"Whoa, dude, I didn't realize it bites!" the guy exclaimed while backing away, then promptly fleeing to the other side of the street.

In a further debasing gesture, Biscuit hopped on top of my head, his dull talons digging into my scalp as he flapped his wings like the malfunctioning turkey he was. "Gold blood! Gold blood!"

"How would you like it if I bit you?!" I shouted, grabbing the handle to pull myself to a proper combat position. Bright red blood smeared across the metal, which glowed as red as a branding iron, then abruptly crumbled apart like a stale cookie. Both bird and human fell silent as the tattoo shop door, now completely handle-free, swung open.

After giving a haughty shake of his feathers, Biscuit leapt off my head and flew inside, leaving me to re-evaluate every single life choice I'd ever made, all of which had culminated in me standing at the threshold of this strange, godforsaken tattoo parlor, stuttering, dumbfounded, and missing a small chunk of my pinky.

Heaving a defeated sigh, I stepped inside.

VI.
INTERDIMENSIONAL FILING CABINETS

As the bell atop the door jingled shut behind me, I was greeted by Biscuit, who was casually perched atop the front desk computer on one foot like a miniature flamingo.

"Have you seen a snake anywhere?" I asked, looking around nervously.

Biscuit shook his head, which was either a coincidental ruffling of his feathers or a negative response. I chose to interpret it as the latter as I took a picture of both runes and saved it on my phone, because, let's face it, I'd probably accidentally lock myself in or out of something at least a couple more times that day. After snapping the book shut, I used my body to heave the waiting area loveseat in front of the broken door to prevent unsuspecting customers from entering. The last thing I needed was a cobra-related, negative review on Yelp. Guilt knotted in my stomach at the thought; I could only hope Roy had fully recovered without requiring too much medical and/or psychiatric intervention (and would, with any luck, skip the poor review).

Speaking of psychiatric interventions.

"If you're in here, Mr. Snake," I called as I minced my way toward the back, "please don't bite me. Or eat the bird," I added for Biscuit's sake.

"Rawk!"

Once safely outside Zayn's locked office, I fished through my purse. The credit card I had repeatedly abused the day prior was in tatters, so I attempted my latest break-in with the grocery discount card I'd borrowed from my mother. As I initiated my tried-and-true lock-jiggering strategy, the small blue rune on the inside of the door jamb caught my eye. I've never been the most observant person in the world, so I had no doubt it had always been there. But I did wonder what the point of a protection ward was if any old dolt like me could break in with a piece of warped plastic.

As the card caught and the door swung open, I pushed that thought to the back of my mind. Zayn's office looked the same as it had yesterday, but I, the intruder, was slightly wiser, and this time I easily recognized the half-dozen runes that appeared on various objects and surfaces. Clutching his book in my hand, I made my way toward the black etching on his filing cabinet, the knot in my stomach growing unrulier by the second. The symbol was small, but far more complex than the one I'd scribbled on the lock outside. I thumbed through the book until I found the coinciding jumble of overlapping circles and squiggles. This one had just over a hundred ordered strokes, compared to the measly thirty-something I'd scrawled outside. As I read the title of the rune, REALM PORTAL, I struggled to swallow the sizable lump that was forming in my throat.

The sound of flapping wings alerted me to Biscuit's presence a moment before he landed on my shoulder.

"I don't get it, Biscuit," I murmured, skimming through the extensive descriptions that surrounded the entry. Unlike the other runes, these didn't go into the symbol's specific purpose or use. The entire page was just detailed steps and directions for creating...well, whatever the hell a "Realm Portal" was. I, for one, had no idea. But I *was* sure about one thing: This was the same symbol Zayn had scribbled on his abandoned mug of coffee for someone to find, even though I had no idea whether or not that "someone" was meant to be me.

Setting the book on Zayn's desk, I let out a heavy sigh as my fingers brushed against the cool metal of the filing cabinet. The cut Biscuit had so graciously bestowed upon my pinky finger hadn't yet scabbed over. Would this symbol respond to my blood the same way the book and door handle had? There was only one way to be sure.

"Isn't this where you start yelling 'gold blood' over and over?" I turned to ask my feathered friend, vaguely dreading the answer.

Biscuit didn't respond. His gaze was glued to something on the other side of the room.

"Fine, whatever. Don't help," I rolled my eyes. At least he wasn't biting me.

Chewing on the inside of my lip, I pressed my bloodied pinky against the rune, half-wishing nothing would happen. No such luck; the black ink immediately illuminated and the surrounding metal began to glow, just like the door handle had. A strange sort of vibration filled the air, one I couldn't exactly hear but could *feel*. Streaks of light escaped through the outer edges of the three drawers, as though a spotlight was shining from the inside of the cabinet. I pulled open the top drawer, the same one that housed Zayn's voodoo ink, and let out a sharp gasp as a blinding light shot out of it like an alien tractor beam. Even as I squeezed my eyes shut against the onslaught, it was bright enough that I could still see it through my eyelids.

When Biscuit started screeching and tugging at my ear urgently, I could only assume it was because the entire room had been set alight. "Don't bite me!" I pleaded, trying to shield both our eyes from the beacon exploding from Zayn's filing cabinet.

The tugging intensified.

"Dude!" I shouted, jerking my ear away. "What's your—ohhhhh shit."

Behind me, less than a foot away from the back of my calf, my scarlet-eyed, scaly black "friend" had reappeared. His flat head was swaying back and forth, hood flared, and sharp fangs bared for battle.

"Biscuit," I murmured, still as a statue, "what do I—hey!!"

Without further tug or preamble, he leapt off my shoulder, folded his wings, and dove head-first into the top drawer.

I ran to the open drawer and peered inside, squinting my eyes against the blinding assault. "Biscuit!" I whisper-hissed. "Come back!!"

The little shit was gone.

A terrifying hiss rose up from the ground as the snake reared its head to strike, its terrible rattle quivering and buzzing like a swarm of angry hornets.

Without pausing to further consider the ramifications, I flung open the bottom drawer of the filing cabinet. A second column of blinding white light shot out of the opening, bleaching the remaining details of Zayn's office completely out of existence – save for the pulsing black rune, which was visible even through the endless, coruscating white.

When the snake lunged, I did the only thing I *could* do: I leapt into the drawer.

I kept expecting to feel the snake's venomous fangs sinking into my bare calf. But there was no pain, not even a scratch, as I plunged into a never-ending sea of bright white light. It continued on forever in every direction, from above and below, blinding me as well as disorienting me. Was I falling? Rising? Standing? Or was I merely suspended, trapped forever in a vast nothingness? *Is this Purgatory?* I bit my lip anxiously. If it was, I wouldn't know. Jews don't talk about the afterlife much. They're too preoccupied with all the inconveniences of this one.

As if on cue, the phone in my back pocket buzzed. *Did they install cell service in the afterlife?* I wondered, squinting against the light as I fumbled to answer.

"H-Hello?"

"So, a Japanese businessman tells his partner of eight years, 'Hiroto, I am very sorry to say, but your wife is dishonoring you with a man of the Jewish faith!'"

"Hi, Mom," I sighed. Look, if I was in fact dead or dying, I didn't want my last words to my mother to be me frantically trying to explain that I'd plunged into the abyss of either death or psychosis. At that moment, both seemed equally plausible since I'd been teetering on the brink of insanity for the past twenty-four hours. But she didn't need to know that.

"Hiroto doesn't believe him, so he rushes home to his wife and says, 'Wife, is it true? Are you dishonoring me with

a man of the Jewish faith?' and she replies, "Husband, that is a lie, I swear it! Where did you hear such dreck and mishegas?"

I let out a mirthless laugh. "Alright, Mom, I'll give you that one. Um, hey, listen..." My voice caught, so I cleared my throat and tried again. "I just wanted you to know – I mean, I know I don't say it a lot, but..." The creeping panic was finally setting in, turning my stomach to heavy, grinding stones. Was this the last conversation I'd ever have with my mother? Was I about to abandon her as well, leaving her both widowed and childless?

"What's wrong? What happened?"

"I just wanted to say I love you," I blurted out. "I'm sorry I didn't – don't – say it more often."

My mom chuckled, almost to herself. *"I love you too, my farshtinkener pain-in-the-tuchus child."*

I opened my mouth, hoping to tell her goodbye. But the call crackled, then faded to static, before I could get the words out. Meanwhile, the white light had begun to dim. Where there was nothing but blinding oblivion before, fuzzy lines and details began to emerge, like fog fading over the ocean.

"Rawk!"

"Biscuit!" I practically screamed as he landed on some insubstantial half-formed thing right in front of me.

"*Tal*-ya!" he squawked with an accompanying flap of his wings.

"Holy crap, Biscuit – look at you!" I gasped, taking in the stunning creature perched before me. The faint decorative lines of tribal scrollwork that were once barely visible upon his plumage now stood out like golden thread, delicate and glinting. And the colors! If I'd thought his feathers were bright before, I may as well have been looking at him in a darkened broom closet. I'd never seen such exquisite purples or greens or blues before, probably because there was no pigment on earth that was saturated or luxurious enough. Cautiously, I stretched out a trembling finger to touch his long, glittering tail feathers, each as brilliant and multifaceted as a finely-cut gem.

He puffed out his feathers and gave his tail a self-satisfied flick. "Almond?"

"Oh. Sure." I obediently handed him the last nut from my purse, which was miraculously still hanging from my shoulder. I was about to ask him whether we were dead or not when a low hiss from behind us made my stomach sink to my knees. "Oh, no," I whispered, slowly turning around. Two eyes, as red as rubies, were staring back at me – from five feet off the ground.

"Gaaahh!" I screamed, flinging myself backward.

A low, hauntingly-familiar voice chuckled. "Don't worry, he won't hurt you."

My own green eyes nearly bugged out of my head once I realized the snake wasn't floating – it was being held aloft, its oil-slick body curled around the tattooed, muscular forearm that was gently cradling it. A muscular forearm that was conspicuously missing its most prominent feature: a colorful bird with flowing tail feathers.

"Z-Zayn?" I choked as the blurry outline of a man began to materialize in the dissolving light.

He stepped into existence, illuminated from behind like some insanely gorgeous cherubim. When the features of his face manifested into view, my jaw literally dropped. His eyes, always such a piercing shade of green, now glowed with emerald fire. His skin shimmered as though dusted with bronze mica, and his dark hair, normally black, was now the deepest shade of midnight blue and perfectly tousled. The planes of his cheeks and jawline were so perfectly defined, it was as though he'd been chiseled from marble. But I nearly choked when I took in the rest of him; there were so many ripples and dips beneath that black, tight-fitting, three-quarter-sleeved shirt, all the blood went straight from my face to my…not face.

"Blood incarnates seldom hurt their creators," he smiled that crooked, heart-wrenchingly beautiful smile of his, "let alone one of the Golden Blooded. By the way, why do you keep calling my familiar 'Biscuit'?" He cocked a bemused eyebrow at me.

"Zayn," was the only response I could muster while my brain was going haywire at the immaculate, almost ethereal sight of him. But it wasn't just him – it was also his office, which was slowly coming back into focus as the light from the cabinet that Biscuit was perched on continued to dim. I kept trying to blink away my muddled vision, but it didn't work – every color in the room was just *wrong*, as if everything had been inverted. And half the items in the room were glowing like bioluminescent jellyfish.

My head was swiveling around so much, I actually began to feel nauseated. "Wh-What…What's going on…?" I stammered, clutching the side of my head. "Where are we?"

Zayn held up his free hand – the one that wasn't enveloped by a cobra – which Biscuit took as an invitation to land on. "Hello, Hibiscus," he murmured, nuzzling the top of the parrot's head.

"Biss-kiss!"

One of my eyebrows hiked in response. "His name is Hibiscus? But I thought he—"

"She. And yes."

"Wait…Biscuit's a *she?*"

At that, Zayn frowned. "Well, I'd always assumed so."

"And the snake?" I all but shrieked.

"You tell me – you're the one who brought it into the world." He waggled his snake-wrapped fingers in the air.

I shook my head wildly, half in confusion, half in fury as the questions tumbled out of my mouth like an avalanche. "Where have you been? What is this place? Why are you holding that snake? What is up with all these tattoos coming to life? And what the hell is going on with your face?!"

He let out another infuriating chuckle and shook his head as though *I* was the one holding a magic butt snake, then said, "My face? You should see yours."

"My face—!" I sputtered, yanking the compact from my purse. "What the hell do you mean, my fa—oh holy hell, what is happening to my face." My jaw dropped even further as I took in the psychotropic sight of my glowing cheeks. Not, like, flushed-with-radiance glowing. But literally glowing. With gold light. As though rivers of hot, molten gold were flowing through my veins. I dropped the compact and held up my hands in astonishment – they, too, were glowing as if illuminated from the inside with golden magma.

Feeling my knees begin to buckle, I promptly plopped to the ground, where I sat cross-legged with my face clutched in my freakishly glowing hands.

When Zayn knelt beside me, I didn't yelp at the sight of the cobra that was now two inches from my nose, but I did burst into tears as my boss's impossibly beautiful eyes took in mine. "I was so scared you were hurt!" I sobbed. "And now I'm pretty sure I'm dead! That, or certifiably insane!"

Zayn cupped his index finger beneath my chin, using his thumb to brush away a stray tear. "C'mon, Goldilocks," he smiled tightly, then stood to help lift me to my shaky feet. "We've got a lot of catching up to do."

VII.
Gold Blood

I sat in front of Zayn's desk while he made us coffee in the breakroom, tapping my foot neurotically as I took in the office that wasn't his office. I mean, everything was theoretically where it should be, but all of the colors were wrong. After Zayn had shut the cabinet drawer and the lighting returned to "normal," I realized it was a lot weirder than the colors simply being inverted. To start, everything was still glowing like one of those trippy black light posters from the nineties, except there was no UV bulb in the room. And then there was the fact that there were colors I couldn't – I swallowed hard – couldn't *name*. As in, I'd never seen them before. It was like someone had taken the tiny sliver of visible light that human brains are able to perceive – you know, good ol' *Roy G. Biv* – and lengthened it to *Leroy Gottfried Biversfort, Esq.* I saw purples I'd never seen before. Reds I'd never dreamed of. A book that used to be "blue" was now…well, it was sort of like magenta and periwinkle got drunk and had a threesome with vermillion. But it was all somehow one color.

Meanwhile, perched on the back of Zayn's empty chair, Bisc—er, *Hibiscus*—glinted and dazzled like a gem-encrusted disco ball. Even the freaking cobra, who had settled into a contented coil beneath the desk lamp, was no longer just *black*; he was made up of hundreds of shifting colored scales that somehow blurred into "black" if I stared right through them, like one of those trippy 3D photos that's just a bunch of static until you unfocus your eyes and look past it to see the hidden image. Trippier still, both animals emitted this bizarre aura that looked like a floating dust cloud of glitter. No matter how many times I rubbed my eyes, it wouldn't go away.

And then, of course, there was me, sitting there polished and gleaming like a goddamned Academy Award. The ring I'd designed for myself was throwing out so many too-many-colored rainbows, I had to take it off – *me*, take off a stunning, custom-designed diamond ring – and put it in Zayn's desk drawer because it was just so discombobulating. I kept snapping open my compact, frantically inspecting my gold-illumined skin, slamming it back down on the desk, and then obsessively picking it up again to check to see if I still looked like Michael Phelps's trophy shelf.

Indeed, I did.

"Hey," Zayn murmured, gently setting a steaming mug of coffee in front of me before taking a seat on the other side of the desk. I resisted the urge to chug it and instead gripped the ceramic between two shaking hands to try to protect my white – well, now purple-fluorescing – tank top.

He took a long sip, set the cup down, and steepled his fingers. After opening his mouth and abruptly closing it again, he ran a hand through that inhumanly gorgeous midnight blue mane with a heavy sigh. "Honestly, Tal, I'm not sure where to begin."

"You could start by telling me why you, me, the freaking *menagerie*, and your entire office look like a bad acid trip!" I gestured belligerently. "And, quick side query, why do I suddenly not have a single bar of cell phone service?!"

"Well, first of all, we're literally in a different dimension than T-Mobile so you're not going to have service here."

"Come again?"

"Secondly, this isn't my office. Not an office you've ever been inside, at least. This is my office in the Fae Realm."

"Fae…Realm?" I blinked stupidly, then shook my head in a huff. "Where the hell did that filing cabinet take us? *Narnia?!*"

"Look, how about this?" he said, leaning back in his chair. "I'll tell you everything, so long as you promise not to interrupt me every five seconds."

"No!" I blurted out, then thought the better of it. "Well, maybe. Just – *ugh!* Talk fast!"

"Fine," Zayn sighed. Biscuit had hopped on his shoulder to seek head scratches, which Zayn was absentmindedly providing. Meanwhile, the snake was still blissfully sunning itself under the unnaturally colored bulb of the lamp, which I guess we were all just accepting as a normal thing at the moment. "You are not on Earth right now. You stepped through the portal—"

"The filing cabinet, you mean?"

He gave me a pointed look.

"Sorry. Shutting up."

"Yes, the filing cabinet, upon which I'd endowed a portal rune. When you stepped through it, you entered the Fae Realm – it's a world that exists directly on top of your world, completely invisible to the human eye. It's a realm of magic, ruled by a different star, which is why you can see colors and auras here that are otherwise invisible on earth."

"O...kay," I ventured, glancing once more at my phone, since at least one of us was in dire need of a seventy-two-hour psychiatric hold.

"Even though our realms – or dimensions, you might say – are interfolded, what happens in the human world doesn't usually affect the fae world, and vice-versa. We coexist side by side, like a room separated by a mirrored window. Those on one side of the glass can see into the other realm, but those on the mirrored side see only themselves, incorrectly assuming they're alone in the universe."

"In other words, humans are just sitting around picking their noses while..." I swallowed, "while *fae* are secretly watching them and laughing? Is *that* what you've been doing for the past two days?"

"No. And to be fair, most fae are unconcerned with the minutiae of human lives, save for those who choose to, um...interact with them." Zayn cleared his throat. "And I haven't been sitting around idly for two days. I literally just came back to grab additional supplies and make sure the shop hadn't burned down. And by the look of things," he motioned blithely toward the snake, the portal, and my skin, "I made the right choice."

My mouth opened to launch an attack, but Zayn quickly interjected. "Anyway," he continued, "in the Fae Realm, all magic is exposed, which is why many fae, including myself, choose to practice our craft discreetly on earth, where we can hide among the mundane. No offense intended, of course."

I shook my head, trying to make sense of it all. "So, you're...a fae?"

He leaned forward in his seat, resting his chiseled chin on interfolded fingers. "Yes."

I racked my brains, trying to remember my limited knowledge of mystical folklore. "And fae are…what exactly? Fairies?"

Biscuit made a sound that sounded alarmingly like a snort, then hopped off Zayn's shoulder to perch on the desk lamp that the cobra was dozing beneath.

Zayn rolled his eyes. "There are a multitude of varieties. Banshees. Changelings. Brownies. Dryads. Elves. Gnomes. Leprechauns. Boggarts. Mermaids. Nymphs. Incubi—"

"Wait, wait, wait – mermaids actually exist?"

"In this realm, yes."

"Holy shit," I breathed, forgetting, in my Disney-esque excitement, to ask exactly what sort of fae was sitting directly across from me. "And, because we're actually in your home world right now, this is what you and Bisc…er, Hibis—ugh!" I shook my head in frustration. "Screw it, I'm just sticking with Biscuit! *Anyway*," I continued before he or the parrot could interrupt, "this is what you two really look like? Because you're both…magic?"

He rapped his knuckle on the book I had stolen from his apartment. "I practice magic. *Hibiscus* was created using Life Magic, similar to what you used with our snake friend, here. But yes, pedantry aside, this is what we look like without the ruddy, dull filter of the human realm." He leaned backward, suddenly appearing uncomfortable. "I'm sorry if it's…unsettling."

"No problem," I squeaked, then cleared my throat. "But, um, maybe you could tell me why *I* happen to look like a polished lemon here, since I don't have a magical bone in my body?"

With a tired-sounding sigh, Zayn rose from his seat to pace. And I may or may not have gotten lightheaded at the sight of those taut muscles rippling under his tight jeans and even tighter black shirt. Leprechaun, mermaid – whatever the hell the man was – he was almost too gorgeous for words in this realm.

"As I said, magic can't be seen on the other side of the portal, which is why I spend most of my time on earth, conducting business." He walked around the desk and knelt in front of me, placing his hands on the armrests of my chair. "It's also why I keep you under close watch."

"Me?" I pressed my body into the back of my seat, my heart thrumming with trepidation and something else I couldn't quite name. "Why would you want to spend your time in some dull, ruddy tattoo shop with me?" I added in a high squeak, once again feeling the blood moving from my face to other parts of my body.

A wan smile appeared on his hypnotically attractive face. For reasons unbeknownst to me, my mind immediately went to terrible, wicked places – places that had no need for clothing or decorum. Places that involved our tangled, naked bodies writhing in ecstasy. Places such as on the bare floor, against the wall, or atop the desk…

Biting my lip, my eyes trailed to where Zayn's hands gripped the chair, where his white-knuckled fingers were digging into the fabric. When I looked back, I could see the reflection of my own face in his eyes, a splash of gold in those lush, bottomless pools. His Adam's apple bobbed as he swallowed, a sharp intake of air that made me wonder if this inexplicable yearning wasn't, in fact, one-sided.

For no reason at all, Biscuit screeched, startling us both. Even the snake lifted its head from its coiled body, then settled back in for another open-eyed nap.

"I'm sorry," Zayn started, rising to his feet. He leaned against the side of his desk, gripping the edge with both hands. He took several deep breaths, shaking his head as if to clear it.

Slowly, gently, he reached forward to take my father's locket in his hand. Where his fingers brushed against the hollow of my throat, my skin became electrified.

"Do you remember the day this necklace broke?" he asked.

I could only nod. The clasp had broken on my first day at work, sending me into a complete panic. When I had finished explaining through mascara-stained tears that it was a gift from my father and I never took it off, Zayn took it to the back and emerged an hour or so later with a repaired necklace, its clasp as good as new.

"Turn it over," he instructed.

I took the locket from his hand, practically jumping as our fingertips touched, and did as I was told. On the back of the locket, a yellow rune was glowing beneath the metal, pulsing in time with my heart.

"How did you—" I choked. "But this…this symbol wasn't there before!"

"This artifact you wear around your neck is a powerful talisman from my world. How you came upon it – or rather, how your father came upon it – I can only guess."

"I don't understand," I gulped.

"It shields magic, making its bearer all but invisible in the eyes of most magic seers. As I can see what certain others of my kind cannot, I saw you for what you were and took it upon myself to add an extra layer of protection to keep you hidden from the others. Unfortunately, neither talisman nor rune is enough to shield you from the magic-revealing properties of this realm."

"But why?" I drew my knees up to my chest. "Why would I need to be hidden? Or protected?"

Zayn wearily rubbed the bridge of his nose before taking a deep breath. "Fae magic," he began, "is sourced and controlled in a multitude of ways. Some fae have ancient talismans that have been passed down by their ancestors – like your necklace."

"But how did my fath—"

He continued as though I hadn't interjected. "Paired with ancient spells and runes, others use catalysts – magic-endowed ingredients – like the ink you thoughtlessly borrowed without permission." His eyes narrowed at me pointedly, making me shrink even further into my seat. "But the root of fae magic – the strongest fae magic – is sourced from blood. And some blood types are more magically-inclined than others. Sadly, the most powerful bloodlines have all but gone extinct in my world."

"And in my world?" I managed to squeak, since the growing lump in my throat had taken up permanent residence by now.

"On Earth, magical blood is extremely rare. There are humans with close fae ancestry that have the potential – and perhaps, the limited aptitude – for magic, though most have no idea. But for those few who become aware of it, the key is in the *type* of blood."

Zayn rose from the edge of his desk and started pacing again. Biscuit, still comfortably perched atop the lamp, was watching him, head rotating back and forth like he was watching a tennis match.

"As you know, there are four basic blood phenotypes that exist – A, B, O, and AB – and each of those is further broken down into positive or negative varieties based on what humans call the Rhesus factor. Where I come from, we refer to those blood types as Extractors, Endowers, Benefactors, and Manipulators, each with Universal and Limited sub-types. O-negative blood types – Universal Benefactors, as we call them – have the strongest capacity to spark magic with the help of a fae-created catalyst. However, they have poor control over their creations. Those with AB-negative blood – Universal Manipulators – have the greatest capacity to control magical incarnates once spawned into existence, but struggle to create them themselves. In short, there is no common blood type in your world that allows a fae descendant to both create and fully control their incarnates."

By then, I'd started to understand where this conversation was heading, and I didn't like it. Not one bit.

"And because we lost so many powerful mages in the recent Blood Wars," Zayn continued, shaking his head, "there are also none who can both create and control incarnates in my own world. Not without additional help, which can be hard to come by. That's where you come in," he added, making me flinch. "What most people, and even fae, don't know is that there are actually millions of blood type varietals outside of the common eight, and the rarest one is shared by—"

"Less than fifty people on Earth," I finished, feeling every last morsel of hemoglobin drain from my face. My blood type, *Rh-null*, was so incredibly rare, I had hospitals reaching out to me every single week begging me for blood donations. On the flip side, if I ever needed an emergency blood transfusion, I'd be completely and utterly screwed.

Zayn had stopped pacing. "I sensed your blood from the moment you walked into this shop, Talia. Yours is what we call gold blood; inside your veins, you possess the key to unlocking magic without a talisman, catalyst, or external magic. Your blood is so valuable, in fact, that many other fae would have killed you on the spot and drained you of every last drop to use for their own magical aspirations."

"That's why you hired me so quickly," I gasped. "That's why you paid me three times what my starting wage should have been and refused to take an apprenticeship fee. I thought you were just insanely nice! Or crazy! But in actuality…" my voice trailed off as the truth hit me. "In actuality, you just wanted my blood."

Zayn shook his head. "I wanted to *protect* your blood. There's a big difference between coveting and safeguarding."

"Protect my blood?!" I exploded, leaping from my chair to go forehead to chin with the infuriating man. "If you were so worried about my damn blood, why the hell did you just disappear and leave me here with nothing but a stupid parrot?"

"Raaawk!" Biscuit screeched indignantly.

"You know what I mean!" I screeched back.

The snake stirred from its open-eyed nap, rearing its head back in alarm. I took a tentative step backward as a disgruntled hiss shot from its mouth.

Zayn wordlessly took my hand in his, sending another bewildering, vexatious zing of electricity through my lower abdomen, and brought his warm lips to the half-healed cut on my finger. As he gently sucked on the wound, I choked back a shuddering gasp, fighting the urge to violently rip his clothes off. I couldn't remember the silly reason I was angry with him a few seconds before, and it didn't matter anyway. I wanted him. *Needed* him. In fact, I'd never needed anyone or anything so desperately in my entire life. Heat pulsed in my core, making my neck and chest and thighs flush with desire. When his bright, probing eyes settled on mine, my fingers twitched uncontrollably.

What the hell is wrong with me?

My eyes widened, first in arousal, and then horror, as he brought his fingers to his mouth, staining the tips gold, then brushed my blood along the edge of the snake's flared hood. "Tell your creation to return home," he spoke calmly.

"G-Go home," I uttered reflexively, caught in the hypnotic trance of Zayn's unnaturally green eyes.

In a flash of bright crimson light, the snake disappeared.

"Where – what the…!" I yanked my hand from Zayn's and spun around wildly, looking for the disgruntled serpent. Twenty seconds later, the phone on his desk began to ring. I arched an accusatory eyebrow. "I thought no one could reach us here!"

"I said there was no *cellphone* service here," he smirked. Smirked! Oh, how I wanted to slap that smirk straight off his face. "That's probably your client, wondering why his missing tattoo magically reappeared. Before you ask, I suspect he has a close fae relative in the family – likely unbeknownst to him – and O-positive blood. Limited Benefactor plus catalyzing ink equals runaway creations."

"Hang on," I shook my head, trying to get rid of the creeping ache in my temples. "Back up. Remind me what a Benefactor is again. And what's the Limited part mean?"

"All fae – and close relatives of fae – with type-O blood are Benefactors," Zayn answered patiently. "People who can spark magic with a catalyst. But O-negative is far more powerful – and far rarer – than O-positive. That's why we refer to one as Universal and one as Limited. Same with Manipulators, and…what?" he asked, cocking his head. "Too much information?"

"Yes," I moaned. My mind was reeling with all this new information. "Could you just, like, explain this whole blood magic system to me like I'm five?"

Zayn tapped his chin a moment. "Okay, so, Extractors harness magic from its natural sources: plants, rare minerals, ancient artifacts – even other creatures, in some cases. Vampires, for example, can temporarily wield the same power as their unwitting victim, for as long as the victim's blood remains in their tissues."

My eyes widened in horror.

"Endowers rechannel that extracted magic into artifacts such as pigments or talismans that henceforth become magical catalysts. Benefactors can then use those catalysts to create, and loosely control, their magical creations and incarnates, while Manipulators are sought after for their infallible ability to seize and maintain control of magic... Pretty simple, really."

I was gaping at the beguiling fae wordlessly, my brain buzzing with at least forty-seven additional questions that I wanted to hurl at him, when Zayn's head whipped toward the door of his office.

"An Intruder Rune has been triggered," he barked as he leapt over the desk and yanked open his filing cabinet. Immediately, the entire office became inundated with brilliant, disorienting light. "Get in the portal, now!"

With an obedient chirp, Biscuit flew off his lamp-perch and dove into the drawer.

"B-But," I started.

"No questions, no argument – just go!" Zayn hissed, pushing me toward the blinding light, now an undulating kaleidoscope of a hundred different colors.

"Fine!" Plugging my nose like I was about to leap off a diving board, I jumped inside, letting the dazzling light bleach away everything else. A few disorienting moments later, a firm hand circled my arm, steadying me as I stumbled into Zayn's *other* office. The one that was dull, dimly-lit, and normal-colored.

Earth! I exhaled gratefully.

The bell out front jingled, though the door was still barricaded by the couch.

Whirling me around with two rough hands, Zayn let out a curse as he took in my face. "Dammit!"

"Zayn?" a woman's voice called from outside the shop.

"What's wrong?" I squeaked.

"Your skin – it's still glowing," he muttered through gritted teeth. He grasped my locket in his hand, turned it over, and let out a low growl. "Talia, listen to me – no matter what happens, no matter what you hear out there, stay right here. Do you understand me?"

"But, but," I stammered, "I already blocked the front door with the couch!"

"A couch won't stop a fae!"

"But how—"

"Talia!" he gripped my shoulders roughly, brilliant eyes flashing. "Unless you want to be drained of every drop of golden blood you possess, you will stay here and be silent. The rune I placed on your locket protected you from being sniffed out in the human world. But after crossing the realms and unlocking your magic, you've become a walking neon sign that marks you as the single most coveted commodity in the entire fae population. Which is why I've told you time and time again *not to touch my damn ink drawer!!*"

"Then why did you leave the mug for me to find?"

"How silly of me not to anticipate you burglarizing my house after one day of missed work!"

I stared at him for a hot second before a string of curses tumbled out of my mouth, most of which would make my own mother keel over from a heart attack. The translation, in non-expletive-laced terms, was essentially, "Perhaps you should have put a lock on the drawer if you knew it would be this much of a problem."

"Zayn!" the woman called again, this time from inside the store.

A frightened gasp tore from my throat.

"Don't. Move," he hissed, then spun on his heel. "Hibiscus, come."

The parrot flew off the filing cabinet in a streak of color that soon became an incorporeal streak of light. In the blink of an eye, he was gone – once more a two-dimensional tattoo embedded in my boss's arm.

"Holy shit!" I whispered, clapping a hand over my mouth.

Zayn rubbed his forearm brusquely, then left without another word, locking the door behind him.

VIII.
Uninvited Guests

After only a moment's hesitation, I ran to the door, cupping my ear against the smooth wood to eavesdrop.

"Zayn!" a woman exclaimed. She had a strange lilt to her voice, but it wasn't an accent I could readily place. "You weren't trying to keep me out with a couch, were you?" A high, tinkling laugh followed.

"Salen," Zayn answered cordially. "I wasn't expecting you so soon. Or at such an early hour."

"As my father said in his earlier correspondence, time is of the essence," she replied, though her next words were too muffled to understand.

I smushed the entire left side of my face against the door as I strained to hear.

"...gathered the ingredients already?"

"I was able to collect all but one, despite the inherent dangers of the wetlands," he answered in a slightly clipped tone. "I must confess, I was rather perturbed that Sol would make such a request without allowing me adequate time to prepare. I very nearly lost my foot to a kelpie."

"Ah, but you came back in one delicious piece, did you not?"

"Barely," he groused, though she didn't seem to notice his tone.

"Frankly, returning empty-handed poses a far greater risk to your personal well-being than those nuisance creatures in the wetlands. After all, we both know Sol is nowhere near as forgiving as I am."

My eyebrows scrunched together at the audacity of this broad, whose smirk could practically be heard through the door. Why the hell was Zayn letting her talk to him like that?

A prolonged beat of silence ensued before he eventually cleared his throat. "As you and Sol both know, the alabaster varietal of delphinium hasn't been seen in several decades. However, I have a connection – a reliable source who informs me that he knows of a place where they may still flourish. I just needed to return for more supplies before making the journey. The first one alone nearly wiped me out of healing tonics, which is bad for business."

"For your sake, I hope this 'connection' of yours comes through, or you'll have far more to worry about than bad business. You, more than anyone, understand the ferocity of Sol's temper. Just because you've managed to remain on his good side for the past few seasons doesn't mean his mood can't be soured."

Carefully, slowly – as slowly as my fingers would allow – I clasped the handle and pulled it down one agonizing millimeter at a time. The door let out the tiniest click as the latch caught and held. I held my breath as I slooooowly pushed the door open, creating a sliver of an opening just wide enough to peer one eye through.

A woman with waist-length, platinum blonde hair and a body straight out of Playboy magazine was standing in front of Zayn, hands placed between her slender waist and wide hips. Her skin-tight pants were made from some sort of maroon, vinyl-like material that almost looked like it was made out of scales, and her blouse was gauzy white and completely sheer. Apparently, I wasn't the only one to have woken up late that morning, because she appeared to have forgotten her bra altogether. I forced my gaping mouth closed and swallowed an uncomfortable gulp. I'm situated pretty heavily on the heterosexual side of the spectrum, but even I would have paid for this lady's dinner – smug, snobby attitude aside.

"I've gathered nearly everything," Zayn answered coolly. I couldn't see his face since his back was turned toward me. "I just need a little more time. It's a highly complex dye for an even more complex rune…the use for which, you still have not deigned to tell me."

"You're the greatest Runemaster in both realms," Salen smiled, taking a step forward. "You've never let us down before, so I don't expect you'll start now, hmm?"

My heart sank to my stomach as she reached forward to pull him in for a deep and sensual kiss that he didn't even try to resist. Fingers knotting through his hair, she pressed her fabulous body against his, moaning seductively. Humiliation heated my cheeks as I watched their private moment from the shadows. No wonder he hadn't shown any interest in me after our one-night stand. I wouldn't have either, if this lady was the alternative.

"I've been so hungry," she gasped into his ear. "And it's been such a long time since…" She trailed off as her inhumanly pink eyes landed on mine, lashes narrowing.

Oh, shit! I spun away from the door and nearly knocked over a chair in the process.

"Do you have company…?" she started, then let out another rapturous noise that made my throat seize up as though it'd been freshly coated in strawberry jam, extra histamines included.

That must have been Zayn returning the favor.

My fists clenched. Alone in the darkness, I skipped the chair and slumped against the front of his desk, too afraid and embarrassed to hazard another glance through the crack in the door. Several agonizingly long minutes later, the two of them must have managed to tear away from each other long enough to exchange a few more murmured pleasantries that I didn't bother to spy on. Finally, the sound of her heels clicking across the floor was followed by the faint tinkle of the bell.

"Tell Sol I need five days' time," Zayn called after her. "Six, to be certain."

"I shall tell him five days, my pet, and not a moment longer. By the way, it looks like your Unchaining Rune could use a bit of work," she snipped. "You're supposed to unlock things, dear, not disintegrate them."

Zayn laughed, which somehow made my blood boil more than their impromptu saliva-swapping session.

When the door finally shut behind her, I didn't move from my spot on the cold tile floor. Instead, I just sat there, hugging my knees to my chest. *Get it together, Talia. You just found out that you're a bright gold sitting duck for any and all fae to come and drain you of your blood. This is* not *the worst part of your morning.* As Zayn's footsteps neared, I furiously blinked away the tears that threatened to spill down my face for no reason whatsoever, then scrambled to my feet.

When the door opened, he didn't enter, just stood there in the doorway gripping the handle. We stared at one another for a long moment, neither of us willing to break the suffocating silence.

Don't be an asshole, don't be an asshole, don't be an asshole.

"Well, now that you're done doling out sexual favors to random fairies, maybe you could help me with a minor skin condition?" I snapped, jerking a finger toward my bioluminescent face.

Eh. I tried.

He winced as though I'd slapped him. Which I very much wanted to do. "Look," he started, then faltered. "About Salen…"

"It's cool, dude," I replied breezily. "Just make me stop glowing like Uranium, and I'll let you get back to…whatever the hell it is you do here." I glared at him accusatorily.

"I create and design runes," he retorted, taking a step into the room. "For very powerful fae from very powerful bloodlines. The ink in that drawer – it takes me days, if not weeks, to make. From ingredient lists that only I know by heart, after…" His voice trailed off as his eyes settled on something far away. A painful memory, from the likes of his tightening expression.

Nope, nuh-uh, I grimaced, digging my heels in the floor. *Don't care, won't ask.*

Zayn shook his head and sighed. "With that ink and my family's grimoire, I alone have the knowledge to create powerful runes and blood incarnates for my most ambitious clients. Salen and her extended family make up the majority of them."

The persistent lump in my throat made it difficult to reply. I was also afraid I might burst into tears if I tried. So, I stayed silent.

"For someone like you – someone with golden blood – you don't need magic ink to summon the spells from runes. You only need to replicate them with decent precision and they'll come alive with a single drop of blood. That's why Salen can't know what you are – a universal skeleton key that can unlock all magic. She and her entire bloodline are the controlling family in my realm. Where there were once kings and high courts that governed the land, the Blood Wars wiped out nearly every member of the royal family – both the summer and winter courts." His shoulders became hunched as he spoke, and for a brief moment, he looked ten years older. "This may not mean much to you as a human, but—"

"My great-grandparents suffered through Auschwitz," I interrupted, sympathy momentarily cleaving through stubbornness. "I understand enough."

"I'm sorry," Zayn said softly.

"I'm sorry too."

We stared at one another for another long moment, then sighed at the same time.

"These people…they're like the mafia of your world, aren't they?" I asked.

He nodded.

I let out a sharp exhale, feeling my own shoulders droop from exhaustion. "That's why you had to leave so suddenly."

"Yes." Zayn took another step into the room. "Sol's order had an impossible deadline, one that also required a long list of impossibly rare and dangerous ingredients. I had to leave in the middle of the night to gather them in time, since a handful only exist at a specific hour, blooming just before dusk or dawn."

"That's…really specific," I blinked, then shook my head. "But why didn't you just tell him to buzz off? Or to at least extend the deadline?" A creeping realization suddenly had me gnawing on the inside of my lip. "Unless...you can't?"

He didn't answer.

"Jesus, Zayn, do you owe these guys money or something? Is that why you were being so shady with the coffee mug and everything else?"

After a moment, he carefully replied, "The journey to acquire some of the materials is...perilous, to say the least. I didn't know if I would come back alive. I didn't have time to tell you, and I certainly couldn't explain."

"So, you left behind Biscuit and a hidden clue to come find you. But why? What good would I have done in the Fae R—"

Zayn held up a hand. "I came back in time, so the answers to that are irrelevant."

"But—"

He strode over to his desk and started thumbing through the spell book I had dropped there before stepping into his teleporting cabinet. "We have bigger concerns, Talia. Like how we're going to hide you now that you've traversed the realms." He closed his eyes and rubbed his forehead, thinking. Part of me wanted to know what was going through his mind. And the other part of me really, *really* didn't. After a moment, he sighed. "You're going to have to come with me."

"Come with you?" I choked out. "Back to the Fae Realm?!"

"Yes," he replied, tracing a finger along one of the weathered pages. "The type of ink that I need to create for Salen's family is the same ink needed for the rune that would permanently shield you from their sight. However, the plant it is derived from has been extinct for decades. Or so I'd thought."

"So why don't I just take a few paid days off and have a Netflix marathon at my apartment while *you* go?"

Even as I said it, the thought of being cooped up in my studio apartment for that long made my chest constrict. I lived and breathed this job. Being a Miami transplant, I didn't have a lot of friends outside of my regular clients. And I didn't have much of a life outside of my job. What the hell would I do with myself for seventy-two hours while I hid from the rest of the world?

Worse yet, what if he never came back?

Zayn shook his head, and somewhere deep down, I felt a tiny glimmer of relief. "I'm not letting you out of my sight… and, frankly, I can use all the help I can get. You got yourself into this mess, so you can help me get you out of it."

"First of all, how is leaving your stupid interdimensional filing cabinet unlocked *my* fault? Secondly, if I come with you to the Fae Realm, I'll stick out like a gold thumb! Not to mention the fact that my mom will lose her mind if I travel to a different dimension!"

"There are ways of shielding you, at least temporarily," he muttered, tucking the grimoire beneath his arm as he approached the cabinet. "By the way, the rune I placed on the inside of this drawer was designed to kill whoever opened it. I'm glad I had the foresight of *not* trusting you to listen to my explicit directions. Otherwise, you'd be dead, and all of that precious blood of yours would have been splattered all over my walls."

"Gee, that's great," I replied, feeling rather nauseated.

He pulled out a vial of ink that was a deep violet hue. "I know you hate needles, but—"

"What…? No!" I practically shrieked, backing away with my hands up.

"Talia," he bit off every syllable of my name, "this is, quite literally, the only way to shield you right now, either here or there. It's a small rune, but extremely powerful. Mixed with your blood, along with the necklace you're wearing, it will be enough to keep you hidden – temporarily, at least, until the ink dissolves into your tissues and the magic runs dry."

"So…it won't be permanent?" I asked, panicked thoughts once more drifting back to my mother.

"With this ink, no. And with the amount of magic that will be needed to shield *this*," he added, gesturing at my glowing skin, "it will last two to three days. Long enough for us to get the delphinium, return, and prepare the ink we'll need for your permanent shield tattoo. But even then, we might have to redo it once a year or so…" he mused to himself, shoulders heaving with a sigh. "For both of our sakes, we'd better find that damn flower."

I grimaced. "Or else what?"

"Or else I'll be dead. And you, glowing as you are, will either be drained of every drop of blood you possess or hooked up to a permanent leeching drip by Sol and his cronies."

"Well, gee, that doesn't sound so bad," I joked weakly.

Zayn's eyes darkened. "Believe me when I say, death would be a merciful alternative to a lifetime of leeching, Talia. If it came to it, I would kill you myself to spare you that fate."

I opened my mouth to blurt out half a dozen follow-up questions in high-pitched gibberish, but Zayn had already turned around and walked out with his ink and spell book.

"Come on," he called over his shoulder. "The sooner we get this over with, the better…for you, in particular."

IX.
THE PLIGHT OF THE INCUBUS

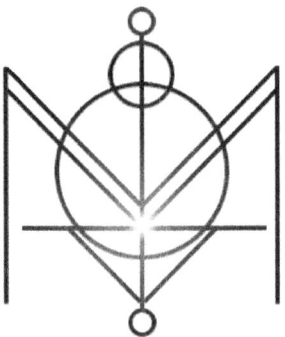

My head felt both heavy and faint at the same time as he motioned for me to follow him into the shop. While my legs moved of their own volition, the damned traitors, taking me closer and closer to that dreaded vinyl chair, I frowned at the couch that was still barricading the front door. *How had Salen gotten in the store, anyway?*

"Sit," Zayn instructed.

I sat, dread filling my chest and tears filling my eyes as he retrieved the fancy-schmancy tattoo gun from his station and carefully started sanitizing and filling the canister with ink. I'd never been on this side of a tattoo gun before and the needle gleaming at the end of it made me want to puke up the last remnants of iced coffee in my stomach, the only sustenance I'd ingested all morning.

"Where do you want it?" he asked. "It will only be about the size of a half-dollar."

Every muscle in my body began to quiver. I hugged my torso tightly to try to stop myself from trembling, but irrational fear gripped me; more than the fae mafia draining me of blood, or our upcoming journey into the perilous unknown, I was terrified of this tiny length of metal with a sharpened tip – three of them, really, since he'd stuck a 7RL tattoo needle on the machine. They'd stuck my dying father with so many of them: needles that infused his body with poison that was meant to kill the cancer but ended up killing everything else along with it; needles that kept his failing organs alive even when he was languishing with every breath; needles that numbed the suffering and the light behind his eyes, until he was nothing but a vacant shell that once housed the warm, vibrant soul of my dad. The tears I had been trying to control all morning started pouring down my cheeks and a choked sob lodged itself in my chest.

"Oh, Talia."

Setting the gun down, Zayn sat on the edge of the chair and wrapped his arms around me, gentle hands cradling the back of my head and the small of my back. I instinctively pressed my face into his chest, squeezing my eyes shut to hold back the tears. After a few moments, the vice grip on my ribcage loosened and my ragged breaths finally slowed – just enough for me to register the intoxicating scent I'd been huffing like a canister of oxygen that entire time. My pulse quickened at the realization, but it was too late. The sudden pang of desire that shot through my core was so intense, I had to stifle a gasp. I pulled away, bracing my hands against Zayn's chest to take in those deep emerald eyes. They were gazing down at me, probing my face with such intensity, I began to tremble all over again.

"Zayn," I whispered, eliciting a soft growl from his throat that set every nerve in my body aflame. His mouth was so close to mine. All I had to do was close that five-inch gap between our parted lips and I would be able to taste him – that sweet, heady nectar I'd been craving ever since I was offered but a sip and nothing more.

Before I knew it, I was inching forward on my knees, spurred by the memory of his powerful hands grasping my wrists above my head, the beads of sweat that trickled down his muscular chest and onto my stomach as he slid his body between my thighs, pressing against the same hot, wet place that was currently throbbing with uncontrolled desire. At that memory in particular, a quiet whimper escaped my lips; the need to feel his touch and taste his skin was almost unbearable.

When my hands slid across his chest and up his shoulders, the sexiest sound I'd ever heard rumbled from out of his chest. Urgency consumed me as his hands reached forward and gripped my waist. His cool hands slid under my shirt, sending goosebumps erupting across my skin while I clenched fistfuls of his shirt to pull our bodies closer. All rational thought evaporated as I closed my eyes and tilted my mouth to meet his.

The moment our lips brushed, a jolt like electricity ricocheted through my veins. My eyes popped open with a gasp. Fire had exploded behind his irises, setting his unnaturally green eyes aflame. With a deep growl, his fingers knotted through my hair. An ensuing moan shuddered through me as his other fingers dug into my waist, drawing me closer. My entire body trembled as our mouths hovered less than a millimeter apart.

"Take me," I whispered against his lips, my voice hoarse with hunger and urgency. "Please."

He let out a ragged gasp and pulled away, holding his hands up like a partition between our bodies. "I can't," he rasped, every syllable enveloped by strain. "I'm sorry."

"Why?" I practically whimpered. "Is it...is it because of...?" I swallowed, unable to bring myself to say Salen's name.

"No, it's..." He raked two hands across his face and through his hair, then shook his head as if to clear it. "I'm so sorry, Talia."

Dazed, disappointed, and dejected, I leaned back in my chair. "I don't understand..." I shook my own head, trying to make sense of it all. Of him.

"Look," he started, then cleared his throat. "I'm sorry for what's happened, for everything you've had to endure these past couple of days," he said softly, caressing my cheek with the back of his hand. "But more than anything, I'm so sorry for that night. You were under my protection, my ward. It was a lapse that never should have happened."

That night. My heart was crashing against my ribcage so hard I wasn't sure which would break first.

"Fae or not, I'm only flesh and blood," he continued, intoxicating and mesmerizing, like a brilliant flame calling to me, his all-too-willing moth. "At times a slave to my incubus nature. I only hope you can forgive me, Talia...for everything."

A sharp stab of rejection twisted in my chest like a knife. My thoughts couldn't help but drift back to Salen, the beautiful creature who was hanging on him less than thirty minutes ago, and humiliation seared across my cheeks. He hadn't pushed her away or rejected her advances.

My mouth fluttered open to ask the one question I'd always been too afraid to ask – then snapped shut. In its place, the image of a frightening, razor-toothed demon standing over the sleeping form of a young woman appeared in my mind.

I immediately recoiled, pressing my back against the chair as my senses finally overcame whatever sexy, demonic spell he must have been projecting onto me. "You're an incubus," I whispered, shock and betrayal etched into every syllable. A flicker of hurt crossed his eyes as he, too, leaned away from me, broad shoulders stooped.

"Yes. But I would never…hurt you," he said finally, his dark irises returning to their pseudo-natural color.

A hysterical sob wedged itself into my throat as I pressed my head to my hands. This was all too much. *Too much.* Gold blood. Tattoo incarnates. Fae mafia. Irresistible incubus bosses that made parts of my body – like my throat – far too dry while simultaneously making other parts far too—

"Ugh!" I raked my hands across my face. I had to snap myself out of this trance, whatever the hell it was.

Zayn glanced at the clock on the wall. "Tal, I know. There's so much more we need to talk about, and questions I need to answer, but—"

"Give me the damn tattoo," I spat through gritted teeth. "Just make it fast. And bring Biscuit back. He can be my emotional support animal."

"She."

Still not believing him, I shot Zayn a piercing glare of fury that would have made my mother proud. What I wouldn't give for her to show up at that very moment and expertly hurl one of her patented diatribes directly at his stupid, gorgeous face.

With a heavy sigh, he gingerly pressed two fingers against the tattoo on his forearm. In a dazzling burst of magenta-and-orange light, Biscuit unfolded his elegant wings and emerged from the design embedded in Zayn's skin, shaking out his feathers as though he'd been napping.

He hopped onto my shoulder, and I settled back into my chair, clasping my hands together like a shackle over my midsection as Zayn pulled on a pair of nitrile gloves. I couldn't help but eye the dozens of colorful designs that laced the thick ropes of muscle in his forearms with renewed interest – and perhaps a tiny pang of lust, which I quickly tamped down.

"What do the rest of your tattoos do?" I asked, a weak attempt to steer the subject away from demons, my failed sexual overtures, and needles.

Ignoring my question, he settled into his chair, where he took the alcohol rub and gently began cleaning the top of my left arm. "Is this spot okay?" he asked. "It shouldn't hurt much at all."

I nodded mutely.

He flashed me a wan smile that didn't quite meet his tight eyes. "As for the rest of my tattoos…well, I suppose you'll find out soon enough. Now, close your eyes and take a deep breath. This won't take long."

I did as I was told, forcing my brain to take me to my happy place where trees were made of chocolate and rivers bubbled with wine, and there was no such thing as needles and my dad was still alive. My eyebrows knit together from the abrupt return of the spastic, flapjack-flipping chef who was once again wreaking havoc in my stomach. Why *had* Dad given me a fae artifact all those years ago? How had he come to possess it? And more importantly, did he know what it was for? Or why I, in particular, would need it?

As Zayn switched on the gun and the yucky, high-pitched whir of the drum filled my ears, those thoughts and questions were replaced with breadstick fences and warm ponds of cheddar fondue – Lunch-Deprived Talia's version of Willy Wonka's factory. Meanwhile, my hands gripped the firm vinyl cushion of the chair while my boss's magic parrot politely preened my ponytail, which was in total disarray from our recent foray into an interdimensional filing cabinet. I flinched and bit back a yelp as the tip of the you-know-what began depositing fae-made ink into my skin, all the while suppressing the frantic, cracking-at-the-seams giggle that had been bubbling in my throat for hours, ready to erupt into full-on hysteria at any moment…

"Talia."

"Unngg," I whined, eyes squeezed tightly shut.

"Talia!"

"What?!"

"It's over. I'm done. You're all set."

My eyes popped open. "It is? You are? I am?"

"Yes. Three-thousand dollars' worth of ink later." Zayn rolled his eyes as he peeled off his stained gloves.

My eyes widened as I took in the purple, geometric design on my arm, which admittedly looked very pristine and badass and…

Wait a minute.

"Why does this tattoo look like it's two weeks old?" I demanded.

"The ointment I formulated for my VIP clients has *droka* compounds added to it, which not only have antiseptic and analgesic properties, but also speed up cellular regeneration." He said all of that with a completely deadpan expression, like some futuristic space doctor on Star Trek.

"Holy crap." I brushed my fingers across the tattoo, which was faintly raised but almost completely healed. No weeping, no angry red lines – nothing. "Why don't we use this on all of our clients?"

"Because it's worth about four-hundred dollars a gram and takes me nearly a month to make," he grumbled as he began to clean and sterilize his work space. "By the way, creating perfectly linear designs on a person's body is painstaking enough when the recipient *isn't* desperately trying to squirm out of her chair."

I grumbled something unintelligible as I continued to examine my first – and unfortunately, not my last – tattoo. "I can't believe how straight the lines are. And you didn't even use a stencil!"

A wan smile formed on his lips. "It's one of the reasons only a handful of true Runemasters exist in the world. A single crooked line or imperfect circle, and the rune becomes worthless."

"Wow." I let out a low whistle. "I'm impressed. What do you think, Biscuit?"

Rousing himself from his snooze, Biscuit hopped from my right shoulder to the left, dull talons digging into my skin as he peered down to look. "Pretty girl!"

"Pretty tattoo," I corrected, mustering a smile for Zayn. "It looks great and it didn't even hurt…much."

"More importantly," he remarked, his workstation once more clean and sterilized, "you're no longer glowing."

"*Gottze dank,*" I muttered, examining the non-illuminated backs of my hands in relief.

"Don't thank God, thank me," Zayn chuckled to himself.

"Wait…you know Yiddish?"

"I know many languages. My ancestors have traveled back and forth to your realm since the dawn of civilization – well, since the dawn of yours. Ours is far older."

"I…see," I blinked.

"Come on," he said, helping me to my feet. "We've got realms to traverse and extinct flowers to unearth."

"But I'm not glowing anymore!" I protested, once-again second-guessing my decision to venture off-planet. "Why can't I stay here while *you* go face the perils of the Fae Realm for a bouquet of enchanted daisies?"

"Delphiniums, not daisies. And I already told you why. I'm nervous about letting you out of my sight. And I could use the help."

My eyes narrowed. His narrowed back, until we were both squinting at each other like near-sighted old ladies.

"Why are you *really* forcing me to go?" I demanded, hands planted on my hips. "Is it because you don't want to let *me* out of your sight or your stupid, precious supply of gold blood?"

Zayn hesitated just long enough for it to sting.

"Wow," I muttered, spinning on my heel to retrieve my purse. "You hired me for my blood, kept me around for my blood, slept with me for my blood—" I bit off the rest of that sentence, feeling a torrent of you-know-what rush straight to my face.

A horrible silence descended upon the room.

When he finally spoke, Zayn's voice was cool and clipped, just like it had been when he was talking to Salen. "What did you just say?"

I couldn't bear to turn around and face him while my cheeks flushed like a steaming bowl of Campbell's tomato soup, so I just stared at the floor. "You heard me," I muttered so softly I could barely hear myself.

The ensuing bout of silence stretched so long, I *almost* turned around to check on him. Thank God, he once again broke the silence before I had to.

"Come or don't, Talia. But if I don't come back, you'll light up like a torch within three days' time, drawing the attention of every human and fae alike."

I whirled around. "So?" I replied haughtily, taking "that" tone of voice that always sent my poor mother up a wall. "I'll just tattoo a new rune on myself."

"Oh yeah? Every seventy-two hours for the rest of your life? How's that going to pair with your needle phobia?" he cocked an eyebrow. "Not to mention the fact that I'm now all out of *Verbena*. Gold blood or no, without that shade of ink, you'll never be able to get the full effect of that rune – if you can even manage to tattoo it on your skin correctly. But that shouldn't be a problem, right? After all, the nightlight look really suits you."

My hands balled into fists. Oh, how I wanted to fling every curse I knew in both English and Yiddish at him, to scream obscenities and rage until my throat was raw – for disappearing on me, for getting me into this mess with his stupid vandalized coffee mug. My nails dug into my palms as angry tears threatened to well up, but I forced them the hell back down. For kissing *her*, right in front of me, drilling the nail into the coffin of the incredible night we'd shared, like it truly had been nothing…

My shoulders abruptly slumped with the heavy weight of realization and self-pity. Because at the end of the day, Zayn was an incubus, and lovemaking was probably nothing but a quick bite for a man – for a *creature*, I gulped – like him. He didn't care whether I lived or died, glowed or didn't. I was just another cheeseburger in his eyes. One he did a favor for when he hired me two years ago because he's a decent guy with a decent heart, and now he was just here to follow through on that kindness. Or protect his investment. Either way. What did it matter?

Once I was sure those damned tears were staying firmly inside their damned ducts where they damn well belonged, I slowly turned around to face him. This had nothing to do with my feelings for him; in three days' time, I would once again light up like the Rockefeller Christmas Tree. If I didn't find a way back to normal, I would find myself trapped in my tiny apartment forever – blasting music to keep the silence at bay, taking nonstop frantic calls from my mother... Not to mention the fact that if Zayn never came back, I'd spend the rest of my lonely, glowing days worrying incessantly about him, whether I wanted to or not.

I let out a low growl. "Well, what are we waiting for? Lead the way, Mr. Fae."

"Don't you want to call your mother first? We may not be back for a few days, and you mentioned she would worry."

I ground my teeth at his stupid, helpful advice, then pulled my phone out of my pocket and punched in her number, doing my best not to look at the freshly-inked aberration on my arm that would send her straight to the cardiac unit if she ever laid eyes on it.

"Hi, Mom," I said when she answered after half a ring, turning my back to Zayn and Biscuit. The latter had perched himself on his owner's shoulder, cocking his head as though trying to listen in.

"Bubaleh, I'm shocked! I can't remember the last time you called me!"

I glanced over my shoulder self-consciously. I'd turned the volume all the way down on my phone, but I was certain Zayn could hear every word she said.

"The reason I don't call you is because I can't go four hours without you calling me first!" I hissed through bared teeth, then took a deep breath to lower my voice to its usual sweet, dulcet tone. "Anyway, Mom, I just wanted to let you know that I'll be out of cell range for a while—"

"Why? Where are you going?"

"Camping," I replied, then flinched. I'd never camped a day in my life. "I'm going with my boss and his, um...dog. Biscuit."

"Raaawk!"

"In Flar-i-da? Who the hell wants to camp in Flar-i-da?"

"Oh, you know, there are plenty of nice places...like near the Everglades," I guessed.

"Oy gotenyu, I'm going to turn on the news tomorrow night to see them dissecting an alligator for my daughter's remains!" she wailed, treading dangerously close to full-on JMZ mode. *"And what do you mean, camping with your boss? Who camps with their boss?"*

I snuck another glance over my shoulder. Indeed, Zayn was looking at me with a horrified expression. It dawned on me that he'd never heard me talk to my mother before, since I always took her calls outside.

As if on cue, she suddenly let out a scandalized gasp. *"Talia! Are you two sleep—"*

"Ma!" I blurted out, cheeks blushing furiously. "First of all, there are no alligators in Florida, they're crocodiles."

"What's the difference?!" my mother demanded at the same time Zayn stage whispered, "Actually, they *are* alligators."

"And, regardless," I continued shrilly, "I'm not going to get eaten by a *crocodile*, because there aren't any giant reptiles where we're going—"

"True, but there are kelpies," Zayn offered unhelpfully.

"Shhh!" I hissed, pressing my hand to the receiver. "Anyway, Ma, I just wanted to give you a head's up so you didn't freak out and—"

"Talia, you listen to me. If you and your boss are sleeping together—"

"Mom!!"

"—I hope you've already asked him for a raise! And for that kind of trouble, he'd better damn well be giving you the best orgasms of your life!"

I stared at the phone in my hand in absolute horror, sincerely praying that God would find it in himself to strike me dead right then and there. When lightning didn't rain down from the sky to mercifully relieve me of my corporeal humiliation, I worked to swallow the sandpaper-covered golf ball in my throat, avoiding eye contact with Zayn at all possible costs.

Mom was still laughing gleefully. *"I guess he's using his package as part of your benefits package! Get it? Talia?"*

Sheer horror had turned my veins to ice. I knew then that I would have to say the one and only thing that could successfully divert the subject away from my boss's package: "Hey, Mom, would it be okay if I came over for dinner Friday night?"

That had the desired effect, thank God, because she immediately launched into several concurrent diatribes, including, but not limited to: why the hell would I ask permission to eat dinner with my own mother, every individual ingredient she'd have to get at the store, which grocery store chain carries the best cuts of meat, and which coupons she'd have to remember to set aside. When she finally stopped to take a breath, I quickly told her that I loved her and would see her Friday, then hung up the phone as fast as my index finger would let me.

Pressing my mouth into a thin line, and not quite meeting Zayn's eye, I scuffed the heel of my sneaker against the floor. "So, um…are we ready to go?"

His face had gone pale. "Is that…how you normally speak to your mother?"

I rubbed the back of my neck. "Uh, yeah, pretty much."

"But all you two did was yell at each other!"

"That's just how Jewish people say 'I love you.' Can we go already?"

Still shaking his head in horrified disbelief, he turned around and motioned weakly for me to follow him to his office. Biscuit flew off his shoulder and landed on top of my head, flapping his wings excitedly.

"*Oy gotenyu!*" he squawked at the top of his lungs, his voice high and shrill – exactly like my mother's.

"Just kill me now," I muttered, raising my eyes to the sky where I was absolutely sure God had made himself a bucket of popcorn and was settling in on his divine couch to spend the rest of the cosmic day laughing at my expense.

"Don't worry," Zayn called from his office. "There are plenty of things that can kill you across the realm."

Please, I rolled my eyes. *How bad could it be?*

X.
A Jilted Glaistig

After gathering a pack of supplies that had been stashed beneath his desk, activating the security alarm for the store – a.k.a., a series of fancy protection runes – and offering to lock up my valuables, Zayn opened the filing cabinet drawer, once more suffusing the office in white light.

"Ladies first," he smiled.

I bit my lip anxiously, wishing I'd had enough time to grab some Dramamine at the drugstore. With an impatient click of his beak, Biscuit hopped off the top of my head and dove in, wings cranked backward like a seagull diving for a hotdog. When the last of his ornate tail feathers disappeared, I took a deep breath, tentatively accepted Zayn's hand for support, and climbed inside. Like before, the room burned away as I fell, leaving nothing but white in its stead. *Unlike* before, Zayn was right by my side, arm hooked through mine, muttering foreign words under his breath. Within seconds, the light dimmed, revealing not an office, but a thickly wooded forest.

"Holy shit," I breathed, swaying precariously the moment he let go of my arm. I wasn't quite sure which way was up until I saw Biscuit – in all of his magical, sparkling radiance – perched on a branch far above us. It belonged to a tree that looked sort of like a massive oak, but its bark was incandescent white, and its leaves were some sort of fusion between lime green and cotton candy pink that made me go cross-eyed if I stared at it for too long. I placed my hand on the gnarled bark while my brain attempted to process this deluge of new information flooding my senses. An inch away from my bandaged pinky, a small hollow in the tree was glowing faintly from the portal rune that had been etched inside.

I shook my head and muttered to myself, "Toto, I have a feeling we're not in Florida anymore."

Beside me, Zayn chuckled as he rooted around his bag. "The Fae Realm is a bit different than the beaches of Miami, isn't it?"

"I'll say," I murmured. In addition to the UV-reactive white bark and the "grink" leaves, we were surrounded by a thick grove of trees, the likes of which I'd never seen before, all towering at least fifty feet over our heads. The ground was covered in dried, multicolored leaves and pine needles that had more blues and pinks than greens and browns, and little clusters of brightly-glowing mushrooms sprouted from the bases of trunks and fallen boughs. A low chorus of insect-like trills made me wonder if it was evening, but it was impossible to tell the exact time since the faint slivers of sky that glanced through the trees were not blue, but greenish-yellow. With effort, I took a deep breath, filling my nose with an earthy scent that was a cross between mulch and nutmeg. The air was somehow thick and thin at the same time – as humid as Miami's, but hard to take in, like we were standing at a much higher altitude.

"How far do we have to walk? And how long will it take?" I asked, feeling the stirrings of delayed panic settling in, because, really, what the *hell* was I doing? I'd blindly followed this man into another realm – another dimension – and I didn't have so much as a granola bar on me.

"All told – three Earth days," he replied. "We'll walk most of today, camp for the evening, and then hike another half-day to the nearest Waypoint in that region. I have all the supplies we'll need in my pack," he added, patting the burlap hanging from his shoulder.

"So, all we have to do is get these special flowers and leave?" I asked, earning an affirmative grunt in response. That made me feel slightly better. For about half of a second.

"Shit," I muttered, patting my pockets.

"What's wrong?"

"I left my inhaler in my…" My voice trailed off as I turned to look at Zayn for the first time since we left his office, his face ethereal and utterly breathtaking in the strange light of this realm. Freed from the dreary filter of the earth and its dull yellow star, his black hair was once more a deep, midnight blue, and it looked like a fine layer of mica had been brushed all over his perfect bronze skin. But it was those impossibly bright eyes and chiseled jaw, dusted with just a shadow of dark whiskers, that would ultimately be my undoing. He was almost unbearable to look at, like a cold, frothy milkshake in the middle of a barren, bone-dry desert – one I wasn't allowed to touch, no matter how hot or thirsty I got.

My breath hitched in my throat and my eyes swiveled around frantically, desperate to look at anything but him. "Could you, like, *not?*" I stammered, feeling my stomach turning itself inside out as delicious, depraved images of our bodies twisting together like Twizzlers pummeled my brain.

"Not what?" he asked, arching a perfect eyebrow at me.

"…Oh. That."

"Yes, *that,*" I grimaced, taking the timely opportunity to thoroughly explore the loose thread hanging from the hem of my shorts.

Zayn sighed. "I'm sorry. It's not something I can turn off, so to speak. Amplify when needed, yes, but not extinguish."

"Is that what you've been doing to me all morning?" I demanded, abandoning the frayed thread to inspect a spotted "blurple" mushroom with the toe of my converse sneakers.

"I've never actively used my glamour around you, Talia, nor would I."

"Not even that night?" the question tumbled out of my mouth.

Silence fell like a curtain between us while angry shadows darkened Zayn's expression. "Is that what you think? That I'd take advantage of you like that?"

"Isn't that pretty much what incubi do?" I shot back, this time mustering up just enough mental strength to meet his narrowing eyes.

"Nice to know what you think of me after two years," he muttered, glancing at the compass he'd retrieved from his bag. "Hibiscus, are we clear from the west?"

"*Rawk!* Clear!"

"Yeah, two years of you hardly speaking to me about anything of substance!" I blustered, falling in behind him as we made our way into the thick groves of strangely colored flora.

"Right, because you've always been such an open book, Talia. Stepping outside every time your phone rings, not talking to me about anything but art projects and movies—"

"First of all, talking to my mother outside was for *your* benefit, obviously." I lifted my arm to brush aside the orange-tinted vines that hung from the greenish-pink canopy of trees. "Apart from that, I've been a completely open book! I just don't have anything interesting to talk about."

Up ahead, Zayn snorted. "Somehow, I doubt that."

"You, on the other hand," I wheezed – holy hell, the air was thin here – "led me to believe you were human, hid the fact that you have magic, cobra-generating ink, not to mention a secret girlfriend who looks like the fairy version of Charlize Theron—"

"I don't have a girlfriend," he snapped over his shoulder. "Watch out for the fireflies, by the way. They're highly flammable."

"Ha-ha, very—aah!" I skittered to the side as a small cloud of glowing red insects flew past my face and landed on one of the taller maple-type trees just behind us, which immediately burst into red flames.

"We call those Phoenix Trees," Zayn called, "because the fireflies congregate inside the old, dying boughs to mate, which ultimately incinerates the tree. From those ashes grow more saplings, which in turn shield the firefly eggs as they mature in the carbon-rich soil. It's a kind of symbiotic thing."

"Lovely," I replied, taking one last glance at the roiling, crimson flames over my shoulder before scurrying to keep up.

About twenty feet above us, Biscuit was flying from branch to branch, making affirmative chicken-like *bawks* that I could only assume meant, "Clear!"

"But anyway, back to you," I continued in a perfectly nonchalant, disinterested fashion. "I guess you and Salen have a friends-with-benefits kinda thing, then?" The memory of her mashing her face against his made my teeth gnash together, so I focused instead on the pretty plants we were passing by – like the bright pink moss that was growing on several of the deciduous tree trunks, or the spiky yellow pine cones that hung from cobalt blue evergreens. Ever-blues?

Zayn glanced at me over his shoulder. "Don't touch the bark of these trees. Your skin will immediately blister and slough off, and I had to use the last of the antidote yesterday."

I snatched my hand away from the tree I was about to lean on, clutching my wrist anxiously. "Don't you think we should have a quick pow-wow or something to discuss all the different things I shouldn't touch *before* we take a perilous stroll through the forest?"

"The list of lethal flora and fauna here is too long for you to even try to remember. Just don't touch anything, and you'll be fine."

A small whimper escaped my throat as I stepped over a large broken bough with a cluster of angry looking, spiked fungi sprouting from the top.

"Salen is neither a lover nor a friend," Zayn remarked, snapping my attention away from the spiny toadstools that had come within millimeters of my bare skin. "Salen is a narcissistic succubus who was taught as a youngling that she could take whatever she desired without any thought of morality or consequence. Because of her looks, and because of who her father is, she has learned that there is nothing she can't get away with."

"So, her dad's the leader of the fae mafia?" I guessed. And then, because I couldn't help it, "You think she's beautiful? ...I mean, yeah, I guess she is, if you're into perfectly flawless women," I muttered, my sullen voice disintegrating into barely a whisper.

"Salen's family operates like the mafia, but without the royal courts to control them or law enforcement to contain them, they aren't gangsters – they're simply the rulers of our realm," he answered, his voice tinged with contempt and something deeper... Regret, perhaps? "Don't step on these *asgera* mushrooms, by the way. They secrete an acid that will both eat through the soles of your shoes and also attract *trows*."

"Trows. Gotcha," I replied, burning the mushrooms' bright red caps into my memory. It wasn't hard – their tops were tall and bell-shaped, and deeper-hued than the deepest shade of crimson. *Ultra-red*, I decided to call the eye-straining color.

"As for Sol's daughter," Zayn continued, making my inside-out stomach twist into a pretzel-shaped knot, "she's one of the most beautiful creatures in both realms."

"Yeah," I agreed, shoulders dropping. "She is."

He glanced at me over his shoulder, an odd expression I couldn't name pulling at his brows. "That wasn't a compliment, Talia. Cobras have fangs, tigers have stripes, and succubi have glamour. It's how they attract and feed on their prey."

"Incubi too?"

"Yes." Zayn's shoulders rose and fell in a silent sigh. "Hibiscus, all clear?"

"*Raawk!*" came the affirmative caw. "Clear!" He'd settled on a branch about twenty feet ahead, shaking out his gorgeous tail feathers for a brief preening session.

I could tell the subject was making Zayn uncomfortable, but be it morbid curiosity or perhaps just nervous prattling, I couldn't stop myself from prying. "So, you literally feed off the sexual energy of humans?"

"More or less."

"But…you feel bad about doing it?" I guessed from his tone.

"Yes."

"Huh." I scrunched my eyebrows together in thought as I carefully scaled yet another fallen bough, this one covered in a blanket of miniature gray mushrooms that Zayn stopped to gather. As he scooped the little buttons into a side pocket of his bag, an uncomfortable-yet-strangely-titillating thought occurred to me. "Do incubi and succubi ever get together? I mean, can you guys, like, feed off of each other?"

His eyes didn't meet mine as he dusted the mushroom residue off his hands. "Sort of."

"Well, if you feel so bad about preying on humans, why not just pair up with a succubus? Like Salen?" I added, ignoring the heavy stone that appeared in my belly. "You could have a nonstop, all-night smorgasbord and never tire. Where's the problem in that?"

"Chafing, for one."

"Real funny," I rolled my eyes. "And also, *ew.*"

Zayn leaned his perfect butt against the fallen tree, crossing his arms with a sigh. "If you must know, that type of…feeding," he scrubbed a hand through his hair, "isn't remotely satiating. It's energy, of a sort, but you end up feeling hollow afterward, like you've spent the entire night gorging yourself on rice cakes."

For whatever reason, my stomach did a little flip at "entire night."

"It's better to save the sexual transactions for humans – willing humans, in my case. Superior energy – think plain, nonfat yogurt instead of rice cakes – which means longer satiety and fewer complications. Succubi are a handful. To say the least."

With an uncomfortable sigh, I sat down beside him, mirroring his body language by crossing my arms. "So, have you had many, um, 'transactions?' With humans?"

Zayn's head lowered almost imperceptibly, and I felt a tiny twinge of guilt. "I've tried abstaining altogether, gorging myself on food and other types of nourishment, but…" he trailed off, leaving the silence between us to stretch for several uncomfortable moments.

I shifted awkwardly, thighs itchy from the prickly moss underneath them, and brain itchy from all of the other questions I was dying to ask but didn't have the courage. More than anything, I wanted to ask him whether *our* night together had just been another evening of nonfat yogurt for him. But I was too embarrassed to ask and too afraid to hear the answer. Because no matter how politely he may have worded his response, I knew there was no way the passionate night we'd shared had been even a fraction as "satiating" for him as it had been for me. The fact of the matter was, after having my appetite sated in such a mouth-watering way, I was honestly worried that nothing and no one else could satisfy me the way he had ever again.

But he didn't need to know that.

So, I opted for the coward's version of that same, gnawing question. "Is that how feeding always feels for you?" I asked softly, praying my cheeks hadn't flushed the color of an *asgera* mushroom. "Like eating stale popcorn or whatever?"

He glanced at me out of the corner of his eye. "Almost always."

I opened my mouth to pester him further just as Zayn made a sharp gesture to silence me. "Shh," he whispered. "Listen."

My mouth snapped shut, teeth painfully clacking together. Biting back a curse, I strained to hear whatever it was that had made his back as rigid as an ironing board. Apart from the distant sound of water – a nearby stream, maybe? – I didn't hear anything. The forest was almost unnervingly still.

"I don't—"

Biscuit let out a shrill, frightened scream that made us both leap to our feet. "Hibiscus!" Zayn called out, spinning in a circle to find him. "What's—"

A terrible, blood-curdling sound sliced through the forest, like shards of glass rubbing against each other while a chorus of fingernails slid across a chalkboard. Nearly toppling off the log, I sank to my knees and tried to cover my ears, but nothing helped. Zayn, too, fell on his knees beside me, pressing his palms to the sides of his head.

"What the hell is that?" I cried, my own screams lost in the terrible cacophony of splintering metal and high-pitched train whistles.

Zayn didn't even try to answer as the earsplitting screech ricocheted between the trees, so shrill I half-expected the boughs to shatter as my eardrums were threatening to do. As horrible as the noise was – worse than a soprano singer matching keys with a fork being scraped against a dinner plate – the sense of dread that had begun to settle in the pit of my stomach like a frozen lead weight was far worse. A small whimper escaped my throat as I glanced at Zayn, possibly for the last time, and wondered what I would say to him if that were, in fact, the case.

As quickly as it had come, the scream subsided, leaving nothing but a terrible, heavy silence in its wake. Fearful tears had gathered in the corners of my eyes; even after a quarter century of aggravating my longsuffering mother up to and beyond her frayed breaking point, I'd never heard such a terrible, piercing sound.

"Banshee!" Zayn hissed, rising shakily to his feet.

"Banshee?" I parroted – another word I didn't fully understand, yet the name alone was enough to make my insides contract in terror.

"We have to go," he instructed, pulling me to my feet. "Her scream is a harbinger of death."

"Her scream is a what?!"

"Something – or someone – is about to die," he growled. "Hibiscus, how much time do we have?" An unintelligible screech from a very frantic psittacine made him curse under his breath.

I shook my head, still disoriented from the echoes of that terrible scream. Was it just me, or had the forest suddenly become much darker? And colder? My teeth had begun chattering at some point, though I wasn't exactly sure when. "I-Is the b-banshee cl-close?" I stammered, hugging my body for warmth.

"It's not the banshee I'm worried about." He swiveled my body ninety degrees to the left and gave me an undignified push. "Move. Now."

"I'm s-so c-cold," I whimpered, stumbling through the forest. "Where did the sun go?"

"Hello, travelers," a female voice crooned from behind us.

I whipped around so fast I nearly lost my footing. Zayn's hand reached out to grab my arm just in time, forcibly yanking me upright and behind him. I peered around him fearfully, afraid of the hideous, nightmarish creature I was sure to find there. Instead, my eyes landed on a woman so beautiful, a soft cry escaped my lips. Long, flowing golden-blonde hair fell a foot below her waist, fluttering around silver-threaded, forest-green robes that billowed against an invisible breeze. Her blue irises flashed like the sun's rays glinting off a cool mountain spring. Extending an inviting hand toward us, her long, slender fingers were so pale they were nearly gray.

Zayn muttered something unintelligible under his breath, pressing two fingers to his bicep.

"Why, hello, my sweet incubus," the woman purred, taking a graceful step forward. Her long robes, trailing far behind her, completely covered her feet. "I can almost taste your sweet nectar from here. Won't you come dance with me?"

As I strained to get a better look at the magnificent creature, Zayn pushed me backward. "Get out of here, Talia," he whispered, pressing a silver compass into my hand. "Head west, and don't stop for anyone or anything until I catch up. Hibiscus will accompany you."

"But—"

His incandescent eyes narrowed into a glare, slanted irises raging with green fire and fury. "Go!"

I stumbled backward in shock.

"Come here, my sweet," the woman crooned, imploring the incubus forward with two outstretched palms. "Please – won't you please come dance with me?"

A flurry of wings whizzed past me as Biscuit grabbed me by the ponytail and tugged. Hard. "I'm coming!" I gasped, stumbling in the direction he was pulling me.

"You'll have to find someone else to dance with," Zayn replied. "I know what you are, *glaistig*."

A flash of silver made me want to look over my shoulder, but the damn bird wasn't relenting. "Biscuit, stop! Let me go!"

"Then you know I can't let you leave, my luscious darling," the woman laughed, the edges of her voice as cold and brittle as glass. "There is no sweeter blood than that of an incubus. Won't you give me just a taste? I promise I won't drink all of it…"

"I'd sooner give a taste of my blood to a shark."

A sweeping cascade of silver light erupted throughout the forest, followed by a terrible shriek – not nearly as bad as the banshee's scream, but not altogether human, either.

"I will have your blood, incubus! Warm or cold, it makes no difference to me!"

"Wait a minute!" I yelped, yanking my ponytail free from Biscuit's stupid claws to whirl around. "Can we all just calm down for a—"

My words broke off as my left toe caught the back of my right ankle, sending me sprawling to the ground. I landed hard, palms-first on the rock-strewn forest floor, all the air whooshing out of my lungs like a deflating balloon.

"*Unggg*," I moaned, rolling over on my back.

"Raawk! Gold blood!" Biscuit shrieked in agitation.

"Oh, no," I regarded my hand in horror as warm, glowing liquid seeped through a wide gash in my palm like molten gold. "That can't be good."

Thirty feet ahead, Zayn – who, to my shock, was wielding an elaborately carved bow and arrow surrounded by ribbons of silver light – had whipped around to stare at me in horror. It took me a moment to understand why – and then the flaxen-haired *glaistig* was straddling me, her water-blue eyes boring into mine as her hands pinned my wrists to the ground. From this up-close-and-personal vantage point, I realized that the pale skin of her face was actually translucent and gray, displaying thin blue veins that faintly pulsed beneath. Worse, her fancy velvet robes had been hiked up to her knees in the scuffle, displaying not skin, but *fur* underneath.

"Holy shit, lady!" I yelped, writhing atop the dry bed of leaves.

An inhuman hiss escaped her peeling, ashen lips. Before I could even register what was happening, she brought my palm to her mouth and slid her cold gray tongue across the bleeding gash. A violent shudder gripped her body as she tilted her head back in ecstasy.

"What is this delectable nectar that illuminates your veins?" she crooned while digging her jagged fingernails into my wrist. Her teeth were bared in a euphoric smile, displaying a horrible set of canines that ended in sharp, jagged points. "I must have more!"

"Get off of me!" I shrieked. Violently jerking my hips this way and that, I flopped around like a fish on dry land, trying to wrench myself out from underneath her. The broad looked like a waif, but man, was she *solid.*

"Raaawk!" Biscuit screamed, snatching the creature's long, blonde hair in his talons and yanking with far greater gusto than he had previously yanked on mine.

With another chilling, predatory hiss, the woman's right arm shot up to grab Biscuit by the throat. The poor bird let out a strangled noise as she squeezed, unbridled glee stretching across her gray, corpse-y face. Her perverse delight abruptly disappeared, however, when my left fist connected with her jaw with a loud and satisfying *thwack.*

She shook her head in stunned confusion, then let out a high-pitched, furious cry. After hurling Biscuit aside, both of her hands flew to my throat, palms pressing against my windpipe with the strength of cold steel. "I will have your blood," she hissed in my ear.

I could only stare up at the branches in mute horror as I felt the tips of those razor-sharp fangs press against my neck, breaking through the skin. Another violent shudder gripped her body, and I honestly thought that was the end of me…until she raised her head, where the business-end of an arrow was protruding from between her eyebrows.

The moment her fingers lost their grip on my windpipe, I let out a bloodcurdling scream, heaving with all of my might to roll out from underneath her limp body. Then I skittered backward and away from her until my spine was pressed against a gnarled tree.

Within seconds, Zayn was gripping my shoulders, prodding my neck and face for injuries. "Are you okay?" he demanded, cocking my chin to the left so he could inspect the shallow holes that had been stamped into the side of my neck.

"Wh-wh—" I stammered, completely at a loss for words.

"I'm so sorry it took me so long. I had to create a special poison for the tip of the arrow, otherwise, even a bullet to the brain wouldn't have done much to stop her."

My eyes bulged in horror as they landed on the *thing* sprawled several feet away from us. Her body was face down in the ground, the tail of a metallic silver arrow sticking through the back of her head and a puddle of black goo pooling beneath her face. Where her robes had bunched around her ankles, hooves were sticking out – *hooves*. Like a freaking goat's. My rational mind shattered into a thousand pieces, and another horrible, shrill scream punctured the silence. This time, it was my own.

"Shh, shh," Zayn whispered, hands fluttering up and down my arms before scooping me into a tight hug. "Shh, Talia, it's okay. You're okay."

After a few seconds, or possibly minutes, my screams died down to hysterical sobs, which eventually devolved into uncontrollable hiccups. "What – *hic* – the hell – *hic* – *was* that?" I wailed into Zayn's shoulder. "And where's – *hic* – Biscuit?"

"Hibiscus is right there," Zayn replied. He pulled away so I could see the disheveled, scuffed-up parrot that was quivering on a nearby log, his right wing drooping unnaturally.

"Biscuit!" I cried. Pushing Zayn away, I flung myself on all fours, scraping my knees on dried leaves and broken twigs to scramble over to him. "Are you okay?"

He let out a pitiful whimper and lifted a trembling claw like he wanted me to pick him up.

My hands worried over his fragile little body as Zayn had done for me. "Poor baby!" I fussed, frantically making sure he had no lacerations or mortal injuries. "What do you need?"

"Almond?" he whimpered in the most miserable, broken little voice I'd ever heard.

"Hibiscus," Zayn admonished. "Cut it out – now."

My eyes shot up to find the incubus standing beside me, glowering at his poor, injured, defenseless animal. I was just about to open my mouth to launch into a furious tirade when Biscuit let out a hearty squawk and flew away, as gracefully as ever, to land on a nearby branch. There, he gave a casual shake of his tail feathers and straightened out his wing, which had apparently never been injured.

With venom and ire spitting from my lips, I jumped to my feet, momentarily forgetting the dead she-goat sprawled less than two yards away. "Are you freaking *kidding* me right now?" I screamed into the branches.

At that, the little shit actually *stamped his claw* like a petulant child. "Want almond!"

"You want an almond?! I'll give you an almond, you little—"

"Come on," Zayn interjected, steering me away from the pile of rocks I was about to hurl at his asshole parrot. "While it appears the banshee's prophecy foretold the glaistig's death and not our own, we don't need to stick around and tempt fate. Hibiscus," he added, "fly ahead and keep watch, please."

The bird shook out his feathers – rather haughtily, I noted – before taking off in a huff.

"What the hell is a glaistig, anyway?" I demanded, taking one last look at the creature's disarrayed robes and splayed-out hooves while Zayn pushed me away by the shoulders. A thick cloud of puce-colored ichor was rising from its body, which – to my disbelief and disgust – had already begun decomposing into a pile of mushrooms. A roiling wave of nausea welled up in my throat as I willingly let Zayn wheel me away and out of the clearing. He didn't open his mouth again until the awful scene had been swallowed up by the surrounding forest, and even then, he kept casting anxious glances over his shoulder.

"A glaistig is a cursed fae – half-woman, half-goat – that often enjoys a nice waltz before slicing open a man's throat and draining him of blood. They don't normally go after other fae," he added, shaking his head. "Good thing I had a few drops of *asgera* extract left because they don't go down easily, especially if they know you've seen their hooves."

"But where did the bow and arrow come from?"

As we walked, Zayn pointed to his left bicep, smiling wanly. A beautifully ornate bow gleamed against his skin, its silver ink slightly faded. "I have perhaps three more uses of it before the magic dries up."

"No way," I whispered.

"The arrows I keep here," he added, lifting his shirt to show me a rune-stamped, half-empty quiver of silver arrows embedded against his ribcage, where thick cords of lateral muscles connected with well-defined obliques.

My eyes bulged. "What other kinds of weapons are you packing under there?"

"Nothing we'll have to use anytime soon, I hope," he replied. His wan smile immediately faded when his eyes fell on my injured hand. "You're bleeding."

"It's nothing," I mumbled, casting a sidelong glance at the gold liquid oozing from my palm.

"Give me your hand," Zayn ordered as he fished a small bottle out of his bag.

I did as I was told, doing my best to ignore the hot pang of longing that knotted my insides the moment our fingers touched. Using his teeth to pull out the cork, he poured a stream of cool, milky liquid over the gash in my hand. I stared in amazement as the pale substance bubbled and foamed like hydrogen peroxide, darkened to black, then evaporated into a dry, crumbly substance. Zayn brought my palm to his lips, eliciting a small gasp from me, and blew away the ashes. Underneath, the cut had become nothing but a pale, flat scar that was faintly glowing yellow.

"Holy shit," I breathed, clenching and unclenching my fully healed hand.

Zayn's eyes flickered from the new scar to my bare legs. A flush of embarrassment rose in my cheeks until I understood why: zig-zagging cuts and scrapes peppered my knees and shins, and unmistakably gold blood oozed through all those shallow lines of broken skin. With another sigh, he rooted around his bag again until he pulled out a shiny, purple square of fabric that reminded me of the scaly leggings Salen had been wearing that morning.

"Take off your shorts and put these on," he instructed. "We need to shield your legs from view."

I took the material in my hands; it was supple and smooth, but also sturdy. Upon closer examination, I could see the tough scales were actually iridescent, blending about ten different colors into what my overworked brain decided to process as "purple" for the sake of conserving my rapidly-diminishing neurological faculties.

I gave the fabric a curious sniff. "What's it made of?"

"Siren scales."

I gawked at him. "Come again?"

Zayn shrugged. "Real sirens aren't the beautiful, long-haired humanoids your species likes to conjure up in fairytales. Sirens, which are a lot more dangerous and nastier than mermaids, are one of the more lethal creatures that lurk in the wetlands. Few of us have ever managed to kill one, but every once in a while, a dead one washes up on land. Their scales make for great protective coverings once the hide is aged and treated."

"O…kay," I gulped, trying not to think of a certain beloved, red-headed Disney character from my childhood. "Um…aren't you going to turn around?"

Zayn, who was standing two feet away with his heavily-tattooed arms crossed, flashed me an uncharacteristically playful smirk. "You act like I haven't seen you naked before."

Scoffing, I whirled away from him and shimmied out of my tattered shorts, praising the creator that I'd put on a pair of halfway-cute, boy-cut panties that morning. I could practically feel Zayn's smoldering stare taking in my backside as I slipped the buttery-smooth siren hide up my bare, scraped legs. Surprise crossed my face as I ran my hand over the gorgeous, kaleidoscopic fabric of the leggings, which somehow hugged my hips just right.

"They fit perfectly," I gushed, turning around to admire my ass. "How did you know my size?"

Despite his ribbing, Zayn was standing with his back toward me, shoulders stiff and neck flushed. When he turned around, he gave me a quick look up and down and then hastily busied himself with a zipper on the side of his pack. "Lucky guess," he coughed, his voice oddly hoarse. I was expecting him to clarify further, but once he'd fixed whatever technical issue he was apparently having, he brushed past me without a second look. "Come on. We still have another five hours to go. And believe me when I say, glaistigs are not the worst of our worries in this neck of the woods."

With a nod and an audible gulp, I shoved my clammy hands in my siren-hide pockets and fell into step behind him, doing my best not to think about the dead creature a few dozen yards behind us, or any of the equally frightening, not-dead ones that almost certainly lurked ahead.

XI.
DAWN OF THE CERULEAN SUN

Save for a few near-misses with a handful of venomous plants and animals, the rest of the afternoon was relatively uneventful. So long as I stayed near Zayn, kept my head down, and avoided the never-ending list of things that could kill or maim me, I even managed to keep cuts and scrapes to a minimum. The tattoo Zayn had given me was doing a great job of masking the glow beneath my intact skin, but it didn't hide any new abrasions or scars – all of which displayed glimpses of my unmistakably gilded blood. At least Zayn had had the foresight to pack a lot of bandages.

After the incident with the glaistig, he'd fallen silent, as though deep in concentration. He steered us away from all rivers and ponds, the hunting ground of many hydrophilic fae, he'd explained, and made sure I didn't travel more than an arm's length away from him. I felt fairly stupid on my invisible, three-foot-long leash, but let's face it – we both knew I was a liability. Not to mention a massive impediment. My oxygen-deprived lungs and aching legs had forced us to stop every so often while I worked to catch a decent lungful of air – a damn near impossibility in this thin-atmosphered alien realm. By the time the blue (!) sun began to sink between the trees, and our long shadows stretched far behind us, I could tell Zayn was getting antsy. He kept glancing at me over his shoulder, a worried expression tightening his brows. I did my best to keep up, but dehydrated, hungry, and oxygen-deprived as I was, it got to a point where I was stumbling more often than walking.

Finally, he sighed and turned around. "I was hoping to get closer to the Waypoint, but we can't risk continuing on in the dark – we'll have to stop here."

"Here?" Teeth chattering from the rapidly dropping temperature, I looked around anxiously. We were standing in the middle of a small, flat clearing, with high trees that blurred into vertical stripes of gray and black surrounding us on all sides. At least the canopy had thinned out; I could actually see a green-tinted sky that was quickly fading to teal, and then twinkling black, as the strange cerulean sun began to set. It was a breathtaking sight to behold – until a cloud of chittering creatures flew overhead, hundreds of their beady little green eyes glinting against the darkness.

I didn't want Zayn to see the fear in my eyes – after all, I'd never even camped in my own glaistig-free realm – so I straightened my shoulders and put on a brave face. "What do you need help with?"

"Here," he said, handing me his spell book and a tall, narrow glass tube that he'd retrieved from his pack. "Turn to page two-nineteen – there's a Greater Protection Rune that you can draw with the salt in this bottle. Use it sparingly, but try to get the angles as close as you can and make sure each line is touching at least one other line. The primary circle will be about ten feet in diameter, enough to ward our campsite against unwelcome visitors."

With a mighty gulp, I reached forward to take the book and salt. "What will you do?"

"I'll set up camp."

Casting a dubious glance at his modest burlap bag – it didn't seem nearly big enough to carry three days' worth of food, camping materials, a first aid kit, and everything else he'd casually mentioned bringing – I went about my work. After studying the rune for a good five minutes, I took my place at the north side of our site and started making a large circle with the salt crystals, which gleamed against the dim light of the rising moon. Once I was fairly certain the circle was as precise as it could be – a difficult feat without a compass – I went back and started adding some of the extra details: on the east side, three ticks of varying lengths, the last ending in an equilateral triangle; and on the south, a circled cross that lay parallel with a set of right-angle diamonds to the north. By the time I finished, I was glistening with cold sweat.

"Hey, Zayn, how's it—"

A lone howl rose up from somewhere in the trees, which was quickly joined by at least a dozen more.

"Werewolves," Zayn remarked casually as he came to stand beside me.

I started to laugh, then thought the better of it. He hadn't made a single joke on this entire trip. Also, the howls were growing louder and louder, sending a wave of goosebumps skittering down my spine.

"This looks good," he murmured, kneeling to inspect my work. "All of the lines are connected?"

"Yes," I answered with more confidence than I felt.

"Raawk!" Biscuit screeched. A warning.

I whirled to my right – there, nested in between the shadowy outlines of the trees, were three sets of glowing yellow eyes staring at us from the darkness.

"Talia, come here," Zayn said calmly. His hand reached out to take my wrist, which tingled with warmth when he grasped it. "May I?" he asked, holding my hand in between us. At first, I didn't know what he meant, but then I saw the sewing needle he was grasping. My eyes went from that, over to the approaching sets of eyes, and back to the needle. I nodded mutely, blinking away the tears that had appeared out of nowhere.

"I'm sorry," he whispered, kissing my fingertip. My heart fluttered to a dead stop as his warm lips brushed against my skin, and for a brief moment, I forgot all about the needle.

Without preamble, he pressed it into my skin, then quickly tucked it out of sight. A single bead of gold appeared on the very tip of my finger. With my hand still clasped in his, Zayn walked us to the edge of the salt circle and held my finger above it, not once taking his attention away from the ominous creatures that peered at us from the forest. As the drop of blood fell on the salt, the entire rune illuminated like a lightbulb, casting a pale, golden glow on the closest line of trees.

The yellow eyes widened, then disappeared into the darkness.

"That should do it," Zayn said softly, flashing me a wan smile that didn't meet his tired eyes. Lifting my finger to his lips once more, he gently sucked away the remaining blood that had gathered at the tip, making my core erupt with heat and desire. To my surprise, his eyes, too, appeared to ignite, but he quickly dropped my hand and turned away before I could be sure.

"Camp's finished," he spoke without turning back to look at me. "We'd better get inside for the night. Hibiscus, come."

Zayn tossed an almond in the air, and with a happy-sounding whistle, Biscuit swooped out of the trees and caught it.

"Time for bed," he murmured, tapping his arm once Biscuit had finished his treat.

"Good night?"

"Mm-hmm."

I'd never seen a bird yawn before, but I was pretty sure that's exactly what Biscuit was doing when he stretched open his beak and ruffled his feathers. Then, in a flash of dazzling light, he was gone, and Zayn's beautiful tattoo had returned to his flesh.

"Good night, Hibiscus," Zayn whispered, then disappeared inside the rune-adorned tent he'd erected.

As I followed him inside, I tried to swallow the massive lump that had made a sudden reappearance in my throat, having little success. *Maybe the tent will be like the inside of the TARDIS,* I told myself. *Nice and spacious and full of—*

Shit.

No such luck. My shoulders sank as the flap fluttered closed behind me. The inside of the tent was mundane and tiny, illuminated by a dim lantern, with only a single sleeping bag spread across the floor.

Zayn flashed me an apologetic grimace. "You can take the sleeping bag once we go to bed. I'm happy to sleep on the floor."

Normally, I'd argue, but with my teeth chattering the way they were, I knew that sleeping bag would be my one and only lifeline to get through the night.

He sat cross-legged on top of it, motioning for me to do the same. When I followed suit, he pulled his burlap sack into his lap, rummaged through it for a bit, and then took out an aluminum-wrapped square of something that vaguely resembled a slice of pound cake. "Have you ever read Tolkien?" he asked.

"I mean, in high school. Why?"

"Well, this was his inspiration for lembas bread," he smiled. "He borrowed the idea from an elf he'd befriended in Blœmfontein."

"I can't tell if you're joking or not," I frowned, not bothering to wait for his answer before taking a bite. The cake was dense and sweet, and it took everything I had to hold back an orgasmic moan as the first mouthful went down. "Oh, God, this is so good."

"Good. A couple bites should hold you for the night, as well as most of tomorrow."

"What will you eat?" I asked through a mouthful of lemon zesty goodness…and then the stupidity of my words hit me. "Er…" I added, swallowing the extra-large bite with an audible, awkward gulp.

He produced a thermos of water from the bag and took a swig from it, then handed it to me. "I'll be fine."

I took the water gratefully, surveying his face in the light of the lantern as I took several deep gulps. He was still as gorgeous as ever, but his skin was paler than usual and dark circles were stamped beneath his eyes. A wave of sympathy welled in my chest.

"Zayn."

He gave me a tired look. "Hmm?"

"You have to be starving. How long has it been since you last, um…"

"It's been several weeks now," he replied with a casual shrug. "I typically try to space out feedings, but I suppose this is taking it a bit far, even for me. It shouldn't be a problem so long as I get some nourishment once we get back."

A pang of cold, bitter jealousy – one I knew I had no right to feel – gripped me by the chest.

"Zayn…" I started, then quickly lost my nerve. Stalling for time, I took another swig of water to wet my tongue, which had gone dry and heavy all over again. I cleared my throat, then tried again. "I mean…if you're hungry, and you need to, um, you know…" Frustrated, I let my breath out in a huff. "I mean, it's not like we haven't done it before."

His eyes widened, then quickly hardened – with anger, I could only presume. When he eventually spoke, the edges of his voice were sharp. "Absolutely not, Talia."

My eyes dropped to my lap and humiliation heated my cheeks. The man was starving for nourishment and still wanted nothing to do with me. Had that night truly been so one-sided?

I turned away in shame, busying myself with straightening out the far corner of the sleeping bag so he couldn't see the pain that had flooded my face. If most of his human "transactions" were like eating stale popcorn, then having sex with me must have been akin to chewing on dried kelp strips. Or better yet, cardboard, since dried kelp actually has some nutritional value.

"Talia…"

My shoulders stiffened.

After a moment, he let out a low sigh. "We should get some sleep. Tomorrow will be another long day of walking."

I nodded, then crawled into the sleeping bag where I shimmied out of my pants and tank top, rolling into a mostly-naked ball to stay warm. Zayn had lain down on his side, back turned to me.

"Are you warm enough?" he asked softly.

"Yes," I lied. I thought I heard him mutter something else, but with the wind picking up and the tent flapping, it was hard to tell.

"Goodnight, Talia."

"Goodnight," I whispered, hugging my knees as the gathering wind carried the frightening sounds of the forest to our shuddering tent. Between the howls, the intermittent high-pitched shrieks and yips, and, most jarringly, the nearby scuffling of leaves and branches, I lay awake for well over an hour, trembling in the darkness. And while thoughts of werewolves, banshees, she-goats, and fire-spitting insects kept me awake, it was the incubus in the corner that eventually tortured my dreams – not with pain, but endless, rapturous pleasure that, even in my dreams, I knew I'd never be able to taste again.

When the warm brush of a half-naked fae stirred me awake, I didn't think much of it; in my half-conscious stupor, I'd just assumed it was the start of yet another forbiddingly delicious, heartbreaking dream...until I felt Zayn's warm breath whisper in my ear.

"Talia?"

My eyes popped open, every muscle in my body tensing as I sucked in a quiet gasp. This had to have been another dream. A dream within a dream, like I used to have all the time as a kid. But then the discomfort of the tent hit me all at once: the freezing air, my numb toes, and my throbbing right hip, which had been pressed against the hard ground for hours.

This was no dream.

I immediately flipped over in my sleeping bag, coming

nose to nose with a wide-eyed incubus. "Zayn," I replied, my voice calm and level – a hell of a feat, because I was a screaming, crumbling mess inside. "What brings you to this side of the tent?"

"Your teeth have been chattering all night," he whispered softly, eyes faintly glowing in the darkness. "I threw my blanket on top of you almost an hour ago, but it didn't seem to help."

This is probably where some sort of response – something like, "Oh, gee, thanks for that" – would have been appropriate, but I was mentally flatlining.

"Turn over," he instructed. "I can't have you getting hypothermia a half-day into our trip."

It wasn't until he gripped my bare shoulders to roll me back over onto my side that I remembered I wasn't wearing any clothes, save for my bra and panties. That must have been about the time he noticed as well, because I distinctly heard a sharp intake of breath just beside my ear.

Zayn, who was shirtless himself, cleared his throat. "I'm going to put my arm around you... Is that okay?" My answering nod was so feeble, he hesitated.

"Yes," I choked out hoarsely. "I mean, if you want to."

He made a dismissive grunt, then wrapped his arm across my stomach, cupping the curve of my waist as he pressed his bare torso against my back. His skin was so warm, I could barely suppress a contented sigh. I'd been shivering since the sun went down however many hours ago, and my teeth had been chattering so hard they physically hurt.

"You're so cold," he murmured, lips brushing against the back of my neck. "Why didn't you say something?"

I stilled, too stupefied to speak or move as he shifted his weight, pressing his hips against the barely-there, sheer fabric of my panties. Heat blossomed in my lower belly, radiating out through my limbs until I could finally feel my fingers and toes again. Within minutes, the sleeping bag had become so toasty warm from our combined bodies, I finally released a deep, building sigh, letting my tensed muscles relax. Forgetting both clothes and coyness, I blissfully melted against Zayn's warm body, infused with heat inside and out.

His breath hitched against the back of my neck, making my heavy, fluttering eyelids pop open. His hand had tightened against my waist, gripping me closer. When he shifted his weight, I felt it – the unmistakable hardness of his arousal, pressed against my back. My own breath caught roughly in my throat. Penises often moved of their own accord – seventh grade sex ed had taught me that – and just because it had…stiffened…didn't necessarily mean it was from arousal. It could have just been from the…friction. Of his jeans. Rubbing against my ass.

My own breaths were coming out short and ragged now, and Zayn's fingers were digging into my side as though he were fighting…

Fighting as hard as I am, I finally managed to swallow. But what was he fighting against? His morals? His nature? His…urges?

Every nerve in my body screamed at me to turn over.

Don't do it, my brain admonished me. *He's just trying to keep you warm, like anyone with half a heart would do. Your gym teacher said it himself – penises have weird, irrational minds of their own. So just leave it.*

A tiny, almost inaudible growl rumbled in Zayn's chest, vibrating against my bare back.

Don't, Talia! the frightened voice in the back of my head pleaded with me. *He'll just reject you, like he did before. He doesn't care about you like that. He doesn't need someone like you when he has stunning, half-naked succubi literally banging down his door…*

I could feel his hot breath brushing against the back of my neck. His fingers clutching me like he couldn't bear to let me go. And the entire length of his hard arousal, which had only grown.

Don't do it.

My heart was threatening to explode out of my chest. The tiny strip of fabric between my thighs was damp with longing. My chest and neck were flushed with a heat that went far beyond a mere toasty sleeping bag. All I had to do was turn around, and he would be right there…

"Talia." He whispered my name in the same ragged, worshipping way he'd whispered it in my ear *that* night, moments before releasing himself inside of me.

And that was the end of me.

I flung my body in his direction, once more finding myself face to face with the heart-achingly beautiful man who'd spent the entire night pleasuring me in my dreams. His eyes, even in the dim light of dawn, burned into mine like fire behind stained glass. A pained expression pulled at his features, as though he were fighting a losing battle.

"Tell me no, Talia. Tell me no and—"

"Please," I whispered, trembling from head to toe. "Zayn…please."

A soft gasp escaped my lips as he clasped my wrists in a single powerful hand, wrapping the other around the small of my back to pull my taut stomach and breasts against his naked torso. His sweet breath intermingled with mine, lips parted with hunger and barely tamped urgency.

Desire pulsed between my thighs, soaking my panties. I wanted nothing – *nothing* – more than to take him deep inside of me, as hard as he could possibly give it.

And for the first time in two years, I knew he wanted that too…

Crash!
 Crack!
Snap!

The sounds of crunching bones tore me out of my primal, coitus-starved state. My eyes flew to the east side of the tent, where faint rays of green-tinted morning light had been eclipsed by a teetering, lumpy silhouette that was quivering and convulsing with every pop and crack.

A strangled gasp had made its way halfway out of my mouth before Zayn stifled it with the hot palm of his hand. His entire body had tensed against mine; when our eyes met, he released my mouth to hold a finger to his lips.

Slubbering, hog-like snorts punctuated the loud crunching, each one sending a fresh chill down my spine. With one last, pleading, "please-don't-scream" gesture, Zayn quietly leaned away from me to grab his nearby boots. Taking his ever-prudent cue, I reached a trembling arm deep into the sleeping bag to retrieve my balled-up shirt, pulling it over my head as quickly and silently as possible, then reached for my pants…

The snorting and crunching stopped.

My fingers froze mid-sleeping-bag as my horrified eyes flew back to Zayn's. He held up a hand, motioning for me to stay put, then carefully crawled out of the sleeping bag to finish tying his boots.

Stay, he mouthed to me.

I shook my head violently, earning me a sharp and silent rebuke.

Talia!

My shaking hands were clenching the sleeping bag so tightly, my knuckles had gone white. But my head bowed in submission, relenting to the fae's command. With one last, backward glance over his shoulder, Zayn unzipped the flap and stepped outside.

With a determined huff, I crawled out of my safe cocoon and ventured after him on my hands and knees, peeking an eye through the narrow slit of the open tent flap. All sounds of life had ceased, but the metallic scent of death hung heavy in the air. At first, I couldn't make out anything in the gray morning light, but as my eyes slowly adjusted, they found the dark smear of crimson that had trailed from the forest and halfway around the salt circle surrounding our camp site. I stuck my head through the opening to get a better look. The salt crystals were no longer glowing, and the trail of blood had intersected the outer line, leading to a mangled deer carcass on the east side of the tent – *inside* the so-called protection circle.

But it wasn't the sight of pooling blood or matted fur or broken bones that eventually wrenched the animalistic, blood-curdling scream from my lungs – it was the horrible giant that was hunched over it.

XII.
What the Fachan?

You know those nightmares you have as a kid – like after an unsupervised night of watching horror movies and drinking one too many artificial, carbonated beverages – the kind that send you screaming awake, too frightened to run for help because the unspeakably terrible things you saw in your dreams might be lurking beneath your bed, ready to grab you by the ankle and gnaw off your leg?

That was the twelve-foot-tall, gargantuan nightmare that was currently towering above me, the pants-less, gawking pipsqueak. When it dropped the twisted deer carcass it had been gnawing on and turned its attention on me, last night's half-digested elf bread welled up in my throat, carried by a roiling wave of stomach acid. I couldn't move. I couldn't make another sound. I could only stare in open-mouthed horror at the rows of jagged teeth that were gnashing beneath its single bloodshot eye. And the entire neckless head sat atop a lumpy torso that had one long, skinny arm protruding from the center of its chest and gnarled, bony fingers that ended in red-stained claws.

But it got worse. So much worse. Because all of that aforementioned hideousness was balanced on a single thick, veiny leg that ended in a huge, hairy foot – a huge, hairy foot that was surprisingly adept at running…

Straight. At. Me.

A fresh scream shattered from my throat as the thing grabbed its bloody club from the ground and lunged, swinging the spiked bat at my head like it was a whiffle ball. Barefoot and clad in only my stupid underwear and tank top, I flung myself away from the one-legged, one-armed, one-eyed monster, flailing my own two arms like a windmill as I scrambled across the forest floor on my hands and feet. Even with half as many limbs as me, the thing caught up to me in three seconds, displaying those serrated, yellowed teeth in a wide grin. My head swiveled around wildly. I was cornered, sandwiched between the club-wielding cyclops and a sprawling cluster of bright red *asgera* mushrooms – the same kind Zayn had warned would melt the soles and skin right off my feet.

"I told you to stay in the tent," the prodigal fae growled, dropping from the tree above to land directly between me and Señor Cyclops. He had his silver bow raised, gleaming arrow trained directly at the creature's massive eye.

I covered my face as the arrow let loose and the giant let out a terrible shriek, then peered between my fingers, expecting to find it face-down in a pile of black goo like the fallen glaistig. Instead, I found a broken arrow on the ground and its furious target lunging at Zayn full-speed. The monster let out a shriek, swinging its club like a hungry kid charging at a piñata.

The incubus ducked and rolled, deftly landing on one knee with his arrow nocked and aimed. It flew through the air, silver tip glinting against the rising sun, but the creature flung its club in front of it, knocking the arrow aside. Zayn had already nocked another one and was preparing to let it fly when the giant flung up its foot and sailed through the air, connecting with Zayn's ribs with a horrible thud. The incubus flew into the side of a tree and sank to the ground, clutching his ribs.

"Shit!" I hissed, looking around for something that might vaguely resemble a weapon. The large cluster of *asgera* mushrooms was just behind me, but I couldn't grab one without my own fingers melting off.

Settling for a large rock, I leapt to my feet and chucked it at the monster's eye as hard as I could, channeling those two summers of softball camp straight into my skillful pitch. The rock *thunked* against the monster's forehead and clattered to the ground. Unfortunately, all that seemed to do was annoy it. Its attention immediately shifted from Zayn to me, the reaction I was hoping for, but it was now lumbering at me at full speed, club raised like a pickleball paddle.

"Shit, shit, shit!" I spun around, frantically skimming my surroundings for an emergency exit. At that particular moment, the field of skin-dissolving mushrooms was starting to look like a pretty good escape route.

"Dammit, Talia," I heard Zayn groan, pulling himself to his feet. Muttering irritably, he pressed two fingers to the inside of his left bicep, where the image of a bejeweled, gold-handled dagger was engraved. In a brilliant flash of blue, the dagger appeared in his right hand. I let out a yelp and fell to my knees as the blade went flying through the air, landing hilt-deep in the back of the creature's knee.

Hooo boy, it did not like that.

With a terrible scream, the giant whirled around, spinning its club in a vicious horizontal arc. It sliced through the clearing, hurtling straight for Zayn's head.

"Watch out!" I shouted.

He dove out of the way just in time; the spiked club sailed straight past his right ear, missing him by a fraction of an inch. A sigh of relief whooshed through my lips – until Zayn took a staggering leap backward. His hand flew to his cheek, where a thin, red line of blood appeared. The monster let out a terrible roar as its knee buckled from the embedded dagger and it fell, hard, on its side. At the same time, the incubus stumbled backward, teetered, then collapsed.

"Zayn!" I cried, jumping to my feet. Making a wide arc around the screeching, flailing monster, I dropped to the ground beside the incubus, cupping his face in my hands. "What happened? What's wrong?"

"T-Talia," he rasped. The cut on his face had blackened at the edges, as had the surrounding veins and capillaries. "The fachan's club…the spines…"

Poison.

My hands flew to my mouth. "What can I do? *Zayn!*" I gripped his limp hand in both of mine. "Please tell me what to do!"

A moan escaped his lips as he grimaced in pain. His skin was so pale, so cool to the touch. A terrified sob had lodged itself in my throat. He'd been so hungry and weak to begin with. Whatever the hell those spines had been poisoned with, they were quickly robbing him of his already dwindling energy.

Less than two yards away, the fachan loosed a furious roar. It had ripped the dagger from its leg and thick, brown blood was seeping from the wound. Dragging itself to where the club lay, the creature picked it up and used it to shakily hoist itself upright. Then, with a rancorous snarl, it began limping toward us, its cyclops eye flashing angrily.

I let out a terrified whimper as Zayn's eyes fluttered closed. His forehead was glistening with cold sweat and his cheeks were almost colorless. Even the tattoos covering his skin looked pale. I didn't know how much of his failing state was from the toxin and how much was from hunger and fatigue, but as the fachan hobbled closer, poisoned club raised high above its head to strike, I knew I had to act. I scrambled to Zayn's fallen quiver, snatched an arrow and stabbed one of the nearby *asgera* mushrooms. The tip of the arrow immediately began to smoke and hiss from the acid. As the fachan let out a belligerent cry and raised its club to smash Zayn's head in, I sucked in a deep breath, gripped the metal shaft with a white-knuckled fist, and flung my makeshift mushroom shish kebab like a javelin; by the grace of God – and sheer, dumb luck – it hit the center of the creature's eye with a sickening *squelch*. The thing dropped its club and screamed like a banshee, clawing at its face as it fell to the ground writhing.

"Zayn!" I cried, kneeling to the ground beside him. He wasn't moving. "Wake up, please!"

No response.

A few feet away, the injured fachan was still screeching and kicking, blindly searching the ground for its weapon. It wasn't about to go down before taking us with it. I didn't know what to do – even if I somehow managed to outrun it, I couldn't leave Zayn behind.

He needed energy – now.

Clambering on top of Zayn's lap, I straddled his hips with bare, bloodied legs, and pressed my ear to the clammy skin of his chest. His heart was beating so faintly, I could barely hear it.

"Please wake up," I whispered, cupping his face in my trembling hands. The blood from the fresh scrapes on my palm left a gleaming streak of gold across the festering cut on his cheek. "Please." Hovering an inch from his face, I hesitated for the span of a single, ragged breath...

And then I dropped my mouth to his.

The moment our lips touched, heat coursed through my own chilled body, radiating from the epicenter of where our mouths connected. A low, throaty rumble sounded in Zayn's chest as warmth spread across his skin. Without opening his eyes, his lips parted to take me in. Cautiously, uncertainly, my tongue gently slid over his and he let out a soft moan. His hands were creeping over the tops of my thighs as he drank from my well, parched and thirsty for more. Every nerve in my body was alight, flooding my veins with electricity. His strengthening hands found my hips, thumbs slipping beneath the lace of my panties as he pulled me against his growing arousal.

"Talia," he moaned against my lips, sending a shudder through my entire body. His hands flew beneath my shirt, gripping the contours of my waist. The low rumble in his chest turned into a deep growl as one of his arms circled my back and the other knotted into my hair, pulling me deeper into the kiss. A soft cry escaped my mouth as he bit my lip, drawing blood.

His emerald eyes popped open, flashing like fire.

Before I knew what was happening, he flung me off of him. Hard. I landed in a pile of leaves in a breathless heap, suddenly too tired to lift my head. The fachan's club crashed to the ground, right where I'd been straddling Zayn a split second ago. The mounting sounds of a scuffle ensued, followed by a series of high-pitched shrieks and, finally, a terrible gurgle. Two seconds later, the fachan collapsed atop its fallen club, its throat split wide open and seeping brown sludge onto the forest floor.

Exhaustion had begun to take precedence over panic – so much so, I couldn't even muster the strength to scream. I felt Zayn's muscular arms encircle my body and for the briefest moment, I thought he was leaning down to kiss me. But when he lifted me against his chest and brought my face to his, his eyes were glinting with fury, not fire. Instinctively, I recoiled, but I had no place to go – his grip was like iron. He ducked into the tent and gently laid me atop the sleeping bag, spreading a warm blanket across my body. Heavy sleep followed shortly after, the entire world fading to black.

But the incubus's flashing green eyes, so deeply etched with anger and betrayal, continued to haunt me in the darkness.

My body was gently rocking back and forth, reminding me of the backyard hammock my father and I used to nap in together when I was very young. The sounds of birds and insects filtered through the heavy daze of sleep, followed by the heady, tantalizing aroma that my body recognized before my brain. My lashes fluttered open and the hazy sight of orange treetops and a green-tinted sky trickled into view. Just beneath that, the beautiful creature carrying me in his arms was gazing into the sky.

"Hibiscus," he was calling. "Come."

A moment later, a blur of color dropped from the sky and landed on his shoulder.

"Zayn?" I asked. My tongue felt dry and heavy.

He gently lowered me onto a moss-covered boulder, holding my shoulder to keep me upright. "Here," he said, the edges of his voice hard. "Drink this."

He thrust something cool and cylindrical into my hands, which I instinctively brought to my lips. The cold water helped clear my head, and as I gulped it down ravenously, a distant memory began tugging at the frayed edges of my mind…

My eyes popped open with a gasp, followed by a coughing fit. When the last of the inhaled water droplets had been expelled from my windpipe, I wiped my mouth with the back of my hand, taking in my new surroundings. The trees had thinned substantially, their leaves more orange than pink. Blue-tinted grass had taken the place of dried leaves and mulch. And the sun was high in the sky, casting dark shadows beneath Zayn's tight expression.

"You're awake." His voice was flat.

I nodded stupidly. "How long was I…was I out?"

"A little under four hours. I've been carrying you for the last two."

My eyes widened. "I don't understand. What happened?"

His irises, no longer glowing with fire, had darkened to simmering coals. "You don't remember?"

I swallowed. "I mean, I remember the…the, um, fack—er, fock—?"

"Fachan."

"Yes, that, and um, you were unconscious, so I, uh—" I rubbed the back of my neck, straining to remember. As the memory slowly pieced itself back together, tendrils of heat snaked and blossomed through my core. My mind may have temporarily forgotten that kiss, but my body certainly hadn't.

"You made me feed on you!" Zayn exploded. That elicited a startled cry from Biscuit, who flew off his shoulder to land on a nearby branch. "Do you know how dangerous that was? How *stupid?!*"

My jaw tumbled open. "I-I didn't… But the fachan! You were in danger and—"

"You had no right!" he snarled.

"Look, I'm sorry, okay?!" I blustered, eyes stinging from both anger and embarrassment. "I'm sorry! You were unconscious, and I honestly thought you were going to die! And I couldn't bear the thought of…of…"

Of never seeing you again.

I abruptly clamped my mouth shut, sealing those terrible words away.

"If you had just stayed in the damn tent like I'd told you to, you wouldn't have been in any danger!"

"What the hell would a flimsy tent have done against—"

"The tent was protected, Talia! Nothing would have been able to touch you in there!"

My head, still so heavy and hazy, was spinning. As a consequence, the string of words tumbling out of my mouth wasn't exactly measured or thoughtful. "Protected?" I gave a derisive snort. "Protected like the stupid salt circle was supposed to protect us?!"

Zayn's jaw clenched. "I asked you if the lines were all connected. You said they were. How stupid of me to trust you to do one simple thing!"

"I have no idea what I'm doing!" I shouted, eyes stinging.

"Oh, that's more than evident!" he retorted. "Seeing as you climbed on an unconscious incubus without first getting approval or consent! Goddammit, Talia! What were you thinking?"

Fists clenched, he spun around and turned his back to me, broad shoulders heaving. I looked up at Biscuit in stunned confusion, but even he seemed to be avoiding making eye contact with me.

I'd never seen Zayn this angry before. Hell, I'd never seen him angry at all, not truly. Not when I'd seriously miscounted the cash in the drawer. Not when he caught me pounding a shot with a nervous client. And not even when I broke into his office to "borrow" his magical, priceless ink…

My hands balled into trembling fists that rested on the purple siren hide he must have slipped back on me at some point. The same kind of hide Salen had been wearing when she—

Oh.

When the realization of what I'd done finally began to sink in, my heart sank along with it. Climbing on top of him like that, kissing him without his permission…I was no better than Salen, who'd barged into his shop unannounced and took whatever she wanted, including him, without asking. Without *consent.* I bit my lip, tasting blood from my half-healed cut. Just yesterday, I'd accused him of taking advantage of people, of preying on women like he was some kind of wild animal, because "isn't that pretty much what incubi do?"

My shoulders slumped with shame. I was the world's biggest hypocrite.

Swallowing my pride, I slid off the rock and stood behind him, too tired and ashamed to hold my head up high. "Zayn, I'm…I'm so sorry," I whispered, the edges of my voice cracking. "I shouldn't have ever taken advantage of you like that."

His shoulders stiffened.

"In that moment, I couldn't think of any other way to help you. I thought you were dying. I was scared out of my mind to lose you. But what I did crossed a boundary, and whether you're human or incubus – it doesn't matter. You deserve respect, and I...I..."

He slowly turned around to face me, one eyebrow arched far above the other.

"I'm sorry," I repeated, feeling like an absolute ass. "I promise it won't happen again."

Zayn blinked, then frowned. After a moment, he started to open his mouth as if about to say something, then closed it again.

As for me, I was just trying my best to look him in the eye.

His hand reached forward – slowly, haltingly – until his thumb gently brushed against the cut on my lip. "Talia..." he whispered. My hands balled into fists as I did my best not to let my knees buckle at his touch. "Don't you understand?"

I shook my head feebly, feeling more confused than ever.

"I never want to hurt you," he murmured, withdrawing his hand. "And that's exactly what I could have done. What I already *did*. Because what you give me...I can never repay." He touched the scar on his cheek, almost entirely healed.

All of the air in my lungs evaporated, leaving me light-headed and dizzy. *He was angry with me...because he could have hurt me?*

Somewhere in the bushes, a twig snapped, and Biscuit made an impatient click with his beak.

Zayn took a step back, letting his hand fall to his side. "It's getting late, and the Waypoint attracts a lot of travelers – of all varieties. We need to get moving, otherwise we won't arrive until nightfall." His eyes traveled to the sun above, and then to my arms, which were scratched and scraped with crisscrossing, glowing scabs. He sighed, then dug around his pack until he withdrew a tiny container. Opening the lid, he swirled his fingers around to remove the last remnants of a shiny balm that reminded me of glittering petroleum oil. Without another word, he took my left hand in his, and then the right, gently rubbing the lotion into my skin. The cuts and scrapes on my arms became infused with cool tingles before slowly fading to dimly-glowing scars.

My eyes lifted to his, wide with wonder and gratitude. If I could have only found the words.

He put the empty container back in the bag and then retrieved his brown leather jacket. "Here. Wear this."

Wordlessly, I took the jacket and shrugged it over my shoulders. It was way too big, but warm and soft on the inside. And it smelled like him. I closed my eyes, forcing away the tears that kept welling from some deep, distant place I didn't understand.

Zayn took one last glance at me over his shoulder, then started walking toward the edge of the trees. Biscuit flew down from his perch and landed on my shoulder, nuzzling against my ear.

"*Oy gotenyu,*" he cooed, eliciting a soft chuckle from me as I hastily wiped my eyes.

Zayn's pace was brisk, but not rushed, giving me the chance to take in my new surroundings. In just a few minutes, the edge of the forest had given way to hills of waist-high, cobalt-blue grass that gently swayed in the cool breeze. The tops were soft and velvety, like cotton. I gently ran my hands over them, enjoying the tickle on my palms as I lifted my face to take in the warm rays of the bluish-white sun. As the last of the morning's fog cleared from my head, I felt invigorated. Somehow.

"Hey, Zayn?" I called out tentatively. "Are you, um…still hungry?"

He stopped walking, tilting his head to glance at me over his shoulder. The color in his cheeks had returned, and while he was once more wearing his black, three-quarter-sleeved shirt, I could see the skin on the back of his neck and forearms had gone back to its normal bronze hue. I wasn't sure if it was a trick of my eyes or the sun, but even his tattoos appeared brighter, more vibrant. A frown was working the corners of Zayn's mouth, almost as if he were struggling to solve a complex math equation.

"No," he eventually replied, shaking his head lightly. "I don't feel hungry at all."

XIII.
The Waypoint

After reaching the end of the forest, we spent the rest of the afternoon walking through low, rolling blue hills that spread out as far as the eye could see. Every now and then, an aggressive neon-yellow grasshopper or venomous red dragonfly would appear, but apart from that, the final part of our trek was thankfully quiet. For the last hour or so, I'd trailed a few feet behind Zayn, entertaining myself by throwing slivers of almonds up in the air while Biscuit performed acrobatic loops and rolls to catch them, leaving trails of glitter in the sky. By now, the sinking sun was approaching the jagged line of plum-colored mountains ahead in the distance, sending bands of turquoise and green streaking across the darkening clouds. My breath caught as hundreds of tiny, twinkling green orbs began to appear above the swaying stalks of indigo wheat, gently hovering like fireflies.

"It's so beautiful," I whispered as I turned in a slow circle to take it all in.

Zayn glanced at me over his shoulder with an oddly wistful expression. "I used to love the sunsets here."

"Used to?"

Predictably, he didn't answer. Instead, he pointed to a tiny, vertical black line in the distance. "We're almost at the Waypoint. We can make it before dark if we keep up the pace."

Biscuit swooped down to land on my shoulder, giving my ear a gentle tug as he did. Absentmindedly, I offered up the coveted head scratches, all the while chewing on the inside of my lip. I didn't want to think about what might lurk in these peaceful plains once the sun dipped below the horizon.

Biscuit let out a soft coo, eyes closed in bliss as I scratched the feathers on the underside of his beak. "Ayluv you," he clucked contentedly.

"You love me?" I started, then laughed. "Are you just saying that 'cause you want another almond?"

"Luv Tal-ya!"

I grinned. "You hear that, Zayn? Biscuit says he loves me!"

"Hmm. Perhaps *Hibiscus* is a male, after all."

"Biscuit, are you a boy or a girl?" I asked. "Squawk once for boy."

"*Raaawk!*"

"Ha! That settles it!"

Zayn shrugged and held up his hands in defeat.

"Hey," a thought occurred to me. "Does Biscuit actually need food to survive?"

"Not a crumb."

"Seriously?"

"As much as he'd like you to think he's always starving, he could go his whole life without it. He just loves eating tasty human food for fun."

"So, if you created Biscuit, and I accidentally created that snake with your ink and Roy's blood, what exactly does that mean? Do they have, like…souls?"

"Blood incarnates do not have souls," Zayn replied.

"Oh." I could feel my heart sink.

"But Hibiscus does."

"He does?" I immediately perked up. "How? Isn't he an incarnate too?"

Something – or someone – howled in the distance, spurring my relaxed walk to a brisk sprint. I caught up with Zayn breathlessly, wishing for the umpteenth time that I had remembered to bring my inhaler.

"The sad and dangerous part about typical blood incarnates – and why it was illegal to have one back in the days of the king's rule – is that they don't feel or think. They're hollow vessels without souls, blindly submissive to Manipulators, and completely untamable for reckless Benefactors."

"Manipulators are those with AB blood, the ones who can control but not create, right?"

"Correct."

"And Benefactors have type-O blood – they can create but not control?"

"Yes. That's why mages who specialize in incarnation often work in pairs. One to create, one to control. And even then, neither can do anything without first having a talisman or catalyst."

"What's a mage?"

"Any creature capable of wielding external – or in your case, intrinsic – magic. Now that the court is gone, blood incarnates are becoming increasingly prevalent. Enslaved, soulless creatures who are compelled to do their Manipulator's bidding. It's…troubling. To say the least."

"No kidding."

Abandoning Biscuit to his own head-scratching devices, I rubbed the burgeoning ache in my temples. The idea of soulless, enslaved blood incarnates was terrifying. If I'd thought an unruly rattlesnake-slash-cobra was bad, what else was out there? Could someone make a glaistig incarnate? Or a fachan? What about a 100-foot-tall Godzilla incarnate? What were the limitations? *Were* there limitations?

"Bisc—dammit, now you have me doing it." Zayn sighed, snapping me from my overanxious reverie. "*Hibiscus* is not a blood incarnate. She—"

"Raawk!"

"Fine! *He*," Zayn amended, "is my familiar. Born of ink and blood, yes, but he also carries a piece of my soul."

I stopped in my tracks. "What?"

He turned to give me a wry, sad smile. "Creating a true familiar is far more complicated, and it also carries far greater risk – if Hibiscus were to die, for example, I might never fully recover – emotionally, or otherwise. But…we can communicate and understand each other on a spiritual level. He's my closest companion. My only companion," his eyes flickered from his colorful familiar to me, "apart from you."

"I…" My mouth opened reflexively, then closed again as I processed those last three words.

Zayn abruptly turned away from me and started walking again, leaving a fifty-pound brick to linger in my stomach. I should have felt elated that after all of this time, he really did consider me to be more than just an employee. Because, in truth, he had long been far more than just a boss to me. Hell, in a world of brief flings and fair-weather friends, somehow along the way, Zayn had become my closest confidant – someone with whom I felt comfortable chatting with throughout the day, or sharing my passion for art, or even disclosing the occasional personal tidbit.

Not that I've ever told him that, I grimaced. Maybe I wasn't as much of an open book as I'd claimed to be. But to hear him say that his only two companions were me and his self-conceived familiar… I swallowed thickly. What about his family? Or the women he "interacted" with? Didn't Zayn consider any of them to be companions?

"Come, Hibiscus," he called, making me jump. Without hesitating, Biscuit flew from my shoulder and landed on Zayn's, gently nuzzling against his ear upon landing. "Talia, the Waypoint is just ahead," he added, turning to address me. "For once, can you please listen to me when I ask you to stay back? Many creatures pass through here, and with night falling, Hibiscus and I need to make sure none of the unseelies are around."

I nodded pitifully, not even bothering to ask what the hell an "unseelie" was.

"Thank you." His smile was small but genuine. "We'll be back in a moment." As Biscuit took to the air, he turned to walk away.

"Wait, Zayn!"

"What's wrong?"

I swallowed. "Your family – your mom, dad, siblings…" I faltered, feeling the brick in my stomach grow heavier and heavier by the second. Oh, God, why had I never asked about this before? Was I *that* self-absorbed? Finally, I mustered up the courage to look him in the eye. "What…happened to them?"

The expression that flickered across his face lingered for less than a second, but I immediately understood it for what it was: a mix of pain, sorrow, and immeasurable grief. I recognized it because I, too, knew the feeling intimately, having felt it each and every time my fingers brushed against the locket my father had given me.

Zayn didn't answer my question, but he didn't have to for me to understand. Instead, he flashed me that same grim, not-quite smile, and said, "I'll be right back, okay? Stay low."

I obediently crouched in the grass, hugging my knees as he walked away. As I watched the back of his head disappear behind the tall, slender stalks of grass, my mind raced with a new and uncomfortable realization: Zayn had no family. No friends. I shook my head, trying to make sense of that. *Could that actually be true? An incubus who survives solely by feeding on the sexual energy of others has no companions?*

But then again, maybe the signs had been there all along. In two years, he'd never once mentioned a girlfriend, never had anyone routinely call or ask for him, never sat in the corner, smiling at secret messages on his phone like even I sometimes did – from time to time, at least. I'd always thought he was just a very private person, but with all of the guilt, sadness, and self-loathing I now understood he suppressed deep down, what if he *didn't* actually have a monthly rotation of lovers on speed dial? What if, instead, his entire existence revolved around a slew of few and far between one-night stands? I hugged my knees tighter to my chest. Far from making me jealous or judgmental, the notion was heartbreaking. With all he knew of sex and passion, did Zayn know anything of love?

How could he? I shook my head sadly. The man had literally cleaved his soul in two so he could have a single lifelong companion in these worlds. And there I'd been, his second closest confidante through sheer proximity, too consumed by my own loneliness to notice.

The tears I'd been holding back for so long began to fall freely. They continued to trickle down my face as the sky grew dimmer and dimmer, until Zayn's shadow returned and blotted out what was left of the sinking sun.

"Tal, what happened?" he asked worriedly, resting his arm on one knee as he knelt beside me. Biscuit was back in his place, sleeping for the night. Frowning, Zayn lifted my chin to get a better look at me. "Are you hurt?"

I took a deep, steadying breath to infuse my trembling limbs with courage. Pushing myself to my knees, I regarded him with eyes full of tears that I didn't bother hiding or wiping away. His own eyes were probing mine with concern, trying to understand. But there was nothing to be said. Without a word, I wrapped my arms around him and pressed my head against his chest, where his heartbeat thrummed in my ears. His entire body stiffened at my touch, and I briefly worried he might try to push me away. But after a moment of hesitation, his arms encircled me, his cheek resting atop my head while one hand gently cradled the back of it. We remained in that tight, silent embrace for the better part of a minute, while dozens of shimmering, green orbs hovered all around us.

Eventually, I mustered up the effort to pull away, just far enough to look him squarely in the eye. "Just so you know, I'm not going anywhere, okay?"

Surprise flickered across his features, followed by a strained expression that I couldn't quite decipher. Finally, that same wan, familiar smile of his returned. "You'd better not. You have an uncashed paycheck sitting in my desk."

I laughed – and shockingly, so did he – as we helped each other to our feet. I'm not sure whose hand moved first, but somehow, our fingers ended up entwined together as we walked across the grassy meadow, where a lone black lamp post stood atop a hill. Faint, flickering runes traveled up and down its tall post, and warm light burned inside the crowning glass panels, though it had no bulb or flame as a source.

Zayn's grip on my hand tightened as we approached. "I don't know what we'll find on the other side," he warned. "My contact sent me his coordinates, but I don't know if he'll be there when we arrive."

"Guess we'll find out together." I smiled, even as a bolt of fear zinged through me.

"Put your hand on this rune," he said, pointing to one of the smaller, purple ones embedded on the post. "And whatever happens, don't let go, okay?"

I nodded, inching closer to him as I pressed my fingers against the symbol. I couldn't help but notice the edges of my fingernails had begun to glow, and I was pretty sure it wasn't from the light of the Waypoint. Zayn must have noticed as well, because his eyes traveled from my illuminated nail beds to the tattoo on my arm, which had definitely faded over the course of the day. He didn't have to remind me why – the power of the ink was already dwindling, just as he'd warned me it would.

His expression suddenly tight, he placed his free hand on top of mine, muttering foreign incantations under his breath. The edges of the faintly-glowing rune began to light up like a neon bulb, heating the tips of my glowing fingers.

"Don't let go, Talia," Zayn whispered, momentarily switching back to English. His grip on my hand tightened as a wash of cold, purple fire surrounded us.

Before I could reply, another explosion of red fire appeared directly to my left. A hooded creature emerged from the crimson flames, turning its "face" to me – a dark, gaping hole that was completely featureless, save for two yellow eyes.

"*Æftelnâh*," it hissed at me, reaching a skeletal hand through the flames. As its fingers – more bone than skin – clasped my father's locket, I cried out, flinging myself backward. There was a peripheral flash of blue and, compliments of Zayn's dagger, the hooded creature shrieked, its shadowy body no longer attached to the bony hand that still gripped my necklace. The wrinkled, black skin was smoking and bubbling where it touched the heart-shaped metal, filling my nose with the acrid stench of burning flesh. A horrified scream erupted from my throat and I stumbled backward, twisting, then falling, as my own hand was wrenched free from Zayn's.

The last thing I saw was his horror-struck expression, completely engulfed in purple flames as he lunged to grab my wrist. Our fingertips brushed – and then both Zayn and the fire disappeared out of sight.

Alone I fell, my screams dissolving into nothingness as blinding white light consumed me.

XIV.
CLIFFS AT THE EDGE OF THE WORLD

    I fell out of the sky like a shrieking comet, landing ass-first on a tuft of grass that was soft enough to cushion my bones, but not nearly soft enough to prevent every last molecule of air from rushing out of my lungs as my body became thoroughly – and abruptly – acquainted with solid ground. With my arms and legs splayed out like a marooned starfish, I could only lie there on my back wheezing for a solid five minutes, fingertips clenching the dirt for moral support. The sky directly above me was concealed by grayish-green clouds, and cold, early-morning rain drizzled against my face and soaked the front of my shirt. At least my siren-scale pants appeared to be waterproof.
    When I was finally able to, I sucked in a hearty lungful of air through my nose. The damp scent smelled familiar, like salt and brine, and I could hear the distant sounds of waves

crashing against rocks. As I slowly drew myself up on one elbow, I found myself perched on the edge of a cliff overlooking an endless, wave-frothed, green ocean.

"Ohhhh, shit," I breathed, eyes bulging as I cautiously peered over the brink. If I had landed just three feet to my right, I'd have had a much, much longer fall – and dense clusters of sharp, jagged rocks to break it. And I wasn't even on the tallest part of the cliffs – I'd toppled onto a much lower overhang, sandwiched between two towering pinnacles of rock that had to have been a thousand feet high. Easily.

"Zayn!" I shouted, momentarily fearing the worst. My voice ricocheted off the adjacent cliff faces, which stretched along the rocky shoreline as far as the fog would allow me to see. The tops of the cliffs were flat and grass-topped, abruptly ending in sheer, vertical rock that met with broken boulders and roaring waves a hundred stories below.

I looked around anxiously. I was trapped on a rocky ledge with no exit in sight, save for a steep climb up the rocky slope behind me or a plunging cliff dive into the churning green waters below.

"Zayn!" I yelled again, as loudly as my protesting lungs would let me.

There was no answer. Was he…could he be…?

No, I shook my head firmly, pushing the excruciating thought away. *No.* He was okay. He had to be okay.

I swallowed thickly, slowly backing away from the edge on my hands and knees while simultaneously working to piece together everything that had just happened: Zayn and I were about to travel through the Waypoint to meet up with his contact; right before we went through the portal, a creepy faceless guy in a hood saw me and immediately launched for my throat; Zayn chivalrously sliced off the dude's hand, which, much like Thing from the Addams Family, kept on trucking despite being a disembodied collection of fingers. And then I fell backward and drop-landed here: a long line of black cliffs at the edge of the world, many time zones away from the Waypoint based on the midday sun. But where was Zayn? Close? Far? On the other side of the dimension?

Oh, God. I fingered the locket at the hollow of my throat with mounting horror. *How will he find me? If he doesn't, how will I find my way back?* And then, of course, there was the question of what the hell that awful *thing* was, and why it had tried to grab me.

My mind continued to race with about a hundred equally-if-not-more-daunting questions – until a flutter of movement two hundred feet below and a few dozen meters down the rocky coastline caught my attention. There, at the bottom of the cliffs, a dozen long-haired women were climbing out of the sea to settle atop the slick, wave-battered rocks.

Forgetting the two-hundred-foot plunge that would almost certainly end in my complete dismemberment, I crawled back to the very edge of the cliff to get a better look at them. Just like parts of Miami Beach, they were all topless from the navel up. Below that, each was wearing various shades of shimmery, lustrous leggings just like mine…

Except…

I rubbed my eyes in disbelief. Their leggings didn't end in feet. They ended in *flukes*. Long, elegant flukes that trailed in the water like diaphanous silk.

"Holy shit," I whispered as they all turned their gazes up to meet mine, their long, blackish-green hair fluttering in the ocean breeze like tendrils of seaweed. Glinting, iridescent scales transformed into green-tinted, alabaster skin at their hips, whiter than my stomach in the winter. And long garlands of pink shells hung across their shoulders and dangled from their necks. As I lay there gaping in wonder and disbelief, the mermaids held out their hands one by one, beckoning to me.

"Come join us!" they cried in unison, voices high and clear as wind chimes.

"Who?" I blinked. "*Me?*"

Several of them nodded, slender arms still outstretched.

"Uh, yeah, except I don't see a ladder anywhere!" I shouted. "Are there any stairs nearby? Or better yet, an elevator?"

"Come, Talia! Come down to us!"

"I don't know how to get to you!"

"Jump!" several of the voices cried. "Jump and we'll catch you!"

What a fantastic idea, I suddenly thought. *Of course, they'll catch me.*

"Jump, Talia!" several more voices cried, their pitches rising in harmony, eventually coming together to sing the most beautiful, haunting melody[*] I'd ever heard.

> *"Come and leap from highland's edge,*
> *The gentle draught shall set you free,*
> *Come and sleep in deep, green depths,*
> *Release your soul unto the sea.*
>
> *Come and hear our lullaby*
> *A lovely dirge of salt and sin,*
> *Come and drift where sea meets sky,*
> *Lay your bones among your kin."*

Tears mingled with the droplets of rain and sea that had gathered on my cheeks. I'd never heard such a magnificent

---

[*] See page 336

song – nay, such dulcet, mellifluous singing – in my entire life. It was like warm honey dripping from a spoon. Like the softest, cushiest velvet caressing the exposed bottom of my soul – *No!* I shook my head. Such uncouth, plain-spoken utterances could never do these sea-borne seraphs justice! I chewed on a bloodied knuckle in enraptured reverence, hardly noticing the glittering wound. These aquatic angels gesturing to me from below were so lovely, so pure, so gentle. And they were crying out in song, calling for me, their most precious friend, to come join them.

Pushing myself up from the damp ground, I propped myself up on shaking legs. I couldn't keep them waiting. I had to get to them. Right now. My obedient feet brought me to the farthest precipice of the cliff, where my toes hung off the rocky, crumbling edge of the world.

"Jump, Talia!" they called out. "Please, won't you hurry?"

"I'm coming!" I cried, raising one foot into the air. A heavy gust of wind whipped at my hair and clothes, making me teeter precariously on the brink. *No matter,* I reasoned. They would catch me.

With a wide, blissful smile plastered on my face, my body pitched itself forward.

Talia, what the hell are you doing?! my mother's voice screeched, yanking me back by an invisible cord.

Staggering to regain my footing on the gravel-strewn overhang, I responded, "I'm going to go swim with the mermaids!"

What have I always told you about talking to strangers?!

My dangling foot faltered mid-air. "Uh...not to?"

Exactly! What if they're psychopaths? Or worse, Scientologists? Did you even stop to think about that?

By now, both of my feet were planted firmly back on the ground while my mother's shrill, imaginary voice partially drowned out the mermaids' hypnotic lullaby. "So...you're saying...?"

Turn around, Bubaleh. Turn around and track down that handsome gentile of yours. What was his name?

I scrunched my brows together, trying to remember. What *was* his name? I tapped my chin thoughtfully, turning on my heel to walk away. *Zach? No. ...Zeb?* Below, freshly agitated waves hammered against the rocky shore as the wind picked up pace, whipping my hair into a wild frenzy. *Xander?* I mused, foot poised to retreat. It wasn't until another blast of wind slammed into my chest, knocking me completely off balance, that his name sprang to my lips.

"Zayn!" I screamed, grabbing at the empty air as I fell backward and over the ledge. "*Zaaaayn!*"

Wrenching my body around in midair, my heart slammed into my throat as the roaring waves and lethal rocks suddenly became much, much closer. With my own bloodcurdling screams drowning out any other possible sound in the region – including homicidal mermaid shanties – I had zero delusions about my rapidly-approaching death. No one was coming to catch me. No one was going to save me.

This was the end.

The wind was blowing so hard, I fell in a diagonal line, just narrowly missing the rocks. But I didn't have time to feel relief. As the brackish water rushed up to meet me, I frantically sucked in the deepest breath I could and plugged my nose, preparing for impact – though nothing could have prepared me for what happened next.

I plunged into the churning water feet first, every nerve in my brain and body reeling from the shock of the collision while sharp pain exploded in both of my eardrums from sinking too fast. But that was nothing compared to the bitter cold that splintered through my bones and turned my blood to icy slush. Instinct alone forced the scream that was tearing at my throat to stay put. My eyes shot open as I sank like a stone, slipping farther and farther away from the dim light of the surface. By now, the green water was nearly black, and millions of tumultuous bubbles were churning all around me, making it impossible to tell which way was up and which was down. My head swiveled around frantically, hair moving about my face in a suspended, unkempt halo as I searched for some sort of static frame of reference. But there was only darkness – crushing, suffocating darkness. A heavy, bone-deep lethargy was beginning to tug at me as my body temperature plummeted and my lungs burned.

Several slow, excruciating moments crept by before the bubbles finally began to dissipate, allowing my muddled brain to register that they were all floating ninety degrees to my left.

Up! My mind screamed. I jerked my body to the side and did my best to follow the rising bubbles, vaguely noticing how my outstretched arms and hands were glowing in the darkness.

I'm a golden jellyfish, I marveled deliriously.

Despite the irradiated flush of my skin, darkness – or rather, hypoxia – was creeping in. My legs, sluggish and numb, could barely kick anymore – and the surface was still a dull, distant green, at least fifty feet away. Bubbles had started to escape from my nose and lips and my lungs were screaming at me to breathe. By that point, I couldn't remember why I wasn't supposed to. They desperately needed air. Shouldn't I give it to them?

Confident in my decision, I had just opened my mouth to take in a lungful of water when something cool and slick latched itself firmly onto my wrist.

My eyes popped open to find two silver, pupil-less orbs floating in front of me.

Gilded One, a voice whispered in my head, *I shall take you to the surface in exchange for a vial of your blood. Are we in agreement?*

My head abruptly tilted forward – partially in a compliant nod, but mostly because that was the moment I finally lost consciousness, transforming those silvery eyes into warm, comforting, endless black.

I woke up on my side some indeterminate amount of time later, coughing up huge mouthfuls of saltwater and slimy chunks of seaweed until vomit and bile took their place. My lungs hurt, my head hurt, my joints hurt, and I couldn't stop shivering from the deep chill in my bones. It took a concerted effort to lift my head and look around. When my eyes were finally able to focus once again, I found myself on a small patch of black gravel beach, surrounded by clusters of rocks and tide pools. On my left, the cliffs stretched as far as the eye could see, both horizontally and vertically. The "shorter," protruding overlook that I had fallen from was casting a long shadow across the beach just ahead, and frothy green waves were crashing against the constellation of large boulders to my right, sending snaking rivulets of foam across the beach that lapped and bit at my frozen skin.

With a groan, I hoisted myself up, brushing away the gravel that had embedded itself in my cheeks and pulling tangled strands of seaweed from my hair. Eventually, my bleary gaze settled on a dark figure sitting a few feet behind me, whose matted hair parted in slimy, black curtains around her face – a face that would have elicited a bloodcurdling scream from me, had my lungs been in any condition to do so. Crouching in the nearest tide pool, the creature had dark purple skin that reminded me of an overripe black plum, and wide, sunken eyes of liquid silver. Her boney fingers – easily twice as long as mine – were webbed like a frog's and clutched the rocks tightly. When she lifted her chin to return my stare, her spine straightened, revealing a distended belly and scaly skin that was so thin and translucent, I could actually see the outline of strange, unidentifiable organs pulsing beneath. That's when I realized that she wasn't crouching, because, like the mermaids, this creature's body also ended in a coiled fishtail – one that was black as oil, with long, tattered fins trailing from the sides.

My eyes darted to the craggy rocks where the maidens had been singing before, now empty and abandoned. Fear prickled down my spine as I heaved myself to a splayed-out sitting position and warily regarded the creature that had been sitting as still and silent as a statue, its cold, predatory eyes glued to me the entire time. If and when she eventually made her move, I wouldn't have the strength to run. I knew it, and so did she.

I am owed a blood debt, the creature whispered in my head, her voice hoarse and deep.

"*You're* the one that s-s-saved me?" I stammered through chattering teeth, bringing my hands to my mouth to blow on them. My fingers were spongy and pale, almost corpse-like – minus the dull golden hue that shone just beneath my skin.

Aye.

"A-Are you a m-mermaid?"

She slowly shook her head from side to side. *Not anymore.*

"Then wh-what are you?"

She held up a long finger and pointed to the leggings Zayn had gifted me, silent accusation ringing through her telepathic voice.

A slash of fear cut through me as Zayn's words echoed in my memory. *Dangerous and nastier than mermaids, sirens are one of the more lethal creatures that lurk in the wetlands. Few of us have ever managed to kill one.*

"Th-These were a-a…gift," I stammered, then immediately winced. "Er, I m-mean, my friend found them. A siren had washed up on the shore, s-so he took the scales. I'm r-really sorry," I added, feeling sick with shame. And here I'd thought showing up to prom in the exact same red dress as Abby Warton had been mortifying.

It is of no consequence to me, she waved a hand that vaguely reminded me of a bat's wing, then retrieved a small, algae-tinted vial from a kelp-woven satchel she wore at her side. *Your blood,* she whispered, tossing the vial in my direction. *Give it to me.*

A pitiful whimper escaped my throat and I very nearly dropped the slippery glass on the rocks as I fumbled to catch it. The container wasn't big, but I wasn't thrilled at the thought of filling it up, either. I looked around nervously. There was no viable escape route. I was practically backed against the bottom of towering, unscalable cliffs, and a mere few yards of craggy rocks was all that separated us from the turbulent, freezing sea that I'd nearly drowned in. Someone else might have tried to book it down the coast, scrambling over the gravel and shattered boulders like a hypothermic crab – but it seemed like a pretty safe bet that she'd be faster on a fishtail than I could ever be on two numb, exhausted legs.

Shoulders caving, I let out a shuddering sigh. "You'll let m-me live once I give this to you, right? P-Promise?"

The siren nodded, then retrieved a small ivory-hilted knife from her tattered bag and chucked it in my direction.

"Th-Thanks," I muttered as it landed point-down in the gravel a few inches from my ankle. I took it with trembling fingers. The handle was intricately carved from some sort of bone – *Hopefully not human*, I shivered, then blushed at my own hypocrisy given my siren-hide leggings – and the blade was long and thin, almost like a letter opener.

Closing my eyes and taking a deep, aching breath, I held the tip of the dagger above my palm, then pressed it against my flesh with a soft whimper. Bright gold blood oozed from the cut, pooling in my hand. The creature's pupil-less eyes narrowed as I popped off the cork of the vial with my teeth, clenched my fingers into a fist, and let the blood trickle inside. It took longer than it should have, probably because the cold had slowed my circulation. Once the little bottle was mostly full, I recorked it and gently set it on the ground before wrapping my hand with a torn strip of cloth from the bottom of my tattered shirt.

You are indeed a Gilded One, she murmured, cocking her head. *But you are not of this world.*

"No, I'm not," I agreed, rising unsteadily to my feet. The sun was beginning to emerge from behind its thinning blanket of clouds, providing a touch of warmth that I so desperately needed. Picking up the knife and vial, I took a tentative step forward, and then another. The siren tensed, the bony vertebrae in her back rising like hackles. The long, slimy tendrils of black hair hung around her sunken cheekbones; with her thin lips, fathomless eyes, and two rows of sharp teeth, she reminded me of an angler fish. It took everything I had not to turn around and run, and the feeling appeared to be mutual. The moment I extended my hand, she snatched the vial from it, glancing from its contents and back to me.

"Thank you," I whispered, handing her the knife hilt-first. "For saving my life."

Be careful who you thank in this realm.

I didn't know what to say to that, so I opted for nothing.

The siren cocked her head, gazing up at me with wide, unblinking eyes. *You are not like the others of your kind.*

"My last three boyfriends would agree," I muttered.

After a moment of thoughtful silence, the siren pulled another vial from her bag – one filled with viscous black ink – and withdrew her dagger. She dipped the tip of the knife first into my blood, and then into the swirling ink. Before I could even open my mouth to ask, she pressed the sharp point into her forearm, where she began carving multiple concentric circles, punctuated by intersecting lines of shimmering black.

"You're drawing a rune on yourself?"

Her jaw was clenched in concentration. *To break the curse.*

"What—"

"*Tal-yaaa!*" A high-pitched battle cry made my head snap up just in time to see Biscuit dive bombing out of the sky.

"Biscuit!" I shouted. "You found me! I can't believe you're..." I trailed off, elation quickly turning to horror as I realized the target of his deranged exuberance. "Biscuit, wait! *Stop!*"

The siren's metallic eyes doubled in size as the unhinged familiar drew back his claws in attack, shrieking like an overstuffed eagle. I dove in front of her, spreading my arms defensively. "Biscuit, stop! She's my friend!"

With a startled *bawk*, he reared up mid-flight, flaring out his wings and tail feathers to narrowly avoid a catastrophic bird-on-Talia collision. After an erratic – albeit impressive – mid-air U-turn, he landed awkwardly atop a low boulder a few feet away, claws scrambling on the slick rock for balance.

"No friend!" he angrily squawked as soon as he'd regained his footing. "Bad!"

"Good!" I retorted. "She saved my life!"

His eyes widened in surprise – almost as wide as the siren's had. Her complex tattoo complete, she quickly snatched her bottle and knife, buried them in her satchel, and then flung her body into the wide rivulet that flowed from the tide pool and out to the sea. She didn't stop to look over her shoulder until she'd swum well into the subsiding waves. Once there, she bobbed along the surface of the water, regarding me with intent, narrowed eyes.

"Wait!" I cried. I grabbed the bottle of ink she'd left beside the tide pool and waved it in the air, stumbling across the rocks to get closer. "You forgot this!"

The ink of a kraken is highly coveted for its unique magical properties, she replied. *Keep it...as a token of our friendship.*

I clenched the vial against my chest, at a loss for words. When she dove beneath the foamy surface a moment later, I let out a little gasp as a patch of iridescent green scales on her tail caught the light of the sun – beautiful, sparkling scales that almost certainly hadn't been there before.

A smile was tugging at the corners of my mouth when a flurry of feathers landed on my shoulder.

"Hii-yii!"

"Biscuit!" I grinned. He let out a muffled coo, nuzzling against the side of my face. "I can't tell you how happy I am that you're here! How did you find me? Where's Zayn?"

"*Rawk!*"

"Ahem!" a gravelly voice called from behind us.

I whirled around at the sound, then immediately stumbled several steps backward and into the surf. The voice belonged to a short, shirtless old man with floppy ears and curled horns who was balanced on a nearby rock…by his hooves. Which were attached to furry mountain goat haunches.

My hand flew to my mouth. "Glaistig?"

"Glaistig!" he sputtered, the horizontal slits of his pupils narrowing sharply. "How rude!" He hopped off his rock, quickly closing what little space I had between the angry sea and the angry goat. "I am a satyr, and a highly distinguished one at that!"

Seeing as my experiences with strange fae had been overwhelmingly negative by that point, my immediate instinct was to flee – as fast as my numb, wobbly legs would carry me. With Biscuit clinging onto my flimsy shirt strap for dear life, I made about five valiant, running leaps down the pebble beach before I tripped and fell over a rock, crashing face-first into a pile of kelp. I'd barely managed to flop onto my back, cursing and sputtering like a drowning fish, when the goat-man loomed over me, his horns blocking out the sun and his bearded face splitting into a wide, murderous grin.

"Hello again, little goldfish."

XV.
A Seder With the Satyr

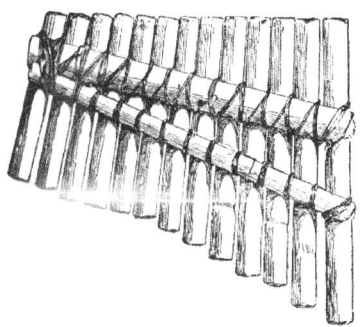

"You must be the caterwauling creature that's been causing such a veritable rumpus!" the satyr boomed. "Are you auditioning to become a banshee, O shrill one?"

Whimpering, I held my hands in front of my face. "Please don't hurt me."

He gave a hearty belly laugh. "Oh, I won't hurt you, my pet – though I can't promise not to steal a bite here and there." His nostrils flared along with his grin. "I will, however, be returning that stolen familiar of yours to its rightful owner. Not sure how you managed to abscond with that, little goldfish."

Biscuit, who had flown off my shoulder just before I tripped and ate a pile of sea salad, landed on top of my head as soon as I pulled myself into a sitting position. Unfortunately, the upright angle brought me a little too close to a certain set of furry balls dangling between the goat-man's equally furry thighs.

"He's not stolen," I muttered, trying to find somewhere – anywhere – else to look. Eventually, my eyes settled on the small set of silver pan pipes hanging from a leather cord around his neck. "He belongs to my, um, friend."

"Biss-kisss!" my glorified rooster added helpfully as he picked small bits of debris from my hair.

"How serendipitous," the satyr replied, stroking his beard. "It appears that you and I share the same friend."

I jumped as a bright orange and aquamarine crab scurried across my fingers. "We do?"

"Indeed, little goldfish." The satyr extended a hand, which I tentatively took, and pulled me to my feet. Toe to hoof, I stood about a foot taller than him – not that he seemed to care a whit as he stared lustily at my damp tank top, which clung to a damp bra and cold, wind-nipped flesh underneath.

I crossed my arms over my chest, arching an eyebrow. "Care to elaborate on this supposed mutual friend of ours? And stop calling me Goldfish."

"But you shine so splendidly, my pet," he smirked, stroking his beard. "Is it your radiance alone, or perhaps a golden nectar that flows through your pretty veins?"

I swallowed. Why, oh *why*, hadn't I just stayed home and binged a Netflix marathon in my bed?

"My name is Lamswyth," the goat-man continued, "but you may call me Lam. I was at my stead, waiting for the incubus's signal—"

"*You're* Zayn's contact?"

"Indeed. I had been preparing for his forthcoming arrival when I heard your wailing and squawking down below. And though the endless cacophony of howls was irksome to my ear, I thought to myself, Lamswyth, you'd better go check and see about that ruckus! For, you see, mermaids don't typically prey on young women. But now that I have laid eyes upon you…" He licked his lips. "I can certainly understand why they tried."

"Is Zayn with you?" I quickly interjected. "Have you heard from him?"

"Not yet, Goldfish."

"My name is Talia."

His eyes sparkled. "Talia. Come. We shall return to my home and wait for the advent of our friend."

My eyes darted around the beach, which was entirely vacant save for the three of us. "No, I think I'll wait," I stammered. "He should be here any minute."

The satyr shrugged one shoulder as he turned to go, tufted tail sagging in what I could only assume was disappointment. "Suit yourself, Pet. I for one wouldn't want to linger in the territory of vicious sirens – or worse, hungry kelpies – but that is entirely up to you."

I clenched my fists and gnawed on my lip. I still had no idea what a kelpie was, but it was the second time I'd heard the name. Zayn had compared them to crocodiles. Or was it alligators?

I sighed in frustration, holding out my wrist for Biscuit to hop on. "Go find Zayn," I whispered softly. "And bring him back here as soon as possible, okay?"

"Talya kiss?" he entreated alongside a series of kissy sounds. "Kiss!"

"Uh…okay," I blinked, pursing my lips for him to kiss. Certainly wouldn't be the weirdest part of my day.

After bestowing an enthusiastic birdie kiss upon my blue lips, he called, "Byeee!" and then leapt off of my wrist. "See you!"

I watched as he flew away, a colorful, shrinking dot against the cloudy green sky, feeling my heart sink to my knees. Not only was I pretty sure that I'd never see him or

Zayn again, but I was also about to follow a strange goat-man into his home where he'd probably squeeze the jelly from my eyes and turn me into a goldfish stew.

"Coming, my pet?" Lam asked over his bare, hairy shoulder.

I hesitated. "What's a kelpie?"

"A kelpie, my dear, is a shapeshifting water horse with a fishtail ending in spiny, poison-tipped barbs and a mane of venomous serpents. They enjoy feeding, in particular, on human flesh. And that's just the freshwater variety! I wouldn't recommend you become acquainted with their saltwater cousins. One of them ate my uncle, leaving nothing but a pile of entrails and horns for us to stumble across the next morning."

"Okay…" I muttered, swallowing back a wave of nausea as I began trudging after him. "I'm coming." I'd take a libidinous goat over a venomous horse-serpent any day.

His white tuft of a tail wagged as I jogged over to him. "Oh, good. My stead isn't far." He pointed to the middle of one of the towering cliffs above us. "Just a few dozen spans up that rock face."

I stopped dead in my tracks. "I'm sorry?"

He frowned, taking in my weak, skinny legs, then sighed. "Fortunately for you, there exists an easy – albeit far less scenic – route. Come, Pet. The entrance is just over there."

Sighing in quasi-relief, I followed him about a hundred feet along the bottom edge of the cliffs, clumsily scrambling over rocks and through shallow tide pools as I tried to keep up with his deft, billy-goat legs. Eventually, he stopped at a low, narrow archway carved into the rock. Barely four feet high, it led to a darkened stone staircase that headed directly into the cliffs.

"Stupid mermaids," I groused. "I'd asked them if there were any stairs nearby and they just told me to jump."

"No doubt they were looking forward to drinking that delectable glowing blood of yours once you hit the rocks," Lam replied blithely. "All the more reason for you not to linger near the water, I daresay."

Blanching at yet another delightfully gruesome image, I ducked my head and shoulders to follow him into the carved-out passage, which sloped upward and into the darkness at a stomach-churning angle. My converse sneakers, which were still soaking wet and full of gravel, squished and squelched all the way up while the satyr's hooves clacked and clattered. Throughout the ascent, I kept both hands pressed firmly against the narrow walls, praying there were no cave-dwelling creepy-crawlers in this realm, but knowing, with my luck, there almost certainly were. Eventually, when my burning thighs were on the brink of going on a permanent strike and my brain was verging on a panic attack, a dim orange lantern appeared at the top of the steps. It was hung beside a heavy wooden door, which was noticeably lacking any sort of knob or handle. Upon our approach, Lam took the pipes from his neck and played a simple six-note tune. The door magically swung open, revealing a small but ornate apartment.

He swept into a low and flourishing bow. "Welcome to my humble abode, Mistress Talia."

I ducked my head and nervously stepped inside the stone chamber. A lit fireplace and cauldron stood a dozen feet in front of me, while lavish tapestries of every color covered the floor and hung from the walls. Apart from a large chest and two stark chairs resting beside the fire, the only other piece of furniture in the room was the low, straw-filled mattress tucked in the far corner. As Lam slipped past me, I eyed my soaked shoes self-consciously, not wanting to track pebbles and saltwater all over his beautiful rugs.

"Please, allow me," he smiled, raising his flute to his lips. This time, he played a more complex melody as his beady eyes trained on my drenched, tattered footwear.

And then the most beautiful, miraculous thing happened: my feet felt *warm*. I couldn't help it; a quiet moan of rapture escaped my lips at the glorious sensation of once again having dry, thawed out toes. Until I felt a strange pressure on the balls of my feet, looked down, and saw that he'd replaced my perfectly practical sneakers with six-inch black stiletto ankle boots.

I raised an incredulous eyebrow. "As much as I appreciate the dry shoes, do you think you could whip me up a pair of bunny slippers instead?"

"Sorry, little goldfish – I can only transform each item once." Except he didn't sound apologetic at all as he eyed my injured hand, which was still wrapped in a dirty strip of my shirt. "Unless you'd like to offer a contribution for another go? If I had but a thimble of your blood, I could produce the most marvelous of transformations, with unlimited—"

"Yeah, maybe later," I interjected, not loving the disappointed look that immediately crossed his face. "How did you do that, anyway – turn my sneakers into heels?"

"I am an Endower, of course," he replied, inclining his head in a small bow.

I rubbed my forehead, my brain sluggish from the cold and lack of sleep. "Remind me what that is, again?"

"An Endower is a master of channeling borrowed magic."

"Borrowed magic?"

"Magic that has been obtained by an Extractor, naturally." Lam had slipped past me again to close the door, locking it behind him with a slightly different six-note melody. "Those are mages who are able to draw out the magical properties from various ingredients – plants, runes, gemstones, and so on – and store them in retention vessels until an Endower comes along to repurpose it. Extractor-Endower pairs are responsible for creating some of the most powerful fae artifacts in history," he smiled, proudly patting the pipes hanging from his neck.

"Is that how you and Zayn got to know each other? Because he's an…Extractor, I guess?"

I had never asked Zayn about his blood type, but that made the most sense given his business of turning ingredients into magical ink. *Except,* I frowned in consternation, *he's also able to rechannel the magic like an Endower. And he created Biscuit, like a Benefactor…* I shook my head, irritated that I hadn't asked him about his abilities when I'd had the chance. I guess there are only so many hundreds of questions you can ask in a day with limited hours and countless monsters.

Lam let out a hearty laugh as he made his way to the hearth. "If he has not told you of his unique lineage, Pet, it's not my place to be remarking on it. After the Blood Wars, it is frankly considered an act of aggression to inquire about one's blood type without invitation."

"Oh," I blanched. "I'm really sorry. I-I didn't know."

"No matter," he shrugged. "Please, make yourself at home."

Even though he'd gestured to the bed in the corner as he spoke, I took it upon myself to sit on the floor by the fire, where strange smells were coming from the lit cauldron.

"I was just about to sit down for lunch." The satyr's eyes gleamed as he spoke. "Would you care to partake? You must be ravished, my pet."

"I think you mean, 'famished,'" I corrected, far more than a little uneasy. Unfortunately, my hollow stomach was making enough noise for a trumpet solo, so, for the moment at least, hunger was taking precedence. "Um, lunch would be great. Do you know when Zayn will be here?"

"Any minute, Pet, any minute," he smiled. Retrieving a ladle hanging from a nail on the mantle, he opened the lid to the cauldron and began ladling food into two shallow bowls. "Here you are. There's plenty more, as well, so don't be shy."

I took my bowl gratefully, though my enthusiasm was tempered when I saw what was in it: runny, wilted greens that looked like parsley, a purple-tinted hard-boiled egg, some sort of root vegetable—

"Oh, and don't forget this." He retrieved a tin of biscuits from the mantle and placed one on the edge of my bowl. Then he took a bottle of red wine and filled a copper goblet for each of us.

A hysterical giggle was bubbling in my throat as I regarded my wine goblet and plate of food, which looked very much like a Passover Seder plate: an egg, bitter greens, horseradish, even a stale, crumbly cracker that reminded me of matzah. But I was starving, and if wilted parsley and a purple-tinted egg with twin blue yolks was all he had, my growling stomach didn't care. I shoveled it all into my mouth, choking everything down with the satyr's overly-sweet wine – all while doing my best not to think about the last Passover my mother, father, and I had celebrated as a family. But the memory surfaced, nevertheless; Dad draped in a dozen tubes and IVs, reciting the Kiddush from the borrowed hospital cot that we'd wheeled from the living room into the dining room just for the occasion.

Baruch atah Adonai, his frail voice echoed in my mind as though it had been just yesterday, *Eloheinu melech haolam, hamavdil beyn kodesh lichol…*

"This special parsley grows atop the cliffs," Lam's voice pulled me from my troubled reverie. "It's highly nutritious, good for both vitality and libido. And I myself plucked these eggs from nearby razorbill nests. They roost in the small hollows of the cliffs. Perhaps you've seen them – the laural- and egwine-colored birds flying along the beach?"

I stared at him blankly. "Laural and egg *what*?"

He popped the entire parsnip-looking root in his mouth, leaves and all. "Egwine, the color that comes after purple, of course."

"Oh, right," I muttered, taking a very large swig of wine. With nothing but a handful of stale crackers and greens in my stomach, it wasn't, perhaps, the brightest idea. But my starved, sleep-deprived brain was craving the sugar. And moreover, I was the uncontested wine queen of Temple Beth-El; I'd polished off an entire bottle of Manischewitz at the Passover Seder my mother dragged me to last year before I even felt buzzed.

Lam, also several swigs into his wine, was cocking his head curiously at me. "So, tell me, sweet Talia, how you have come to travel this realm with our friend, the incubus. Your blood glows with magic, that I can see, but I don't believe you are of this world…?" He let the unfinished question dangle in the air.

"No," I shook my head. "I'm human. From Earth. Um, Zayn and I work together at his shop there, and uh…" I hesitated, wondering how much the satyr knew – about my boss, our journey, or anything else he'd recently disclosed to me in confidence.

"Never fear, Pet," the satyr waved a hand. "I have known Zayn since he was but a beansprout of a boy. He is a gifted Runemaster in search of ingredients for his coveted pigments. That is no secret to me."

My shoulders relaxed at that. I quickly polished off the rest of my wine, which Lam was already poised to refill.

"I am curious about your role in his journey," he said, arching a furry eyebrow. "As he has not claimed you, I can only imagine he keeps you close for the occasional snack. Or perhaps he routinely taps the golden syrup in your veins for his runespells?"

My eyes bulged. "Claimed me? *Snack?*"

"Why yes, my pet. The symbol on your arm is a complex warding rune – no doubt as to its purpose," he added, caressing one of the glittering scrapes on my arm, "but I see no other marks on your skin publicizing his claim. Being such a succulent morsel as yourself, I can only imagine he would want his mark to be prominent, so as to avoid any unnecessary confusion. Therefore, since you have obviously not been claimed, I can only imagine your purpose is to serve as his traveling snack. And an endless supply of unlimited magical potential, of course. What has he offered you in return for such a splendid arrangement weighted so heavily in his favor?"

By now, I was staring at him with eyes so wide, I imagine they were showing white all around. My brain felt sluggish and heavy as I worked through all the implications of the satyr's remarks. Snack? Limitless blood tap? *No,* I shook my head, trying to clear the fog. *Zayn's not just using me. We want the same thing – a flower that will produce the ink we both need.*

Lam had leaned forward to guide my goblet of sweet, syrupy wine toward my mouth. Dazed and dehydrated as I was, I drank it.

"I'm not a snack," I mumbled, setting my empty plate down to rub my temples. "And he's not using me. He's my..."

"Lover?"

I blinked. "Well...no."

Lam shook his head and *tsked*. "How strange. And also a pity. For him, at least." He smiled widely. "For me, it is my gain. One does not step between an incubus and his victim – claimed or not – without losing a testicle or two. Fortunately, it seems that is not the case here! Anyway," he patted my hand, "you must be very tired, my pet. Come."

Before I knew it, I was on my feet, being guided toward the corner of the room that housed the satyr's hefty bed. Somewhere in the back of my mind, at least one voice was screaming an indistinguishable warning at me. But my eyelids were so heavy, and the words all sounded like gobbledygook anyway, so I ignored them while letting myself be led like the near-comatose person I was. What was the harm in taking a nap?

Thump, thump, thump! "Lamswyth!" a voice yelled from outside the door. "Open up!"

"Don't mind him," the satyr cooed as he laid me down on the bed. "There's a ward on the door. We'll just pretend there's no one home so he won't disturb us."

"Mmkay," I murmured, laying my head on a lumpy potato sack of hay. With my eyelids drooping from several days' of lost sleep, it felt like the softest, most comfortable silk pillow. My body sank into the scratchy mattress like I was floating on a cloud. As sleep rapidly overtook me, I heard Lam whisper, "Just close your eyes, my pet…"

"Talia!" The voice outside shouted again, jolting me back awake.

I knew that voice.

My eyes popped open and immediately recognized three simultaneously-occurring phenomena: One, I was most definitely drunk; Two, I was lying in a satyr's bed with my shirt all twisted and tangled around my waist; and Three, the angry-sounding person shouting and banging on the door was none other than Zayn.

While Lam started to hoist himself onto the bed beside me, my fist moved before my brain told it to. It connected squarely with his scruffy, bearded jaw, which let out a terrible crack as his teeth smashed together. A scandalized bleat erupted from his mouth as he tumbled off the bed, hooves flailing in the air. With instinct and reflex alone spurring me through my drunken haze, I dove out of the bed, leapt over the writhing satyr, and scrambled toward the door.

Unfortunately, there was no handle.

"Zayn!" I banged on the door with my palm. "I can't get out!"

"Wait!" Lam rasped, crawling toward me with a bloodied lip.

"Talia! Get back!" Zayn shouted.

I plastered myself against the wall beside the door, flinching as the entire thing – all five inches of solid wood – flew off the hinges less than two seconds later. Zayn stepped through the doorway, head swiveling until his wild eyes landed on me – damp, disheveled, and shivering with my shirt hiked up to my bra – and let out a growl that sounded far more animal than human. In a flash of magenta light, Biscuit tore from his arm and immediately dove straight for Lam, who was cowering on the floor with his arms raised over his horned head.

"Ow!" he shrieked as Biscuit sank his powerful, almond-crushing beak into the fleshiest part of his furry haunches. "Begone, loathsome seagull!" Lam blindly swatted at the bird, missing him by a mile. Biscuit flew up and away, landing safely on the edge of the fireplace mantle with a menacing hiss.

Zayn, who had already strode halfway into the room, picked Lam up by one flailing hoof and held the satyr aloft and upside down. A blue dagger gleamed in his other hand, its glowing tip pointed at Lam's rotund, hairy stomach. "Give me one good reason why I shouldn't send your entrails flying across this floor, goat," he snarled.

Lam let out another frantic bleat. "Sh-She wasn't claimed, boy! I didn't – *couldn't* – have known—" He let out a shrill yelp as Zayn's dagger pressed against his skin.

The incubus's eyes flew to mine, glowing as bright as I'd ever seen them. "Did he touch you?"

"Not exactly," I swallowed, still hugging the wall behind me.

Zayn dropped the satyr to the ground, eliciting a strangled yelp from his victim as Lam's horned head connected with stone, then knelt beside him, dagger glinting against his throat. "I swear to you, Lamswyth, if you had touched a single hair on her head, your innards would already be splattered across this rug."

The goat's wide, horizontal pupils flew from his to mine. "I'm s-sorry! I swear I didn't kn—"

"And now you do." Zayn jerked the satyr's face toward his. "Touch her again and I'll ruin you," he hissed. "Do we have an understanding?"

"Yes!" Lam gasped. His wide eyes had flown back to the dagger pressed against his jugular. "I won't touch her! I swear it!"

Zayn rose to his feet, leaving the satyr panting and sweating on the ground, and was standing before me in three strides. "You're sure he didn't touch you?" he whispered, finger curling beneath my chin.

"Yes," I swallowed. "I'm sure." Hastily tugging at my shirt to cover my exposed navel, I took several deep, shuddering breaths. Zayn's fury, while not aimed at me, was terrifying. And while I should have been grateful for his timely appearance, my racing heart still felt firmly lodged in my stomach. Had he lost his temper and threatened Lam because he was genuinely worried about me…or because the satyr had broken some sort of fae bro code?

As his eyes probed mine, full of molten fire and fury, I honestly couldn't tell. According to Lam – someone who had supposedly known him for most of his life – Zayn would have "claimed" me, whatever that meant, if he'd given even two shits about me.

I could feel my eyes begin to sting, but God help me, I wouldn't cry. Instead, I quickly pulled myself away, shoulders sinking with rejection and cheeks blazing with humiliation, to sit alone by the fire. I hugged my knees to my chest in an effort to keep myself from shaking. Once again, I'd forced this man to swoop in and save my pathetic ass. And now, on top of that, I had to wonder all over again what the hell I meant to him – if I meant anything at all.

"Gather your supplies," Zayn was snapping at the satyr. "We're leaving. Now."

"The delphiniums won't bloom for another seven hours, and the hike is a mere hour or two from here," came Lam's surly reply as he rose shakily from the ground. "Do you want to linger with the girl in prime siren territory for five hours' time?"

My hand instinctively went to the kraken ink tucked away in my pocket.

"No," Zayn finally replied, gaze flitting to me. "We'll rest for a few hours and then go. But you will behave, *sheep*, or you will find my dagger embedded in your bowels – delphiniums be damned."

Surprisingly, Lam let out a wry chuckle. "Oh, my boy. We both know you won't return to Sol empty-handed, seeing how he has you on a domesticated varg's leash. Considering I'm the only one who knows where to find these precious flowers of yours, you may want to rescind your hollow threats of disembowelment."

My head jerked up suddenly. "Why?"

The men turned to look at me quizzically.

"Why does Sol have you on a leash?" I demanded. "What is it you owe this man?"

At that, Lam's chuckle turned into a hearty laugh. "Oh, come now, Zayn. You haven't told her?"

"Told me what?"

Zayn gritted his teeth, but said nothing.

"Zayn," I pressed. "What is he talking about?"

Still chortling, Lam moved to pour himself another glass of wine. "Don't worry, my dear boy, I won't spill your secret. Though I must say I'm surprised the girl doesn't know the lurid details of the mess you've gotten yourself – and her – into. Ah well, I suppose *snacks* don't need more than the bare minimum of details," he flashed me a condescending wink.

Rising to my feet, I turned to Zayn angrily, expecting him – *needing* him – to rush to my defense. To tell Lam to shove it up his furry asshole, that I was so much more than a goddamned granola bar for him to prey on. Or, even better, to explain what the hell the crusty old goat had been talking about with respect to some fae gangster's proverbial claws being stuck in my boss.

Instead, he said nothing. And my fractured heart was crushed even further.

XVI.
SOL'S DOMINION

With Zayn there to guard me from the lusty satyr, I eventually plopped back down on the lumpy, scratchy mattress and curled into a ball, desperate to get some sleep before dusk. And though both figurative and literal pain welled in my chest, the fog of heady wine and the warmth of the fire eventually lulled me into a fitful, dream-fueled sleep.

I found myself being chased down a long, white corridor by a dark-haired siren with blood-caked goat legs in place of fins. There were no doors in the pristine hallway, save for one at the very end. I ran and ran, lungs burning even in my dreams, but no matter how fast I pumped my aching legs, the corridor seemed to stretch on forever. When I finally burst inside and locked the door behind me, I found myself in a windowless hospital room with my father. He was unconscious, hooked up to a dozen tubes and IVs that were pumping bright gold liquid into his frail body. Beside his bed, an old rotary phone was ringing. I fumbled to answer it, each time nearly dropping it. When I finally held the receiver against my ear, my mother was crying on the other line. No words, just deep, mournful sobs, as though someone she loved had died. One of my father's machines started beeping rapidly just then. As I whirled around to shout for a nurse, his hand reached out to grab my wrist. But it wasn't my father – it was Zayn, pale and weak, crying out in a silent plea for help. The hospital room had begun filling with black water that rushed up past my knees and thighs, nearly knocking me down. I reached forward to help Zayn to his feet, but he was gone. From floor to ceiling, the entire room was submerged in opaque, inky water, obscuring my view from anything else. Only the telephone floated in front of me, still ringing, but I couldn't answer it because icy liquid was filling my nose. Just as I opened my mouth to scream, two yellow eyes appeared in the darkness, and long, bony fingers reached for my locket…

I started awake, covered in a cold sweat, just as Zayn was draping a heavy fur blanket across my body. After that, my sleep marathon went mostly undisturbed…until the loud pop of a burning log interrupted my slumber. A strange pressure on my hip made me open one bleary eye to seek its source. Biscuit had balanced himself atop the blanket on one foot while the other was curled up and tucked beneath his underfloof. His eyes were closed and he was swaying gently on the round of my hip, fast asleep. A smile tugged at the corner of my mouth as I closed my eyes again, not wanting to disturb him.

"I have never seen a familiar become so attached to anyone apart from its bonded," Lam remarked quietly, making my ears perk up.

"I left him to look after Talia when I had to leave," Zayn grunted in response. "If I didn't come back, Biscuit would have guided her."

"Biscuit?"

"It's what she calls him. He's taken to it."

"I see…" the satyr replied. "So, your familiar has not only bonded with the girl, but has allowed her to re-christen it as well?"

Zayn didn't reply.

Lam heaved a great sigh. "My boy, you must not hold onto your anger. I had no intention of hurting the girl. I've been sitting idly in this cave since the fall of the court and had forgotten how potent fae wine can be to a human. Besides, I merely meant to curl up beside her, and that is all. I am an old, lonely man, but I am no monster. You, of all people, should understand how one may choose to rise above their inborn compulsions."

Zayn still didn't reply. I wanted so badly to turn my body so I could see his face, but that would wake Biscuit and alert the two fae to their captivated audience. So, I remained as still as a log, not caring a whit that I was intruding on what was meant to be a private moment.

"Why have you not claimed her?" Lam pressed.

A chair creaked. "Be quiet or you'll wake her."

"The girl sleeps like the dead."

"Still."

"You must understand, Zayn. I truly thought she was but nourishment for your journey. Now that I've been made the unwitting subject of your ire – and witness to the bond she's clearly forged with your familiar – I can see my assumption was an erroneous one. So, please, indulge an old man his curiosity. What is the reason for such an obvious lapse?"

In the ensuing silence, I was honestly worried they might have heard the mounting thumps of my heart from across the room. I sucked in a breath and held it until Zayn finally released a long sigh of his own.

"For one, the concept of branding one's mark on another living creature offends me."

Lam let out a harrumph. "Entirely understandable, given your history."

I frowned, having no idea what that meant.

"But even if I weren't opposed to it for the obvious reasons, I still would not claim her because it would result in an entirely one-sided arrangement."

My crossed arms squeezed my body tighter, trying to hold myself together. His reply was the one I'd been waiting for, but that didn't make it hurt any less. In fact, it somehow hurt more than I'd ever expected it to. I worked to keep my breathing steady as the sharp stab of betrayal intermingled with aching self-pity. Why the hell hadn't he rejected me two years ago, instead of stringing me along in ambivalence? What was his problem, always acting so sweet and caring over the years?

Why did he call me his closest companion, as though I actually meant something to him? My teeth ground together angrily. If he had just told me that we would never happen, that my feelings were "entirely one-sided," I could have protected my heart from the get-go – erected walls, kept him at an arm's length like all the others. And I probably would have been okay in the end. Because back in the beginning, my feelings for him had been entirely superficial, born and rooted in the smell of his cologne, the soft, tousled waves of his hair, the Adonis-like beauty of his stupid face. Basically, all of the outward qualities that nature had designed to draw an incubus's prey straight to his bed.

If I had known how "entirely one-sided" things would forever remain, I never would have allowed myself to fall in love with the way he would absentmindedly chew on his thumb while doodling yet another jaw-dropping design on one of the dozens of post-it notes he left sprinkled throughout the shop. Or how his mouth would quirk into this adorable half-smile whenever I cracked a joke, biting back the laugh I could plainly see hiding behind those twinkling eyes. Or the way he was constantly looking out for me – not just through his recent habit of slaying monsters on my behalf – but also quietly, subtly, like bringing extra sandwiches to work because I almost always forgot my lunch at home. Or the fact that he remembered the names of all my favorite metal bands and routinely gifted me vinyl records to play on nonstop loops in the shop…

I swallowed tightly. *Even though he hates metal.*

"I see," Lam murmured after a long beat of silence, then elaborately cleared his throat. "Well, my boy, now that you are no longer threatening to redecorate my home with my still-warm entrails, could I offer you some supper?" I heard the metallic scrape of him removing the heavy lid from the cauldron, and shortly after, the sulfuric scent of eggs and bitter greens made my nose crinkle. "Since the girl is not, in fact, your dedicated snack for the road, I can only imagine you're famished."

"I'm fine, thanks."

"Nonsense! How could you not be half-starved after the week you've had?"

Zayn hesitated for a moment before answering. "I don't know," he replied cautiously. "To be honest, I've been asking myself the same question lately."

Lam let out a low, rumbling chuckle.

"What's so funny?" Zayn asked, echoing my own perplexed sentiments.

"Egg!" Biscuit screeched suddenly, scaring me half to death. He launched himself off my hip, letting those damned tail feathers graze across my face and nose as he did. I lurched bolt upright as a series of rib-cracking sneezes hit me one after another.

"Bless you," Zayn offered when I'd finally finished with my fit. He was leaning forward in one of two wooden chairs sitting beside the hearth, resting a goblet of wine on his knee. "Biscuit, that was rude. You woke her up."

"Want egg!" his familiar demanded from his new perch – the curled horn that grew out of the left side of Lam's shining dome. "Gimme egg!"

"Take your damned egg, confounded beast!" Lam bellowed, tossing an egg that was still encased in its spotted green shell. Biscuit leapt off his head, gracefully catching it with one outstretched claw, and then landed on the edge of the mantle where he happily began unpeeling the shell with his beak. A pile of broken bits was accumulating on the floor below, which Lam eyed in obvious annoyance.

I rubbed the remainder of sleep from my eyes, doing my best to act like my heart hadn't just been ripped from my chest and repeatedly stomped on. "Biscuit eats eggs? Isn't that a little cannibalistic?"

"As cannibalistic as a human drinking milk," Zayn replied with a quick glance at his watch. "Biscuit is as closely related to a razorbill as you are to a cow."

"Oh," I replied, feeling my traitorous cheeks flushing gold the moment our eyes met.

"Speaking of cows," Lam mused to himself. He strode across the room, hooves thudding on the upholstery, until he came to the large wicker chest. After lifting the lid, half of his body disappeared as he knelt inside, sending various articles of clothing flying out and around him. "Here we are," he called a minute or two later, holding some sort of corset out in front of him. "See if this fits, won't you?"

I caught the shirt after he tossed it to me, frowning at the fabric. The sleeveless, black top was made from a tough hide of some sort and was laced up the front. "Not really my style, but thanks," I muttered, tossing it aside.

"Your shirt is in tatters," Lam said matter-of-factly as he returned to his chair beside the fireplace. "And you seem to have gotten quite the scrape on the beach," he pointed to a patch of glowing skin on my stomach, which was perfectly visible beneath the ratty, gaping hole at the bottom of my shirt. "This corset was designed by one of the king's tailors, one of the few pieces from the castle I was able to escape with, after…" he faltered, horizontal pupils darting over to Zayn. "Well, after the Fall."

"The Fall?" I asked, eyeing the fabric again. "You mean, when the two courts fell in the Blood Wars?"

Lam nodded as he topped off his goblet with more wine. "The very same."

"Are you saying you were inside the king's court when it happened?"

"Indeed," he replied. "We both were."

My head whipped in Zayn's direction. "You were?"

He gave Lam an irritated, sideways look. "Yes. Not that it matters, since the entire summer court is long gone, either slaughtered for their blood or in hiding, like Lam."

"It is a wonder we survived at all." Lam shook his head slowly, his words tinged with bitterness. "So many fae had lost their lives in the war that gripped the entire realm, incited by those who had been born to inferior bloodlines."

"Inf—" I bristled, swinging my legs off the side of the bed. "What the hell does that mean?"

Lam waved a hand as he swallowed about half of his goblet in one gulp. "I do not refer to any class or race as being inferior, but rather, innate magical ability. There were nobles from inferior bloodlines who had very little proclivity for magic, and impoverished paupers born with gold blood in their veins. The cycles of Blood Wars were the only battles in the entirety of recorded fae history that were *not* the result of clashing religions, cultures, or a ruthless king. Noblemen and laymen, various species of all sorts, fought side by side in battle, either thirsty for more power or desperate to cling to it. Unfortunately for…" he glanced at Zayn, who was scowling into his empty glass, "well, for the royal courts, there were far more powerful bloodlines inside the castle walls than there were outside. After all, power begets power."

The incubus, clearly irritated by Lam's impromptu history lesson, glanced at his watch again. "Enough chatter, Lam. It's getting late."

"I am nearly finished, dear boy!" the satyr crooned, emptying his glass. "To cut a long story short, my dear, both courts were utterly destabilized after years of external and internal fighting, with many of the most powerful royalty hiding away to avoid proffering up their greatest weapon – their blood – to the enemy. During this time of immense bloodshed, there was one influential family that had gone completely dark. They were so quiet, in fact, that the king's advisors – myself included – all assumed they'd been wiped out. It was a terrible miscalculation," he shook his head. "One I will never forgive myself for."

I opened my mouth in a feeble attempt to offer my condolences, but Lam was already barreling on with his grim tale.

"In any event, Sol's first – and final – blow was swift and savage; in the midst of the closing stages of the collective ceasefire and proposed truce, when both courts and laypeople had lain down their weapons, we were accosted – outnumbered, outplayed, and out-savaged. The surviving members of court were all slain in the massacre, save for a handful who brokered deals with this new syndicate of blood-hoarding overlords."

"Holy shit," I breathed. "That's…that's…"

Despicable, evil, and *reprehensible* were a few of the words spinning through my head when my eyes darted over to Zayn. A terrible chill snaked down my back as a sickening realization began to click into place.

"Oh my God," I whispered. "*That's* what Sol has over you, isn't it? That's why you jump when he says jump, why you routinely put your life on the line for him and his family. You made a literal deal with the devil…didn't you?"

The condemnation in my tone hadn't gone unnoticed by Zayn, who was clasping his hands tightly, jaw clenched, eyes rooted to the ground.

"Don't be too hard on him," Lam said. "He was a young lad when it happened. And besides, had he not possessed the talents he did – enough to warrant such a deal – he'd be long dead." He rose to his hooves, gathering up the pile of broken eggshell bits that Biscuit had scattered all over the rug. "Along with the rest of his—"

"Enough," Zayn snapped, startling us both. "It's getting late."

Rising to his feet, he lifted his arms over his head to crack his back. I noticed then that he had changed his clothes as well, and was now wearing a brown, sleeveless leather vest that looked similar to mine. It collared around his neck and hugged his broad chest, revealing his chiseled, elaborately-tattooed arms. It also gave me a glimpse of his shoulders, which I'd never seen before. (His apartment had been rather dark the one night we'd been naked together.) More runes curled up and over them, spreading across his bronze skin like vines. Tattoos that held so much raw power in them, like the ability to conquer giant monsters and smash through warded doors unharmed. And he was giving that same power to gangsters and murderers. *For them to do what? And to whom?* I swallowed as I regarded the man standing in front of me, more of a stranger to me than he'd ever been.

Clutching my own vest in my hand, I stepped off the bed and turned around to peel off what was left of my tank top. The neckline of the leather corset was low and had thin straps, so I yanked off my damp bra as well. Lam let out a low *baaaa* as I did, which quickly turned into a pained grunt. Embarrassed, I threw on my new shirt as fast as I could, lacing the crisscrossing leather cords up the front.

With a sigh, I held my arms out to my sides as I turned around. "Does it fit okay?"

Lam was intent on looking in every direction except at me. But Zayn crossed his arms in appraisal, nodding slowly as he looked me up and down. As much as I hated myself for it, his gaze literally made my knees quiver.

"We'll need to cover those scratches on your arms and I'm completely out of healing balm. Lamswyth, would you mind?"

"Not at all," he replied, returning to his chest of pilfered clothing.

I took a timid step in Zayn's direction, which he mirrored, until the two of us met halfway between the bed and the fireplace.

Rubbing the back of my neck, I grumbled, "Thank you. For coming to rescue me. Again."

His tone was equally sullen when he replied, "You're welcome."

Awkwardness simmered between us, which I was all too happy to pretend to ignore…until the tangle of thoughts and questions I'd been inwardly trying to unravel rushed out of my mouth without permission – as it so often did.

"Your family was murdered," I blurted, more of a statement than a question.

His nod was almost indiscernible.

"But you made a deal in exchange for your life? How did you manage that?"

"As Lam already took it upon himself to divulge, I possessed a certain set of skills that were highly coveted by Sol and his family. They also had no way of reading my family's grimoire." He nudged the bag lying at his feet with the toe of his boot. "If I'd been killed along with the rest of my family, that knowledge would have been lost. The spells inside were designed to die off with the last of our bloodline, which Sol somehow knew."

My eyebrows flew up in shock and dismay. "So you decided to *work* with him, even after all of the unspeakable things he'd done to the people you loved?"

Zayn's eyes darkened. "From the moment the deal was forged – my life for a lifetime of service – I swore to myself I'd kill him. I had devised a plan as well, honed all the way down to the very last, bloody detail…" He trailed off, lost in a terrible memory I could not see or even begin to understand.

"What happened?" I asked softly.

His broad shoulders dipped as though a great weight had settled on them. "Sol doesn't have half the knowledge of ink and runes that I do, but he knows enough to be dangerous."

My eyes widened as he abruptly began to unbutton the row of metal clasps on the front of his vest, then peeled it away. Naked from the belt up, he turned around to display the intricate scrollwork of tattoos that continued on his back. Thorny vines that were just visible over the tops of his shoulders and biceps knotted across his muscular back in overlapping tendrils, coming together to create a tangled mosaic of leaves and exotic flowers that incorporated at least a dozen runes, each skillfully entwined into the complex design. Though the immense beauty and vibrancy of it took my breath away, one distinct symbol stood out from the rest: a spiky, insect-like symbol haphazardly placed in between his shoulder blades. Heavy-handed and the color of dried blood, the lone tattoo was nothing like the rest of the design.

"Four of his sons held me down while Sol himself branded me with this," he tapped the ugly red lines. "A Dominion Rune. Which means my body – and what I do with it – is the property of Sol and his family."

No. My hand flew to my mouth in horror. *He can't mean—*

"The rune binds me to Sol by three laws: I will not harm him or his family in any way. I will not intentionally harm or kill myself in order to escape them. And I will dutifully carry out whatever they ask of me, provided it doesn't break the first or second law."

I swayed in my spot as the full force of his disclosure hit my mind like a truck. Zayn, the last of his bloodline, had been forcibly enslaved by the very same murderer who slaughtered his entire family. My hand ached to reach forward and cup his cheek, to comfort him, but I clenched it in a fist by my side instead. I would never, *ever,* touch his body without his express permission again. To be violated in the way he had been, over and over again during the course of years… I swallowed forcefully, trying to coax the acid from my stomach back down. What had been done to him – what *Sol* had done to him – was unspeakable.

"Hey, it's okay." He took a step closer, flashing me a wan smile that didn't come close to touching his eyes – as though he were trying to make *me* feel better. "It was a long time ago."

"What if we removed the tattoo with a laser?"

"The ink is impervious."

I bit back a curse. "What if you ran – skipped town and never looked back so he'd have no way of controlling you? Then what?" My fists were shaking, fingernails cutting into the skin of my palms. But I hardly noticed.

Zayn's answer was soft and matter-of-fact. "He would hunt me down and kill me."

Anger sliced through me, hot and sharp. "I won't let him," I growled, the intensity of my words surprising even me.

"And I believe you." Zayn offered me that same sad, crooked smile. "But in the meantime, there's no reason to put that declaration to the test." His gaze sank to my shoes before he heaved an exasperated sigh. "Lamswyth, how the hell is she supposed to walk in those?"

The satyr pulled himself from the chest, holding a pair of fingerless, elbow-length leather gloves by his teeth. Spitting them out and into his palm, he shrugged sheepishly. "Guess one of us will just have to carry her up the cliffs."

Zayn rubbed the bridge of his nose while Biscuit flung his last bit of crumbly, blue egg yolk at the satyr.

"No egg! Want almond!"

Flicking a hunk from his cheek, Lam gritted his teeth. "Any chance we could leave the seagull here while the rest of us—" Zayn shot him a withering look, and the satyr's hairy shoulders slumped. "I didn't suppose so. In any case, my five-toed friends, it's time to go. Your quest is very nearly at its end."

Zayn and I exchanged bone-tired glances, and I knew we were thinking the same thing: *It damned well better be.* But as he turned to gather up Biscuit and the rest of his belongings for the final leg of our journey, my thoughts drifted to other, far more pressing matters – like how I was going to do everything in my ineffectual, untrained, gold-blooded power to help free my boss from the soulless son of a bitch who took everything from him... No matter what.

XVII.
ALABASTER DELPHINIUMS

Lam took us up another steep, pitch-black stone staircase that led to the top of the cliffs while I muttered about bloodthirsty mermaids and aching feet the entire time. At some point around the twenty-story mark, I removed my heels and continued to plod up the steps in bare feet, wishing more than ever that the stupid sheep had bequeathed me a pair of fuzzy bunny slippers instead of ankle-snapping stilettos. At around forty stories, Biscuit settled in for a nap inside his ink home on Zayn's right arm, which was holding a lantern aloft so I wouldn't trip and die. Finally, somewhere around the five-hundredth step, I sank to my ass, panting to the point of hyperventilating, and wiped the beads of cold sweat from my brow.

"I can't go any further," I wheezed, hugging my ribs. "Just get the – *pant* – damn flowers – *pant* – without me."

With a sympathetic sigh, Zayn set down the lantern and fished around in his bag until he retrieved a tiny bottle of bright pink liquid. He unscrewed the top, which was connected to an internal glass dropper, and plopped down beside me. It took everything I had not to rest my head on his shoulder and go to sleep. But that would be problematic for a handful of reasons.

"Stick out your tongue," he instructed.

"Seriously?" I asked, then begrudgingly did as I was told.

Zayn squeezed a tiny drop of liquid on the tip of my tongue, which immediately tingled like peppermint.

"Wuhdiz?" I asked, my tongue still hanging over my lower lip.

"Revitalizing serum," he replied. After twisting the top back in place, he tucked the bottle back into his Mary Poppins bag of requirement. "I try to use it as sparingly as possible since I haven't been able to find *corbana* seeds in months. Fortunately, a small drop goes a very long way. You can put your tongue back now," he smiled.

Blushing, I stowed my tongue back where it belonged, marveling as the tingle spread from the back of my throat to my belly. An electric *zing* jolted through my nerves, like I'd just chugged a gallon of triple shot espresso upside down from a kegger. With my toes and fingertips buzzing, I shot to my bare feet like I'd been fired out of a cannon, bouncing on the edge of the step on tingling toes.

"Holy-*craaaap*-this-stuff-is-*amaaaaazing!*" I exclaimed, swapping my shoes for Zayn's lantern before darting up the steps like an amphetamine-addicted rabbit, chronic asthma be damned.

"How much of that stuff did you give her?" I heard Lam grumble as I sailed past him with a shrill and echoing *"Weeeeeeee!"*

"Hardly any. Talia's apparently a cheap date."

"Hurry up, slow pokes!" I yelled over my shoulder, bounding up the stairs two at a time with Zayn's stolen lantern.

Within no time at all, I came to a square-shaped, wooden door embedded in the low ceiling at the top of the steps and burst through, letting the rusty hinges bang shut behind me. Setting down Zayn's lantern, I stretched my arms over my head and filled my lungs with the crisp, salty smell of the night. From where I stood, I couldn't see the dark outline of taller cliffs on either side, and the distant sound of waves was so faint, I had to assume I was standing atop one of the highest bluffs. Like the distant clifftops I'd spied earlier that afternoon, this one boasted a flat, grass-topped plain that stretched behind me for as far as I could see – which wasn't far, given that the sun had long ago sunk beneath the turquoise horizon.

To help pass the time while I waited for the boys, I started doing a series of barefoot cartwheels in the soft tufts of grass, hooting with glee. Eventually, the two of them emerged from the square-cut hole in the ground, both with glistening sheens of sweat on their foreheads. While Lam set about placing fresh wards on the door, I breathlessly continued my acrobatics, eventually falling into a cackling heap a few feet from Zayn's boots.

"Oh man, I haven't done that since middle school!" I gasped in between peals of laughter.

He knelt beside me, suppressing a smile. "Sorry, Tal. I guess the revitalizing serum worked a little too well on you."

"Dude, you should sell that stuff! You'd put all those energy drink companies out of business in a week!"

"If *corbana* seeds grew anywhere outside of the swamplands, believe me, I would," he chuckled. "Try to conserve some energy, though, otherwise you'll crash hard when it wears off in a few hours."

"Aye-aye, Cap'n!" I grinned.

"Kindly try to keep the centaurplay to a minimum!" Lam whisper-hissed as he dusted off his hands on his furry flanks. "We may not be near the water, but that doesn't mean there aren't other creatures lurking in the night that might try to eat or maim you, little goldfish."

Well, *that* certainly sobered me up quickly.

"Be nice, Lam," Zayn clicked his tongue. "Talia's held up surprisingly well, all things considered. Glaistigs, fachans... Hell, she even made it out of *your* place in one piece."

"Don't forget the mermaids. Oh, and the siren too!" I added proudly.

"The *what?*" Zayn whipped his head back in my direction. "When did you get anywhere near a siren?"

"Come along," Lam called. "We must make our way to the far side of this cliff, where the northern face receives the most moonlight. Alabaster delphiniums are a highly lunarphilic species." He gave a little kick, furry tail wagging, and started trotting across the grass.

"I want to hear all about your sea folk misadventures the second we get back," Zayn muttered as he stood up. "In the meantime, take these." He handed me the stiletto boots he'd been carrying for me. "I know they're not particularly comfortable, but neither is stepping on a pod of poison-barbed *miricelles*."

Sighing, I slipped them on and brushed off my pants as I clambered to my feet. Lam had already started making his way across the plateau, but I took a few steps toward the edge of the cliff – a safe twenty feet away, mind, you – to survey the distant horizon below. There, ribbons of light were rippling across the obsidian ocean from the reflection of a pale white moon. That alone was a breathtaking sight, but I let out a gasp when I realized a second moon – a much larger, pinkish satellite with rings like Saturn – had already risen several degrees above it. Its delicate silver halos circled it in two different directions, crisscrossing in the center.

My jaw dangled open. "You have two moons?"

"Four." I felt Zayn's hand on the small of my back. "Stay close. You never know who – or what – might be lurking nearby."

"No kidding," I muttered as we fell into a brisk step a dozen yards behind the satyr. "Hey, I've been wanting to ask you – what the hell was that hooded thing back at the Waypoint, anyway?" Shivering, I instinctively reached for my necklace, which was still safely in place. "And why—"

"Did he attack you?" The muscles in Zayn's jaw clenched. "I have no idea, but you can be sure he won't be bothering us again. Lucky for his remaining appendages, my greater priority was rushing through the Waypoint to get to you."

My throat tightened at the memory of the creature's disembodied hand dangling from my neck. I shook my head to try to clear it, but images like that don't just fade away.

"At least you didn't land too far off course," he muttered with an angry shake of his head. After eyeing the twin moons steadily rising in the sky, he called out, "Lamswyth! How much further?"

The satyr extended an arm and pointed just ahead. "The north edge of the cliffs is just over there. Now all we need to do is make our way down and gather your flowers."

"And then we can go home?" I asked Zayn, the thought of my mother bringing an unexpected wave of homesickness.

"And then we can go home," he agreed, casting a glance toward the faded tattoo on my arm, now barely visible against the strengthening glow of my skin.

I stopped, looking up at Zayn with a worried expression that I could tell he was doing his best not to mirror. "How much longer do I have before the effects of the tattoo wear off completely?"

"The talisman around your neck is helping, but you'll be shining at full strength by morning," he replied tersely. We were both peering around the clifftop, which was still mercifully bereft of life, save for a handful of gulls, their dark silhouettes hovering above us as they scavenged for food scraps. "Come on. We'd better get a move on."

I nodded, jogging alongside him as he set the pace. "My father's necklace – you really believe it's a fae talisman?"

"Yes. I'm sure of it. The magical signature it emits is unmistakable. Kind of like yours when you stumbled into my shop," he smiled.

"But how do you think it fell into his hands? I mean, he was just an accountant working in Brooklyn before I was born."

Zayn cast a sideways glance at the gold locket around my neck. "I can only guess."

There was obviously much more on his mind and plenty of things I was dying to know. But we were getting so close to the end, and I was already planning on accosting him with a few dozen more questions on the long trek home. Questions like, "How are you able to create, extract, and endow magic when you don't have gold blood?" and, "Do you think Ancestry.com can help me figure out which one of my great-grandparents got frisky with a fae?"

At that moment, however, we'd caught up to Lam, who was leaning over the edge of the cliff at a stomach-churning angle to survey the vertical rock face with a scrutinizing expression. "Not many hoofholds," he was muttering to himself, "but certainly not the worst precipice I've scaled in the dark, not by a long shot."

"And you're sure they're down there?" Zayn asked, peering over the edge.

"Not at all, my boy!" Lam hooted, dusting off his hands on his woolly haunches. "I can only be sure they were there several months ago. Made a delicious salad," he rubbed his belly. "If only I had known they had…certain medicinal properties?" His left eye narrowed at the incubus, as though trying to coax information out of him.

"Something like that." Zayn unslung his bag from his shoulder and rummaged around until he'd retrieved a small leather pouch that he tossed in Lam's direction.

The satyr caught it, opened it to inspect the clinking metallic contents, then deftly weighed it in his palm. "This isn't enough, boy, not by half."

"Half now, Lamswyth." Zayn's smile was hard and didn't come close to meeting his dark eyes. "And the other half once you've retrieved my alabaster delphiniums. And don't forget to preserve as much of the stems and roots as possible, please."

Lam opened his mouth as if to argue, then closed it with a shrug. "As you wish, *Your Highness.*" Then, with a mighty *harrumph*, he vaulted off the edge.

I let out a surprised gasp. My wide eyes darted back and forth between the thousand-foot ledge that the satyr had casually leapt from and Zayn. The latter had visibly stiffened while the former was zig-zagging down the side of the endless cliff, hooves clattering and scraping against the black rock. I chewed on the inside of my cheek, thoroughly confused, until I scoffed and shook my head. It was just the satyr's snarky way of being passive-aggressive, since he didn't get his full payment up front. Hell, I'd probably be feeling feisty too if I had to scramble down a rocky, sky-high precipice in the dead of night.

Zayn cupped his hands around his mouth and called, "What do you see down there?"

"Rock!" came the irritated reply.

"Smartass," he muttered.

"What are delphiniums used for?" I asked suddenly.

"Hmm?" Zayn glanced at me.

"You said that the only way to permanently conceal my, uh…" my eyes swept to my dully-glowing skin, "well, my 'condition,' was to use ink made from this plant. And Sol wants it, too. But…why? What's so special about this flower over, say, a purple daisy?"

"Ah. You're asking about its magical properties," Zayn cleared his throat. He glanced over the edge to check on the satyr's progress, seemingly satisfied when he saw he was already about a hundred feet down, one hairy arm digging around in the cliff's hollows by the light of the moons. "As far as Lam is concerned, it's just another run-of-the-mill ingredient I need for my ink. But in actuality, this specific variety of delphinium can work in one of two ways, either as a powerful alterant or as a neutralizer, depending on the rune it's paired with."

"What's an alterant?"

"Anything that can permanently change the appearance of something else." Leaning closer, he pitched his voice even lower. "Many years ago, my old mentor told me that the delphinium's roots, once broken down, secrete enzymes that can have blood altering capabilities. I haven't tried it out first-hand, and I've never heard of anyone else attempting it – or even being aware of such a property. But he was the most knowledgeable Extractor I've ever known. If he said it can be done, I trust him."

I frowned. "So, you're going to try to alter my blood?"

"Not directly, no. The rune I will be pairing with it will only allow the pigment to alter the observable magical signature of your blood. Superficial camouflage, of a sort, like scattering a powerful beam of light into a trillion different particles. You'll still light up a room, figuratively speaking," he smiled, which made my heart skip a beat. "You just won't be a bright gold neon sign anymore."

"Oh," was all I could muster after his casual yet perplexing compliment.

Silence fell, leaving only the faint scraping of hooves, the distant rush of waves, and about a thousand unspoken words suspended in the cool, breezy air between us. My own quick, shallow breaths sounded deafening in my ears. As close as we were to the very brink of the cliff, with twin moons rising above us and an endless black ocean below…well, it would have taken anyone's breath away, let alone an out-of-shape asthmatic's. But pair that with the heavy trepidation of what lay ahead, not to mention all those damned incubus pheromones, which were teasing my nose and filling my lungs with every ragged breath I took, and it was like I was falling from the sky all over again.

Something brushed against my skin. With a start, I glanced down at our hands – the same hands that had readily found their way into one another's yesterday – and realized our pinkies were touching. When I looked up at Zayn, he was watching me intently, the moonlit depths of his eyes probing my face with an intensity I almost couldn't bear. And then that stupid, crooked smile suddenly appeared on his stupid, handsome face – one that not only touched his eyes but illuminated them – as though I were somehow the magical sight he wanted to see instead of the endless, moon-kissed ocean before us.

I yanked both my hand and my eyes away, chewing the inside of my cheek to shreds. For all the pain and confusion and turmoil the man caused me, I wanted nothing more than to hate him… But I didn't hate him.

I couldn't hate him.

In fact, I…I…

No, I shook my head, crossing my arms over my breasts so tightly they ached. But it was a welcoming kind of ache, one that distracted me from all the hurt that simmered directly underneath. Because at the end of the day, it didn't matter what I wanted, or even how I felt. Zayn was the most selfless, good-hearted man I'd ever met, apart from my father. It was time I stopped putting my own self-centered whims and desires first, and started focusing on his.

We both opened our mouths to speak at the same time, but I clamped mine shut, shaking my head. "No, sorry, you first."

Zayn cleared his throat. "Ah, while you were sleeping," he started, the edges of his voice strangely hoarse, "I informed Lam that your skin is only glowing because you accidentally ingested one of my more potent illumination inks, which should naturally leave your system in a few days' time. I can only assume you didn't tell him – or anyone else you may have stumbled upon – the real reason for your glowing blood?" He ended his statement as a brow-arching question.

I swallowed, immediately remembering the lovely chat I'd recently had with a certain cursed siren.

"Uh, no. Nope," I shook my head. "But, hypothetically speaking, if I *had* said something, what's the worst that could happen?"

"Your blood can unlock magic across two realms," Zayn replied dryly. "No talisman, catalyst, or, in some cases, rune needed. If a golden key to unharnessed power such as that were to fall into the wrong hands…well, use your imagination."

"Right, right," I swallowed again and rubbed at the goosebumps appearing on my arms.

The crisp breeze was nipping at my bare skin, and it was only getting colder as the night went on. Zayn and I had instinctively huddled closer as we watched and waited, so close our arms were pressed together. Where we touched, my skin tingled with electricity. But he wasn't pulling away, and because I was cold and stubborn, neither would I.

"So, uh, back to the delphiniums," I asked through chattering teeth, "what does Sol want with blood-altering ink, anyway?"

"Oh, ho!" Lam suddenly yelled from somewhere far below. "I may have found something!"

Zayn's whole body tensed. He'd opened his mouth to answer me, then abruptly snapped it shut upon Lam's proclamation. After a long moment, he scrubbed two hands through his midnight blue hair and let out a heavy sigh. "Salen refuses to answer me when I inquire and I'm not familiar with the runespell she's provided me. I can only hope and pray it's for some sort of neutralizing spell. But if Sol has somehow been made aware of the little-known properties of delphinium root *and* has managed to find the right rune to pair with it, he could theoretically alter – or even enhance – his magical abilities."

"Seriously?" I gawked at him.

Zayn's nod was curt. "Sol is a powerful Manipulator. He can control sparked magic, but needs people like me to create and endow it, something he's always resented. Like I said, I'm not aware of any sort of rune that could allow a person to alter their blood type, or whether anyone could even survive such a thing, but if anyone could dig up such a spell, it would be him."

"But what if he has found something?" I pressed, clutching his arm tightly. "You can't take the chance! You can't just give someone like him that type of..." I swallowed. "I mean, with power like that—"

"I know."

"Indeed, my friends," Lam bellowed triumphantly, "the delphiniums are in bloom!"

Zayn bowed his head in resignation as I whirled to face him. "You're not actually going to bring this stuff home, are you?" I asked, eyes wide. "I mean, I know Sol's got some sort of control over you, but there has to be something we can do to keep this pigment out of his hands...right?"

He struggled as though he wanted to answer, but couldn't. His face was contorted in a mix of grief, dread, and something else. Something...dangerous.

"We could hide it from him! Or just lie, and say the flowers were all gone... Or even—"

"The Dominion Rune forbids it, Talia. It forbids me from even talking...about certain things," Zayn choked out.

I don't know what clicked in my head just then. Whether it was a delayed understanding or maybe a rush of adrenaline from seeing him look so inexplicably broken. Whatever it was, it made my own emotions mount – and at the very forefront of those emotions, I felt sharp, cold fear.

"Why did you leave your familiar behind when you left?" I rounded on him. Before he could reply, I kept going. "I heard you tell Lam that Biscuit was supposed to guide me if you didn't make it back, but *why?* I could have stayed home, far away from glaistigs and fachans and stupid horndog satyrs! So, why did you want to bring me here, Zayn? Tell me!"

"I've got them!" Lam hollered from far below, his voice oddly muffled. "On my way – kindly stand ready to assist!"

Zayn still hadn't replied; he looked as though he were fighting with himself, fighting some internal power that I couldn't hear or even begin to understand. Finally, he gritted his teeth. "I am bound to Sol in ways you can't begin to imagine – but *you,* Talia, are not." A startled cry escaped my lips as Zayn reached forward, gripping my arms so tightly it almost hurt. "You are the most talented artist I've ever met. Capable of creating complex runes with the precision and skill of a Master. And powerful, far more powerful than you realize. But more than any of that – more than anyone else in our two worlds – I trust you, Talia. Completely."

By now, my eyes had widened into two gaping saucers. "Zayn…wh-what are you saying?"

He reached into his vest pocket and pulled out what appeared to be a crumpled ball of blank paper. "Do you remember how you were able to read my spell book?"

I nodded quickly, recalling how my blood had caused it to light up with words – words written in plain English the moment I wished for it.

"Before you or I say anything else, take these papers from my hand and put them somewhere safe."

Obediently, but still utterly bewildered, I reached forward to take the weathered pages from him, frowning at the weight. When I cautiously unwrapped an edge, a smooth gray stone with intricate carved etchings peeked up at me.

"It's a Waystone," Zayn murmured softly. "All it needs is a drop of your blood and a clear thought of your destination.

Hide it from sight and don't take it out until the moment you're ready to use it. And make sure there's no one else around when you do; it'll only work once, and even so, it's worth more than my entire shop and everything inside it."

Stunned, I quickly stuffed the priceless wad of paper and stone beside the vial of kraken ink into my pocket. "Why would *I* use it? Where will you—"

My question ended in a sharp gasp as Zayn leaned in close, cupping my face between two hands. Eyes locked onto mine, the following came out in a whispered rush: "When Lam comes up with the flowers in a few minutes, I'm going to reach for them. I have to. I need you to take them before I can get my hands on them. And then I need you to run."

"*Huh?*"

Zayn pressed his finger to my lips and continued, "Once you have the flowers, run as fast and as far from here as possible. Only when you're absolutely sure the coast is clear of Lam, me, or anyone else within a hundred yards, use the Waystone to get back to my office in the Fae Realm, and then use the Portal Rune to get back to yours. Those pages I gave you will tell you – and you alone – everything you need to do."

I was staring at him like the crazy person he was. "You want *me* to somehow get back to your office – all by myself? Are you *insane?*"

The clatter of hooves on rock made my eyes jerk back to where Lam was scrambling back up the side of the cliff, less than forty feet down, with a mouthful of white flowers in tow.

"Talia." Zayn turned my face back to his, where the toll of immense effort was beginning to appear. "Delphinium extract is almost unparalleled in its ability to neutralize, but few people realize that paired with the right rune," he took a labored breath, "it can also be used…to counter—ugh!" His eyes squeezed shut as a painful groan slipped between his teeth.

"Zayn," I whimpered, my hands fluttering across his face uselessly. "Please, I don't understand. What's hurting you? How can I—"

He clasped his hands over mine and took a deep, shuddering breath. "The ink that Sol so desperately needs, the ink that may give him the key to altering his blood—" he grunted with exertion, "—is also the ink that will...counteract...the Dominion R—*augh!*" He doubled over, clutching his stomach as though he'd been kicked. To my shock, a trickle of bright red blood appeared on the edge of his mouth. He quickly wiped it away with a trembling hand.

"Shh, shh," I pleaded, kneeling beside him. "Please, don't hurt yourself. Okay. I understand. I need to use the stone to go back without you and make this pigment. And then what? What will you do?"

He took several wheezing gulps of air, then straightened unsteadily, clutching my shoulders for support. "Before anything else, you have to make sure you have enough ink to tattoo yourself with the Concealment Rune provided on one of those pages. Salen will be back in two days to make sure everything is prepared for her father's arrival, and she cannot see you as you are. Do you understand? Concealing your blood is your first and utmost priority."

"Almost there!" Lam announced, his voice no more than twenty feet away.

Staring at Zayn in slack-jawed, dumbfounded horror, I somehow managed a nod.

"Secondly, when I come through the portal – and I will travel back the longest and slowest way my compulsion allows – I need you to find a way to tattoo the Counteraction Rune on my body, using the leftover ink. I am giving you my express permission," he added, his face as hard as I'd ever seen it, "to do whatever you need to do to me to get that tattoo somewhere on my body. No matter what I do or say. Are we completely clear?"

By now, I was so stunned, I couldn't even nod. Words had escaped me entirely.

Zayn took my hands in his. "I need you to understand that you can say no. We can return to your realm together where you'll be free to leave my shop and never look back. I would pay you enough to ensure you wouldn't have to search for a new job for at least a year, that I swear. But," he swallowed, as if every word cost him dearly, "if you can help rid me of Sol's binding, there is a chance I can finally avenge my family…and more importantly, save this realm from his terror."

Lam's arm reached up to pull himself from the cliff. "A little help, if you don't mind?" he huffed through gritted teeth – gritted teeth that held a half dozen white flowers, their delicate petals gleaming in the moonlight.

I stared at the satyr dumbly, then whirled back to face Zayn. He took both of my hands in his, squeezing them tightly, and I licked my lips, doing whatever I could to put moisture back into my mouth.

"If I do this…you'll be free?" I managed to whisper.

"Yes," he forced out. "And then…I could teach you…everything. And finally…t-tell you…everything…" A small sound like a sob escaped his throat. "I'm sorry, Talia. For dragging you into this. For what I'm asking of you. I will never be able to repay you. Never." His glassy eyes darted to the flowers in Lam's teeth and I knew I had only seconds to make my decision.

"Zayn," I whispered, clasping his hands. The tortured look he gave me – those eyes as full of sorrow and guilt as I'd ever seen them – nearly broke my heart in two. What it must have taken for him to muster up the courage to ask for help, knowing the weight of his request. Knowing his very life would be on the line if I failed him.

Which meant now, more than ever before, failure wasn't an option.

I wrapped my arms around his neck and pulled our bodies close. "In case I never get the chance to tell you," I softly whispered against the side of his cheek, "I care about you. So much." A tear trickled from the corner of my eye, wetting both his skin and mine. When I pulled away from him, it was still glistening on the edge of his jaw.

Squeezing his eyes shut, he leaned down to kiss my forehead, his warm, trembling lips whispering against my skin, "And I you, Talia. More than you could ever know."

"Perhaps this ill-timed declaration of affection would better be saved for later?" Lam grunted over the side of the cliff, his bearded jowls contorted with effort. "There's a satyr in need of assistance over yonder!"

Blue light glowed on Zayn's skin before he withdrew his favorite tattooed dagger from his arm and pressed the golden hilt into my hand. He then took his jacket from his bag and draped it across my shoulders before taking a step back, his face hardening. "Biscuit will guide you," he choked out hoarsely. His feet were planted in the grass, but his knees were shaking with the effort of keeping them there. "Go. Please."

As I turned to go, something in his expression flickered. I hesitated for the span of a single breath, because for a second there, his eyes looked almost…

"Go!" he snarled, making me jump.

Answering his command, Zayn's familiar burst from his arm in a kaleidoscopic flash of feathers and light. In an equally quick motion, I knelt down and snatched the flowers from

Lam's teeth, leaving him snorting and sputtering in confusion. With one last, fleeting look over my shoulder, I bid a wordless goodbye to the man I'd come to care for more than anyone else in the two realms.

And then I ran.

XVIII.
A Hot Pursuit

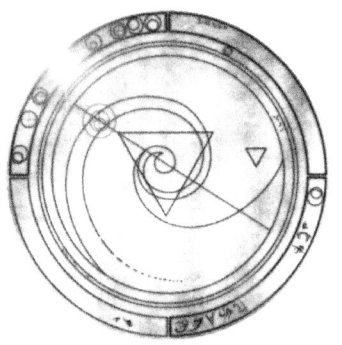

After pilfering the unguarded lantern from the ground with two outstretched claws, Biscuit charged ahead as though he'd been anticipating Zayn's command, a blur of sparkling color and light that spurred me away from the cliffs and across the grassland as fast as my wobbling ankles would carry me. The unmistakable sounds of a physical scuffle echoed behind me, including the shrill, indignant bleat of an affronted satyr, but I refused to check over my shoulder. If I had, I almost certainly would have tripped. Or worse, found my mafia-controlled "incu-boss" in hot pursuit, and that was the one thing I could not handle at that exact moment. And so, with Biscuit's encouraging whistle, I launched every frantic step from the balls of my stiletto-clad feet, grateful for all the drunken nights spent dancing in high heels that had prepared me for this moment. It also helped to have a heady dose of fae-powered revitalizing serum still coursing through my veins, and I had to wonder if Zayn had knowingly given it to me for this purpose. He was good at big-picture plans – unlike me, who always figured everything out as I went.

After ten minutes of hard running, asthma started to overtake magic-fueled adrenaline, and I was forced to slow to a panting jog. I could no longer hear the waves or the ocean breeze at all, and as far as I knew, there were no flower-hungry men or goats directly at my heels. I'd tucked the delphiniums away in an inside pocket of Zayn's jacket, opposite the Waystone and papers, but the dagger I kept clenched in my fist, point-down as I ran. Biscuit dropped the lantern into my other hand before making a wide circle in the air to survey the land, swooping down to nudge me to the left or right every so often. Another ten minutes later, seemingly displeased with what he saw, he glided past me and made a sharp left, which I followed. Within moments, we came across a narrow dirt road.

"Which way, Biscuit?" I wheezed, resting my elbows on my thighs to catch my breath. He landed on my left shoulder and gave my ear a gentle tug. "Left?"

He moved his head up and down in a gesture I presumed was a nod, then regarded the lantern I was clutching and clucked, "No lamp."

"You want me to put out the lantern?" I all but whimpered.

"No lamp," he repeated firmly.

"Okay," I sighed. Licking my fingers, I opened the glass on one side and pinched the flame. Darkness and bitter cold immediately enveloped us, as though the tiny flame alone had been keeping it at bay. Grateful for the gloves Lam had given me, but lamenting the lack of fingers, I zipped Zayn's jacket up to my chin. Its familiar smell should have been soothing, but instead brought hot tears to my eyes. I was reminded of my father's jacket, the one I used to wear every single day after his death, until the leather was worn and his scent was long gone.

"Go, go," Biscuit tugged on my ear again.

"Okay, okay!" I sniffed, furiously rubbing the tears from my eyes.

Abandoning the lantern behind a tall tuft of grass, I made a left at the dirt road and started walking, too afraid to run. Without the warm, flickering light, I felt like I'd lost my safety net. I clutched Zayn's dagger like a starving man with a shish-kabob as my eyes adjusted to the darkness. Luckily, the light from the two moons illuminated the gravel beneath my feet, and after a few minutes, it didn't even seem all that dark anymore. I would have given my right pinky for some tree cover, though. Walking out in the open with only low grass on either side made me feel incredibly vulnerable and, as much as I hated myself for even thinking it, I almost wished Zayn would catch up to us so I could have the comfort of his company, his protection. But that would mean that his hands would be on the delphiniums, and those hands, bound as they were, would be forced to use the ink for Sol, not himself. I couldn't let that happen.

"Can I use the Waystone yet?" I whispered to Biscuit.

By this point, cropped grass had been replaced by low plants and shrubbery – squat, wide bushes the color of robin's eggs that were all but glowing beneath the moonlight. Bright white berries that reminded me of pearls grew among the clusters of six-pointed leaves, and while my growling stomach tempted me to stop and try one, I knew better than to touch anything in this realm.

Biscuit jumped off my shoulder to take another look from above, but when he landed a few minutes later, he seemed particularly agitated, tugging on the front of Zayn's jacket and urging me to hurry ahead. With images of murderous glaistigs and fachans spurring me on, I followed the winding road as briskly as I could, trying my best not to jump and shriek at every cricket chirp or breeze. As for my much braver traveling companion, Biscuit stayed on my shoulder about half the time; the other half, he flew in a wide figure-eight pattern, keeping a close lookout behind and ahead like he had always done for Zayn. For now, at least, the road in front of us appeared to be empty, save for the faint orange dot beckoning to us from far ahead. That must have been the Waypoint for this region – the one I would have landed at had I not been thrown off-course by that creepy yellow-eyed thing.

I was still bristling at the awful memory when something rustled in one of the nearby shrubs. "Zayn?" I whispered, whirling around. "Lam?"

There was no answer. My hand gripped the dagger even tighter as I thought of the paper-enfolded Waystone in my pocket, fingers itching to use it. But Zayn had given me strict instructions not to use the stone until I was absolutely certain no one else was around. I'd disregarded his instructions enough times on this nightmare of a journey; I wasn't going to muck anything up now, not when I was so close to getting out of here.

From somewhere above, Biscuit let out a low whistle that my brain perceived as, "Hurry up, don't slow down."

"Okay, okay," I muttered, trying to ignore the throbbing of my feet and the blisters on my toes. Even so, my pace continued to pick up the closer we came to the glowing lamp post at the end of the road, until I was all but running to get there. I wouldn't be using the Waypoint since I had no idea how – and I was pretty sure it couldn't get me back to Zayn's office anyway – but I was drawn to its warm light like a lost moth flitting about in the darkness.

It had been at least fifteen minutes since I'd heard any sounds behind me, and while my lungs were threatening to erupt in flames, a sigh of relief was forming at my lips. A cluster of dark clouds had rolled in, enshrouding the moons and casting the land in darkness, but I could clearly see the outline of a glowing lamp post just ahead. Thank God for the pale gravel beneath my feet and Biscuit leading the way; without him, I probably would have accidentally run off the side of a cliff. Or straight into some werewolf's den.

When his glittering outline dove from the blackened sky moments later, I expected him to nuzzle up against my cheek to let me know that everything was okay and it was time to use the stone. Instead, the moment he landed on my shoulder, he began tugging on my ear anxiously and glancing at the nearest bush to our right, one that was markedly larger than the rest – about four feet high. The sound of crunching gravel not far ahead made me immediately understand. As quietly and quickly as I could, I skittered toward the bush and crouched behind it, doing my best not to brush my exposed fingers against its pale leaves or white berries. Biscuit was padding at my shoulder with his claws, clearly agitated, and raising his head like a meerkat trying to peer around the leaves.

After a few tense, silent moments, the clouds above began to part. I stuck my head out as far as I dared to try to locate whatever had gotten Biscuit so worked up. As the path reemerged in the mounting light of the moons, three figures appeared halfway between our shrub and the Waypoint, no more than fifty feet away. They were all tall and lanky, humanoid in stance and stride, though their graceful steps made them look like they were gliding in the direction of the Waypoint. At the sight of them, Biscuit began to tremble like a leaf. I raised my hand to give him a comforting head scratch, but he butted my hand away – a first in our entire relationship.

"What are they?" I whispered as softly as I could while craning my neck to get a better view. The three men (at least, I assumed they were men by their narrow hips and pale, bald heads) were walking side by side. One of them was dragging a large, lumpy object behind him.

Biscuit let out a low noise that sounded like "Bam-pie."

"A *what* pie?" I started to ask, then abruptly broke off.

Even though the moons were once more shining brightly from above, and the Waypoint was casting a lengthy shadow across the road, the three skulking men cast no shadows behind them. Nor did they leave footprints. In fact, the only thing they left in their wake was the long, dark streak that trailed behind their cargo and across the gravel where their shadows should have been. A long, dark streak that looked a lot like blood.

My hand flew to my mouth to stifle the cry clawing at the back of my throat. "*Now* can we use the Waystone?" I whispered shrilly.

"No blood," Biscuit clucked. "Bam-pie!"

"First of all, why the hell would you take us *toward* the Waypoint if we have to avoid other people in order to use the stone?" I snapped, my temper flaring. He shrank away, looking about as chagrined as a magical parrot could. "Secondly, I don't know what the hell a 'bam-pie'—" Abruptly I froze as I heard the word in my own mouth. "Wait… Are you trying to say '*vampire?*'" I hissed, high and quiet enough that only dogs could have heard. And probably werewolves.

Biscuit nodded vigorously, ducking behind me when one of the figures looked over his shoulder.

"Oh fuuuuck," I cursed under my breath.

Slowly turning his head from side to side, the *vampire* appeared to be sniffing the air. As he did, the light of the moons illuminated the taut, white skin of his face and his smooth, hairless scalp, making the hollows of his cheeks appear nearly black and his dark, beady eyes look like empty cavities. For a moment he hesitated, that deathly stare resting directly on our hiding spot.

I recoiled in silent horror. *Keep walking, keep walking, dear God, please keep walking!* My hand was clenching the dagger at my side so tightly, I could feel my heartbeat throbbing in my knuckles. The visceral reaction from his vacant gaze was so powerful, it threatened to liberate the scream I'd been doing everything I could to tamp down.

A few feet ahead, the vampire that had been lugging the trio's bloody cargo made a sharp sound. With an answering hiss, the straggling sentry gave one more slow survey of the land, those dead, black eyes glossing over us twice more, then turned to fall into step with the other two. I held my breath, too afraid to exhale. Just a few more yards and they would be there, free to teleport wherever the hell they wanted – so long as it was far, *far* away from us.

Seconds passed like long minutes. When they finally arrived at the post, only then did my grip on Zayn's dagger start to loosen. The vampire at the front held up a pale, bony hand. A rune near the top of the pole glimmered awake, casting a pulsing green light that would soon trigger a portal.

"It's okay, buddy," I whispered to Biscuit with a sigh of relief. "We're going to be—"

A horrible scream shattered the silence from every direction, discordant and shrill and steeped in despair. It made every hair on the back of my neck stand stalk-straight, shrouding me from head to toe with the looming certainty of death. Biscuit let out a stifled cry, hiding his face beneath my chin. Even the vampires covered their ears against the blood-curdling cry, far worse than a dying cat scraping its claws across glass.

Banshee! the voice in my head shouted, and the urge to run was almost insurmountable. My eyes darted behind us, calculating how far we might be able to get if I tugged off my shoes and bolted as fast as I possibly could. But there was nowhere to go; behind or ahead of us, the promise of death hung in the air like the tangy scent of ionization just before a lightning strike.

Nevertheless, I'd started slipping off my shoes when the noise ceased as quickly as it had come, leaving a deathly silence in its wake that was nearly as bad as the scream itself. Before I even had time to collect my scattered thoughts, the not-so-lifeless bundle the vampires had been dragging behind them jumped to its feet, yanking its startled keeper to the ground. With the other two vampires still doubled over in the aftermath of the banshee's cry, their victim began staggering away from the Waypoint and its captors as fast as it could – which wasn't very fast. It staggered up the road with the frantic desperation of a wounded gazelle fleeing a pack of lions, tripping and stumbling with every odd step.

Having finally shaken off the residual shock from the banshee's scream, the vampires all let out angry, terrible hisses and started chasing the tottering figure…straight toward us.

"Oh my God," I gasped, my heart lurching painfully against my ribs. "Biscuit, we have to use the Waystone!"

"No blood! Bam-pie!"

I let out an agitated groan. "Look, I know you hate bam-pies! I hate them too, even the handsome, sparkly kind, but—ohhh, fuck."

The gazelle – who I could now see was a middle-aged fae with pointy ears and hair so blond it looked white – stumbled to the ground, landing no more than twenty feet away from our hiding spot. Stupid as it was, I actually made a move to help him. But Biscuit yanked my hair sharply, distracting me just long enough for me to understand how futile that would have been.

Propped on bloody knees and elbows, the man was working to scramble to his feet when the fastest vampire was on him. A horrible sound, like a ripping sheet, filled the air. The man let out an agonized scream, which ended in a gurgle – and then abruptly cut off. In the blink of an eye, the two other vampires had leapt on top of his unmoving body, feeding and convulsing as bright red blood sprayed from his neck and trickled down their chins.

Bile and vomit filled my throat, and I had to clasp a hand over my mouth to keep from retching all over the ground. On my shoulder, Biscuit had become as still as a statue, though his wings were half extended – as though preparing to attack if they took even one step closer.

No! I mouthed, shaking my head at him pleadingly.

The three of them – the sentry, the courier, and the butcher, as I'd labeled them – pushed and elbowed at one another as they gorged themselves on blood, completely oblivious to the rest of the world. It was like they hadn't eaten in months. Based on their skeletal appearances, maybe they hadn't.

Still crouching, I shifted my weight off of my groaning left knee as slowly as I could. Immediately, the sentry shot his head in the air. My breath hitched in my throat and I froze, one hand clasping Biscuit's skinny little leg to keep him from doing anything stupid, just as he had done for me. A moment later, the vampire let out a primal hiss and jerked back to his prey, shoving his bloody comrades aside to seize the coveted spot above the femoral artery.

The hand that wasn't clutching Biscuit's leg carefully set the dagger on the ground, then crept toward my pocket one millimeter at a time, creeping…creeping…until it clasped the paper-wrapped bundle. Doing everything I could not to let the paper audibly crinkle, I used my thumb to unfold one edge, exposing a small section of cool, carved rock.

All it needs is a drop of your blood and a clear thought of your destination, Zayn had instructed me. Like sharks, I had to assume vampires could smell a drop of blood from a mile away, which is probably why Biscuit didn't want me to trigger the Waystone. But since they were practically bathing in it, there was no way they'd be able to differentiate the scent of my blood from their prey's.

At least, that's what I told myself as my heart rate skyrocketed toward full-on cardiac arrest.

"Biscuit," I whispered quietly, so quietly I almost couldn't hear myself over the nearby sounds of slurping and flesh-tearing. Another wave of bile filled my mouth, and I had to take a moment to recover before attempting to whisper again. "Biscuit, bite me. Now." I raised my finger to his beak.

He flashed me what can only be described as a look of pure exasperation, which was interrupted by the shrill hiss of one of the ashen, black-eyed vampires. The butcher was looking right at us.

"*I sssssseeee yoouuu,*" he whispered, his sharp, curved fangs dripping with blood. Both the courier and the sentry immediately snapped up their heads, flashing their own fangs like vipers. "*Your familiar's magic calls to this blood. Come to me,*" he beckoned with skeletal fingers.

"Bite me – *now!*" I yelped, thrusting my thumb against Biscuit's beak.

The stupid bird hesitated – *hesitated*, after all the other times he'd bitten me! – and flared his wings as though preparing to launch a solo kamikaze attack.

"Oh, no, you don't!" I tightened my grip on his leg as the three vampires started crawling toward us like a trio of venomous spiders. "Just BITE ME!"

"Yessssss." Through the leaves, I could see the gruesome smirk spreading across the butcher's face. It made me want to crawl into a hole and die. *"Bite her – I command it."*

And then Biscuit did – harder and more violently than ever before. His beak sliced straight through leather and the soft flesh between my thumb and forefinger, eliciting a sharp yelp from my throat. When he flew off my shoulder a moment later, I could only stare in horror at the bright gold blood dripping from the gash in my hand.

"Very good." The butcher nodded as Biscuit landed on his outstretched arm, calmly and obediently, as though... I licked my lips, desperate to put moisture back in my mouth.

As though he'd been Manipulated.

Vampires were a type of Extractor, Zayn had told me – those who rob mages of their magic along with their blood. If their most recent victim was a Manipulator, and they'd used his stolen magic to seize control of Zayn's familiar, what fresh hell would they be able to wreak on the land after stealing *my* blood?

"Come out, watcher," the courier cackled hoarsely, *"or we shall command it to crush its own skull against a rock."*

"Get away from him!" I scrambled to my feet, clutching the dagger in a shaking fist.

The courier cocked his eyes at me, as black as pitch and entirely without reflection. *"A Gilded One,"* he mused.

"Yesss...I can smell its honeyed blood," the sentry rasped.

I stood my ground, eyes darting between the three vampires, the ravaged corpse at their feet, and Zayn's familiar – the stupid creature I loved almost as much as I loved his creator.

"Let him go," I choked out, my throat as dry and scratchy as sandpaper. "I'll give you whatever you want… Just let him go. Please."

"Come and take him," the butcher grinned, his snake-like fangs gleaming in the moonlight. Behind him, the other two laughed – hoarse, voiceless croaks that chilled me down to my marrow.

"Why don't you come and bring him," I retorted, the overwhelming desire to protect superseding all other common sense – like basic self-preservation. "That is, if you want to be the first to get a taste of this." I held out my hand, where liquid gold oozed from a deep, beak-shaped wound.

"Stay!" the butcher hissed at Biscuit. Then, with a guttural snarl, he flung the poor bird to the ground and charged, his dead, black eyes flashing with unsatiated hunger. Blood-stained saliva dripped down his jaw as it became unhinged, transforming into a gaping maw about to strike.

Clutching Zayn's dagger in front of me, my free, bloodied hand flew to the Waystone in my pocket. "Biscuit!" I shouted. He was staring up at me from the ground, wings drooped and body shaking. "Biscuit, come!"

The butcher lunged for my throat. I flung myself to the side and stumbled, falling to one knee as he sailed past. I twisted around just in time to see him skittering face-first in the shrub I'd been hiding behind, long arms flailing wildly. Jumping to my feet, I gritted my teeth, preparing for his next attack. But instead of whirling around and launching himself at my jugular, he staggered out of the bush, screaming and clawing at the pallid gray skin that was sloughing off his cheekbones like melted wax.

My stomach lurched violently. My own face had been hovering inches from those leaves for the last fifteen minutes. Fortunately, and unfortunately, I didn't have much time to ponder that thought because the other two vampires had just joined the party. They circled me like two skulking hyenas, completely disregarding the shrill, agonized shrieks of their friend.

"Biscuit," I pleaded, eyes darting between him and the vampires that circled between us. "*Please* – come here!"

He cocked his head but made no move to obey, even as one of the vampires sprang into the air. With a cry, I flung up my fists to shield myself in a pitiful boxer's stance, forgetting the dagger I held in my hand. The blade plunged into his stomach with a sickening squelch, leaving me just as surprised as he was when bright red blood from his recent victim began spurting out. Screeching something awful, he began frantically trying to scoop the fountain of blood back into his mouth, not even bothering to remove the blade embedded in his gut.

I stumbled away from him, head whipping around queasily. There was no way these guys were fighting at full strength, or I'd have long since been dead. But even if that were the case, how long did I have before the energy from their most recent meal kicked in?

Behind me, the butcher was still screaming, his face now more bone than skin. Neither he nor the courier – who was too busy trying to drink from the hole in his own stomach – were much of a threat for the moment. But just ahead, the third and as-yet-unwounded vampire was crouched on the ground, preparing to strike. The sentry eyed my bleeding hand hungrily – a hand that was now completely weaponless.

Between us, Biscuit hadn't moved from his spot on the ground. He wasn't hurt, at least not from what I could see, but he was clearly dazed. If I could just get the little twerp to listen to me, to lure him over to me in some way, I could use the Waystone to snap us out of there. But what could I possibly—

I gasped. My hand flew to the breast pocket of Zayn's jacket, where my fingers closed around something small and pitted.

"Hey, Biscuit!" I shouted, flashing the nut in front of me. "Want an almond?"

That did it.

Eyes rounding with excitement, he sprang from the ground, greedily eyeing the nut. At the exact same moment, the sentry launched, his own greedy, black eyes trained on the blood-stained hand that held it. The second Biscuit landed on my outstretched arm and snatched the almond from my bloody fingers, I grabbed the Waystone in my other pocket.

"Zayn's office!" I screamed, clutching both it and the bird for dear life.

Blinding white light exploded from the stone, streaking between my fingers as though I were clutching a star fragment as bright as the sun. It erupted from my hand and all around us, hot and blazing as it stole the very darkness from the night. The other two vampires managed to stagger away from the inferno, one still clutching the remaining tatters of his face, the other trying to salvage what was left of his own seeping gore, but the sentry crumpled to the ground with an agonized scream, shielding his inky eyes with smoking, blistering hands. Determination to get home overruling my terror, I held the Waystone aloft, raising it high above my head as a shaft of light as wide as a redwood tree and as bright as a laser shot into the air, splitting the clouds wide open. The pressure on the balls of my feet disappeared as my body floated up from the ground. Five feet, ten feet, fifteen feet, I held onto both bird and stone for dear life while suspended in the air as though caught up in an alien tractor beam. And then, like a silent lightning strike, a curtain of coruscating light enveloped the entire world, blotting everything – the land, the stars, and the moons – completely out of existence.

Taking in one final breath, I hugged Biscuit against my chest as he and I surrendered to the light, dissolving into nothingness alongside everything else it had obliterated in its wake.

XIX.
THE STOWAWAY

It took about sixty seconds for my eyes to adjust to the darkness enough for me to recognize Zayn's fae-bound office; sixty-five seconds for Biscuit, who'd been busily attacking his beloved almond, to let out a loud, alarmed squawk; and sixty-five-and-a-half seconds for the vampire curled in the fetal position beside Zayn's desk to leap to his feet, snarling ferociously. The skin on his face and hands was peeling and bleeding, as though he'd come face-to-flames with a pizza oven. The three of us gaped at each other wordlessly for a single, protracted second before the vampire let out an enraged roar and sprang at my face like a wounded hyena.

Biscuit leapt from my shoulder. Crying out, I too tried to flee but instead smacked into a chair, knocked it over, and toppled to the ground beside its spinning, upturned wheels. The vampire bounced off the desk and made a swift one-eighty, rounding on me with fangs bared and claws flashing. His hollow cheeks had filled in significantly since draining his victim of blood, to the point that he no longer looked skeletal – just angry. Which meant my luck had all but run out.

My eyes darted around the room frantically. The door was less than eight feet away, but an hour of uninterrupted running and panic had turned my entire pulmonary system into an anaerobic wasteland. I couldn't make my legs move, not for the literal life of me. My breaths were coming in short, wheezing, ineffective bursts that left black spots swimming in front of my eyes.

The vampire lunged, soulless black eyes flashing with rage and unsatiated hunger, and I closed my eyes in defeat. This was the end. I'd survived a nonstop marathon of glaistigs and fachans and sirens, only to collapse a yard from the finish line.

I couldn't save you, Zayn. I'm so sorry.

Something tickled my nose, making my eyes pop open. Biscuit had plunged from the safety of his filing cabinet perch to dive between us, wings and tail feathers flared as he let out a shrill battle cry.

"No!" I screamed as the vampire unhinged his jaw to strike. "Biscuit, *no!*"

My screams cut off with a ragged gasp as every feather on Biscuit's body, each one as multi-faceted and dazzling as a precious stone, erupted into an identically-colored flame. Crimson red, sea green, lapis blue – every color I could ever try to name and countless more – consumed and surrounded his body. He hung in the air, wings spread majestically, a breathtaking creature of rainbow fire that was nearly as blinding as the spire of light that exploded from the Waystone. Shimmering waves of heat rippled away from his body in a targeted blast that assaulted the vampire while leaving me unscathed.

The vampire screamed, a blood-curdling, agonized scream that rivaled even a banshee's, and flung himself away from the dazzling inferno. He smashed into the opposite wall and immediately began clawing at it frantically, leaving jagged, bloody lines embedded in the plaster. His head whipped around desperately, blindly searching for the door. Just as his charbroiled hand brushed against the handle, his skin burst into flames. The screams heightened into a dying crescendo and then broke away as the fire consumed him, scorching skin and bone until nothing remained of his body but smoke and ash.

Still suspended in the middle of the room, Biscuit turned to glance at me over blue and violet flames, his beautiful, gold-flecked eye reflecting the rainbow of fire that engulfed his little body. "See you, Tal-ya," he cooed softly – and then all at once, the flames went out. His feathers, now completely black, crumbled away.

And in the blink of an eye, he was gone.

"No," I whispered. I crawled toward the pile of black, glittering ashes resting in the middle of the floor. "No, no, no." I reached forward with trembling, bloody fingers to touch his remains. They were still warm, twinkling like thousands of distant stars embedded in the night sky. "Biscuit," I whispered, tears spilling down my cheeks. "Come back, Biscuit. Please."

I truly expected him to reappear, to rise from that pile of ashes, shake out his feathers, and pester me for an almond. I held my breath, waiting, not daring to look anywhere else. The clock ticked softly as seconds turned into long, agonizing minutes.

A strangled sob tore from my throat. "Biscuit!" I cried, planting my hands on either side of his ashes. "Please, come back! *Come back!!*"

But the mound of ashes didn't stir.

Sorrow clawed at my chest, clawed and clawed until it tore from my throat – a raw, primal howl of grief that racked my body to the core. I crumpled to the floor sobbing, curling my body around his remains as though trying to protect them. I wept and wept, until my tears had gathered into a small puddle that caressed his ashes like a salty ocean meeting a black-sand shore. I must have lain there for the better part of an hour, waiting – praying – for him to reappear. But nothing happened. And nothing ever would.

He was gone.

Though silent sobs still racked my body, I forced myself back into a sitting position, hugging my ribcage as Zayn's soft voice echoed in my ears.

If Hibiscus were to die, I might never fully recover – emotionally, or otherwise.

My hands clenched into trembling fists. Whatever pain I felt, I couldn't begin to comprehend the agony he must be suffering from the death of his familiar, a loss he no doubt would have felt at any distance. The two of them had shared a spirit. And now a piece of Zayn's soul was gone forever... All because of me.

Another sob welled up in my chest but I forced it down. I couldn't think about that. If I did, I would never be able to rise up from that floor. And now, more than ever, Zayn needed me.

Biscuit's sacrifice wouldn't be in vain. I couldn't let it.

Repeating that thought like a mantra, I mustered the strength to pick myself up, just as I'd done the day my father died. I dusted off my clothes and pushed the pain as far down as I could, to a deep, walled-off place that I'd created long ago for the sole purpose of surviving one day, one hour, at a time.

Moving as though on autopilot, I found a bible-sized, hinged silver box resting on Zayn's bookshelf, and carefully scooped every last bit of Biscuit's ashes inside. I nearly broke down again as I worked, but I buried the heartache next to all the grief I'd buried years ago, inside the gaping void my father had left.

With a deep, shaky breath, I gently cradled Biscuit's ashes in the crook of my elbow. Then I wiped my eyes, activated the Portal Rune on Zayn's filing cabinet, and turned my back to the one corner of the universe I prayed I'd never have to see again.

XX.
Home Again, Home Again

Home. In all the realms in all the universe, there is no greater combination of four letters.

I wanted to bend over and kiss the ground the moment my toes hit that earthly tile, but knowing first-hand how infrequently that office floor was mopped, I merely stood there, savoring the sensation of breathing moist, oxygenated Miami air into my battered lungs. When the wave of interdimensional nausea finally passed, I slammed the portal shut and trudged over to Zayn's desk, where I carefully set the silver box in the top drawer, next to my cellphone, purse, and garish diamond ring. After adding the kraken ink from my back pocket, I gave Biscuit's remains one last, tearful look, then gently closed the drawer.

Once I'd taken a moment to re-collect myself, I emptied the rest of my pockets onto the desk. I smoothed out the wad of crumpled papers and carefully set the delphiniums on top of them. Their petals had gotten smashed and tattered but their roots, thankfully, were intact. The Waystone had broken cleanly in two after we arrived, so I unceremoniously dropped the two halves beside everything else. After peeling off my bloodied gloves, chucking off my shoes, and hanging Zayn's jacket on the otherwise empty coat rack, I opened the door and stepped into the shop. It was pitch black inside, save for the purple neon light that filtered in through the darkened storefront. Even the street outside was quiet, which meant last call had ended a long time ago. Not bothering to turn on the lights, I made my way to the bathroom, where I flipped the light switch and shut the door. After using the facilities – the existence of which, I'd never felt so grateful for – I leaned against the sink, gripping the porcelain for support. A smear of blood had dried on the edge – almost certainly from Roy hitting his head.

When I finally gathered the courage to look in the mirror, I gasped at the haggard reflection staring back at me. My bangs were a mess, the rest of my dirty hair fell in limp ringlets around my face, and my eyes had dark circles beneath them, making my irises look pale and washed out. But my skin…my skin glowed like one of Lamswyth's polished goblets. No amount of make-up would or could ever hide it completely – probably not even spray paint. Unless I planned on donning a head-to-toe burka for the rest of my life, I'd never be able to show my face in public again. I'd never be able to see my mother again. And if the fae mafia happened to stop by during one of my shifts—

No, I shook my head firmly. *Zayn won't let that happen. I won't let that happen.*

Pumping out handfuls of freesia-scented soap from the dispenser, I furiously scrubbed at my hands, arms, and face, scouring as much of the blood and filth off my body as I could while working delicately around various scrapes and bruises. I splashed cold water over my skin to rinse everything off and dried myself with paper towels. Then, after raiding the first aid station for gauze to wrap around my hand – feeling an unexpected wave of grief as I did – I made one final pit stop to the Keurig machine at the back of the shop.

And then I got to work.

Like before, a drop of blood was all it took to reveal the text and images on the pages Zayn had torn out of his grimoire. One was an Extraction recipe to create Delphinium ink that included five numbers scrawled at the top in his handwriting. The other two pages were runes. One of them – the Concealment Rune – seemed straightforward enough. Not much more difficult than the Unchaining Rune I'd cast however many days ago, although I did have to remind myself that I'd accidentally broken the front door when I attempted it.

Still, it was the Counteraction Rune that gave me pause. While it somehow looked vaguely familiar, it had so many perfectly-round circles and straight lines and weird angles – every single one of which had to be measured perfectly in order for it to work with Zayn's blood – that I may as well be trying to write a poem in Chinese kanji. Free-handed. With a needle.

I shook my head in mounting despair. How the hell was I supposed to get that rune on Zayn's body if Sol's Dominion Rune made him resist my efforts? And speaking of resisting, just how much control did that tattoo have over his actions? Would he run – or even worse, try to fight me?

The ticking clock in the corner – just after 3:00 a.m. – was the only thing that kept me from having yet another meltdown; that would have to wait till later. With a deep breath, I smoothed out the page detailing the ink recipe and scanned it, feeling increasingly anxious with every line. The list of ingredients wasn't terrible, but the process was even more complicated than my mother's infamous challah recipe. Worse, this recipe specifically had to do with making ink from the flower petals, not the roots, but Zayn had crossed out certain sections in lieu of hand-scribbled notes in the margins, which only made the page even more jumbled and hard to read.

"Clean the petals – er, *roots* thoroughly… Mash into a fine-grain paste using a mortar and pestle…" I muttered to myself, running my finger along the many, many steps. "Pure marble is necessary to ensure an uncontaminated Extraction… blah, blah, blah… Mix paste with a clear solvent such as ethanol, one to three parts, and distill over a flame for one hour per gram…yadda, yadda…making absolutely sure not to under- or over-process, as the former will render the ink inert, and the latter will cause the solution to emit a dense plume of poisonous vapors…"

My eyes widened. "Oh, I am so royally screwed."

I seriously doubted I'd find a noxious-gas mask in any of Zayn's drawers, so I spent the next twenty minutes obsessively reading and re-reading the instructions to make sure I didn't miss a single detail.

Only when I had all but memorized them did I start raiding all the secret nooks and crannies around Zayn's office. I marauded every drawer and cabinet, snooped through his mini fridge, used the numbers written across the top of the page to open the safe embedded in the wall – while trying not to drool at the mountain of cash tucked in the corner – and rifled through a collection of hinged, black containers I found resting on top of his bookshelves after climbing on top of his interdimensional filing cabinet to get a better look. They reminded me of cookie jars, except they were filled with dried ingredients that I'd never seen before, like bright green mushrooms and scaly, coiled things that I could only pray were *not* lizard tails.

By 4:00 a.m., I'd gathered nearly all of my supplies: 1) a mortar and pestle, 2) a container of ethyl alcohol, 3) two strips of cannabar bark from one of the black not-cookie jars, 4) a Bunsen burner and a handful of glass tubes and beakers, 5) Ræṣhur sea salt, 6) a set of silver scales that measured to the nearest hundredth of a gram, 7) a container of distilled water, 8) a small, glass thermometer, and 9) tælcome powder for inspissation... Whatever the hell that meant.

I carried everything out of his office and into the back room, which had a nice, long countertop for mixing pigments, and spread everything in a neat line in front of me after clearing the mess of ink bottles I'd left sitting out days earlier. With a steaming mug of coffee that had already been twice refilled and a stale energy bar clamped between my teeth, I set to work cutting the delphinium roots two millimeters beneath the start of the green stem and cleaning them with distilled water. Since there was barely enough root material to make the pigment, I tied my hair back with a rubber band and taped clumps of tissues to my forehead, terrified that a single drop of sweat might ruin the whole batch. Bangs managed, I put the chopped roots in the mortar and began grinding them into a smooth paste, the smell from which made the inside of my nose go numb and tingly. With glass droppers half the diameter of my pinky and scales to measure everything down to each individual salt granule, I set about making my pigment.

When I finally got to the part where my sickly-sweet-smelling, honey-colored goop needed to rest atop a blue flame for exactly one hour, forty-six minutes, and eighteen seconds – I checked my math six times and prayed to God I'd gotten it right as I set the timer on my phone – I sank to the ground, breathing a huge sigh of relief…which was then followed by an immediate jolt of panic when I saw morning light trickling in between the blinds at the front of the store.

What day is it? I wondered, pulling out my phone to check the lock screen. *Oh, God. Friday already?!* I knew Salen wasn't supposed to arrive for at least another day or two, but how much time did I have before Zayn eventually showed up?

I reached up and behind me to snatch the page from the counter, skimming through the last quarter of the delphinium recipe for the twentieth time. After the ink cooked and cooled completely, I would still have to "inspissate" the liquid – which my good buddy Google told me meant to thicken – with *tælcome* powder until it reached the proper consistency, at which point the color of the dye would supposedly change from burnt honey to yellow to white. And that was it. No more instructions.

But when is it safe to use? I wondered, turning the page over to check for more text, though I already knew it was blank.

With a groan, I pulled myself back to my feet and reached for the paper detailing the Concealment Rune that I'd promised Zayn I would tattoo on myself before doing anything else. The thought of having to press a needle into my skin – a needle filled with homemade fae dye that might very well be acutely toxic with all I knew of concocting magical ink – made me want to throw up.

I raked my hands over my face and through my hair, trembling from head to toe as I did. Not only would I have to tattoo myself, but I'd have to do it accurately. As in, straight lines that didn't waver with every sob and/or hysterical hiccup, or else the rune wouldn't work. Or, hell, maybe it *would* work, but in the wrong way. Like turning me into a toad or something because I got one of the angles wrong.

The image of me as a red-headed frog mutant hopping around the shop and eating flies made me sink to the floor all over again. *Why the hell would anyone ever want to permanently tattoo a magical rune on their body?!* I wondered, then winced at just how much I sounded like my mother. She'd said pretty much the exact same thing when I finally mustered up the nerve to tell her I'd been hired at a tattoo parlor: *What kind of meshuggeneh would want to permanently scribble cartoons all over their body? What's that butterfly on their tuchus gonna look like when they're ninety years old and their butt cheeks are flapping behind them in the wind?*

The memory of the conversation actually made me chuckle – until I remembered the wrath my mother would unleash upon me when I finally mustered up the courage to call her back. I pulled my phone from my pocket, wincing at the number of voicemails I had from her, and quickly skimmed through them. Each one made me cringe with increasing severity, until I was stooped over my phone like Quasimodo. By her sixth and final message, I had to hold the phone three feet away from my ear to avoid rupturing an eardrum.

"Talia Judith Kestenbaum, I have been sitting on shpilkes for three days! If you don't call me back in the next three hours, I will send an entire SWAT team to the Everglades! And don't you think I'm joking! If I find out you got eaten by a

crocodile, I'll dig you out of its stomach, resuscitate you, and then kill you all over again!"

I glanced at the timestamp – she'd left the message at midnight, well over four hours ago – and sighed, finger poised to dial her number. Sure, I'd probably incur at least an hour's worth of nonstop kvetching, but at least it would stop her from harassing the entire Miami Police Department, if she hadn't already. My finger wavered as a huge yawn made my jaw crack. Apparently, not even the combined powers of Revitalizing Serum and excessive caffeine could keep exhaustion from setting in with a vengeance.

I'll call her in five minutes, I yawned again. Curling up on the floor, I pillowed my head on my arm so I could rest my eyes for just a few seconds.

Just...a few seconds, I promised myself, *and then I'll... I'll...*

The sound of my own, open-mouthed snores was the last thing I heard before slumber triumphed over consciousness.

I awoke from a dream about roaring chainsaws that sounded suspiciously like my own snores with a panicked start. An alarm was going off somewhere, but for the life of me I couldn't remember what it was for or where it was. Or where *I* was, for that matter...

My eyes settled on the bright yellow morning light streaming through the front of the store.

Oh, shit! I scrambled to my feet, trying to shake the fog from my head and the bleariness from my vision, and fumbled to silence the alarm. Thank goodness the second timer hadn't gone off yet, which meant I still had—

Beep! Beep! Beep!

The first timer clattered on the ground. My hand jerked forward of its own accord, snatching the beaker of dye from the Bunsen burner, and then almost dropped the molten-hot glass on the floor.

"Augh!" I yelled, abandoning the glass on the counter so violently, it nearly tottered over. I sucked on my fingers with a pitiful whimper as I knelt to inspect the beaker's contents, very much praying I hadn't somehow overcooked it.

My heart sank to my knees when I saw the color.

"No," I whispered hoarsely. After snatching a wad of tissues to protect my fingers, I grasped the neck of the beaker and swirled the liquid around gently. This couldn't be right. The instructions specifically said the solution needed to fade from brown to white. Instead, the contents were still a sickly, pus-colored yellow.

I shone my phone's flashlight against the swirling contents of the vial, then snatched the page of instructions to reread it for the hundredth time. I skimmed through the entire page again, mumbling furiously to myself, before my shoulders sank in relief.

"*Tælcome* powder," I breathed. "First, the liquid has to cool down, and *then* I stir in this weird stuff until it turns white," I warily eyed the tiny jar of what looked like purple baby powder, then turned back to the instructions:

Once the suspension reaches 315 K, stir in the tælcome powder one half-gram at a time until proper viscosity and color is achieved.

315 'K'? I rubbed my temples, then reached for the old-fashioned mercury thermometer I'd grabbed from Zayn's

office. Indeed, instead of reading degrees in Fahrenheit or Celsius, it had a fancy K at the top. *For Kelvin, maybe?*

Only the metallic taste in my mouth made me realize I'd been chewing on my glowing lip hard enough to make it bleed. I had absolutely no idea how long it was going to take Zayn to get back, but I still had to sketch the Concealment Rune somewhere on my body, wait for the delphinium ink to cool, thicken, and hopefully lighten, and then inject it under my skin and pray I didn't die from blood poisoning. And then, oh yeah, I had to come up with an idea for how I was going to ambush my boss, restrain him against the influence of his Dominion Rune, and then tattoo one of the most complex designs I'd ever seen onto his squirming body.

"Biscuit, how the hell are we—" I started to ask. And then my voice cut off as the same massive lump from before abruptly reappeared. "...Oh. Right."

After snatching the angriest, loudest, most discordant vinyl record we had – a signed copy of *A Different Kind of Truth* by Van Halen, which Zayn had spontaneously gifted me late last year – and turning the record player up to its max volume, I snatched one of the surgical tip skin markers from the drawer, hoisted my bare foot on the counter beside the cooling ink, and set about sketching the Concealment Rune on the inside of my right ankle. I thrust my full attention into the design, blocking out everything else but the strokes I was drawing on my body and the screaming singer who was blissfully accosting my ears. When my favorite song of theirs, aptly named *Tattoo,* began to play, I hummed along while I worked.

Here's a secret to make you think
Why is the crazy stuff we never say, poetry in ink?
Speaking dayglow red

Explode-o pink, purple mountain's majesty
Show me you, I'll show you me…

My eyes darted back to the thermometer sticking out of the ink every so often. By the time I had finished sketching, checking, and re-checking the design on my ankle, the liquid had cooled to 317K – which meant it was time to get the purple baby powder ready. I measured it out in tiny half-gram piles, dropping them in one at a time the moment the thermometer ticked down to 315K. Each time I dropped in a scoop, I swirled it around with a glass mixing stick until it was completely dissolved, watching the color of the liquid like a hawk since I had no idea what the viscosity was supposed to be. Just as I was getting ready to sprinkle in a sixth scoop of *tælcome* powder, the solution began to steam and hiss. I staggered back, eyes as wide as saucers as I threw an arm over my nose and mouth to block out the fatal fumes.

…And then the steam abruptly stopped.

Within seconds, the solution faded to a perfect, milky white.

A heavy sigh of both immense relief and terrified, selfish disappointment rushed between my lips. Once you add potentially-lethal homemade ink to the bundle of needles I'd have to stab into my body thousands of times, I was treading deep into breathing-into-a-paper-bag-so-I-don't-pass-out territory. Except we didn't have any paper bags at the shop.

Suffice it to say, there were tears. There were hysterics. There was cursing. Not to mention the five or six times I gave up mid-tattoo, firmly deciding to instead live as a mountain recluse where no one would ever see my gleaming skin…only to force myself to grab the tattoo gun yet again and pick up where I left off.

Finally, after nearly an hour of emotional bargaining with God and uncontrollable blubbering, I had just three more strokes to go. Three more clean, straight strokes, and then the stupid thing would be done, and I could go about the far more crucial business of freeing Zayn from his forced servitude.

Sniffling, I pressed the needle against my ankle, dragging it across my skin in a nerve-wracking motion that felt a little too close to self-mutilation, then blotted away the excess ink and blood.

Two lines left.

The record finished, plunging the rest of the shop into deafening silence as the whir of the tattoo machine buzzed in my ear like a hornet. I gritted my teeth together, hurriedly finishing the right side of the triangle before another series of sobs could grip my body. When the ink was blotted away, I breathed a shuddering sigh of relief, wiping the sweat from my brow and the tears from my eyes.

Just one line to go.

I pushed the button and the little handheld torture machine whirred back to life. When I went to press it to my skin, however, it coughed and sputtered…but no ink came out. Not even a drop.

"Oh, come on," I muttered irritably, flicking the side of the cartridge. "Don't you dare run out on me now!" With a deeply aggravated groan, I slammed the stupid gun back on the counter and reached for the corked beaker of ink, which I'd been trying to be as stingy with as possible given the complexity of Zayn's rune.

The bell on the front door jingled.

My head shot up so fast I nearly knocked over the beaker. The intruder couldn't have been a customer; our shop didn't open for two more hours. And even then, there was still a couch firmly wedged in front of the door.

"Zayn?" a woman called in a high, singsong-y voice.
My entire body froze in place as though I'd grown roots.
Salen.

XXI.
The Early Bird Gets the Ink

"Oh, Zaa-ayn!" she called again, honey dripping from every elongated syllable. "I was flying overhead and saw the lights were on, so I thought I'd pop in early to check on your progress."

I spent a whole precious second trying to figure out what she meant by "flying," then shook my head fiercely. The only thing that mattered at that moment was getting the hell out of here. But there was no exit out of the back room, save for the door that led directly into the shop. Judging by the brisk click of her heels, I had five, maybe ten seconds to act, which meant I had enough time to do one of two things: hurry up and try to finish my tattoo so she wouldn't see my glowing blood, or hide the ink so she couldn't take it before I had the chance to get the Counteraction Rune on Zayn's body.

"Hello-o?" Her voice was literally right outside. I could hear the hinges squeak as she started to push the door open.

Without the luxury of another second to squander, I hastily put the ink in the nearest drawer, slammed it shut, and whirled around.

"Zay—" she started, then gasped when she saw me. "You! What are you—" Her magenta-pink eyes abruptly doubled in size as she took in my glowing face.

"Oh, h-hey," I waved like an idiot. "How's uh…how's it going?" As casually as I could, I scooted the right cuff of my pant leg back down with my shoeless left foot, praying she hadn't seen the fresh delphinium-ink tattoo I was thirty seconds away from finishing.

"Gold blood…" she whispered. "All this time, he's been hiding one of your kind right here? Right in front of us?"

"Who, me?" I blinked innocently. "Oh, you mean this?" I forced out a laugh as I scrubbed my glowing hands together. "That's a really funny story, actually… Um, you see, Zayn has this illumination ink, and I, uh, accidently drank some, which is, yeah, that's why I currently look like a lightbulb. But he should be back in a couple of days to fix me right up. Three, tops. Oh, and I'm sure he'll have, um…well, whatever it is he promised you! Not that I really know anything about that…"

While I rambled on like a drunk politician, a smile began to creep across her radiant, gorgeous face until she was openly grinning at me with teeth that were strangely pointed, almost as though they'd been filed.

I swallowed thickly. "Anyway, I'll, uh, be sure to let Zayn know you stopped by!"

"Mm-hmm." She crossed her arms over a very full bosom that was popping out of the low-cut, see-through blouse she was wearing. "What have you been making back here?" she asked, looking over my shoulder at the mess of beakers, petals and rumpled pages on the counter.

I glanced behind me, feeling the panic rising in my chest. *Please don't let her read them,* I fervently prayed. I stifled a gasp as the letters instantly faded from sight, making the pages look like plain parchment paper.

Salen pushed past me, eyes narrowing as she surveyed the blank pages. When her eyes fell on the delphinium petals, her back stiffened. "Where is he?" she asked softly, not bothering to turn around.

"He's... He hasn't returned from his business trip yet. I think it'll be another day, or maybe even two..."

She didn't reply. Instead, after scooping the wilted delphinium petals into the side pocket of her siren-hide pants, she pulled up her sleeve to reveal several tattoos – including an ugly reddish-black tattoo on the inside of her wrist. It looked just like the Dominion Rune her father had carved between Zayn's shoulder blades. She pressed her perfectly-manicured fingertips against it, and the ink glowed bright red.

"Zayn, you will return to your Earth-bound shop immediately," she commanded, then withdrew her fingertips as the ink faded back to the color of dried blood.

When she turned around to face me again, a look of pleasure appeared on her face the moment she saw the horrified expression on mine. "You sweet little thing," she smiled. "You haven't said a single true thing since I set foot in this store. But how can I be mad at a face like this?" she cupped my chin in her hand, those inhumanly pink eyes flashing.

Somewhere in the back of my head, it occurred to me that now might be a prudent time to run. But the longer her gleaming eyes bored into mine, the further that thought slipped. She was so beautiful, with her long, flowing platinum-blonde hair and perfectly painted lips, it took my breath away. It was an odd feeling, since I couldn't remember ever being physically attracted to a woman before. But *this* woman was special. This woman was the most beautiful lady in two realms, a powerful creature who exuded a raw, irresistible sensuality that you could nearly taste in the air.

Why doesn't Zayn like her again? I wondered, genuinely confused, then shrugged. Whatever his reason, it must not have been a very good one.

"Let me have a taste," she purred, and my stomach did a little flip. Before I knew it, her glossy lips were pressed against mine.

She tasted so sweet, like maraschino cherries coated in sugar. Her lips rolled across my open mouth, roughly, hungrily. A small whimper escaped my throat. She was almost too sweet, like a spoonful of aspartame. When she flitted her tongue against mine, black spots floated in front of my eyes and my knees nearly buckled.

Something's not right, a fearful voice whispered in the back of my mind.

"And here I thought your employer was delicious," she murmured against my mouth. "Do you know how long it's been since I fed on someone like you?" Her fingers traced their way up my stomach, stopping at the ties dangling from the top of my shirt, beginning to unlace them.

"Wait…" I wanted to push her hands away, but I suddenly felt so faint, so drained, it was hard to stand.

While her fingers worked to undo the laces of my corset, she traced her sharp teeth over my lower lip. "Sol would be cross with me for sampling your blood before him, but what he doesn't know can't hurt me… Don't worry, it won't hurt," she cooed, nibbling on my lip. "Much."

I cried out from the pressure of her teeth, so close to tearing through my skin. *No!* a voice shouted. *She can't have it! You can't let her!*

With effort, my hands reached up to grab her wrists, wrenching them away. "No!" I gasped.

Her eyes widened like saucers. "How—"

"I said *no*," I choked out. As my grip tightened around her wrists, the spots in front of my eyes dispersed, and my knees began to steady. "Or is that a word you haven't heard before?"

"Get off of me!"

"No!" The cry tore from my chest, where the hatred for what she'd done to Zayn simmered hot and deep. "I won't let you hurt him anymore!"

"What are you doing?" she grunted, trying to wriggle free.

I had no idea. But whatever it was, I was beginning to feel stronger by the second while her cheeks were growing paler and paler.

Her dimming eyes flew to her trapped wrists. Beneath her gauzy chiffon blouse, I could clearly see the outline of thorny rose vines wrapping around her slender forearms. It was Zayn's work, that much was obvious. Not only because of the style – he had a distinctive way of 3D shading that most tattoo artists would kill to be able to emulate – but because in the center of every rose blossom lay a different rune. And about half of those runes were beginning to fade.

"Stop it!" she cried out, eyes widening as they darted from her arms to mine.

With a startled gasp, I shoved her away. She fell against the counter, panting, while I held out my arms in front of me, gaping at the faint designs that were just beneath my skin.

Runes. At least a half-dozen of them.

Salen let out a strangled cry as she shoved up her own sleeves to get a better look at the damage. A half-dozen of the runes embedded within the rose petals were so faded, you could hardly see them against the surrounding scarlet ink. We gaped in disbelief at one another's tattoos for a long, protracted minute.

She was the first to snap out of it, shaking her head furiously. "How dare you!" she snarled. "Give them back!" She lunged at me, though her movements were slow and unsteady, like someone moving through molasses.

I, on the other hand, felt like I'd just woken up from the best sleep of my life. I dodged her easily, surprising even myself when she skittered past me. With a furious cry, she pivoted off the counter and raised a quivering hand to strike, her pristine fingernails extending into two-inch, razor-sharp claws. Beneath those demonic magenta eyes, pulsing black veins appeared and a terrifying smile spread across her face.

I'd barely had time to shake off my horrified expression when her hand shot forward to grab my throat. "I'll suck you dry, pretty girl, and leave your used up corpse for my father to—"

"Salen," a deep voice growled.

Features fading back to normal, she whirled around to find Zayn standing in the doorway, emerald eyes flashing with unrestrained fire. He had a smattering of cuts on his face and arms, and an angry bruise beneath his right eye.

"Zayn," she gasped as she quickly smoothed out her blouse. "That was awfully quick, even for you."

"I was nearly home when you…summoned me." His gaze fell on me, lingering on my still-glowing skin and the collection of stolen tattoos that had appeared on my arms. Only the near-imperceptible narrowing of his eyes gave away his emotions.

Salen was running her fingers through her tousled hair. A glossy, papier-mâché smile had already plastered itself back on her face. "Well, I'm so glad you're back," she purred, doing her best to appear unperturbed by the thousands of dollars' worth of tattoos she'd just lost. "I was also pleased to see your sweet little ingénue had already gotten started on the delphinium ink. I didn't know you had trained her to do so."

Zayn said nothing, but the Adam's apple in his throat bobbed.

"Then again, I didn't know you were safe-keeping her prized blood for us, either," she smiled primly. "Father will be so pleased when he finds out. So long as you provide him with his completed order and the accompanying rune, I won't even tell him you've been hiding her away." She sauntered over to the doorway, where she pinched his cheek. "Your face is just too pretty to be beaten to a bloody pulp. Now, I'm sure I'm correct in assuming that you'll get to work on the ink immediately?" she smiled, retrieving the petals from her pocket. As she sprinkled them into his open palm, she cast me a biting look. "This order is far too important for an apprentice. You will make the ink yourself, and have it ready in twelve hours when I return with Sol."

She made a move like she was going to squeeze past him, then gripped his arm in two hands and stood on her tip-toes. "You will not let the girl leave this place until I return with Sol," she murmured against his ear, eyes darting back to me in a smug look of satisfaction as she sucked his earlobe between her teeth.

My hands balled into fists, but Zayn shot me a warning glare.

"At that time, you will Endow him with the rune we've supplied, then immediately present *her* as the long-anticipated gift you and I have been secretly readying, together. That is a direct order," she smiled as she touched the glowing Dominion tattoo on her wrist once more. "I've grown far too fond of you to see you get yourself killed through sheer stupidity. Tell me you understand, darling."

"I understand," he spoke through gritted teeth.

Salen's magenta eyes once more fell on me, angrily gripping the counter so I wouldn't rip off her smug, predatory face. Her gaze lingered on the tattoos I'd partially Extracted from her before she flashed me her dazzling, predatory smile. "It was an honor to meet you, Tania. I look forward to spending much, *much* more time with you at my father's mansion." Something vicious glinted in her eyes. "By the way, I love the color of your pants. We've been setting traps for sirens all year, but we've yet to ensnare a hide of that color and quality."

A growl was building in my throat, threatening to erupt in a long, custom-designed string of profanities, but I choked them back down for Zayn's sake.

"Anyway, I'll be taking those, along with the runes you stole, when I return. Unless Zayn would like to help me tear them off of you now?" she licked her lips hungrily.

He stepped between us, blocking her from my view. "I'll need every minute I can spare to get the ink ready and prepare before you return with Sol tonight."

"Fine, but I'll expect you to fix *this*," she jabbed a finger at the washed-out runes on her arms, "and properly punish *her* for her insolence the moment you finish with Sol. In fact, I'll be overseeing that punishment to ensure she learns a valuable lesson."

At her savage smile, Zayn's hand clenched at his side.

Salen tossed her hair over her shoulder as she turned to walk away. "Oh, and one more thing, Zayn. Would you be a dear and go retrieve whatever it was the girl was trying to hide when I came in?" She pointed to the drawer behind me, which I was still firmly wedging my body against. "Right now, darling, if you don't mind."

"Wait—" I started.

Zayn squeezed his eyes shut, rubbed his forehead, then stiffly strode over to where I was standing.

Don't, I mouthed, looking up at him with a pleading expression.

The look he gave me was one of pure defeat as he gently pushed me aside. After hesitating for a long moment, he pulled the drawer open and retrieved the flask. When he turned around, he was clenching the corked vial in a shaking fist. My heart sank to my knees.

"What kind of ink is that?" Salen asked innocently. "Do not lie to me."

"Dandelion," I blurted out before Zayn could respond.

Anger flashed in her eyes. "What did I just say about lying, Tania?"

"It's Talia," I glared. "I've worked here for two years."

"Tania. Talia. It literally makes no difference… But lie to me again," she smiled serenely, "and I will have my brothers break every bone in your pretty little face – starting with your jaw. Because, much like your name, it doesn't matter if your body is mangled or whole when we drain you of your blood, does it? Now," she turned her attention back to Zayn, "is that the delphinium ink, yes or no?"

He nodded stiffly.

"In that case," her lips curled into a predatory smile, "I'll be back with my father right after lunch. Provided she made it correctly…?"

"Honestly, I think it needs a little work—" I started.

"She made it perfectly," Zayn replied, his voice completely devoid of emotion.

My shoulders wilted.

"Wonderful!" Salen clapped her hands together. "Keep that safely on you at all times until Sol arrives, won't you? After all, it belongs to him." She pinched his cheek again, then stood on her toes to kiss him on the mouth. Like the other day, Zayn stiffened, but made no move to stop her. As she smirked at me over his shoulder, crimson fire flooded my vision and I had to dig my fingers into the edge of the counter to keep myself from head-butting her to the ground.

After what felt like hours, she pulled away the kiss, blotting a smudge of lipstick from Zayn's mouth as she did. "In the future, darling, when you train another nameless tramp to take this one's place, don't let her anywhere near my father's property. If it weren't for *Tania's* blood, I'd have already killed her."

With that, she twirled on her stiletto heel and sauntered toward the door.

Zayn rounded on me the second she turned her back. "How the hell did you get those?" he hissed, motioning toward my arms.

I glared at Salen's back as she stopped to inspect the bowl of lollipops sitting at my station. "I think I accidentally Extracted them from her."

A look of surprise flickered across his face, which immediately contorted into a labored grimace. When he spoke, it was through gritted teeth and under his breath. "That...one..." he pointed at the faint swirly triangle embedded at the top of my left forearm, "is an Animalia Rune. It's used...to transform you...or a-another," he winced as he sucked in a deep, labored breath, "into any creature...found in...natural world."

My head jerked toward the front of the store where Salen was busy unwrapping a stolen lollipop. "What do I do?" I hissed. "Hypothetically, I mean! How would I use it...you know, on myself?" I added for good measure.

He opened his mouth to answer, then stifled a cough into a closed fist. Whatever hell the Dominion Rune was doing to him, there were specks of blood on his hand. "Touch th-the rune...then imagine...any c-creature—*ungg!*" With a silent groan, he doubled over and clutched his stomach.

Standing in front of the couch-blocked door with a pilfered lollipop between her lips, the succubus held out her arms and began to shimmer as though she were getting ready to walk through it.

"Hey!" I shouted frantically. "Hey, Salen!"

"Hmm?" She glanced at me over her vanishing shoulder, those awful pink eyes of hers appearing almost red in the early morning light. "What's the matter?" she smirked. "Miss me already?"

"Oh, I...just wanted to wish you a pleasant trip," I smiled innocently, my fingers brushing against the Animalia Rune on my forearm.

She rolled her eyes, turned around, and then, in a puff of red smoke, she disappeared.

XXII.
Unchained

For a moment, I thought I was too late – that she had already disappeared and was on her way back to tattle to Daddy.

And then I heard the squeaks.

They were coming from a little white rat with magenta eyes – the very same rat that was racing around a fallen lollipop on the floor in frantic, agitated circles.

When the shock of what I'd done had worn off, pride swelled in my chest like a birthday balloon. Little old me, art school dropout and perpetual abandoner of hobbies, had successfully Extracted magic! And then used said magic to save the day! A wide grin crossed my face as I turned to Zayn to crack a joke – something about a rat's favorite game being "Hide and Squeak" – but the joke evaporated as soon as I opened my mouth.

He was frozen in the doorway of the supply room, pivoted on one foot as though caught between two choices. Pain and doubt carved into his features as he reached out to grip the door frame for support. I chewed my lip anxiously. Did this count as hurting one of Sol's family members? I wasn't exactly sure. And for the moment, at least, it didn't seem like he was, either.

Before his Dominion Rune could decide for him, I quickly shoved past him, grabbed a glass Tupperware container from our miscellaneous mug-and-bowl cabinet, and then darted back into the shop. Rat-Salen was screeching furiously, trying desperately to claw her way to the top of one of the couch cushions, when I slammed the container down on top of her, flipped it over unceremoniously, and snapped the lid on.

"Ta-da!" I grinned, balancing my trophy on my palm.

When Zayn made a move like he was going to intervene, I yelled, "Wait!" and dashed over to the front counter. There, I grabbed a pair of scissors to stab a small hole in the lid.

"Look," I said, holding up the soup container for him to inspect from afar. "She's not hurt. She's doing just fine. In fact, I'll even drop a few shreds of cheese in there, okay? So, tell your Dominion Rune to chill the F out. She's perfectly safe and unharmed." I tapped on the glass. "Isn't that right, Salen?"

She bared her ugly little teeth at me and her tiny little claws scratched furiously at the inside of the container. But for the moment, at least, she wasn't going anywhere. I set her on top of the front desk, next to the computer screen, and set a pyramid-shaped paperweight on top of the lid so she couldn't escape.

Zayn appeared to relax, though only slightly.

I tried to give him my best reassuring smile. "So, what happened to the other guy?" I teased, gesturing to his cheek.

"I don't recommend picking a fight with a satyr," he muttered, wincing as his fingers brushed against the gnarly bruise. "He head-butted me like a damn goat."

"What?! Why didn't you just pay the dude and leave it at that?"

Zayn sighed tiredly. Even at a distance, I could see the dark circles beneath his eyes, as though the last few weeks of not feeding had caught up to him all at once. "Because I needed to provoke someone into keeping me away from you long enough for you to escape."

"You didn't!" My hands flew to my mouth. "Are you okay? Shit, is *he* okay?"

"Let's just say he fared better than I did."

"Oh my God, Zayn," I shook my head. "I'm so s—"

He held up a hand to silence me. "How badly did she hurt you?" he asked quietly. His voice was so soft, it took me a moment to understand what he'd meant.

"I'm fine," I answered quickly, and he frowned at my mouth. Chagrined, I quickly wiped off her stupid pink lip gloss with the back of my hand. If I had been feeling at all badly for what I'd done to her, the guilt immediately evaporated at the memory of what she had tried – and very nearly succeeded – to do to *me*.

Zayn closed his eyes, and even from afar, I could see the muscle in his jaw spasm.

"No, really," I insisted. "For a second, it wasn't going so well. I got really tired—"

"Because she drained you of your energy," he seethed. Hot anger burned in his eyes, contorting his expression into something that, for the first time ever, made him look almost inhuman. "Just like I did when you…you…"

"When I straddled you like a horse?" I joked weakly.

He cast me a sharp look.

"Look, it turned out to be okay." I forced a smile as I took a few steps toward him. He still hadn't moved from his spot in the supply room doorway. "In the end, I showed her who's boss. And I got some cool, needle-free tattoos in the meantime!" I held up my arms to admire the six – well, *five* – runes that I'd absconded with, since the faint outline of the Animalia Rune had disappeared right after I used it. I frowned at the empty spot at the base of my wrist. I could have used that rune for something much cooler, like transforming myself into a dolphin. Or, even better, a parrot, so I could fly around with—

The smile wiped right off my face.

Biscuit.

"Zayn," I started, but when my eyes fell on his right forearm, my throat caught. Instead of Biscuit's colorful portrait, only a faint, raised scar remained. It formed a perfect outline where his tattoo used to be. A sob lodged itself in my throat. If a broken heart could break all over again, mine would have crumbled at that very moment. "Zayn," I tried again, "I'm so sorry…" I took another timid step forward. All I wanted to do was hold him, to share some of the burden. But he held up a hand and backed away from me.

"Don't come near me. I'm not safe for you to be around."

"But I trust you—" I started to say.

"Don't!" he snapped. Though he appeared to be looking anywhere other than at me, I could see the anger flashing in his darkened eyes. "You can't trust me. You shouldn't be anywhere near me right now! *Augh!!*" he slammed his open hand against the supply room door, making me jump. "I never should have gotten you involved in any of this. It was so fucking selfish of me! And now…now…" He raked a hand through his hair. "Now the worst possible thing that could have happened, has happened."

"But Salen can't hurt us now," I protested. "She's—"

"Right here. Right where Sol will come looking for her. And so long as she lives, whether as a succubus or a rat, her commands rule my decisions. I can't give you this ink. I can't leave. And I can't...I can't let you leave, either." His hand reached for the hollow place on his arm where Biscuit used to be, hovered a few inches above it, then dropped to his side. "I'm just...I'm so sorry, Talia. For everything."

"Hey. It's okay," I tried to smile. "You have nothing to apologize for. I'm the one who messed up. I didn't make the ink in time. I couldn't finish my tattoo in time. I..." I swallowed, fighting back tears. "I'm the reason we lost Biscuit." My voice cracked. "It's all my fault. All of it."

His head shot up. "What do you mean, you didn't *finish* your tattoo?"

I lifted the cuff of my pants to show him my bloody, weeping tattoo, which would almost certainly become gangrenous since I hadn't had the chance to properly clean it. "My stupid cartridge had just run out of ink when Salen walked in. If I'd had just thirty more seconds...or even better, three more drops of ink—"

Zayn's hand that was holding the bottle of ink started shaking. I knew he desperately wanted to give it to me so I could finish my tattoo and run, but he physically couldn't. He was bound in ways I couldn't even begin to imagine, bound with invisible, unbreakable chains.

...*Wait*. My breath hitched. *Chains?*

My eyes jerked to the front entrance, where my Unchaining Rune had obliterated the locked door handle, then doubled in size. It wouldn't work for his curse, that I knew, but there was something else on that page that might be exactly what I needed...

While keeping my face as smooth as I possibly could, I casually retrieved my phone from my pocket and pulled up the picture I'd taken of the inside of Zayn's grimoire Wednesday morning. Two side-by-side runes stared back at me: one for

Chaining, and the other for Unchaining. After zooming in on the one on the left, I glanced up at Zayn, swallowing tightly. He was staring at the ground with a look of pained concentration on his face. More than likely trying to figure out a way around Salen's command, if I knew him – which I did. Based on her calculated wording, I doubted there was a way to circumvent it. But it was better that he was distracted, so he couldn't see the wheels turning in my own head.

On the front desk, right next to the one-room rat hotel, was a sticky pad and a cup of sharpies. I meandered over there casually, trying to make it look like I was just shuffling off nervous energy. While Zayn started pacing in the corner of the store, muttering to himself, I grabbed a marker and began to sketch, using the picture on my phone as a reference. The rune wasn't terribly complex, but there was a specific order of strokes I had to memorize, just like before.

Salen's front claws were pressed against the inside of the container while she watched me copy the design one line at a time. If a rat could glare menacingly, this one was definitely doing it. But she stayed quiet, and that was good enough for me. Peeking every so often to make sure Zayn wasn't looking my way, I drew and redrew the rune over and over again, making sure I had the order of operations down. Finally, when I was absolutely certain I had it memorized, I held it up and admired my work. *Perfect*, I thought. Then I crumpled up the design and tossed it in the trash with the dozen other discarded sticky notes.

Unfortunately, memorizing the rune was the easy part. Because in order for the rest of my plan to work, I had to bank on a single, miniscule chink in Zayn's otherwise impenetrable armor. And in order to take advantage of said chink, I'd have to power through the many, many chinks in my own, which included, but were by no means limited to: perpetual self-doubt, major insecurity paired with way too much pride, and a fragile ego that made me shrink away from even the slightest hint of rejection.

Except…

My eyes darted back to the pink-eyed rat that was glowering at me from beside my elbow. Somehow, I'd managed to extract magic from an assertive, sexually-confident, and criminally-beautiful succubus. Which meant, alongside the single-use tattoos I'd pilfered, some of those skills now belonged to me. A smile was tugging on my lips. For the first time in a long time, I was filled with a strange and unfamiliar feeling.

I could do this. With her magic, I *knew* I could.

After taking a moment to position the computer screen directly in front of the Tupperware container so the succu-mouse wouldn't be able to witness anything that was about to happen, I slipped a permanent marker in my back pocket after double-checking that it was the odorless variety. For good measure, I reached just behind the cash drawer, where I'd long ago hidden a small, dusty bottle of tequila that a client had gifted me – the same client I got busted doing shots with in the middle of my shift. I snatched it from its long-forgotten hiding place, unscrewed the top, and took a long glug of liquid courage before slamming it back down on the desk.

With a deep, shaky breath, I made my way to the corner of the store where Zayn was pacing, acutely aware that the top third of my corset was still unlaced. My fingers desperately itched to retie the laces but I couldn't afford to feel self-conscious. I couldn't worry about the tangles in my hair or the stains on my clothes. And I certainly couldn't whither or flee at the first sign of rejection.

I stopped two feet away from him.

"Zayn?" I whispered.

He started but didn't lift his eyes from the floor.

"Zayn," I tried again, making my voice as low and husky as I could. "I'm just…so scared. You know, about tonight." Borrowing some of Salen's magically-imbued confidence, I slipped my arms underneath his, then pressed my body against him. Embarrassment colored my cheeks, so I buried my face in his leather vest.

His entire body stiffened. "Talia, what—"

"Please, Zayn," I murmured into his chest. "Would you please just hold me?"

"Talia." He started to gently push me away. "I keep trying to tell you. You're not safe around me."

"Please." I looked up at him with very real tears in my eyes. "Please, just this once. Don't push me away."

He hesitated, his face contorting with effort, then gingerly wrapped his arms around me as though I were made of porcelain. I could feel the bottle of ink pressing into my back. He was still clutching it in his hand, just as Salen had commanded.

Shame and guilt gripped my entire body for what I was about to do, which was no better than anything she'd already done to him. But he had ordered me, begged me, really, to do whatever I needed to do to get that tattoo on his body. And it was time to fulfill my promise. Because now that the ink was firmly in Zayn's possession – which meant it was as good as in Sol's possession – his worst fear had come true. In Zayn's mind, there wouldn't be any counteraction tattoo, our plan was ruined, and all hope was lost. With all of his thoughts shifting to how the hell he was going to get me out of here safely, despite Salen's command not to let me leave, his guard would otherwise be completely down.

I couldn't hesitate. Couldn't second-guess myself.

It's now or never.

I pulled away from Zayn just far enough to look up at him. His eyes were tightly closed, as if he couldn't bear to look at me. "Zayn," I whispered softly, rising to my bare tip-toes. Without waiting for him to respond, I pressed my lips against his. A jolt of electricity from where our mouths met nearly made my knees buckle, but I gripped his vest and instead pulled myself deeper into the kiss.

Zayn's eyes shot open and he staggered backward, breaking my hold on his vest. "What—" his voice cut off sharply as I casually started to untie the rest of the laces on my shirt.

"We have no chance of escaping," I replied as calmly as I could, tapping into my stolen succubus power. The top of my corset was already undone, exposing the upper part of my breasts. So, I started with the laces at the bottom, casually pulling them free one eyelet at a time. "If I try to leave, their compulsion over you will make you kill me. If I stay, Sol and his family will drain me of my blood and then most likely kill you since your services will no longer be needed."

"Talia," Zayn growled, side-stepping away from me and farther into the shop.

I turned and followed him, continuing as though I hadn't been interrupted. "Since I really don't want to die completely pent-up and horny, the least you can do is grant me this. Besides," I added hastily, before he could interject, "if we have any chance at all of getting out of this alive, you'll need to be as strong and clear-headed as possible tonight. Since you're not allowed to go feed on someone, and I'm sure you wouldn't risk inviting anyone else into the danger zone, I'm all you've got."

"It's completely out of the question." He was straining to look anywhere but at my unraveling shirt laces.

I swallowed tightly, ignoring the screaming doubt at the back of my mind, and took another step forward. After pulling the final cord free, my shirt was now completely unlaced, exposing a wide strip of skin from my collarbone to my navel, and the tequila was starting to warm my belly.

"I'm not asking, Zayn."

Before he could say another word, I reached forward and pulled his face to mine, pressing my parted lips against his. His body went completely rigid. The hand that wasn't holding the ink flew up to form a barrier between us, meeting naked flesh as it did. A shudder ripped through both of our bodies as his fingertips raked across my stomach. He tried to take another step back, and I followed, pushing him farther into the store as I clung to him like moss on a bough. As my tongue rolled over his, his hand gripped my waist, torn somewhere between pushing me away and pulling me closer, but I made the decision for him. My hands dropped from the back of his neck and found the row of buttons on the front of his vest, tearing them apart one by one.

"Goddammit, Talia," he growled into my mouth, but he didn't try to pull away. Instead, his hand was frozen, digging into the curve of my waist as though stuck by magic.

Thanks, Salen, I thought wryly.

I tore his shirt open and yanked it off of him, pausing to admire the gorgeous dips and planes of his deeply chiseled abs. He too was staring at my exposed torso, where I'm sure he was provided with more than a glimpse of my bare breasts. His eyes, full of fire and arousal, flew to mine while his stubborn mouth was still opening to protest. Without thinking, I draped my arms around his neck, pressing my naked stomach and breasts against the heat of his skin. With a helpless moan, his mouth dipped to meet mine as my fingers entwined in his thick hair, pulling him deeper into the kiss. He groaned against my mouth, setting my entire body aflame. One hand still clutching the beaker of ink like a live grenade, his free hand slid into the untied opening of my shirt and around my back. I shuddered as his fingertips brushed the side of my breast, surrendering to his forceful embrace.

I didn't feel drained the way I had after trying to save Zayn from the fachan. I felt powerful and revitalized, electrified from head to toe as our bodies twisted and tangled. Zayn, too, was growing stronger by the second. His grip on me strengthened, his cheeks flushed with vigor, and his eyes burned into mine like kryptonite – fitting, since this man's intoxicating power over me had become my greatest weakness.

We stumbled into the shop the way we'd stumbled into his home two years ago, clawing at one another like starved animals, until we reached my tattoo chair. With all my strength, I pushed him into the chair and immediately climbed on top to straddle him. He let out a surprised gasp as I ran my fingers across his chest and shoulders, leaving faint red streaks across his bronzed skin. The moment his lips parted, I dropped my head, crushing my lips against his. A husky, hungry growl rolled from his chest as I ground my pelvis against the hardness of his arousal, all the way up and back down again until we were both gasping with pleasure.

"Talia, you have to stop," he moaned against my mouth, though he made no move to make me.

I responded by taking his lower lip between my teeth and sucking on it until the bulge in his pants became a steel rod.

He let out a curse as his fingertips dragged down my bare back.

Drunk with desire and stolen confidence, my thoughts drifted to all the places of his body that I'd long believed were forbidden to me. I imagined myself sliding between his legs to peel away the layers of clothing that separated his body from mine. I yearned to touch and caress every single one of those forbidden places, to run my tongue across his skin and taste every inch of his body, as he'd once tasted mine. To bring that body to the very edge, only to climb atop his arousal at the last moment and take him deep inside of me until… until…

No.

The booming thought rang out in my mind, eradicating all other thoughts of lust and longing. I was here for one reason, and one reason only.

And that reason was right where he needed to be.

With one hand roughly entwined in his hair, my other hand snaked to my back pocket to withdraw the marker. In doing so, my back arched and my breasts pressed against his chest. The moment my erect nipples dragged across his, a hot rush of arousal throbbed between my legs, making me feel faint with desire. I don't know how I managed to keep that marker in my trembling fingers, but somehow, I did.

Zayn knotted his fingers into my ponytail, tilting my mouth deeper into his. A low, shuddering moan erupted from my throat as his tongue danced and swirled over mine. He thrust his erection against me, and even between two layers of clothes, I could feel the ridges of his arousal rubbing between my legs. I arched my back and cried out as his mouth found my breast. Whimpering from the waves of pleasure coursing throughout my entire body, I took the opportunity to pop the lid off with my thumbnail and bring the tip of the marker to the back of the chair, just above his shoulder. His tongue lapped and traced the aching peaks of my breast, which made my eyes blur with euphoric tears. I literally had to bite down on my lower lip to bring myself back from the brink

Focus, goddammit!

With a shaking hand, I began to draw the rune on the vinyl, one hard-fought line at a time. I just about dropped the marker when his teeth grazed my stiff nipple, and I nearly came right then. Sensing that, he thrust his erection even harder against the junction of my thighs, making me cry out in rapturous bliss. He wanted me to come. Was doing everything he could to bring me to climax right there on his lap.

Tears and stars swam in front of my eyes, but I persisted on drawing that godforsaken rune, even as Zayn's fingertips dug into my hip and he turned his attention to my other, even more sensitive, breast. Goosebumps erupted down my spine, and I let out a whimpering moan as he tugged and sucked on my right nipple, sending a fresh torrent of arousal straight to my already-drenched panties.

In the battleground of Talia's Impending Orgasm – whereby Zayn was doing everything he could to bring me to it, and I was desperately fighting it – he was very clearly in the lead.

Thank God I only had one more line to go.

Quivering with gritted teeth and a clenched fist, I finished the rune, letting the marker drop to the floor the moment I was done. For this spell, it didn't matter if the lines were shaky. All that mattered was that they were all touching, and I triple-checked that they were.

Zayn's free hand gripped the back of my head, bringing my mouth back to his. His taste was so intoxicating, I felt lightheaded. When his tongue slid across mine, I caved against his chest, moaning into his mouth. But I couldn't give in to the ecstasy. I was so close to finishing this. So close to saving him.

And so, *so* damn close to climaxing, which would obliterate any trace of intelligence and logic my mind was desperately clinging to.

With the determination and willpower of a reformed alcoholic at a family reunion, I brought my thumb to the back of my earring post and pressed it until I felt it pierce the skin. Then I begrudgingly pulled away from our kiss and shifted my body, feeling the entire length of Zayn's arousal sliding between my thighs as I did, and ducked beneath his ear to leave a trail of kisses against the side of his neck. He gasped as my tongue skimmed the edge of his jaw, which turned into a rumbling moan as I gently caught his earlobe between my teeth.

Once his attention was completely captured, I pressed my bloody thumb against the symbol on the back of the chair until it glowed with power. My power.

"I'm so sorry," I whispered. My lips swept across his forehead to rest in a trembling kiss.

Then I roughly pinned his shoulder to the rune.

"What the—" Zayn started to choke out.

The Chaining Rune beneath his shoulder hummed with electricity, trapping his entire body against the chair as though someone had coated the backs of his arms and legs with glue. He stared at me in shock as I cleared my throat and awkwardly scrambled to my feet – even though every inch of distance I put between us physically hurt. I've heard stories about withdrawals, and I was pretty sure my body was already having them.

After taking a moment to straighten my pants and lace up the front of my shirt, I turned to give him a sheepish look…then immediately took a frightened step backward. His beautiful green eyes had gone ruby red, and the look he was giving me was one of pure venom. Every muscle in his body was straining against the Chaining Rune – which meant Sol's compulsion had also been triggered. I didn't know how much time I had. I didn't even fully understand the extent or limits of the hasty rune I'd managed to cast. All I knew is that I needed to get that ink into his exposed skin – fast.

"I really am sorry," I murmured.

I reached down to pry his fingers from the ink bottle, one at a time. The way he was gripping it, it felt like I was trying to bend back metal. After finally wrestling it free, I held the ink an arm's length away as I tiredly leaned against the chair.

"Okay," I panted, "we're almost there. Zayn, if you can hear me in there, I'm just gonna grab my tattoo machine and then we'll get this tattoo on you ASAP…okay?"

Save for a brief flicker in his crimson eyes, his face remained completely impassive.

Turning to go, I shivered…and then let out a startled cry as one of Zayn's arms jerked free from its binding. Before I could react, his fingers had closed around my neck.

"Zayn," I croaked. "Don't—!" My free hand flew to my throat. I tugged and clawed at his fingers, but they were like an iron vice, digging into my trachea and cutting off my air.

His eyes flickered from scarlet to jade. "Please, Talia," he choked out, his insanely powerful grip pressing down on my windpipe. "Please, I'm begging you. Let go of the ink."

Spots swam in front of my eyes, but I wouldn't let go. I couldn't. I tried to hold the bottle as far away from him as I could, but he was pulling me closer and closer. Just visible above his shoulder, the Chaining Rune was still glowing green – save for one dim line, which had somehow gotten smudged.

I gave up on trying to tear his hand away and instead wedged my palm against his bare chest. With all my strength, I pushed myself away from him, but his grip was unyielding. Tears filled my eyes as I unsuccessfully gasped for air. It was like drowning all over again. Except, this time, my life wasn't the only one hanging in the balance. And there would be no siren waiting to rescue me.

Zayn panted hoarsely. "Please, Talia! I'm not worth—"

He abruptly cut off as his irises shifted back to red and his grasp on my throat tightened, crushing my windpipe.

The edges of my vision were turning to black. "*We…are…worth it,*" I rasped.

A sharp rap made my bulging eyes jerk to the front door, where a blurry, yet familiar, outline was frantically banging on the glass. Zayn's grip loosened slightly, allowing me to suck a wheezing mouthful of oxygen back into my lungs. I squinted, then let out an astonished squeak as the short, round figure came into focus.

My *mother* was standing outside, banging both hands on the glass, her wide eyes doubling and then tripling in size as she gaped at us through the window. At my bright gold visage. At my shirtless, demon-eyed employer, who was magically pinned to the chair save for his outstretched hand, which just happened to be clenching my windpipe.

"Mom!" I tried to croak. "It's not what it—"

She opened her mouth to suck in the deep breath that would fuel her imminent verbal assault while I braced myself against the onslaught of ranting and raving that I expected to follow. But nothing prepared me for what happened next.

A high-pitched, ear-splitting scream tore from my mother's throat like a train whistle, rising in pitch until it was almost unbearably shrill. And then the proverbial locomotive screeched to a metal-ripping halt, producing a strident, nerve-scraping howl like nothing I'd ever heard before…

Except…

I *had* heard that sound before.

The moment that realization hit me like a crate of lead ingots, every window in the shop shattered into a million pieces, sending an explosion of glass shards ricocheting throughout the front of the store as though a nuclear bomb had gone off on the sidewalk. The bottle of tequila sitting on the desk burst open as though shot by an invisible bullet. The Tupperware container splintered down the middle and a frantic white rat went scurrying for its life. And the glass bottle I was gripping in my hand detonated like an ink grenade, casting a torrent of milky-white delphinium ink splattering all over the floor.

XXIII.
Purple Banshee's Majesty

"Get away from my daughter!" my mom screamed through the windowless front door. The air in front of her mouth shimmered and surged like a shock wave, culminating into a sonic boom that slammed into Zayn's chest with the force of an invisible battering ram. He cried out in pain, his entire body jerking and spasming, but the Chaining Rune held him to the chair.

"Zayn!" I croaked.

His scarlet eyes flickered shut and his head slumped forward. The moment his hand fell from my throat, I sucked in a sharp mouthful of air that immediately turned into a violent coughing fit.

"Talia!" my mother cried out while attempting to hoist herself through the blown-out entrance and over the couch. Her curly, bottle-blonde hair was in disarray, and the rest of her outfit – which was perfectly coordinated from her purple pumps to her purple manicured nails – was uncharacteristically rumpled, as though she'd rolled out of bed and right into the car. "What the hell is going on? Are you okay? Did he hurt you?"

I managed a quick shake of my head as I cautiously slipped two fingers against the side of Zayn's throat. He had a pulse, though it was going a mile a minute. "What the hell just happened?" I wheezed. My own erratic heartbeat was thundering in my ears as I looked around the shop in confused horror.

"You tell me!" she shot back.

"No, *you* tell *me!*"

She had just finished clambering over the top of the couch, straddling the cushions like a drunk sorority girl atop a mechanical bull, when Roy – *Roy*, my inauspicious client with the magical butt-serpent – popped his bandana-clad head through the adjacent glass-less window.

"Uhh… Did I catch you guys at a bad time?" he asked, climbing the rest of the way through. He surveyed the front of the shop with a low whistle while kicking aside shards of broken glass with a steel-toed boot. "I was on my way here, hopin' to catch you before you opened, when I heard what sounded like a herd of cats going through a blender!"

"Oh my God," I croaked, raking my hands down my face. This was it. This was the end. The City of Miami was going to cart me off to a loony bin and throw away the key, because there was no way in hell I would ever be able to explain this.

As if to validate those concerns, my mother let out another high-pitched shriek – her usual variety, not the new and terrifying sonic boom kind – and jumped back on the couch. My head shot up just in time to see Salen zig-zagging across the floor, trying to find a clear path to the exit among the broken rubble and stomping shoes.

"Stop that rat!" I cried out hoarsely, knowing it was too late.

"Don't worry, I got it!" Roy jumped between the shrill, squealing creature and the rodent. "Monty, come!"

My mother's screams rose to an absurd crescendo as a black cobra tumbled out of the back of Roy's leather vest, shook out its flattened hood, and let out a menacing hiss.

"No, wait!" I shouted, jumping to my feet. "Not like that!"

Fangs bared, the snake reared its head, then launched itself at the screeching rodent like a coiled spring.

"Wait!" I yelped, skidding to a barefoot stop at the edge of a field of broken glass.

One blink of the eye and two cobra bites later, Salen was gone.

My hands flew to my mouth, which had tumbled open in horrified revulsion.

"Atta boy, Monty!" Roy whooped, then rounded on my mother, who was quivering on top of the couch. "You saw that too, right? I ain't crazy?"

"Oy gevalt!" she wailed at the sky. "What is this? Am I dead?!"

With the sea of coffee in my stomach churning like an ocean tempest, I staggered over to the cobra, doing my barefooted best to skitter around the shattered windows.

"Talia, what the hell are you doing?!" my mother shrieked. "Get away from that thing!"

"Open your mouth," I demanded as I knelt beside the snake. "Monty" obliged, and I shone my phone's flashlight down the long, dark tunnel of his throat.

There were no rats to be found.

"Shit," I muttered, rising to my feet. I couldn't say I felt bad, exactly, not after learning the full extent of what Salen

had been doing to Zayn for so long – and even worse, what she had been taking from him. But I certainly wouldn't wish that kind of ending on anyone. Not even her.

I guess that's what you get for legalizing blood incarnates, I sighed as I apprehensively regarded Roy's "pet." Completely oblivious to the murder he'd just committed, he was looking up at me with big, glowing eyes as red as the Ruby ink I'd deposited into Roy's backside.

I let out a long sigh. "Go home, buddy."

Eliciting a flash of light – and a high-pitched yelp from Roy – the cobra returned to his two-dimensional home on Roy's backside.

"Where did it go?!" my mother demanded, swiveling her head from side to side.

Roy peered over his shoulder, lifted up the back of his vest, and let out a gasp. "Well, I'll be damned! Monty Python only listens to me 'bout half the time, and he certainly don't listen to a damn thing my wife says! What's your secret, Talia?" As he turned to look at me, a frown was beginning to unfurl beneath his scruffy beard. "Hey, have you been hittin' the tanning beds or something?"

Head reeling, I shuffled back into the shop, checked Zayn's still-galloping pulse, and then slumped down on the far edge of the chair, well out of his reach. How much time did I have before he woke up? And who would I have to answer to when he finally did – my Zayn, or Sol's?

As I surveyed the delphinium ink pooling on the floor in front of me, contaminated with broken glass and bits of dirt, angry tears swam in my vision. There was no way it would work now, not unless my end goal was to give both of us blood-poisoning.

"Talia Judith Kestenbaum, I want answers and I want them *now!*" Using Roy's offered hand for support, Mom stepped off the couch and made her way toward the tattoo chair I was sharing with my unconscious boss. With every step, her eyes grew wider, so much so that I began to wonder if they might fall out of her face.

"What the hell happened to your skin?" she demanded, her expression one of twisted horror.

"Oh...that." My shoulders slumped even further. "That would be the gold blood."

"Not that," she snapped, jabbing a manicured finger at the faint tattoos on my arms. "What the hell are *those?*"

"They're just temporary!" I started to groan, then immediately shook my head in stunned disbelief. "Hang on a second. Let me get this straight – I'm over here glowing like a freaking jack o' lantern, and it's the *tattoos* that are causing you concern?"

Her mouth tumbled open.

"Furthermore," I barreled on with increasing belligerence, "would you mind telling me what the *hell* just happened? Or are we just going to gloss over the fact that the mere sound of your voice just shattered every window in my store and *knocked my boss unconscious?"*

"Hmph. Serves him right for touching you," my mother sniffed primly. "And I was able to break the glass for the same reason your blood is glowing. Though I would certainly love to know *why* it's suddenly glowing since your father and I spent half our retirement savings on that *farkakteh* locket! *Feh!"* She threw her hands up in frustration.

I stared at her as though one or both of us had completely lost our minds. "What. The. *Hell.* Are you talking about?"

She waved a dismissive hand in the air. "I'll tell you over dinner."

"Hey, can I come too?" Roy interjected. "'Cause I got a lotta questions myself," He shuffled around his pocket, then pulled out a crumpled piece of paper. "My wife even sent me with a list to make sure I didn't forget any!"

My mother shrugged. "Do you like brisket?"

"Now just hang on a minute!"

I tried to jump to my feet, but the tiny woman pressed a surprisingly-firm hand against my shoulder. "I'm not answering a single question until you tell me what the hell that man was just doing to you."

"It wasn't what it looked like," I muttered, averting my eyes as I leaned forward to press the back of my hand against his glistening forehead. It was surprisingly warm, considering how cold and clammy he'd felt when he first returned from the Fae Realm.

"Not what it looked like," she rolled her eyes. "Then why the hell is he shirtless? And speaking of shirts, what the hell are you wearing?" Her eyes narrowed at my corset. "Is this some sort of weird new BDSM *mishegas* you haven't told me about?"

"Mom, no!" I cast a mortified glance in Roy's direction, who was thankfully preoccupied with scribbling a note into his wife's honey-do list of magical tattoo maintenance. "Look, can you just tell me how long he's going to be out?"

"Forever, if he knows what's good for him!" she retorted. "It's been a long time since I lost my temper like that. He's lucky he's not dead!"

"Yeah, but you still haven't told me how you—"

"Later." My mother's eyes flashed with fire and brimstone, signifying that that was the end of it.

"Fine!" I snapped, then rubbed the skin of my throat tenderly. "Look, Zayn would never intentionally hurt me. He's...he's cursed, for lack of a better word. And the only way to break the curse is – *was* – with that ink." I pointed to the white puddle on the ground. "Now that it's gone..." I shook my head in disbelief as I heard myself say the words out loud. "I have no way to break the curse."

"Aw, now see, that's too bad," Roy stuffed away his list and crossed his beefy arms over his vest. The intricate sleeve tattoo I'd given him earlier in the year flexed beneath the fluorescent lights. "My ex-brother-in-law had Crohn's Disease. You wanna talk about a curse, I tell you what – that man was cursed to a miserable life on the toilet."

"Oh, poor thing," my mother tsked. "My neighbor has the same problem whenever she eats dairy…"

As the two of them nattered on about various intestinal ailments, my eyes traced the colorful design on his arm. It was one of my tattoos that I'd been particularly proud of, featuring a rich scarlet and violet sunset that started at his shoulder, then faded to sun-streaked gold and vermillion before meeting a frothy indigo ocean at his elbow. There were distant palms on the beach in the background of his forearm, whose fronds fluttered in an imaginary breeze. And there, sitting in the foreground, was a busty, topless mermaid combing her blonde hair with long, slender fingers. Seeing her stirred something in the back of my mind. Something faint and distant and shrouded by a perpetual lack of sleep.

The memory of a pair of bottomless silver eyes made me gasp out loud.

The answer has been in your pocket the whole time.

"Oh my God," I whispered, then jumped to my feet. "Oh my God!"

"Would you please stop saying the 'G' word like that?" my mom snapped as though she hadn't been clucking it herself all morning.

"Hey, Roy?" I piped up shrilly, "Would you please give us a minute…alone?"

"Yeah, sure," he shrugged. "There's a hardware store just down the block. I'll head over and get some plywood to patch up these busted windows of yours. The bars'll be open soon, so I expect you'll be gettin' a lot of the hair-of-the-dog crowd comin' round to see what happened."

"Thank you," I breathed. "I'll pay you back, I promise."

"Nah," he grinned. "I still owe you money for the killer tattoo you gave me – literally! Isn't that right, Monty?" he murmured lovingly over his shoulder before moving the couch away from the front door and sauntering out of the shop.

"...Right," I mumbled. Between his runaway snake tattoo, my mother's cavalier attitude about weaponized screams and magic blood, and Salen's, uh, untimely swallowing... It was all just too much.

But all of that, even the laundry list of questions I had for my mother, would have to be dealt with later.

"I'll be right back," I shouted to my mom as I darted out of the shop and into Zayn's office. Excitement and dread welled in my chest as I pulled open the drawer with Biscuit's ashes.

There, sitting beside them, was the bottle of black kraken ink. My hands trembled as I carefully lifted it from the drawer. I remembered now why the Counteraction Rune had looked so familiar to me when I first saw it. It was the same complex tattoo the siren had carved into her skin moments after telling me she needed my blood and the kraken ink to break whatever "curse" had been placed on her. I didn't know if the Dominion Rune on Zayn's body could truly be considered a curse, whether this ink had any chance at all of working or becoming yet another failure on the long and growing list of Talia-Related Screw-ups... But I knew I had to try.

When I returned to the front of the store a few minutes later, I found Zayn beginning to stir and my mother sweeping up the glass while shooting him the occasional scathing look. I gently placed the kraken ink and a charged tattoo gun on the stand, then took a moment to fix the smudged line on the Chaining Rune. That should keep both of his arms bound...I hoped.

As I double-checked his shoulder to make sure it was in direct contact with the adjusted rune, a muscle in his jaw flexed.

Hurriedly, I began sanitizing my tools and the work station.

"What are you doing?" my mother asked suspiciously.

I didn't look up from my work. "I think I know how to help him, but I need you to give us a minute."

She snorted. "Like I'm going to leave you alone with that man. He's lucky I haven't called the police."

"Mom, listen to me. I fixed the rune that's currently trapping him in his chair—"

"Rune?" my mother stopped sweeping. "What do you know about runes?"

"I should ask you the same thing!" I snapped as I unpeeled a sterilized liner needle for fine detail work. "Suffice it to say, Zayn won't be able to lift a finger, let alone try to hurt me. If – *when* – this Counteraction Rune lifts his curse, you'll see what a kind and gentle person he is."

Well, to everyone other than a handful of fachans and glaistigs, I conceded to myself. But that was neither here nor there.

By now, Mom was gripping the broom with two white-knuckled fists. "Is that what you've been doing here? Messing around with runes and magic?"

"No," I replied, pulling on a nitrile glove. "Up until three days ago, I had no idea any of that stuff even existed. *You*, on the other hand, seem to know a lot about the subject. Of course, you could just continue to deny it, since you've apparently been lying to me my entire life."

I expected her to puff up and get defensive like she usually did when I copped an attitude. Instead, she turned to the ground and nodded. "I'm sorry for that, Talia. I really am."

"Well, that makes everything all better," I replied drily. "Now, would you *please* give us a minute and stand watch outside? Businesses are going to be open soon, and I can't have people sticking their heads in here while I'm trying to concentrate."

"Talia—" she started.

"Mom, please! Just trust me on this, okay? This man…" I swallowed, trying to find the right words. "To say he's been through hell and back wouldn't even begin to cover the pain he's lived through. Yet somehow, despite everything, he's still the most selfless, generous, kindhearted person I've ever met. If I don't help him…" I let the words trail off, unable to say them out loud.

Zayn's eyelids fluttered as he let out a soft groan.

Mom's narrowed eyes lingered on him for a long moment, as though she were thumbing through her mental Rolodex of a thousand-and-one ways to win an argument. Just as I was gearing up for another exhausting round of back and forth, she…nodded.

"I can't predict when people will die, certainly not like your *bubbe* could, but I do know when bad things are about to happen." She gave me a wistful smile. "That's why I'm always so anxious all the time. Having a constant feeling of dread and despair about all of the bad things that can and will happen…well, it can do that to a person over time. But now that I'm here and you're close, I know you'll be okay for the time being." She nodded to the street outside. "It's the rest of the *meshugge* world I need to keep my eye on."

By the time she finished, it took me a few tries to unglue my tongue from the roof of my mouth. "*Bubbe* was a banshee? Does that mean you're a…?"

"Not like the kind you're probably thinking of," she smiled. "But yes, of a sort."

"But how—"

"*That,*" she interjected, "is a long story that needs a whole lotta Manischewitz to tell. Man with a Cobra Tattoo will be back soon, so whatever you need to do to your boyfriend, do it now."

"He's not—"

"Whatever he is, just be safe. And keep it PG, if you don't mind." She raised a scandalous eyebrow at Zayn's half-naked state. "I will only say this once: If he touches you again – curse or no – I will break his arms and legs."

She shot him one more dirty look, then gave my hand a reassuring squeeze before she turned to go.

As I watched her leave, a strange feeling was welling up in my throat. All this time, I'd just assumed I'd inherited my gold blood from my father. It didn't even cross my mind that my neurotic, anxious, loud-mouthed, overly-protective Jewish mother had fae magic running through her veins. But seeing her march outside to yell and shake her broom at all of the potential onlookers both near and far, it all made perfect sense. As far back as I could remember, whether she was shrieking with laughter, fury, or just her usual excitement, my *chutzpahdik* mother had always screamed like a banshee. Honestly, what Jewish mother didn't? The only real difference between yesterday and today was the knowledge that she actually was one. Or at least related to one.

Oy, I sighed in resignation. *We're gonna need a lot more than a bottle of Manischewitz to make it through tonight's dinner.*

XXIV.
RUBIES AND EMERALDS

Despite the proverbial bombshell my mom had just dropped on me, as well as the literal one she'd unleashed on our store, I did my best to focus on the here and now as I sat beside Zayn. I emptied the last of the isopropyl alcohol onto a cotton ball and gently rubbed the base of his forearm, just above Biscuit's empty frame.

"I'm so sorry, little buddy," I whispered, brushing my fingers across the pale, pink scars that marked his grave. "I wish I could have thanked you for saving my life."

"Talia..." Zayn muttered under his breath. His eyes were squeezed shut, as though he were straining against something. Whether it was the Chaining Rune or himself, I couldn't be sure.

"I'm right here."

I lowered myself on one knee beside the chair, since his arm was all but glued to the vinyl. Clutching the grimoire page in my left hand, I used a surgical marker to sketch out the complicated symbol as carefully as I could, checking each line at least three times. Zayn began to stir at my touch, but the Chaining Rune kept him from moving.

What felt like hours later, when I was absolutely certain the symbol was flawless, I carefully set the page aside and uncorked the kraken ink. After only a moment's hesitation, I picked up the tattoo gun, closed my eyes, and pressed the needle deep into my fingertip. Then, just as the siren had done, I squeezed a few drops of blood into the vial of ink. The Department of Health and Safety would have had me fired on the spot, but this was blood magic, and I wasn't going to take any chances.

I poured about half of the vial into the ink cartridge, inserted it into the tattoo gun, and pressed the power button. A small, shimmering black bead was forming at the tip of the needle, ready to be applied, but I found myself hesitating. I'd never given Zayn a tattoo before since he'd always insisted on doing them himself. Now, of course, I knew why that was. But that didn't mean I wasn't terrified to make a mess of this, the first and most important tattoo I would ever give him.

Quit it, a voice in my head chided. *Don't psych yourself out – this is just another tattoo for another client.*

With that, I took a deep breath and pressed the needle into his skin.

Zayn's eyes popped open before I'd even finished the first circle, his irises glowing as red as an enchanted cobra's. He ground his teeth and tensed every muscle to try and jerk free, but the binding held – much to my relief and his silent, seething fury.

"Hey, it's going to be okay," I murmured.

He shot me a dirty look before his gaze fell upon the half-emptied bottle of ink. "What is that?" he hissed in a voice that didn't sound at all like his.

"Kraken ink."

His ruby eyes flashed and the vein in his temple bulged. "Get that away from me!"

"I can't do that," I replied, feeling a sharp stab of guilt as I did. "But if this works, it will be the last time someone touches your body against your will, I promise you that."

"Get off of me or I'll kill you!"

"That seems a little harsh," I muttered, doing my best to concentrate. "Still, I really am sorry for this."

"You should be sorry." His lips curled into a vicious grin. "Because even if I don't kill you for this, he will."

"Well, luckily for me, that's Future Talia's problem," I smiled tightly, head bowed over his arm. "Present Talia has a tattoo to finish, if you don't mind."

Doing my best to ignore the venom and ire pouring from his inhuman eyes, I continued to deposit the glittering kraken ink into his skin one centimeter at a time, pausing only when I needed to wipe away excess ink or get a better grip on him. His arm was tensed and shaking beneath my hand, but it was no worse than a regular, unbound client trying to squirm away from my needle. And besides, I had been trained by the best Runemaster in two realms. It took more than a possessed incubus to frazzle me, even if the two were one and the same.

After about twenty minutes, the rune began to take shape, a series of complex circles and overlapping squares – exactly like the tattoo the siren had cut into her own skin, I was sure of it. Zany – as I'd dubbed Evil Brainwashed Zayn – continued to fight and strain against the Chaining Rune, hurling threats at me the whole time, but I did my best to ignore him. Meanwhile, my mom was still sweeping and yelling at people outside, when she wasn't casting anxious glances into the shop every so often. Somewhere around the fourth circle, Roy returned from the hardware store. Which meant, in addition to trying to ignore Zany's many grievances and threats, I also had to tune out the obnoxious sounds of hammering – as well as my mother's kibbitzing about the way he was hammering – as Roy dutifully began nailing plywood over the broken windows.

And of course, all of this was happening as I painstakingly crafted one of the most complicated designs I'd ever done. Seriously. Those big, detailed, colorful sleeve tattoos? Compared to this, they're a piece of cake. You sketch it all out, throw on some color, make a mistake, go over it with fresh ink and just cover it up – kind of like painting with acrylics. As Bob Ross said, "There are no mistakes, just happy accidents." But once you start getting into perfectly straight, individual lines – or worse, perfectly round circles – you're treading into any tattoo artist's living nightmare. Paired with the immense responsibility of creating home-brewed magical ink that could kill you if you heated it for literally one second too long, and I finally understood why Runemasters like Zayn were in such outrageous demand.

Thank God, my peculiar taste in music – which also happened to feature a lot of unleashed rage, banging, and screaming – had prepared me for that morning's cacophony. Expertly tuning out all other external stimuli, I concentrated on the Counteraction Rune with steely, single-minded focus. Line after line, circle after circle, the marker had become almost completely covered in kraken ink, its edges as clean and crisp as a laser etching.

It wasn't until I heard the sirens in the distance that my concentration began to waver. I chewed on my lip, waiting – praying, really – for them to fade, but they kept growing louder and louder until red and blue lights were flashing against the back wall.

"Shit," I muttered, forfeiting a precious second of attention to glance outside, where a police car had just pulled up. Two officers came striding out, slamming their doors behind them.

"Good morning, ma'am," one of them said, tipping his hat to my mom. "We received reports about screams coming from this area." His eyes swept the floor, where tiny fragments of glass still glittered in the morning sunlight. "Uh, is this your establishment?"

"Nope," Roy grunted as he hefted a piece of plywood against the window. "Just helpin' out!"

"Okay…? Well, can you tell us what exactly happened here?"

"Oh, well, it was the strangest thing," my mother chuckled nervously. "You see, my daughter likes listening to this terrible death metal music – you know, the real scream-y kind…"

I let their voices fade out as I returned to my assiduous work, not daring to pick up the pace, but not willing to waste another precious moment, either. If anyone could charm a pair of Miami cops into eating out of her hand, it was my mother.

"Let me go," Zayn said suddenly, nearly making me jump. His voice sounded much calmer than it had a few minutes ago.

When I casually looked up at him, I nearly dropped the tattoo gun. His eyes were glinting like rubies caught in a ray of light, and his face, already achingly-beautiful, literally sucked the air from my lungs. The fluorescent lights had dimmed around his silhouette, as though all light was emanating directly from him. He was so radiant, so breathtaking, I almost couldn't bear to look directly at him. But when I tried to pull my eyes away from his face, they only made it as far as his shirtless body. There, my thoughts became ensnared in the carved perfection of his well-developed pectoral muscles, which flexed above perfectly chiseled, six-pack abs and terminated in a lean, muscular V-shaped arrow... One that pointed to the substantial bulge in his tight, dark-washed jeans.

"Talia," he whispered, his sultry voice dripping down my spine like warmed honey. "Please. Let me go, sweetness. I would never hurt you."

"You w-wouldn't?" I stammered, once more lost in those crimson red eyes, so beautiful and hypnotizing as they bored into mine.

"Of course not," he purred, licking his lips. "Come, little one. We can finish all this later. For now, let's lock ourselves in my office so we can pick up where we left off before you bound me to this chair."

My jaw dropped. "Come again?"

"Exactly." A sinful smile curved the edges of his lips. "I want to lick that deliciously sweet rosebud of yours until beads of sweat and ecstasy drip between your thighs like hot nectar. I'll make you climax again and again, until you beg me to stop."

A wheezy gasp barely escaped my throat.

"After that, I'll make love to you all day long, tending to every inch of your body in a way you've never been pleasured before. Only when you collapse with bliss will I finally allow you to sleep, wrapped safely in my arms...until I wake you for more." His eyes flashed wickedly.

The tattoo gun slipped from my hands and clattered to the floor, making me jump.

Glamour, I realized with a mortified start. *He's using his glamour on me.*

I swallowed hard, forcing oxygen back into my lungs and blood back toward my brain. This was the predator that Zayn had been warning me about, the beguiling creature that fed on its victims wantonly and without remorse. This was the side of Zayn that he loathed. The side of him that he was ashamed of, that he spent his life running from. The dark, hidden side of him he never wanted me to see.

"…So you're saying it was your daughter's death metal music that made all the windows break into pieces?" one of the officers was saying outside, every syllable infused with incredulity.

"If an opera singer can shatter glass, why can't Black Sabbath?" my mom retorted.

Avoiding Zayn's piercing gaze by dropping my own to the ground, I scooped up the fallen tattoo machine, re-sanitized the needle, and brought it back to his arm. My tongue had gone dry and my panties were, embarrassingly, soaking wet. I felt positively faint from all the blood gushing to other parts of my body thanks to Zayn's consummate powers of seduction.

But I wouldn't give in.

Pressing the power button, I did my best to focus on the low hum of the machine, drowning out everything else – my irresistible, hijacked incubus, the police officers just outside the shop, and my mother's impressive recollection of a music genre I knew she absolutely despised.

"I know what you're doing," I finally spoke up, directing my comment to the rune on his arm so I wouldn't have to look in his eyes.

"I'm not 'doing' anything except telling you the truth," he replied in a velvety smooth voice. "I want you, Talia. And I know you feel the same way about me. For two years, I've felt the sexual energy you exude every time you look my way. I can taste your desire for me in every breath you exhale. Let me go, please, and I swear to you, I'll drop the pious, masochistic act and give you everything you could ever hope for. Everything. As often as you want it. Whenever you want it."

"Because all I care about are your looks, right?" I muttered through gritted teeth, concentrating on getting the final, largest circle as perfect as possible. "I've stuck around this long because I just want to bone you, and nothing else."

"What else am I good for?"

I paused, lifting the needle from his skin, and forced myself to look up. "You truly believe that, don't you?"

He would have shrugged if he could. "I am a bastard son, born from an illicit affair. My mother's husband would have slit my throat if she hadn't begged him not to, and even then, every time she bothered to look at me, I felt her immense shame." Zayn's eyes flickered for the briefest moment, betraying a shadow of green. "I feed and prey on the sexual energy of all who lust after me. Like the demon who spawned me, it is what I was made to do. It is all I was made to do."

I could feel my vision blurring. "Oh, Zayn," I whispered. "I had no idea."

"I am but a slave to the sexual beast that lives inside me." His eyes once more glinted with crimson wickedness. "Come. Let me put that beast inside of *you*. We'll bask in the pleasure I've been denying us both for so long."

"Ma'am, Miami PD was already called to this address earlier in the week," one of the officer's voices wafted from the sidewalk outside. "So, I'm asking you for the last time. Where is the owner?"

"Um, well, he's just a little busy at the moment," my mother was stammering. "Could you maybe come back later? Like, say, tomorrow?"

"Ma'am—"

"Okay, okay, I'll call him! Oy, stop hocking my *tchynik*!" my mother held up her hands defensively. "But before I do anything, I have to tell you the hilarious story my rabbi told me the other day. Okay, so, there's this Japanese businessman named Hiroto—"

One of the officer's radios chirped. "Okay, if you could just step aside, ma'am, we're going to take a look around the store."

"I don't see a warrant in either of your hands!" Roy retorted.

"That's for a house, sir."

Focus, Talia!

I blinked away the tears in my eyes furiously, forbidding my vision to blur. Zayn didn't need my pity. He needed this rune. And fast.

"So, what do you say?" he murmured in that stupid, seductive voice, completely ignoring the commotion outside. "Shall we abandon this silly endeavor for something a little more…edifying?"

By then, I'd finally come to the last line of the rune. As I hovered the needle above his skin, my eyes lifted to meet his. "You are so much more than what you've been made to believe. I hope, deep down, that you know that."

His eyes narrowed imperceptibly.

"No matter what happens next," I continued, "I want you to know, it was all worth it. *You* were worth it. And if this doesn't work, you have my word. I will find a way to free you."

Zayn opened his mouth to speak, but the only sound he made was a ragged gasp as I connected the final line to the first, completing the rune.

Hurriedly tossing aside both gun and glove, I took his hand in both of mine and held it with bated breath. Several angry voices were on the rise just outside, but I remained as frozen as a statue, waiting for the rune to burst to life. Waiting for Zayn's eyes to return to that beautiful, verdant green.

Instead, his face contorted with pain and his back arched against the Chaining Rune. Every muscle in his body spasmed as though he'd been electrocuted and his hand was clenching mine so tightly, I worried my fingers might break.

Still, I refused to let go.

"Zayn," I tried to whisper, but my voice stuck. He cried out in silent pain, unable to move or scream. With a sob, I flung my body on top of his, pressing my face against his chest, where his heart was thrumming like a jet engine. His body had become so rigid, it felt like I was embracing a bronze statue. "I'm sorry – I'm so sorry," I quietly wept.

"Is there a problem in there?" one of the officers called into the store as his partner radioed nearby officers for backup.

"There's no problem!" I cried out. "No need for backup, either! I'll...I'll be right there!"

I knew I needed to get outside before tensions between the cops and my mother spiraled even further. But I couldn't make myself leave Zayn. I clung to him like a blanket as a series of violent spasms gripped his body and a fresh sheen of sweat broke across his forehead, which burned feverishly hot.

The ink, I realized with a jolt. *It's killing him!*

A sob lodged itself in my throat as I cupped a trembling hand against his face. "Don't you leave me," I whispered hoarsely. "Don't you dare!" Stifling a sob, I pressed my hands against his chest and my forehead against his brow.

Please, God. Please don't take him too.

Fresh grief welled inside the hollow void I'd carved out, and the one memory I'd spent years trying to staunch began to trickle from the splintering cracks, pooling in front of my vision no matter how tightly I squeezed my eyes shut.

July seventeenth.

It was the week before my final project was due, some stupid mixed-media painting I'd been agonizing over all semester. Overflowing with pride from actually having finished it, I'd schlepped the still-damp canvas to the hospital to show my dad, knowing he probably wouldn't be awake to appreciate it. But to my surprise and delight, he sat up in bed when I arrived, in better spirits than I'd seen him in months. Lucid and buoyant, he actually cried when he saw the painting. Said he couldn't wait to go see it hanging in the college's permanent gallery. I knew then that he was going to be okay. That all of the invasive procedures, the poking and prodding, the pain and suffering had been worth it. So when my mother started blowing up my phone later that evening, hocking me to go back and see him because she had "a bad feeling," I ignored her. It was the opening night of some big-budget comic book blockbuster, and all of my art school buddies and I were going to go drool over the CGI since we knew a couple of the compositors. I even silenced my phone for the first time in six months. Mom was just pulling her usual neurotic crap; Dad would be there in the morning, excited to hear all about the movie. Maybe I'd even ask his doctor if I could take him to see it next week since he was finally on the mend.

By the time the movie was over, I had twenty-four missed calls.

I burst into my father's room just in time to see him take his final breath. To watch the light dim from his eyes as his pupils lost focus, staring straight through me instead of at me. The last time I told him that I loved him, he couldn't hear me.

As long as I lived, I would never forgive myself for that.

A fresh wave of spasms seized Zayn's entire body, and I squeezed him tighter.

"I love you," I whispered against his forehead, cool and damp with sweat. "Please. Please come back to me."

Several agonizing seconds passed before the spasms began to cease and his arched spine sank back into the chair. When his racing heart abruptly slowed, I feared it had stopped altogether. Sinking terror froze every nerve in my body – more than the glaistig or the fachan or even the vampires, I feared I'd lost him. Lead filled my stomach as I pulled away, terrified at the thought of what I might find when I looked up.

A low moan rumbled from his throat.

"Zayn?" I whispered.

His eyes fluttered open a moment later. Green as I'd ever seen them, they glittered like a pair of emeralds.

"Zayn!" I managed to choke out. "D-Did it work?"

He shook his head slowly, wincing as he did. It took a moment for his eyes to focus, but when they did, they landed directly on me. "Talia," he whispered. He tried to lift his arm, flinching when he realized it was stuck in place.

"Are you…" I swallowed, "back?"

"I don't know…" He hesitated, squinting around the room uncertainly. He seemed surprised to see the police officers outside.

"They're coming to talk to you," I whispered urgently.

"No! …No," he shook his head. "You can't let me out of this chair until we know for certain."

"How?" I pressed.

"Ask…" He opened his mouth, then closed it again, licking his lips. "Ask me something I couldn't answer before."

"Like what?" I frowned. "What couldn't you answer before?"

"Ask me…" He paused for another long moment. The Adam's apple in his throat bobbed as he swallowed. "Ask me if I love you."

My breath caught, and for a moment, I couldn't find a single word to utter. All I could do was sit there dumbly, trying to rack my brain to figure out what he had meant, what he'd really been trying to get me to ask.

And then a strange voice whispered from the recesses of my mind.

Why have you not claimed her?

I shook my head, trying to push away the memory. But Zayn's soft, broken voice answered nevertheless.

Because it would result in an entirely one-sided arrangement.

Shock took hold of me like a lightning strike, freezing me in place. *He wasn't talking about* my *unrequited feelings.*

I looked up to find his eyes boring into mine, his fiery gaze burning away every last dreg of fear and uncertainty in my heart.

He was talking about his.

It was a hard-fought battle to make my mouth work again. When I finally managed to speak, my voice sounded low and hoarse. "Zayn, do you love me?"

He closed his eyes and took a deep, shuddering breath. When he opened them again, they were glassy and filled with emotion.

"More than anything in the two realms."

I gaped at him for a split second longer before throwing my arms around his neck. "You idiot!" I sobbed. My lips crushed against his, passionately and full of ferocity, until I felt his mouth break into a wide smile.

"I am indeed an idiot," he chuckled against my lips, just as two more police cars pulled up to the store. "And as much as I *really* don't want this moment to end, you should probably let me out of this beautifully-crafted binding spell so I can go put my store back together."

"Umm..." I blinked, then anxiously looked around for the one crucial thing I already knew I wouldn't find.

"What's wrong?"

"Well, I-I..." My shoulders dipped sheepishly. "I drew the Chaining Rune in permanent marker."

"Pfft," he grinned. "You scared me for a minute. Just go and get some rubbing alcohol. That'll take care of it."

"I would, except..." I chewed my lip.

One of his eyebrows crept halfway up his forehead. "Except?"

"Except...I forgot to order more when you told me we were running low last week."

I winced, half-expecting Zayn to heave an exasperated sigh – after all, he'd reminded me at least twice to order more cleaning supplies. But to my immense shock and delight, he let out the loudest, most genuine laugh I'd ever heard come out of his mouth. And he continued laughing – shirtless and pinned to the chair as he was – well after the police arrived, with tears of joy pouring down his bruised, battered face.

XXV.
New Beginnings

Mom once again took up the hero's charge and ran to the drugstore for a bottle of alcohol, so I did eventually manage to casually expunge the Chaining Rune from Zayn's chair…about twelve minutes into his awkward, shirtless interrogation. When the officers saw my glowing skin, we all blurted out fake explanations at the same time. Unfortunately, we hadn't synced up beforehand, so those explanations ranged from Day-Glo body paint (me) to radiation poisoning (Mom) to a spray-tan gone terribly wrong (Roy, obviously), while Zayn just sat there looking exasperated. Suffice it to say, by the time the cops were finished with their cross-examination, all four of us had been subjected to a series of detailed sobriety exercises. I was the only one who failed thanks to the powerful whiff of tequila on my breath, but I managed to get off with a warning after insisting I'd walked to work. It's not like I'd normally condone lying to law enforcement, but telling them the truth – that instead of driving, I'd arrived via an interdimensional filing cabinet – would have almost certainly landed me in that seventy-two-hour psychiatric hold I'd been actively trying to avoid.

After the police slapped us with a pretty hefty fine for blasting loud, glass-shattering music and then went merrily on their way, Zayn – who was regrettably fully-dressed by this point – gave me a quick lesson, then put me to work drawing Restoration Runes on the larger pieces of glass. Each time I finished a symbol, the shard and all of its accompanying pieces returned to their respective frame, until there were no more pieces on the ground or embedded in the soles of my feet – quite a handy party trick, to be sure. Once the windows were back to being whole and unbroken, I dug up a small piece of the disintegrated door handle from its hiding spot beneath the couch and managed to restore that part of the entry hardware as well.

All the while, my mother had cozied up on the couch – now back to its rightful place beside the unbroken door – to play *Words with Friends,* periodically exploding whenever some *mamzer* on the other end managed to score more points than she did.

Zayn, unfortunately, had the hardest task of all. Under the guise of retouching a couple of rough spots on Roy's tattoo, he cleverly hid two small runes among the snake's scales. One was a modified version of the Chaining Rune, to temporarily keep the serpent bound to Roy's derrière; once we created the proper neutralizing ink with the delphinium petals, we'd invite him in for a free "touch-up" session to permanently neutralize the magic. The other tattoo, sadly, was an Obliteration Rune, which Zayn used to erase all of the relevant, trouble-causing portions of Roy's recent memories.

I cast my favorite client a sad smile as he stood from Zayn's vinyl chair thirty minutes later, looking faintly dazed but in good spirits.

"Make sure you apologize to your wife for playing such a lousy prank on her, okay?" Zayn patted Roy's shoulder as he surreptitiously tossed the man's crumpled-up magical honey-do list into the trash. "It sounds like the rubber snake you used was really lifelike."

"Yeah," Roy muttered, scratching the back of his head. "It sure must have been..."

"If Dottie has any lingering questions about it, bring her in to see us right away. And in the meantime, why don't you take her out to a nice dinner tonight? On me." Roy's eyes bulged when Zayn handed him a nice, fat wad of cash from his pocket.

"You got it, man!" he grinned, promptly stuffing it inside his vest. "And hey, thanks a lot for touching up Monty Python. Even though he seemed pretty dang near perfect to me."

"Even total pros can make mistakes," Zayn winked at me.

"From time to time," I shrugged sheepishly.

"Alright, well, thanks again, you two!" he grinned. "It was nice to meet you, Mrs. K!" He nodded his head at my mother just before the door swung shut behind him.

"Mmhmm..." she muttered, frowning at her phone. "'Juxtapose?' Are you kidding me?! ...Oh!" She looked around as the door jingled shut. "You fixed the windows already?"

"Sure did." I crossed my arms proudly.

"I'll be back for you," she muttered at her phone. Then, after relegating it to the fathomless bowels of her massive purse, Mom pulled herself off the couch with a grunt. "*Oy-yoy-yoy!* As your grandfather used to say, *starość nie radość.*"

"Indeed, getting old is no fun," Zayn smiled, offering her a hand.

"You speak Polish?" my mother's eyes widened, then narrowed as she swatted away his help.

"*Tak. Aun a bisl Yiddish.*"

Mom stood at her full height, which barely came to Zayn's chest, to look him up and down. "What kind of gentile knows Yiddish?" she intoned in her trademark Brooklyn inflection, planting her hands on her hips. Abruptly she gasped and whirled in my direction. "Unless he's Jewish?"

"Why are you asking me?" I demanded. "The man's standing right in front of you!"

"Sorry," Zayn smiled ruefully as she once more rounded on him. "Not only am I an unabashed *goyim*, but I'm not even technically human."

"Are you *crazy?*" I hissed, elbowing him in the ribs. "Why would you say that?! It's bad enough that you're a gentile!"

"Eh," she shrugged, and the bottom half of my jaw all but dislocated as it toppled open. "Human, Schmooman. So long as he's willing to convert one day, I'll allow it."

At that, Zayn actually laughed.

Mom's face broke into a mischievous smile as she reached up to pat his cheek. "Ooh, *tateleh*, you'll look so handsome in a *yarmulke!*"

"Are you out of your mind?" I exploded. "First, you're threatening to break the man's legs, and now you're talking about *converting* him?"

"*Oy gotenyu*," she rolled her eyes skyward. "God forbid you make a joke around this one!"

"But that wasn't a joke!"

"Well, anyway," she barreled on, "now that your shirt is back on and you're not trying to throttle my daughter, I need to get to the deli before all the good briskets are gone. You are coming to dinner…*right?*" Her eyes narrowed alongside the emphasis, making it very clear that Zayn's presence would be non-negotiable.

"I wouldn't miss it," he replied quickly.

"Good, because the three of us will need to figure out a way to fix…" she gestured blithely at my bioluminescent skin, "well, *that*."

Zayn was nodding, though he looked troubled. "Mrs. Kestenbaum, I just wanted to say—

"Call me Dee Dee. Mrs. Kestenbaum was my mother-in-law and she was an absolute *chalerya*."

"Literally?" Zayn frowned.

She gave a non-committal shrug.

He glanced at me – and I too threw up my hands in mystification – then continued, "Anyway, Dee Dee, I know you have no reason to trust me, but I just want you to know that I would never harm Talia. Earlier, when you arrived, I…" He rubbed the back of his neck, faltering as he stared at the ground. "Truly, I'll never be able to express how profoundly sorry and ashamed I am."

I opened my mouth to defend him – what he'd done was entirely against his will – but my mother held up a hand.

"Shush. If I had the slightest inkling of a premonition that you would hurt my daughter again, you would already be dead. And speaking of which…" She pulled a bottle of Advil out of her purse and dumped a sizeable pile in his hand. "You're gonna want to take a lot of these. The aftermath of a banshee scream feels a little like taking a mallet to the head. I'd tell you I'm sorry," she shrugged, "but that would be a lie."

"Ma!" I gasped.

"What?" she said innocently. "I'm old and senile. I say crazy things. Anyway, see you both at five!"

"Mother," I groaned. "We've been over this. What kind of person eats dinner at five in the afternoon?"

"Ancient people like me. I'll be dead one day, so don't complain. And don't be late – it's Shabbos!" Without waiting for my forthcoming snarky response, she reached up to hug and kiss me, leaving a smudge of coral lipstick in her wake, then patted Zayn's cheek lovingly. "I'm glad my daughter was here to help you with your problem. You should give her a raise for the trouble."

"I couldn't agree more," he flashed me a genteel smile.

"And, seriously, do make sure she's getting her needs met in the bedroom, would you?"

"*Mom!*" I screeched.

"This is what I'm talking about!" she held out her palms as she lamented. "Maybe if you got laid every once in a while, you wouldn't be so uptight!"

My mouth fluttered in stunned disbelief as I worked to construct some sort of face-saving falsehood about my admittedly-wanting sex life, but she was already well on her way out.

"See you both at five!" she waved over her shoulder.

"See you then," Zayn called as the door jingled shut, then immediately locked the door behind her.

When he turned around to look at me, my face was flushing *asgera*-red. "I get laid!" I protested a little too fervently. "It's just been a few—"

Zayn's arms were around me, pulling me tightly against his chest. "How will I ever be able to thank you for what you did?" he murmured into my hair.

In a striking reversal of roles, I stiffened. "It was nothing," I muttered before quickly extricating myself from his grasp. "Seriously, you don't have to thank me."

"How can you say that?" he demanded. When I didn't answer, he gently curled his finger beneath my chin and tilted my head to look him in the eye.

I twisted away from him and trudged over to the front desk, where the Tupperware container was resting in pieces. Picking up the lid, I spun it between my hands as I spoke, keeping my eyes glued to the plastic. "I know you told me to do anything I could to get that tattoo on you, but..." My lip trembled as I thought about Salen, and all the terrible ways she'd forced herself on him over the years. "But what I did – how I did it – was wrong, and I'm so sorry. I'm the last person you should be thanking."

Zayn was giving me a funny look. "Wrong? In what universe is freeing me from forced servitude wrong?"

I tossed the stupid lid on the desk, disgusted with myself. "Because the only way I could think of 'freeing' you was to exploit you – just like *she* did! I used her powers against you, Zayn! I-I..." I bowed my head, ashamed to even look at him. The half-dozen faded tattoos on my arms stared back at me like cancerous sores. "I used Salen's succubus magic to manipulate you into wanting to sleep with me. It's the only reason you're free."

Zayn had gone completely quiet as he processed my confession, and the awkward silence between us seemed to stretch on and on. After a long, torturous minute, I finally mustered the courage to lift my head and look at him.

To my horror, his face was pressed to his hand, and his shoulders were shaking. When he regarded me with tears in his shining green eyes, my entire body wilted like a shriveled delphinium.

My chiseled-as-a-stone, stoic-as-a-statue boss was *crying*, and all because I was the absolute worst human being on the planet. Just as I was about to prostrate myself before him and beg for forgiveness, he let out the loudest, most hysterical howl of laughter I'd ever heard.

"L-Let me get this straight," he somehow choked out in between peals of laughter. "You think you used your *stolen succubus powers* to lure me into that chair?"

"Yes!" I gaped at him in wide, Gollum-eyed shock. "Because that's what happened!"

"I'm sorry!" He held up his hands as he tried to calm himself down. "Really, I'm not trying to laugh!"

"What could possibly be so funny?" I shrieked, jabbing a finger at the tattoos on my arms. "I took her tattoos, her magic—"

"You stole some of her runes, yes," he agreed as he wiped away tears. "Which is extremely impressive. But there's a difference between magic and *essence*. When you Extracted those tattoos from her skin, it's true that you Endowed yourself with some of her own borrowed magic. But to say you stole her "succubus powers" – that's like saying you stole the spots off a leopard. Or the color from a sunset. You can't *steal* someone's nature, Talia."

"Wait," I held up a hand while I used the other to steady myself on the desk. "Are you saying…what happened earlier…" I swallowed. "That was…?"

"That was all you, my little succubus-in-training," he replied, laughter still tugging at the corners of his mouth. "And may I say, your powers of seduction are formidable. That may have been the sexiest thing a human has ever done to me."

My head jerked up. "Wait – so that means a non-human has done something sexier to you?"

Zayn's cheeks colored.

"Tell me! I want to know!"

After choosing that specific moment to busy himself with collecting an armful of tattoo guns from his station, he strode toward the office. "Come on. We don't have much time."

"Don't change the—Wait, much time?" Still barefoot, I jogged to keep up with him. "Much time 'til what?"

"Until Sol shows up, looking for his completed order. And his AWOL daughter, for that matter."

"Oh. Right," I muttered, feeling an icy stab of anxiety shoot through my belly.

"I give it 'til tomorrow evening – tops – before he shows up with his legion of thugs in tow."

"So, what are we going to do?"

"Ha! *We* aren't going to do anything." He thrust open the door to his office and started darting around the room, stuffing a half dozen charged tattoo guns, spare batteries, and the entire cabinet of enchanted ink into his Mary Poppins bag. "I've put you in enough danger, Talia. The only thing *we* are going to do is finish your tattoo, attend your mother's non-optional dinner, and then part ways." He glanced over his shoulder to look at me. "At least until I can figure out a way to take care of Sol and keep you safe."

"Oh, yeah, sure, definitely," I nodded like a bobblehead in a windstorm. "You go off to Fae Land and take out the mob boss and his entire family all on your own, and I'll just hang out here and keep an eye on the shop 'til you get back."

His head popped out of the cabinet he was rummaging through. "Really? Just like that?"

"No!" I snarled. "Now tell me what I need to pack. And this time, don't let me forget my inhaler!"

"Talia—"

"Nope, nuh-uh," I held up a hand, channeling the bossy spirits of all my Jewish ancestors before me. "I am sleep deprived, starving, and somehow *still* glowing like a radioactive chemical! So how about we skip over the part where the two of us engage in an epic battle of stubbornness and I end up wiping the floor with you because *no one* is more stubborn than me. Not you, not my mother, not the entire goddamn fae mafia! Now," I continued through gritted teeth, "tell me what to pack."

He stared at me for a long minute, and I could see those damned cognitive wheels turning in his brain as though he were trying to solve complex trigonometry. Finally, a smug, evil smirk crossed his face. "Okay, Talia, you win. I'll take you with me to face certain death in the next realm over. Right after dinner – when I tell your mom all about the mortal peril and dangers that await us there."

I slapped my hand on the desk to emphasize the empty threat I was about to make, but the shining, Sacajawea-gold-dollar sheen of it distracted me from my would-be tirade. "Look, we can fight about this later, okay? For now, what the hell am I going to do about *this?*"

Zayn glanced up from his half-emptied safe. "Go get me the tattoo machine you were using."

"Why?"

He rolled his eyes. "Just do it, please."

Muttering, I headed into the supply room, snatched the gun from the counter, and then brought it back to the office where I sullenly dropped it in his hand. "Look, I did everything right," I started, "I just ran out of ink at the very end, and then…" My voice trailed off as he unscrewed the needle and ink canister to inspect it, then let out a mighty sigh.

"What have I told you about these rotary machines?" he asked, then charged on without waiting for an answer. "If you don't clean them out in between ink changes, they dry out and clog."

"But I didn't do an ink change," I protested as he slipped past me. "It just had the delphinium pigment!"

I followed him into the supply room where he'd grabbed a jug of distilled water from the cabinet. After carefully setting down the used, worthless ink cartridge, he snatched another liner needle from the drawer, unwrapped it, and turned his back to me.

"Yes, and much like tattoo ink, acrylic ink, and any other water-based solution, Endowment Ink dries out – extremely quickly."

"Yeah, I know, but—"

"Let me see your tattoo."

"Here." I hoisted my ankle on the counter, rolled up the cuff, and continued defending my perfectly good needle-cleaning technique. "And anyway, what's the point of lecturing me if—"

"Hey, what's that?" Zayn asked, motioning into the shop.

With my foot still propped on the counter, I twisted my torso around to look. "What's what? Hey, wait—*Ow!*" I tried to jerk my foot away, but Zayn was gripping my ankle like an iron shackle as he pressed the needle into my skin, pulled a lightning-fast line, then wiped it off with Green Soap and slathered a layer of ointment on it in less than eight seconds.

"Done."

"What do you mean, d—oh my God!" I squealed, gaping at my foot. The finished tattoo was shining as bright as a lightbulb, sucking the glow right out of my skin. My normal, cream-colored, *not*-glowing skin. "How did you do that?!"

He smirked. "As I was saying, my dear apprentice, you clogged yet another needle."

"Oh my God!" I shrieked again, yanking my foot off the counter to throw my arms around him.

"Well? Go look at yourself," he laughed.

Without another word, I skittered across the shop, tore open the bathroom door, assaulted the light switch, and spun toward the mirror. When I saw my face, I screamed triumphantly.

"ZAYN! I'm not glowing!"

"I know!" he hollered back. "And guess what, there's even better news!"

"What could be better than this?!"

"There's still a few drops of ink left!"

I did a giddy tap dance and let out a child-like squeal of joy at the sight of my regular, pale-ass, anemic reflection before darting back toward his office.

"This is so great!" I exclaimed, bursting through the door. "I don't have to stock up on spray paint after all! I can blend into the darkness like a ninja! I can—"

My mouth abruptly snapped shut as I skidded to a stop in his doorway. Zayn had just opened the top drawer of his desk, where Biscuit's remains were sitting in a hinged silver box.

"Wait—" I started, but he'd already removed the box from the drawer and was flipping open the lid.

"What's this?" he frowned.

"That's..." I swallowed tightly. "It's..."

"Hibiscus," Zayn whispered. He delicately set the open box on the desk, staring at the glittering ashes in disbelief. "I mean, I felt it. I knew, that is, when he..." he shook his head slowly, unable to finish the thought. "But I didn't want to believe it. I couldn't." His eyes trailed to the gaping vacancy in his tattoo sleeve, where he was absentmindedly fingering the hollow scars Biscuit had left behind.

"It was my fault," I said, slumping into the chair in front of his desk. "We were running, just running and running. I was no help at all. And, finally, for whatever reason, he led us straight to the Waypoint. Which turned out to be...crowded."

"*That* was entirely my fault." Zayn sank into his own chair, staring at Biscuit's ashes with red-rimmed eyes. "I was following you too quickly. I did everything I could to hold myself back, but…" He leaned forward, pressing his palms against his forehead. "It wasn't enough."

"You did everything you could! And we would have been fine, if it hadn't been for the stupid vampires!"

Zayn's head shot up, and all the color leached from his cheeks. "Vampires?" he demanded in a hoarse voice. "What do you mean, vampires? They didn't touch you, did they?" His eyes shot to my bandaged hand.

"Ah, no. That was actually Biscuit's doing." I grimaced at the memory. "One of the three vampires—"

"*Three?!*"

"Yeah. The three of them had just finished, uh…eating. Anyway, I guess the poor guy they took down was a Manipulator, and um…" I shifted uncomfortably, not wanting to recall that particular series of events. "Well, I was surprised, to be honest, at how quickly they were able to take control of Biscuit like that."

"Because he'd never been Manipulated a day in his life," Zayn raked his hands through his hair. "I allowed him complete free will, which is part of why he was such…"

"…a pain in the ass?" I offered, sniffling.

"Exactly. So, how the hell did you escape?"

I quickly explained what had happened as best as I could in my tired, delirious state, starting with the skin-dissolving shrub, all the way until we used the Waystone to get back to the office. By the time I'd finished, white shone all the way around Zayn's irises.

"Jesus." He shook his head faintly. "Those vamps had to have been starving. Near desiccation, even. Otherwise, there's no way in hell… I mean, I don't even think that *I* could have—

Wait a minute," he frowned. "If the two of you were able to get back to my office, then how did Biscuit...?"

My shoulders slumped. *That* part of the story was much harder to tell, but I did my best not to leave out any details about Biscuit's final moments. I owed them both that much.

"I'd be dead if it weren't for him," I reiterated once I'd told him everything. "I had no idea he could even do that. And then it all happened so fast... I didn't even have time to say thank you." I wiped away a tear as I looked up, expecting Zayn to be doing the same.

Instead, he was leaning across the desk, eyes wide and back rigid, as though I'd just announced that aliens had taken over South Beach.

"Hang on. Back up," he demanded. "You were saying that when you returned from using the Waystone, he had just finished eating an almond."

I stared at him stupidly for a long minute. "*That's* the part of the story you're choosing to focus on?"

"Talia!"

"Yes!" I snapped. "He'd just finished eating an almond."

"And that almond had your blood on it?"

"I..." I gulped, trying to remember. "I...I think so?"

"And when you say he erupted in flames, do you mean literal flames?"

"Yes!" I all but shouted, feeling my temper flaring. I more than anyone understood that everyone processes grief differently, but we'd skipped right over grieving and straight into asinine questions, which I was neither expecting nor comprehending. How about, 'Gee, Talia, I'm awfully sorry that extenuating circumstances forced you and my beloved pet straight into a trio of hungry vampires,' or, better yet, 'Good heavens, I'm so very sad to hear about the death of my closest feathered companion, who also just so happened to carry a piece of my soul!'

"What did you do with his ashes?"

I glared at him like the flaming lummox he was. "You're looking at them!"

"*Before* you put them in this box. What exactly were you doing when you gathered them up?"

"Oh," I faltered. "I, uh...well, I cried. A lot. And then I scooped them up—"

"With what?"

"With my hands!"

Zayn leapt to his feet, nearly giving me a heart attack as he did.

"What are you—"

He held up a hand to silence me. Then, as slowly and as carefully as a father reaching for a newborn child, he reached into the box and gently began rooting around the ashes. After a moment, he lifted something from the cinders, cradling it in his palms as he blew away a layer of fine dust.

Eyes wide, I leaned in to look at the object, which was small, round, and black. *No, not just black.* I blinked at its surface, which glittered with thousands of multi-colored, iridescent sparkles.

My hands flew to my mouth. "Is that... Can it...?"

Zayn was shaking his head in wordless disbelief. "So, *this* is why I was able to persevere...why I felt numbness, not anguish, when he disappeared."

"Did you know about this?" I demanded. "Has this ever ha—"

"No." Zayn carefully set the egg atop the ashes, then sank back into his chair. "No. I have never heard of this happening before."

"But I thought a phoenix—"

"He's not a phoenix."

"Then what does it mean?!"

He was quiet for a long moment, studying the egg intently with a deep-set line of concentration furrowed between his eyebrows.

Finally, he licked his lips, resigning himself to the back of his chair. "Your tears. Your blood. The immense gratitude and grief you must have felt when he sacrificed himself to save you—"

"Oh, God," I whimpered. "What did I do?"

He looked up at me with a mix of wonder and astonishment. "Your blood imbued him with power – far more than before. And your love, your sorrow... Talia, I think you gave him a piece of your soul."

A small gasp escaped my lips. "You mean...?"

"Yes," Zayn nodded. "You created a familiar, but not just any kind of familiar. I believe this egg is carrying a piece of us both."

As he said that, I felt a strange flush spreading from my head to my toes, one that made me feel as though I were standing buck-naked, teetering on the edge of a crowded abyss.

"No. That can't be," I forced out a weak-sounding laugh. "I have no idea how to make a familiar. And I'm pretty sure I would know if I'd given up a chunk of my soul. It must be something else."

He weighed my words for a long time, nodding slowly to himself. After several moments, he glanced at the clock in the corner of the room and sighed. "Listen, Tal, I know it's been a very, very long night, and we still have another long day ahead, but do you think you have it in you to create just one more tattoo for me?"

"Another…?" My gaze followed his, from the glittering egg on the desk to the vacant space on his arm. "Y-You want *me* to…" I stammered. "I mean, you would trust me to do that?"

Zayn reached forward to take my hand. "Talia, there's nothing in this world I wouldn't trust you to do…apart from properly restocking our shop, of course."

"Heh. Touché." I managed a weak smile as electricity thrummed through my core. "Okay, so first I give you this tattoo, and *then* we flee the mob?"

His smile wavered. "I already told you, it's too dangerous for you to come with me."

"Oh, please!" I threw up my hands and rolled my eyes. "We're already about to do something *way* more dangerous than take down an entire family of magical gangsters."

"Oh?" he asked, arching an incredulous eyebrow. "And what, pray tell, is that?"

I glanced down at the luminous, impossible-to-miss tattoo that was advertising itself on my ankle like a flashing neon sign, then let out a heavy sigh.

"Have dinner with my mother."

To Be Continued…

Talia and Zayn's adventures will continue in the second installment of *Gilded Blood*: **JINXED**, out now!

By the way, if you enjoyed **INKED**, please consider leaving a review! 🖤 More than anything else, your words help indie authors get the exposure we need to create new stories to share with you, our readers.

In the meantime, keep reading for a **ton** of awesome bonus content at the back of this book!

And don't forget, you can always follow me for exclusive news, updates, sneak peeks, and awesome giveaways!

Rachel ♡

⭐ www.RachelRener.com
(You can order signed books here!)
📘 www.facebook.com/authorrachelrener
🐦 www.twitter.com/RachelRener
📷 @AuthorRachelRener
♪ @AuthorRachelRener

COMMON BLOOD TYPES AND THEIR MAGICAL CLASSES

Blood Type	Magical Class*	Commonality	Brief Description of Abilities
O-	Benefactor (Universal)	Rare 6.6%	Has unlimited capacity to create magic/incarnates with the support of a catalyst, but with limited control of creations. Catalysts include: magical pigments, enchanted talismans, wands, conduits, or any other artifact that has been Endowed with magic.
O+	Benefactor (Limited)	Common 37.4%	Has limited capacity to create magic/incarnates with one or more catalysts. Limited Benefactors are unable to control even their own magical creations without the help of an amiable Manipulator.
A-	Extractor (Universal)	Rare 6.3%	Has unlimited capacity to harness magic from objects, ingredients, or other fae, thereby rendering their target magically-bereft. The extracted magic can then be stored or temporarily mimicked by the Extractor.
A+	Extractor (Limited)	Common 35.7%	Has limited capacity to separate magic from ingredients or objects, often rendering them weaker, though not entirely inert. Harnessed magic cannot be repurposed or channeled without the cooperation of an Endower.
B-	Endower (Universal)	Very Rare 1.5%	Has unlimited capacity to channel, bestow, and sometimes restore extracted magic into another item or conduit for indefinite use. Powerful Endowers of the past created

			ancient talismans that are still used to catalyze magic today.
B₊	*Endower (Limited)*	*Rare* 8.5%	Has limited capacity to repurpose magic obtained by Extractors into another artifact, though the Endower will not be able to rechannel the magic without the help of a willing Benefactor.
AB₋	*Manipulator (Universal)*	*Very Rare* 0.6%	Has unlimited capacity to seize control of magical creations and incarnates through a talisman, catalyst, or conduit – even the creations of others. However, their capacity to create magic is extremely limited.
AB₊	*Manipulator (Limited)*	*Rare* 3.4%	Has limited capacity to control magical creations; wholly unable to spark magic or bring incarnates to life without the assistance of a Benefactor.
Rh_null	*Gilded* ∞	*Extraordinarily Rare* <0.0000005%	Only 1 in 2 million fae (and 1 in 6 million humans) carry Rh-null blood, meaning their blood cells contain no magic-inhibiting properties that human scientists refer to as antigens. All known fae carriers were exterminated or lost in the Blood Wars. On Earth, fewer than 50 humans have the extremely rare condition. To date, only one living fae descendant has "gold blood," thus allowing them to spark, extract, endow, and control magic.

* MAGICAL CLASS APPLIES ONLY TO FAE BORN UNDER THE POWER OF THE CERULEAN SUN. HUMANS WITH THE SAME BLOOD TYPES ONLY HAVE MAGICAL ABILITY IF THEY ARE DESCENDANTS OF FAE LINEAGES. EVEN THEN, THEIR MAGICAL POTENTIAL IS SIGNIFICANTLY DAMPENED WITH EVERY GENERATION THE FAE ANCESTOR HAS BEEN REMOVED.

Glossary For The Goyim

Used by Ashkenazic Jews, Yiddish is a language that is related to German (but also has many Slavic, Hebrew, and Aramaic loan words). Though originally written in Hebrew, the below definitions are an American hybrid of Yiddish and English called Yinglish.
Enjoy!

Bubaleh
(BUB-e-leh) n. | "little grandma"; a general term of endearment, esp. for children

Bubbe
(BUB-eh) n. | Grandmother/Grandma (Zayde is Grandfather)

Chalerya
(hal-AIR-re-ah) n. | a mean-spirited woman; a shrew; harpy.

Chutzpah
(HOOTZ-pah) n. | nerve; insolence; sass; confidence
    var: **Chutzpahdik** *(HOOTZ-pah-dik)* adj. | Showing chutzpah

Farkakteh
(fuh-KOK-teh) adj. (vul.) | lousy, messed up, ridiculous; shitty, full of shit.

Farshtinkener
(fuh-SHTOONK-eh-neh) n. | stinky person; smelly person; adj. smelly, stinky, rotten

Gottze dank
(GOT-zeh DAHNK) phr. | thank God / heaven / goodness

Goyim
(GOY-im) n., pl. | non-Jewish persons, gentiles

Ho(c)k a tchynik
(hok a CHIY-nik) phr. | to nag or talk incessantly; "Stop hocking my tchynik" is Yinglish for the original Yiddish, "hoch mir kein chinik" which literally means "don't bang my tea kettle."

Kibitz
(KI-bitz) v. | to meddle; to make unwanted and intrusive comments; to needlessly interfere.
    var: **Kibitzer** *(KIB-bit-zer)* n. | one who kibbitzes

Kvetch
(kVETCH) v. | to gripe; complain; to bemoan one's fate.

Mamzer
(MUM-zer) n. | Derogatory reference to a difficult or unpleasant individual; bastard.

Manischewitz
(man-i-SHEV-itz) n. | Cheap, kosher wine that is often associated with Jewish Passover seders.

Meshuggeneh
(me-SHOO-ge-neh) n./adj. | Crazy; a crazy person.
    var: **Meshugge** *(me-SHOOG-eh)* adj. | crazy; insane.

Mishegas
(MISH-eh-goss) n. | madness; craziness; insanity

Oy!
(OIY) excl. | a lament, a protest, a cry of dismay, a reflex of delight; *Oy!* is uttered in as many ways as the utterer's histrionic ability permits.

Oy gevalt!
(OIY ge-VALT) phr. | an exclamation of fear, panic, astonishment, etc. A cry for help, such as "Oh my God!" or "Good grief!" (Literally, "Oh, violence!")

Oy gotenyu!
(OIY GOT-en-yoo) phr. | "God help us!" An exclamation of panic, pain, shock, or dismay.

Schlep
(SHLEP) v./n. | to haul or carry (something heavy or awkward); a tedious or difficult journey.

Schlocky
(SHLOCK-ee) adj. | cheap or low in quality; shoddy

Shabbos
(SHA-bus) n. | Ashkenazic term for Shabbat or the Sabbath; Judaism's day of rest that starts just before sundown each Friday and ends at nightfall on Saturday

Shpilkes
(SHPILL-kehs) n. | nervous energy; restlessness; "ants in the pants," "nerves." (literally: "pins") to "sit on shpilkes" means you are very nervous or anxious

Tateleh
(TAHT-e-leh) n. | a term of endearment for a boy or man; lit., "little father"

Tuchus
(TOO-kus) n. | rear end, bottom, backside, buttocks

Yarmulke
(YAH-muh-kuh) n. | a Jewish head covering, esp. for males during prayers or prayer service

A Dirge of Salt and Sin

Lyr. Rachel Rener
Comp. Alora Carter & Rachel Rener
Arr. Lauren Prendergast

337 • GILDED BLOOD

(You can listen to the MP3 **here!**)

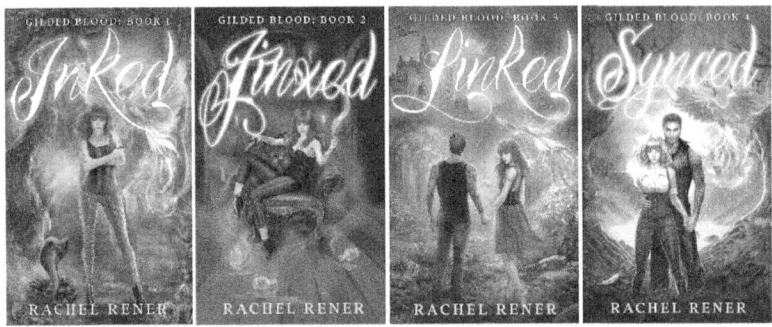

THE GILDED BLOOD SERIES

When Zayn, your smoking hot boss, tells you never to touch the cache of deluxe tattoo ink locked away in his office, you listen to him... until the day you run out of your own ink, your squirming client is on the verge of peeing his pants, and your boss is nowhere to be found. Desperate times call for desperate measures, right?

I fully expected Zayn to yell at me when he returned to the shop. What I didn't expect was the fresh cobra tattoo on my client's butt magically springing to life. Or the interdimensional filing cabinet hiding in the back of Zayn's office. And, oh, did I mention that my gorgeous, magic-ink-hoarding boss is actually an incubus?

Now – through (mostly) no fault of my own – we have to venture into a strange and distant land where a never-ending list of lethal flora, fauna, and fae await us. When you add in my Jewish mother's string of poorly-timed, hysterical phone calls, there is one thing I'm grateful for: there's no cell service in the fae realm.

THE LIGHTNING CONJURER SERIES

Three years ago, I woke up in an abandoned cabin without a single memory – not even my own name. Since then, I've been doing my best to stay off the grid. But this week? Well, that's proving to be a problem.

From freak tornados to exploding fireplaces, strange things are happening all around me. Aiden, my new (and irritatingly attractive) college professor, says he knows "what" I am. A strange car is following me everywhere I go. And now an organization of people claiming to be "like me" are entreating me to join them. But the deeper I venture into this world, the more I wonder – is this organization a safe haven or a cult?

Whatever it may be, I can't turn back now. Because the only way to unearth my past, my name, and this growing power deep within me is to brave the lion's den...

Even if that means disclosing the one secret about me that will shake the very world to its core.

THE BONE WHISPERER CHRONICLES

Things change around Lilah. Like actually change.

An apple disintegrates. People age.

Dogs transform into puppies.

Or bones.

These changes seem to be tied to her epileptic seizures which is why she has to take that daily little blue pill. In fact, the pill works so well that Lilah seems like any other normal teenager.

Until the day she chooses not to take the pill. That day changes everything and Lilah begins to wonder what could happen if she let the seizures happen. But can she control them or will they control her?

THE LITTLE MORSEL

Feral, a retired war hero with ancient bones and thinning scales, has been living in a dragon retirement home for several centuries. There, his daily routine is always the same: wake up with creaky joints, force down the stale protein bars from Bites of Knights, avoid the caterwauling old females on the shuffleboard court, and then return to bed to dream of flying.

But when a tiny stray human shows up at his front boulder, Feral's ho-hum world is turned upside down. Once a tentative agreement not to eat this strange little 'morsel' is forged, the two of them embark on a journey for applesauce that ends with each of them saving the other's life – in more ways than one.

THE LITTLE MORSEL is a warm, lighthearted adventure that shines a delicate light on loneliness, neglect, found family, and purpose. Multifaceted and relatable, it is a story that can be enjoyed by children and adults alike.

ACKNOWLEDGEMENTS

I owe a huge debt of gratitude to Sara Lawson, who is not only a brilliant editor, but a cheerleader, fan, and champion of my work. It was kismet that one of my characters shared your name before we even met!

Aaron, you are literally sitting next to me as I write this, which is only fitting since you've been by my side throughout this entire writing process, from page one of *The Lightning Conjurer* series. Thank you for seeing the magic in my work even when I'm about ready to swear off writing for good and move to Timbuktu.

I must offer bushels of love and gratitude to my own outrageous Jewish mother, who has provided me with endless comedic source material over the course of my life (while at the same time putting up with my never-ending assortment of smart-ass retorts). I love you and I'm sorry for being an interminable pain in the ass. Oh, and, uh, thank you for being cool about the sex scenes. I had no idea that's how I was brought into the world until you reminded me.

Thank you to my parents and late grandparents for imbuing my childhood with old country Yiddishisms, even (especially) when you were yelling at me. A special thanks to my dad for his extra help with this book's glossary, as well.

To my lifesaving (line-saving?) proofer, Ashlynn, I cherish your scrutinizing eyeballs almost as much as our 20+ year friendship. Thank you for everything!

A tremendous thank you to Kristin Jones, my brilliant and incredibly talented tattoo artist who provided me with a veritable treasure trove of information (that I then took great artistic liberty with). You are amazing!
(Check out her incredible work @ www.kjonestattoo.com)

A special thanks to my early readers, Aaron, Jess, Sara, Constance, Travis, and my mom, who let me talk their ears off about tattoos and fachans throughout the entire writing process. "Incu-boss" is all thanks to a certain grumpy dragon! And to my ARC readers, who were so ready and willing to quickly read and share with the world – thank you so much for celebrating this book with me and getting the word out!

Dziękuję Adam Burry, for the Polish tips! As well as my late grandfather who provided many Polishisms to the family – even if many of them were confusing and oddly derogatory toward cows.

Thank you to those friends who supported my shift from 9a-5p drudgery to writing all hours of the day and night. Far too many people look down on writers, especially in the fantasy genre. To those who have offered kind words and encouragement, it truly means more than you know!

Terrance, even though you can't read, I'd like to thank you for being my favorite feathered buddy and providing lots and lots of silly ideas for your literary rainbow counterpart. Ayluv you!

Most of all, to my readers, I offer you my profound thanks for taking a chance on small-time author such as myself. I quite literally could not do this if not for all of you. Thank you from the bottom of my heart for embarking on this adventure with me. 🩶

About the Author

Rachel Rener is the author of THE LIGHTNING CONJURER Series, a critically-acclaimed contemporary fantasy with elements of magical realism and romance. Her standalone novel, THE GIRL WHO TALKS TO ASHES, was an Amazon #1 new release and a BBNYA (Book Bloggers' Novel of the Year) semi-finalist.

She graduated from the University of Colorado after focusing on Psychology and Neuroscience. Since then, she has lived on three continents and has traveled to more than 40 countries.

When she's not engrossed in writing or hanging out at Indie Fantasy Addicts, Rachel enjoys art of all kinds, riding her motorcycle, reading fantasy books, going to rock shows (both musical and mineralogical), Vulcanology (the lava kind as well as the pointy-eared variety), and playing video games. She lives in Colorado along with her husband, the world's best bonus kiddos, Josh and Leah, and a feisty umbrella cockatoo named Terrance (a.k.a "Jungle Chicken") that hangs out on her shoulder as she writes – whether invited or not.

Made in United States
North Haven, CT
07 November 2023